# One Day I Shall Astonish the World

## NINA STIBBE

VIKING
*an imprint of*
PENGUIN BOOKS

First published 2022

003

Copyright © Nina Stibbe, 2022

The moral right of the author has been asserted

The publisher is grateful to the following: for permission to use the epigraph
text on p. vii, reprinted by permission of David Sedaris. From *To Make a Friend,
Be a Friend* originally broadcast by National Public Radio. © 2001 by David Sedaris.
For permission to use the text on pp. 286 and 294, reprinted by kind permission of
Lucy Ellmann. From *Sweet Desserts* originally published by Virago Press © 1988.
For permission to use the text on pp. 269 and 366 reprinted by permission
of Wim Hof, Ebury Publishing. From *The Wim Hof Method* originally
published by Sounds True © 2020.

Set in 12.5/15.25pt Garamond MT Std
Typeset by Jouve (UK), Milton Keynes
Printed and bound in Great Britain by Clays Ltd, Elcograf S.p.A.

The authorized representative in the EEA is Penguin Random House Ireland,
Morrison Chambers, 32 Nassau Street, Dublin D02 YH68

A CIP catalogue record for this book is available from the British Library

ISBN: 978-0-241-45116-8

www.greenpenguin.co.uk

MIX
Paper from
responsible sources
FSC® C018179

Penguin Random House is committed to a
sustainable future for our business, our readers
and our planet. This book is made from Forest
Stewardship Council® certified paper.

*For Stella Margaret Heath*

Some friendships are formed by a commonality of interests and ideas: you both love judo or camping or making your own sausage. Other friendships are forged in alliance against a common enemy.

David Sedaris
*To Make a Friend, Be a Friend*

# Preface

## Vice Chancellor's Office
## November 2019

For the first time in all my years at the university I find myself struggling to write a decent contribution for the newsletter. There've been few highlights this semester, certainly nothing newsworthy, and not much on the horizon for the Vice Chancellor's Office nor the institution as a whole, not like last November, when I was able to trumpet the VC's OBE, and his broadcast for BBC Radio 4's *Thought for the Day* in which he pondered the benefit of year-round crop availability: 'Is it good for us, or bad? And might waiting until June for strawberries and falling gratefully on asparagus in May make us better people?' Plus there was his involvement with the new staff bicycle initiative. Joyce Ho, our head of Human Resources, had had to *cut* words in order to fit in details for the Christmas lunch. The year before that, the VC had come second in a national punning competition, we'd been among the first to be awarded TEF Gold after a lightning-strike inspection, a visit from celebrity smallholder Dick Strawbridge had made the ITV news, and the VC's monograph *The Bovine Imperative* had been published to rave reviews.

It seems to have been all lowlights this term; starting

with disastrous student recruitment and dropout statistics, a death threat to the VC leaked to the press, a cyber-bullying incident when a member of staff was sent a photograph of Thora Hird with the message '*Bobbly cardigan crime*', and all culminating, yesterday, with the news of our Deputy VC's freak accident at a stately home. On top of all that, my plan to mention a new collection of articles for and against mega-dairies, *Farmageddon*, has just been ruined by a review in the *FT* describing the VC's chapter as 'worthy, verbose, old hat' and mocking him for using the term 'cowshed'. Again I have to wonder at his wife not stepping in to improve his written vocabulary, her an award-winning poet, known for being pithy and germane. Out of curiosity, I search for the book reviewer and find him on Instagram, @PeteDwight, tall and handsome in buckled gaiters, kissing a horse on the lips, 250K followers, and make a note to invite him to the centenary gala dinner. Finally, with no other option, I write two hundred words on the subject of *next* semester and leave campus for an appointment with my GP. Driving to the other side of town, I reflect that it hasn't been a great time for me, personally, either. My husband Roy and I have been at odds, starting when I accidentally called out the VC's name during an unusually playful moment. All I can think is that I somehow got the names 'Roy' and 'Professor Willoughby' muddled. I have never had sex with Professor Willoughby and have never wanted to, unless deep in my subconscious (which doesn't count), but it has to be said, we do have a laugh, the VC and I, and that, I think, is the problem. Roy and I stopped having any fun in 2012. I made it up to him afterwards (Roy) by watching him play table tennis against another veteran, but on the way home it turned out I'd cheered every time the opponent won a point.

'Ping-pong is a fast game, Roy,' I said. 'I can't always follow what's happening.'

And he said, 'Please can you stop calling it "ping-pong".'

It's not just that. I was looking after a neighbour's dog while she took a bereavement cruise of the Rhine, and though Roy was used to me fostering via the Blueberry Trust and perfectly taken with the dog, he was offended at my having agreed on this occasion without his consent (talk about looking for trouble), so much so that he came home for lunch to discuss it.

'I'm the bottom of the pile these days, Sue,' he said.

And I replied, 'I hate it when you call me Sue,' and he looked at me with such sad eyes that I said, 'Well, if I'm not allowed to say "ping-pong", I don't see why I should put up with being called Sue.'

And with that he went back to work without eating his quiche, slamming the front door so hard that the bell rang of its own accord, and Honey came crashing downstairs thinking it was her Depop delivery.

'No, it was Dad going off in a huff,' I said.

That reminded her that her counsellor had asked to meet me.

'Meeghan thinks it would be good to chat with you,' was how Honey put it.

'Who?' I said.

'My counsellor.'

'What about?' I asked.

'I don't know – things, you know, about me, and you and Dad, I don't know, she's a counsellor,' she said, looking down, picking at her nail varnish. 'So, is that cool?'

'No,' I said, 'it's not cool.'

And I'm now examining twenty-eight years of parenting *and* marriage, wondering which particular aspects of either Meeghan the counsellor might want to take me to task for. The time I cut a picture of Helen Mirren out of the paper and asked my hairdresser for the same style, and then, in front of Honey, criticized the actress for saying she found childbirth 'disgusting'. My habit of smoothing Honey's hair down and suggesting baggy tops with tight bottoms, the year I served meals on portion plates. The time, twenty years ago, she fell over and I asked about the toy horse she was holding before checking she was OK (it was antique). The times I deliberately sound clever, like yesterday, when I said 'Byzantine art' for absolutely no reason, and all the times she's heard me say 'As an English graduate . . .' which I'm not. Anyway, I'm now thinking I should have agreed to meet Meeghan the counsellor, even though I'm wondering what in the name of God the world has come to, that people are indulging this nonsense? I mean, shall each of us haul our parents over the coals for every tiny retrospective thing? For our congenitally thick hair, our fear of giraffes, the amount of amalgam in our molars, their failure to teach us card games? I could sue my mother ten times over but I don't. I mean, I could literally have her thrown in jail, right now, today, but I don't.

*

Veg-wise, Roy will only eat baked beans and iceberg lettuce and I honestly thought it would be the least nice thing about being married to him, and, believe me, it has rankled, watching the rest of the world tucking into chargrilled asparagus and green beans with garlic and herbs. And then, when he started his quest for longevity, I thought *that* would be the worst thing, and now, to cap it all, he's started putting his fingers in his ears when I speak.

I'm telling Dr Z. Tang the above, intermingling it with our discussion about my dry cracked hands (which I've presented with) and I expect her to be aghast, and sympathetic, especially about the veg, knowing first-hand how keen she is. She's on the Board of Governors and I once had to pick her up at home and while waiting I noticed, on her granite worktop, an array of vegetables – broccoli, cauliflower and celery – all immersed in water, like cut flowers.

'Oh,' I said, 'veg in vases?' and she explained that storing vegetables in this manner keeps them fresher, and more vitamin and mineral rich, than dry refrigeration, and more like they were when newly harvested.

Now at the surgery, waiting as she searches the database for an ointment, my eye is caught by an encapsulated diagram of the human ear, and I realize it's an exaggeration to say Roy 'puts his fingers *in* his ears' – what he does is press the *tragus* into the opening of the ear, which has the same effect but can be achieved quite subtly if you're looking at a device of some kind. Simply rest your chin in your spare hand and stretch your middle finger up and close out all unwanted noise.

'Should I be concerned, do you think,' I say, 'about my husband blocking his ears when I speak to him?'

Dr Tang doesn't respond; she's lost the cursor and after moving the mouse about frantically for a few moments she gives up, swivels to face me, suggests an over-the-counter hand cream, and a blood test to confirm menopause, which she reckons to be the underlying culprit.

'A lot of women suffer epidermal dryness,' she says.

I accede to the diagnosis but decline the test and when I start to say, 'But my husband—' she interrupts.

'No, I wouldn't worry, I frequently put my fingers in my ears when my husband speaks, it doesn't mean I don't love him, it's just because we've been married so long.'

'*Really?*' I say.

'Yes. Also, women's voices hurt men's ears – fact.'

'Really?' I say again (thinking what a whizz she is).

'Yes, unless very childlike or gravelly,' she says, 'hence Marilyn Monroe.'

'OK – but he wants to live to a hundred,' I remind her and describe the breath-holding exercises every morning that make the mattress quiver ever so slightly, as if he's being asphyxiated by an assassin crouching beside the bed, the running backwards up hills, the sloping block in the bathroom for ankle strength, the stool-stool for total bowel evacuation, the vitamins, the nagging worry as to where it all might lead (extreme old age, cryogenics, journalism).

Dr Tang laughs. 'Don't knock it,' she says. 'I have women coming to me exhausted, wishing theirs were *more* that way.'

'But he won't eat veg,' I remind her, and immediately regret saying 'veg' again.

'That's his problem,' says Dr Tang. 'If you want to eat vegetables, eat them.'

For a moment it feels slightly as though Dr Tang is on Roy's side, and making me seem unreasonable, and if only I'd chargrill some courgettes, and stop talking in such a high voice, everything would be fine, but then it occurs to me that a broken marriage must be as financially burdensome to a medical practice as unwanted pregnancy, smoking and loneliness, and I agree.

'You're right,' I say. 'I'll get myself some broccoli.'

I leave via the pharmacy and buy a hand cream recommended by the Norwegian navy. I do not apply it in the car, in spite of the fast-absorbing claims. I eat my lunch and give the newsletter piece one last proofread before sending it to Joyce in HR.

## NOTES FROM THE VICE CHANCELLOR'S OFFICE

We're looking forward to 2020!

The VC's Office has been fairly quiet this semester, though preparations continue apace for next year's centenary events. A week of activities and celebrations, commencing mid-March, will include:

- 'One Hundred Years of the University of Rutland' lecture, delivered by [a person]
- Games afternoon including a tug o' war against staff from the University of Leicester

- UofR collection of essays, poems and anecdotes by staff and students, past and present
- Charity Gala Dinner Dance, music by Happy Days Jazz Band

In other news, the new Arts in Society module has got off to an interesting start with its striking mural visible from the VC's Office, splendid anticipation of greatness to come. Our stronger links with the Confucius Institute have meant many interesting ideas flowing, and, to avoid further accidents, the wall-mounted hand-dryer in the female staff toilet has been moved to a more sensible position.

# PART ONE
# Friendship
## 1990—2000

# I

I met my husband Roy Warren for the first time at the Two Swans café in the town of Brankham, in late June 1990. I'd always thought of it as a place of romantic encounter because of its wall-sized mural featuring a pair of swans, beak to beak, with amorous eyes and whose necks formed a heart. I'd finished my first-year exams and had come home to work for the summer at the haberdashery where I'd been a Saturday girl, but arriving at the shop that Monday morning found it locked and a note on the window reading '*Late opening due to power cut*' and so went across the road to the Two Swans to watch from the window for developments and have a cup of tea.

Almost immediately after I'd taken my seat Roy Warren, not then known to me, tried to enter through the wrong door, causing both to open noisily at once, and came in smiling with his hands in the air, apologetic and charismatic at the same time. He ordered breakfast at the counter, sat down at the next table but one to me, and waited until I looked at him before saying, 'Good morning!' and it turned into a conversation. He was handsome, wiry and very pale, with purplish shadows around his eyes. Cafés were an extravagance back then and to be in one without a good excuse seemed wrong, so I began by giving my reason for being there, and then Roy stated his. First, he liked a fried egg before work but his landlady had banned pan-fumes since having a baby, and only allowed cereals first thing, which didn't satisfy him after years of straight-up protein. Second, he was early for work after dropping the same lady's cat at the nearby veterinary surgery, and I don't recall the other things, but altogether he had every right to be there. I asked what was ailing the cat. He didn't know, he'd only taken the basket as instructed and left the landlady to describe the symptoms to the veterinary nurse over the phone. Once we'd got the cat out of the way, our conversation was wide-ranging and impressive – him mentioning the Serengeti plains, and me the white horses of the Camargue – and I liked him. Everything was a high score except when we exchanged opinions about the greatest living writer, after I'd said Graham Greene with him in mind, and he'd said John Fowles, whom I detested, and I had to object.

'I'm afraid I'm not a fan,' I said, putting it mildly.

'I suppose he's more of a bloke's bloke,' said Roy, which I felt a reasonable recovery, and we agreed I probably knew best, being an English undergraduate.

His breakfast arrived and I watched him attend to his eggs, placing a sprig of watercress in the ashtray and generally moving things about on the plate. He was such a pro, that's what hit me, knowing to pierce the yolks before attempting to sandwich them, and his buttering the eggs *not the bread*, it being just-baked and too fresh to butter. And asking, 'What's the biggest effect on salt intake?' as he tipped a tiny pile into his hand.

I worked it out on the spot, and said, 'The size of the hole in the shaker?'

'Correct,' he said.

Normally, I'd consider all this fuss a bit much – it might put me off a person – but at some deep unconscious level I suppose I was sizing him up as a husband and father because I very much required someone with high self-esteem and analytical skills. And, goodness me, that chirpy 'Good morning' followed by this egg-and-salt performance was impressive indeed – for a man wearing tracksuit bottoms, and with chipped front teeth.

Before I left the café, which I wouldn't have, except I'd seen the sign turn round on the shop door opposite, I found I had butterflies in my stomach. How apt! I thought, given the earlier mention of John Fowles.

'I have to go – my boss is opening up,' I said.

'Well, Susan, it's been lovely chatting,' he said, offering his hand.

I shook it gently, 'I hope all goes well with your land-lady's cat.'

He nodded solemnly. 'Let's hope so.'

'I shall think about him, or her, all day now,' I said, and I meant it, but as it turned out, I had other fish to fry.

I ran across the street and entered the shop, as usual calling out, 'Morning!' and went to put the milk with the coffee things, but before I could slide the door across, a stranger blocked my way, thinking me a customer, and said, 'I'm afraid that's a private area, madam.'

And it turned out the reason for the shop's delayed

opening was nothing to do with a power cut, it was because the Pavlous' daughter, Norma, had, unbeknown to me, taken over as manageress, and, finding herself to have overslept, stuck the note up while she got dressed. I don't know if I thought to myself that morning, wow, it's not even ten o'clock and I've already met my future husband and my best friend for life. But I should have, because I had.

'But I work here,' I told the woman, and held up the carton; it being UHT proved my identity because no one had UHT in those days, only the Pavlous having no truck with perishable foodstuffs.

'Goodness!' said Norma. 'Are you Suzanna?'

And I said, 'I'm Susan, yes, who are you?'

And she said, 'Gosh, I was expecting someone a bit older. I'm Norma Pavlou – daughter of the proprietors.'

In all my time at the Pin Cushion I'd never set eyes on Norma-Jean Pavlou, so this was quite something. I'd heard a lot about her, of course, from Mrs Pavlou; in fact, Norma-Jean had been one of her favourite topics of conversation and I used to wonder why she'd given me the job when she had this daughter available. I soon heard that Norma-Jean was not permitted to work in the shop, and because no explanation was proffered as to why this should be the case, I imagined her to have extremely poor manners, a hatred of the public, an allergy to lint, to be bedridden, insane, a figment of the imagination, a rehabilitating juvenile delinquent, or even dead, and I longed to catch a glimpse of her.

It wasn't for some months that I finally understood:

Norma-Jean was being protected from the drudgery of shop work on account of being a scholar and needing every hour for her books and experiments and not to have her brain fuddled with dressmaking concerns. Her subject was geology, with a specialism in sand, and in particular non-tropical silica. I knew it all backwards, and Mrs Pavlou was in constant awe of Norma-Jean's brilliance and the extraordinary nature of sand. I knew also that she had passed her driving test first go after only twelve lessons and now motored all over the county, even venturing into Lincolnshire to take samples and photographs of certain rocks and soil (and sand) on her own, with nothing but a sausage roll and a few screw-top jars.

Mrs Pavlou never had a moment's worry because of Norma-Jean's innate common sense, and so, frankly, it was a bit of a shock to meet the girl. I'd imagined a younger, bespectacled version of her mother – small, warm and kind, a funny old hippy with twinkly eyes – but Norma (she shortened her name to just that) was tall, aloof, and her wary eyes were always hunting for clues in your face as you spoke, and then never seeming satisfied. 'Really?' she was fond of saying, and thrusting her head back, and exaggerating a long blink.

Norma explained the situation. She was about to graduate (as above) and the plan now was to switch to the arts. She just couldn't see herself as a scientist, she said, and though I very much could, I kept the observation to myself because if there was one thing I'd learned in my first year at university, it was that scientists like to appear creative, and artists to appear relevant. If, she said, it turned out she'd done well in her exams, her tutors (at the University of Leicester) would railroad her onto their MSc course.

'It'll be difficult – nay, churlish – to turn them down,' she said. 'Academics take it personally when you don't choose their course.'

'I suppose it's like being rejected,' I said.

'Whereas,' Norma continued, ignoring me, 'a mediocre result will at least slightly justify a swerve to Bloomsbury, Manderley, and –' She paused, struggling to come up with a third literary setting, so eventually I offered, 'Or the Deep South,' just to move us along, and she said, 'Exactly.'

The above conversation took place before I'd even got the milk away, as if it were the most important thing in the world, more so than the customer who'd come in and stood at the counter, moving her head about, trying to get our attention.

'And so, why are you here all of a sudden?' I asked Norma.

'I need a new horizon,' she said, and we both glanced out of the window, where we saw Roy Warren exiting the Two Swans and lighting a cigarette.

After selling some fat squares to the customer, I watched as Norma crouched over the worktop to prepare our beverages in the utility area. The kettle not quite having come to the boil before she poured it and consequently undissolved granules swirled like tiny oil slicks. I reached for the teaspoon but she got to it first, stirred her drink vigorously, and then plopped it into mine quite abruptly. Even so I thought it impressive, a manageress making coffee, and reflected that old Mrs Pavlou never lifted a finger in that department, and thinking that prompted me to make mention of her.

'Your mother is really nice,' I said, or something bland and friendly along those lines, and Norma paused to take in what I'd said before replying, 'My parents are an idiot,' like that, as if they were a single entity. She wiped up a little spillage with a sheet of kitchen roll and flung it into the flip-top bin.

Norma looked older than twenty-four, partly because of a height-disguising stoop, and a habit of holding her hand at her throat in a defensive gesture, as if slightly aghast at the world, but mainly because of her awful clothing, in particular the home-made poly-cotton dress she wore that morning, the bust darts so sharp and pointed, and ill-fitting, and all ironed shiny so that the hemming showed up in relief like a wax rubbing. It took me some weeks to appreciate that she was attempting to dress like the 1960s in an approximation of her mother at that time, who, by her own account, had been very attractive, eccentric and arty, carving ornaments (mice, clogs and tulips) in a miniskirt (the first outside London) to sell to the tourists of Amsterdam. The shop had one of Mrs Pavlou's original works outside – a giant painted wooden bobbin, with a hole in the top for a plant pot – which had to be heaved inside every evening to stop men peeing into it as they stumbled home from the Brankham Arms on the corner of the street.

There was a lot to see in Norma's appearance and it took the whole day to process it all. Black hair piled up into a sort of beehive effect that, like the dress, was incredibly ageing. Her inward-sloping incisors were from most angles in shadow, giving the impression of a mouthful of black teeth, but a well-placed beauty spot on the left side above her chin was pretty and, when not smiling, she was all in all the healthiest-looking person I'd ever seen, her bare arms and shoulders quite muscular, and I could easily image her working a geologist's hammer and scrambling about looking for the Precambrian crust.

'Who would you say,' she said, 'was the greatest author?'

Here we go again, I thought.

'Living or dead?' I asked, and she said, 'Greatest of all time,' and I said, 'I think that would have to be John Donne.'

And Norma said – and I'll always remember this – 'But I thought he was just a poet.'

'*Just a poet?*' I gasped, and, realizing she'd said something against the laws of literature, she grabbed my arm.

'You see, Susan, I really need your help – imagine if I blurted that out in an interview.'

And so, there it was – she wasn't after a new horizon, she was there for literary conversion, and though it was never quite spelled out, from that day forward it was my job to prepare her for interview. It was perfectly pleasant playing teacher to such an attentive and well-behaved pupil, but I can't deny I did miss discussing the history of Harris Tweed with Mrs Pavlou as we unfurled a new bolt of shirting, or wondering why the Americans will use the term 'haberdasher' to mean gentlemen's outfitter or hat maker, or the chance to run up a simple beach robe on the

Bernina with an offcut of towelling and then question the wisdom of trimming it with a nylon zigzag binding in a contrasting colour, with shrinkage in mind, as I had in the time before Norma.

Now it was all, 'Is Woolf considered anti-Semitic or misogynist?' 'Is Flaubert too fond of metaphor?' 'Should I read *Petals of Blood*?'

This was a time when three years of learning, if you include A Level, gave you the edge on others and I disliked admitting I didn't have all the answers.

Once she asked me, 'What writer was it who compared women to empty museums filled with men's art, Susan? Because whoever it was I hate them.'

And I said, 'Oh, I believe that was John Fowles.'

I don't recall every one of her questions that first day, but she seemed to be writing things down, and I do remember telling her quite firmly, 'The thing is, Norma – you have to read the books yourself, it has to be at least partly your own interpretation. I mean, it's not like science, there's not a right and wrong.'

'I know it's subjective, thank you very much, Susan,' she said. 'Give me credit for a bit of intelligence! I'm being interviewed for university courses, not to host the *South Bank Show*.'

Later in the day, I made reciprocal enquiries about her specialism. 'Sand is so fascinating,' I said.

'Please let's not talk about sand,' she said. 'I'm sick of it.'

'But it's very literary,' I said.

'Is it?'

'Are you kidding? Metaphorical sand is sprinkled all over literature!' I said. 'To see a world in a grain of sand . . .'

'Oh, yes,' said Norma, urging me to continue. I mentioned the hourglass – sand falling from the upper chamber to the lower – and she got it straight away. 'The inexorable passing of time,' she said.

'The sands of time,' I said, 'a footprint in the sand, sandstorms, burying one's head in the sand, the rare and ever-changing beauty of the dunes, the cleansing tides that wash away marks in the sand – this is what you say when you're asked how your degree in geology is relevant.'

She wrote all this down, and then, bang on five-thirty, turned the sign round on the door and said, 'Very good,' as if it were the end of a school day.

It had been almost impossible to find a Saturday job in my home town, back in those days. Every position was filled, before it was even vacant, by nephews and offspring of the management, and the only jobs advertised were in warehouses or pubs where you'd be run ragged or mauled at by drunks. My problem was that I came from one of the few outsider families, only unlike other outsiders, I had nothing to commend me. Not like the Jacksons, who'd arrived from London and were cockneys and so confident, in-the-know and charismatic they were soon running the place and the dad was known as 'Del Boy' and everyone loved him in spite of his noisy motorbike and mean streak. There were the Warrens (Roy's family) and the McNamaras; both families had come from Corby,

Northants, to start a new life but within striking distance of family, and having authoritative Scots accents (Corby, Northants, being at that time over 30 per cent Scottish) were in great demand for jobs that involved speaking. There were the Patels who got everyone onto fresh herbs, and the daughter, a solicitor who championed the underdog, and the brother, easily the handsomest boy in town, who sang and danced by the Corn Exchange to fund his place at drama school, and now you see him on TV in all the medical soaps. And there was us, the Cohens, my parents, my brother and I, who had come from High Wycombe after my mother's accident in 1978. We'd been settled in Bucks with friends galore, and a much-admired front garden, but she'd insisted on a move, dreading that folk would witness her slow decline, and she held a peculiar grudge against a neighbour called Cynthia, and so we'd come to Brankham, a well-appointed, bombproof market town seventy minutes from St Pancras with rolling countryside and affordable housing. Practically everyone else, back then, born and bred – no tourists and no big industry, no ego.

The Pavlous arrived after us. Greek Mr Pavlou and Dutch Mrs Pavlou and their extended family scattered around the area offered many services, including bespoke tailoring, made-to-measure ceremonial gowns, property surveying, and non-domestic veterinary services. J. & T. Pavlou set up their haberdasher's shop, the Pin Cushion, in a pretty double-fronted premises with deep bay windows either side of the door. It wasn't in the busiest location but a haberdasher doesn't have to be, customers find you and then come especially and soon, because the Pin Cushion was there, a florist sprang up in what had been a dentist's and crowded the pavement with buckets of blooms, and a long, narrow table against the window crammed with jam jars of grape hyacinths and violets and Alchemilla mollis, and then a shop selling modelling paraphernalia, which had a railway running all around the walls at eye level, that didn't mind people just looking – in fact, encouraged it. This quaint industry was all very good for the Two Swans café which had previously been a bit of a run-down canteen above the hardware, but now, on account of the increased footfall, had splashed out on a job lot of rustic furniture and changed their menu to include salads and pasta. And, because they lent their ovens to Roy's landlady, who was trying to launch a catering company and needed to roast meats and birds after a failed marriage, and in a too-small oven, Roy had come to hear of it and went there for egg breakfasts, as you know.

I remember noticing the haberdasher's for the first time, where the Snuff Box, an old antique and bric-a-brac shop, had been, and it seemed perfect, with its painted wooden bobbin outside and, inside, the dresser with a hundred tiny drawers and each drawer handle being one of the beads or buttons contained inside. The reels of ribbon in every colour, and thread in forty-six shades, and the six-foot-deep shelving along the entire back wall groaning with rolls of fabric. The spinner bedecked with zippers, poppers and all manner of needlework accessories, the sewing table with an electric Bernina machine which customers were welcome to use. I'd gone home to

22

change and get my hair shipshape and then called in. The bell tinkled merrily and out came Mrs T. Pavlou and I said to her, 'I'm looking for Saturday work and she said, 'Here, in the shop?' and I said, 'Yes,' thinking to myself, where else? And she said, 'Yes! How fortuitous, we need someone.' We discussed the terms and conditions and she said she'd prefer I wore home-made garments, it being so encouraging to customers. I explained this would be difficult and she said she'd run something up and measured me on the spot. I started the following Saturday wearing a dress with actual smocking at the neck, in a chequered pattern with roses, and it was most nostalgic, a feeling reminiscent of my mother before the accident, brushing me down, straightening my collar and generally sorting me out with such tender care, and it was all I could do not to burst into tears.

At the end of my first day with Norma, I'd been rolling the ornamental bobbin back into the shop when I saw Roy Warren, leaning on the wall outside, hands in pockets, like someone out of a black-and-white film, but in colour, and in sports clothing. Men hadn't quite stopped wearing proper clothes back then and a sporty look usually meant a sporty life, which his was. He ground out a cigarette with his training shoe, holding the smoke from the last drag until the job was done and then exhaling through a small gap between his lips, like someone whistling for a trusty dog.

'Hiya,' he said, 'just wanted to let you know, the cat's OK.'

'Oh,' I said, 'thank you, that's good news.'

'Yeah, home and lapping at a saucer of milk,' said Roy.

'What's its name?' I asked, for something to say, but Roy couldn't quite remember.

'Timmy, Tommy, Jimmy, something like that. Anyway, do you fancy a drink?' he said, nodding at the Brankham Arms across the road.

And I said, 'Yeah, OK, a quick one, but I'll have to just see if my colleague wants to come.'

He shrugged.

Back inside, Norma was gone but there stood Mrs Pavlou.

'Oh,' I said, 'hello.'

And she said, 'Hello, ducky, how did the day go?' She looked eager and anxious with her hands clasped at her breast.

'It was great,' I said. 'I really like Norma.'

'And you can help her with the English literature?' she asked.

'Oh, yes, she's so keen.'

'And bright, yes?' said Mrs Pavlou.

'Yes. I was just going to ask her to come across to the pub for a drink with me . . .' I gestured outside, and was quite taken aback by the reply.

'Thank you,' she said, 'but I should tell you straight away, I don't think you and Norma-Jean will be friends in that way.' And with that, she waved her hands and shooed me out into the street.

At the pub I was impressed to see Roy speak confidently to assorted people, about football and golf and the likelihood of rain at the weekend, and that he had his own set of darts. I drank enough shandy in an hour to become quite inebriated and Roy drove me home in his car, because men still did in those days, even if they'd had three pints.

'Thank you for letting me know about the cat,' I said, outside my house, and we went on chatting for a while until my brother, James, tapped on the passenger window with one finger. I alighted from the car and looking at the house, saw my mother peering out and through the gap in the curtains I could see she was in her underwear.

Roy leaned right over and looked at us both through the open door, and James said, 'At least park round the corner next time, can't you,' and, to prevent Roy replying, I slammed the door shut, and the car moved slowly away.

James was dubious about Roy. 'Isn't he a gardener at the golf club?' he said.

'Yes, but he's planning to take over the running of the place, in due course,' I said and laughed at the pun.

Roy called for me at the shop almost every weekday night over the summer, for beer and kissing and home early, so as not to be too exhausted for work the next day (him) and not to upset my mother who liked to lock up at nine. I was sorry for Norma going upstairs to her parents every evening, but, quite honestly, a whole day with her was enough.

# 2

Norma had come in above me, as manageress, in spite of having no idea at all how the shop worked, or how to cut fabrics – how, with some types, you can make an initial snip with the scissors and run them along, half-cutting, half-tearing, for a good line, and how satisfying that is, the noise, the sensation of the rending, the slight dust remaining on the scissor blades. And how you must always let the customers have a few inches to play with, and never reveal that we keep rolls of fabric in the toilet and sometimes dry our hands on it. Norma was actually hopeless except for measuring, and in her authoritative manner with the customers, not caring what they thought of her. She once told a lady trying to buy snow-washed denim for a sexy trouser suit, 'I don't understand the fascination with this fabric – it's uncomfortable, expensive, scruffy, unwieldy to work with, a faff to wash and dry, it shrinks, wears badly, and is worn exclusively by idiots.' The customer took it all in and switched to a cotton moleskin in a silvery brown. I wasn't unaffected myself and soon shared her attitudes about cheesecloth and, for a while at least, loved anything spotty, until she went off it and said people who wore polka dot had something wrong upstairs. I came to sympathize with her squeamishness regarding velvet; the way it felt cool then warm to the touch, changed colour at a stroke, its tendency to baldness suggesting decay, and though I'd loved it as a child, I joined her in rejecting it, to the extent that we never had it on display, even at Christmas when customers went mad for it.

Norma telephoned me at home every Sunday evening, at seven on the dot, to read me the rota for the following week. This became a ritual for us.

'Hello,' she'd say, 'how are you?'

And I'd reply, 'Fine, thanks. How are you?'

And she'd reply, 'I'm ringing with the rota, do you have a pencil?' and then she'd begin, always ending on a forecast. 'It's the Harborough show a week on Saturday, so I expect they'll all be in for fancy-dress materials.' Or, 'It's going to be hot, we'll probably have the sun-dress crew in.'

As the summer went on Norma and I had a lot of fun, and if Mrs Pavlou hadn't said on that first day that we wouldn't be friends I'd have thought we very much were. Norma didn't laugh easily but if something amused her properly she might need her inhaler. Such as the time I'd pluralized the word 'bust' to 'busts' and she almost died of oxygen starvation and I'd had to turn the sign round on the door until she recovered. Or the time I realized that when Norma said 'Lippety Print' she meant Liberty Print, our stock being 'slight seconds', the selvedge smudged and the B looking like a P. I knew the brand not because I was a fabric expert but because we had curtains at home in *Strawberry Thief*, and my mother was always collecting nick-nacks to match (handkerchiefs and an egg cosy). And the time I'd thought Norma's gloved hand was a pin cushion and tried to stick a needle into it and, hearing her scream, a customer knocked the spinner over in her dash for the door, thinking a violent robbery was under way.

Or the times customers dragged husbands in to choose trouser fabric and Norma would ask them, 'Are you sure the inside leg measurement is *accurate*, madam?' before she'd take them seriously, and the wife might say, 'I *think* so?' with a tiny note of doubt in her voice, and Norma would grab the tape measure and say, 'Shall I just . . .' and the wife would step away from the man and look at the sequins out of decency, and we'd hear Norma ask, 'Which side do you dress, sir?' And the man would say, 'Oh, um –' and have to imagine the precise location of his genitals, at that moment, in relation to the crotch seam on his trousers, and slightly shift his weight from one leg to the other, to make certain of it, and then he'd sometimes say, 'To the left.' But more often, 'To the right,' and Norma would bob down, all the time looking him in the eye. Once she'd said, 'Oh! I thought you said the left, sir,' and the man said, 'Sorry, I get mixed up with my left and right.' And Norma insisting there was nothing remotely amusing about this procedure when I'd have the giggles afterwards, asking, 'What's so special about men that you fall about laughing? Perhaps you're not suited to haberdashery.' A rebuke I'd throw back at her when she failed to be at all delighted by our matrimonial fabrics and appurtenances.

Weddings were laughable to her: 'Spending hundreds of pounds to get trussed up like a virgin, it's idiotic,' she'd say and the fact that our white and ivory silks were double the price of silk in any other colour seemed to corroborate this. She refused to wear cotton gloves to handle the ceremonial fabrics, and, when a bride-to-be stepped up onto the bridal stool to have the proper adjustments made to an unfinished dress and Mrs Pavlou, talking through pins, might say, 'Oh, yes, this is really so beautiful,' with the mother-of-the-bride in tears, lips trembling, hands fanning her hot face, Norma would clear her throat and move around noisily to make the moment mundane and ordinary. But she also used to claim not to believe in sex before marriage.

I asked her one day, 'When are you going to have sex then, seeing as you're so against marriage?'

And she said, 'I'm all for marriage, I'm against the absolute nonsense of weddings.'

One day a middle-aged man came in, on his own, and that was unusual – him a man and old and in a business suit – and he was looking at sewing patterns for glamorous nightgowns and we were assuming they were for his own use and sniggering, because back then, I'm sad to say, people were prone to laugh at things of this kind, it being a mainstay of television comedy etc. and he left the shop and Norma, overcome with shame at our behaviour, had run out after him to apologize, and had caught up with him in the butcher's, waited behind him and while the butcher sliced him a quarter-pound of ham, wafer thin, she told him we stocked all sizes and could advise on fabrics, etc. and invited him back to browse. And then, finding herself at the front of the queue, unable to avoid it, bought some lard. The man (known as 'the Ham Man' after that incident) called in occasionally to browse, and apart from the time he bought some tailor's chalk, said not one word to us.

We always had a box of Maltesers on the go and made them last all day, taking them few and far between and not just guzzling them, as one would bored to death at the theatre. For some while, almost daily, a dear little old woman would come in and ask us to thread a needle for her because of arthritic fingers and poor eyesight. Norma, one day, very sweetly, gave her a little felt book she'd made, containing a line of needles ready threaded with different-coloured cotton.

'This should keep you going,' she'd said.

Afterwards I said, 'That was kind of you, Norma, but I think she liked the excuse to come in for a chat and a Malteser.'

And Norma said, 'Well, she should say so and not waste our time pretending she needs help.'

Towards the end of the summer, in spite of not being officially friends, we started to have occasional outings which involved driving into Leicester just as the night clubs were opening – admission being half-price and the music down low – where we'd dance in front of the few old men at the bar and allow them to buy us Britvic juices, and then leave, before it got too frenetic. One club was called Norma Jeane's and another Bailey's but Norma's favourite was Genevieve's because of its clean lavatories and secure cloakrooms. She would always smooch with one or two of the men after requesting the DJ play 'What Becomes of the Brokenhearted' or some equally slow song, especially for the purpose, and I'd wait on a bar stool with our coats ready and try not to catch anyone's eye. It really was very odd but for a while I said nothing, thinking that as she'd driven us there I should be grateful. But later when I felt I knew her well enough, I thought it my duty and after a few weeks I said, 'You can't just dance with men like that, looking furious – you have to smile and look reasonably happy.'

'Why should I?'

'You just should – it has to seem as though you're enjoying yourself, but don't laugh.'

'I am enjoying myself,' she said. 'I'm doing it for me, not for them.'

'It doesn't look like it,' I said. 'It seems as though you want a fight.'

Soon Norma and I reached the stage that married couples do, where their principal joy is in the condemnation of others. In the shop we derided the customers who came in to ask for samples, and returned wanting boudoir brocade for curtains, or robust fabrics for upholstery in reds and oranges. We scorned anyone wanting patterns with large flower heads, especially poppies. And we criticized our neighbours too; the florist next door for sticking pins into tulip stems to prevent them drooping, when any fool knows the whole point of a tulip is the way they lean away from the vase, and being able to see inside them – and Norma should know, being half Dutch. We sneered at the Brankham Arms for their ploughman's lunch with the brown-mottled, insufficiently pickled onions, and the Two Swans for their notice tacked up above the counter, 'One serviette per customer'.

Our favourite person to dislike was a man called Hugo Pack-Allen, whom I'd never met in person, but whom the Pavlous had got talking to in the Brankham Arms earlier that summer, and Mrs Pavlou had asked him to consider investing in the Pin Cushion and he'd agreed, paperwork pending. Further meetings ensued and soon without anything being signed, he had the authority to rethink our opening hours, to demand that we stock novelty items such as the Ronco Buttoneer and other gadgets, glues, kits and nasty things that would diminish us in the eyes of our traditional and loyal clientele, and display them in the window instead of beautiful printed silks. I'd not even met the man and he was knocking my professional esteem.

In early September, Norma told me she'd been invited to take tea in the Two Swans with her parents and this silent partner and we'd laughed at the idea of him ordering a fondant fancy and eating only the icing. When the day came, Norma put on a show of reluctance, but I felt left out as I locked up and watched them cross the road with their hair brushed. Mr Pavlou muttered something to Norma, presumably along the lines of 'Try to be nice, Norma.' And Mrs Pavlou was looking nervous.

When Norma telephoned me the following Sunday evening with the rota, she told me all about the tea. How Hugo Pack-Allen had invested not only in the Pin Cushion but that he also had a financial interest in the Two Swans and to prove it, he'd torn down the notice about serviettes, saying it looked common. Not the notice, the word 'serviette'. Also, that the teatime meetings were to be weekly events while the business settled and I was to attend the next one.

The following Friday, we all four of us went over to tea and sat at the same window table I had sat at that first time I'd met Roy Warren. While we waited and the Pavlous tried to remember what type of tea or coffee Mr Pack-Allen had ordered the previous week, I gazed out into the street hoping to see him rushing along. Instead I saw a man looking at our window display, and taking photographs. I nudged Mrs Pavlou. 'Oh, yes,' she said, 'that's Mr Pack-Allen,' and as he turned to cross the street I saw that he was the man who had come in for nightwear patterns, whom Norma had run after and caught up with in the butcher's. He was none other than the Ham Man. He'd not come in to buy anything, he'd come in to spy on us and the stock, and Norma, I guessed, had suddenly realized and that was why she'd chased him to apologize.

'Why didn't you tell me he was the Ham Man?' I said.

Norma shrugged. 'I didn't think it was important.'

Soon he appeared with a briefcase and said he was delighted that we were all present as he wanted to tell us about the exciting new partnership he had formed with a franchise called Curtains For You which ran national advertisements for drapes, nets and blinds for windows, doors and conservatories. 'From blackout curtains to drapes so sheer you feel your home breathe.' We would be required to do home consultations across a twenty-mile radius, he told us.

'Home consultations? You mean go to people's houses?' said Norma, aghast. 'Could the customers not phone their measurements through to us?'

'No,' said Hugo Pack-Allen, 'the accuracy of the measurement is paramount and it is the Curtains For You USP.'

'I can't go round to people's houses,' she said. 'I'm studying.'

'Well,' said Hugo Pack-Allen, 'maybe other staff will fulfil our obligations.' And it was left like that.

That was how we went on: me doing the shop work while she read the classics in preparation for interviews at English departments across the Midlands, in which she'd call John Donne 'emotional' but quote by heart 'At the round earth's imagined corners', and if questioned about her science background, knew to say, 'Where would Milton and Tennyson be without their fascination with earth sciences, where Thomas Hardy without the Jurassic coast? And Blake without his love of the earth itself? Where the Brontës without the uniqueness of the moorland? Dickens without the Kentish marshes?' Though it was all a bit rum, you must admit, it sounded learned.

Occasionally the phone rang and Norma would tell the caller, 'There's a six-month waiting time for curtain consultations.' And they'd ring off with instructions on how to measure their own window frames.

Mrs Pavlou offered to come downstairs from time to time on the days that Norma had university interviews and other engagements. If we had a rush of customers, I was to ring the little handbell on the stairs and she'd pop down to help. I did ring it one day and she attended to a cluster of children needing kilts, blouses and hockey socks, her shop being the sole supplier of uniform for Brankham House School for Girls. Afterwards, instead of going back upstairs to her dressmaking, she stayed with me, chatting. She apologized for Norma.

'You mustn't take it personally,' she said, and I said I didn't know what she was referring to and she said, 'That she can be a bit brittle in her manner.'

I laughed it off. 'Oh, I like her directness,' I said.

And Mrs Pavlou with tear-filled eyes said, 'She was snatched, you know, at Disneyland when she was eight years old—'

'Oh, no,' I gasped, interrupting.

'No, no, she came to no harm, don't worry – but she poked the man's eye out with her fingers and left him in a heap.'

'Oh my God,' I said, and remembered with a chill Norma's fascination at the 'Out, vile jelly' scene from *King Lear*.

'Yah, it left her a little cynical, you know,' said Mrs Pavlou.

'About men?'

'About all things – life, love, Disney, everything.'

I didn't ring the bell again, and by the end of the summer holidays Norma had secured offers from three institutions and eventually settled for the English MA at the University of Rutland, just up the road from the shop.

And then, later, just as I was about to go back to university and Norma to start her Master's, she learned that she'd earned more money than I had (having nominally been manageress) and insisted on sharing the difference of just over two hundred pounds, but, not wanting to let me 'waste the windfall', she took me to a gallery and in the shop attached told me to choose something. I couldn't decide between an embroidery of some strawberries which I could give to my mother, or a still life of a Savoy cabbage cut in half. I didn't particularly want an artwork and would have preferred the cash. It reminded me of the time my father and I had walked past a homeless man and I'd wanted to give him my loose change. 'No,' my father had said, 'money is no good, he'll spend it on drugs.' And instead he bought a Scotch egg and, as we passed again, handed it to the man, who threw it after us as we walked along, and my father turned, just in time, to kick it away into the gutter with the toe of his shoe. 'What a waste,' he said under his breath, and I thought he meant the man's life but now, thinking about it, he probably meant the egg. Anyway, I chose the still life of the cabbage and still have it and, yes, it reminds me of Norma, but also the homeless Scotch egg.

# 3

It wouldn't be fair to say that Roy Warren was more fun than Norma, but he was easier to talk to – and whereas Norma was going to disappear off and become a Professor of Geology or Literature, whichever got the better of her, I felt sure Roy and I could make a life together. He'd grown up in some rough suburbs and on the few occasions he'd been allowed out of the house he'd had to dodge gangs of kids, and negotiate roads of four and six lanes. One morning, while fishing in an urban setting, he and a pal had seen two men throw a body into the canal.

'We called 999,' he said, 'but when the policemen turned up at my house, they were the same two men and so we had to agree that we'd probably imagined it – but we hadn't.'

Sensing him getting emotional, I changed the subject abruptly. 'Did you have any pets as a child?' I asked, because really, what can you say about murder and corruption in someone else's distant past? And I didn't want him crying on me, plus, I knew how soothing a list of dog names could be and that interesting animal facts – a dog can be allergic to thirteen different types of grass, and cats, fewer than five – can be quite diverting. And though Roy had little interest in the subject compared with that of ball sports, he remembered two pets and talked quite nicely about them.

'We had a yellow budgerigar and a tortoise,' he said, which perked us both up.

'Oh, how lovely.'

'The tortoise shares my birthday,' he said.

And though I was delighted to hear this and encouraged him to continue, his stories about animals couldn't rival mine for the simple reason that he hadn't befriended them, integrated them into his daily life, or even really played with them properly. I mean, imagine having a yellow budgie and not teaching it to swear or to pick racehorse winners for you, or walk the plank, or something? My stories were epic in comparison. Take the time Mitch our bearded collie saved our lives by alerting us, with frantic barks, to the smell of North Sea gas, and then when my brother had been about to kill himself by drinking turps, Mitch had leapt up and knocked the bottle out of his hand with his nose. It occurred to me to say that if Mitch had been with him on the canal bank he'd have growled at those two policemen and given the game away. But I didn't want to dredge all that up (excuse the pun), so I didn't say it. Instead, I relayed the old, possibly apocryphal tale of my mother's Dandie Dinmont who jumped out of the car window at the traffic lights, into another car, and the driver of that car following my mother to the pharmacy to deliver the dog back – albeit I do not recall that dog's name, because I was only a baby. (Rusty? Crumpet?)

Apparently the body in the canal was the final straw for Roy's mother and she grounded him for the rest of his childhood, and used to corner him, and talk into his face, warning of every different kind of danger: illness, evil people, parasites (internal and external), taking a lift with a careless driver, walking barefoot, splinters going septic without you even knowing until it's too late and you've got gangrene. There was the danger of choking on bread-bag ties, running with scissors, accidental dishwasher cutlery stabbings, sudden unexpected death syndrome, falling out of bed – a bigger killer than the rest put together. She didn't like him mixing with other species unless they were beatable in a fight, or caged, or only in a picture. She didn't like her boys facing danger of any kind, except playing in the garden with the tortoise after she'd gone over it with an antibacterial wipe, and occasional super-vised non-contact sports. Just around the time Roy started to show a talent for golf, Lee Trevino was hit by lightning and they'd had to hide the newspaper, and when Roy and his brother showed intellectual flair she'd remind them not to get any big ideas about university, and would list the harm they could come to in that context: drugs, debt, sperm theft, intellectual burnout, depression, compara-tive despair syndrome, thinking too much – plus, she said, even if *they* stayed safe, the worry of it all would likely give her cancer. Eventually Roy had no option but to move into a bedsit, aged twenty, and have therapy to get her off his back. He never did go to university, though against her advice he got an aquarium.

My mother, who had been perfect and adventurous in my early years, had been injured in a railway accident at High Wycombe station when I was ten, and woke from a short coma having turned nasty and developed a West Country accent. This incident, by the way, is replicated with such bizarre accuracy in the novel *On Chesil Beach*, that I wondered when I read it many years later, whether Ian McEwan might know of it, or have read the station-master's report. 'As the train moved into the station, a passenger on board opened the door before the train had come fully to a stop, the lady in question was knocked down by the door and found to be unconscious by two alighting passengers. The train steward gave assistance until an ambulance arrived.'

Or McEwan might have been there, seen the whole thing. He might have been the actual man who in his haste to meet with his editor, opened the door while the train was still moving, and knocked her down and then rushed on, in a great hurry, looking back briefly before exiting to Totteridge Road. He'd be the right kind of age and build. I'm not really blaming him, I'm saying he must have got the idea from somewhere.

My mother was fearful afterwards, not in the way Roy's mother was, but entirely selfishly, and there was no one she wouldn't trample to save herself, and she only once offered an opinion on my health and well-being; informing me as I breakfasted on toast with margarine and blackcurrant jam that God would hate me if I had an abortion and didn't give up smoking. And though this was preferable to having been kept prisoner in the garden, like Roy had, it had a sinister side, the fact that she had me search the wardrobes and understairs cupboard every night for hidden assailants and to taste food prepared and served to her by my father, to check it wasn't poisoned and meant to kill her.

'Switch plates, Sue, he won't want *you* dead,' she'd say.

My brother was also recruited – to perform regular checks on the car, making sure no one had tampered with the brakes.

With Roy I could simply drone on about anything that took my fancy and, because he paid so little attention, I could lure him into conversation by starting on something that intrigued him, say Antarctic exploration, but rather than focus on practical details (ponies versus dogs, Scott's credentials as a leader), I might give it a twist to suit my own preoccupations e.g. Scott's mental health.

'Do you think he was suffering from chronic low self-esteem?' I'd say.

And Roy would say, 'Oh, blimey, I don't know, I hadn't thought about that.'

'Well, think about it now.'

Roy would gaze off into a corner, sip his pint, and say something like, 'I suppose he might have.'

'And what about his wife's attitude?' I might say. 'I heard she was a bitch to him all the time, and he went off on that final expedition feeling wretched, and while the other men had tins of home-baked fruit cake to share with the team, he had nothing, only the demand that he make sketches of ice and snow.'

Then Roy would say, 'Poor bloke.'

'And,' I might continue, 'don't you think it a bit convenient that she was a sculptor and could fashion his likeness in granite for the nation afterwards?'

And Roy might say, 'Yes, I suppose it was.'

I might continue again, 'Maybe that was a factor in his

decision to marry her, because what else could it have been – her, acquainted with Isadora Duncan and Auguste Rodin, and him, a naval officer who'd barely seen inside an art gallery.'

Then Roy, getting the hang of pointless conjecture, would agree, 'Yes, they were chalk and cheese,' and go on to describe what he'd like as a send-off before embarking on a voyage, and I honestly don't think he'd ever had such interesting chats before in his life. He even said as much.

Norma, on the other hand, was attentive and discriminating. If I began, 'We used to have this sweet little dog—' she'd interrupt, 'I can't bear little dogs,' and it wasn't that I didn't want to bore her so much as she didn't deserve the little dog and so I'd stop and swerve to a literary topic.

'Graham Greene is addicted to the television, apparently,' I once told her.

And she wondered, 'Do you think he saw *Twin Peaks*?' which seemed ridiculous but then made us wonder if J. R. R. Tolkien had watched *Miss World*, or Igor Stravinsky had listened to Bowie, or if C. S. Lewis liked the Rolling Stones, and if Simone de Beauvoir went to see *Jaws* and *Jaws 2*, but drew the line at *Jaws 3*. Norma disliked her own and other people's memories, which rendered much of my usual repertoire (personal anecdote and ambling digression) entirely dismissible, unless about sex scandal, which it rarely was. She liked to talk about the future not the past, and she had a pretty bleak view of it. There'd be no grapes, and no Christmas trees due to climate disasters, farms would be factories, meat would be lab-manufactured or made out of locusts, and if people didn't stop taking pebbles from Chesil Beach, there'd be nothing to prevent flooding in Abbotsbury, where she'd been on a field trip and heard from locals that tourists frequently loaded their car boots with the pale flat stones to pile up at home, like modern art. If I inadvertently mentioned something quaint or tedious she'd stare out of the window until I'd finished, and punish me by predicting an imminent and horrific Third World War. If I mentioned my love of cattle, she'd drop out that Nina Simone had attended a bullfight.

I remember once asking her opinion on a hairstyle I was considering and her saying, 'You do realize women will soon go bald as young as men, don't you?'

And when I asked why, she listed dispassionately, 'Contaminated water, anxiety, cling film, aluminium, the contraceptive pill, anxiety,' and then added, 'I hope you appreciate the luxury of having a hot shower every day, Susan, because it won't be possible for ever.'

To which I replied, 'We don't have a shower. I have my mother's bathwater after her.'

And I honestly thought she might be sick.

There was no chance of combining the both of them. Norma would sneer at Roy because of Disneyland and men in general, and though Roy wouldn't notice, I would. They'd not enrich each other, they'd cancel each other and each be less not more. Since my previous boyfriend had been stolen by a friend, I didn't want to risk it, especially after my having learned the hard way that girls who don't believe in sex before marriage can suddenly find themselves fondling the boyfriend of a friend on an impromptu lift home, and Norma holding that belief, and Roy having a car and being that bit older and therefore susceptible. Also, Norma would be appalled by Roy's tattoo – and fair enough, tattoos in those days being unironic and intensifying whatever it was that made you *you*. Roy's made him more Roy and those few which adorned my university classmates made them even more *not* Roy. One boy in my Victorian Poets class had '*Hamlet*' in copperplate on his shoulder. Another had a tiny struggling beetle (upside down) and the word '*Nihilism*'. Roy's roaring bear holding a rose was so innocent and decorative. The red part still swells slightly when he uses sun cream.

Anyway, I *did* believe in sex before marriage, and Roy and I were soon having it in the car, my home being untenable, Roy being too old to take to one's bedroom, and Roy's landlady being the old-fashioned type and with a young child. I knew things were serious between us when, just before I just went back to university that first September, Roy took me to meet his mother. We had afternoon tea in their back garden and it struck me that she was the opposite of my mother. Where mine was unable to care for others, that's all his could do. While mine looked at clouds and knew their names, ditto every kind of bird – its call, its lifespan, its preferred habitat – his watched TV with her lumpy feet up on a pouffe, worried about toxins in the upholstery. While mine was like a blackbird who'd fledged her babies early and didn't want to be reminded of them, his was a catastrophist who didn't entirely trust

Jesus but talked about him so often that Roy used to think he was related. And though he had described how the little woman beside me had cornered him and spoken her worries into his face, my opinion at the time was that her worst crime was not having trained her sons to drink coffee or tea, which stranded them in childhood for ever, because who wants to meet someone for coffee if they'll only have a glass of Oasis? Or afternoon tea with someone who has diet Ribena? Or breakfast with someone who has a glass of water with their eggs?

Roy's mother, Grace, had heard lots about me, she said, and thinking it just up my street, invited me to accompany her to see Frendini the stage spiritualist – and though I had no interest in that kind of thing, and Roy seemed against it (shaking his head behind her back, and frowning), I accepted in order to be polite, and to be in her good books. The following Saturday, off we went to the afternoon performance. We arrived early at the Corn Exchange and after buying a 50p leaflet about Frendini took our seats near the front.

'I hear you're fond of animals,' said Roy's mother, for something to say.

'Yes,' I said, 'are you?'

'Well, do you know about our tortoise?'

'I heard you had one.'

'He was my brother's, but he wasn't looking after him properly, so I brought him home and gave him to my husband,' she said. 'Little did I know we'd still have him, all these years later.'

I laughed politely, not quite knowing who the villain

was in this story; the brother for not looking after the tortoise, or the sister for basically stealing it and giving it to her husband.

'And do you know what, Susan? A neighbour *reported* us, for cruelty – for painting a letter H on his wee shell. We thought that was what you did with tortoises, we'd seen it on the television,' she said, 'and the RSPCA sent a warden, and I told him, "This tortoise has a semi-tropical diet and I wipe him over with TCP every other day, he's borderline pampered," and thank God, the warden saw sense, and wrote a report stating, "As far as I can tell this creature is well cared for," so that was that, but I felt awful, taking him from my brother, and then being reported ourselves – it was mortifying.'

After digging about in the straw basket between her feet, she showed me a blurry photograph of two small boys with what must have been a tortoise but could have been a teapot. She seemed all sweetness and light, almost in tears recalling this long-ago mortification, and I decided she must have done it for the best.

Frendini the spiritualist didn't even try to not seem like a con man, and seeing the hundred or so women in the audience – and they were all women except for the odd husband who'd had no choice but to come along – turn into sad fools, Roy's mother included, was surprisingly upsetting, the only moment of lightness being when someone threw a single gladioli onto the stage and Frendini punched it away like a bad goalkeeper and inadvertently said, 'P*ss off!' At that moment he seemed exactly like the Ham Man, not so much his looks, but his aura.

'I'm getting an urgent message for a Margaret,' said Frendini.

No response.

'A Margaret G.?' he said. 'Margaret *Jean.*'

Nothing.

'Maggie, Maggie G., Maggie J.?' he said, touching his temple. 'Margaret, Mary, Mary G. – is there an M.G.?' said Frendini. 'Jean, or Joan, Margaret G., or J. – or Jane? Come on, Margaret, speak to me, don't be shy, I've got a message for you.'

Roy's mother gazed about.

'Margaret G.? Is there an M. G., a Mary-Jane, a Jean, a Joan, or even a G. M.?' Frendini called, walking up and down the stage, and Roy's mother gripped my arm and let out a yelp. Frendini shaded his eyes and looked in our direction, nodding slowly, breathed in and out, and whipped the lead on his mic.

'Here she is. Margaret G., is it?'

'Grace Margaret,' said Roy's mother.

'Well, you're forgiven, love, you're to let it go now – does this make sense?'

'Yes, it does, thank you,' she croaked.

On the way home she said, 'That was me, Margaret G. Only the other way round, G. Margaret.'

'So do you feel better?' I asked. 'Did it help?'

'Yes, very much so. I feel absolved,' she said. 'You see – and you mustn't say anything – but Hector's not Ted's, and it's been playing on my nerves all these years.'

I thought about this – was Hector the tortoise? I wondered. Yes. H for Hector?

47

'Who's Ted?' I said.

'Ted's my husband, but anyway, I'm to let it go, and stop worrying.'

'Oh, good,' I said, 'so you're glad you went?'

'Yes, it's a weight lifted.'

At home she went straight upstairs for a lie-down.

'How did that go?' asked Roy.

'It was a bit grim, if I'm honest, but your mother seems to have got something out of it,' I said, 'and that's the main thing.'

'Was she contacted from the other side?' he asked.

'Yes, she was.'

'What, really?'

'Yep, something to do with your tortoise,' I said, 'it belonging to her brother, and not being your dad's.'

'What?' said Roy.

'I know it sounds mad, but she believes it, so, you know, be merciful.'

'The *tortoise*?'

'He's not your dad's,' I said, 'but we're not to say anything.'

Roy looked puzzled. 'What?'

'That's what she said,' I whispered. '"Hector's not Ted's, but don't tell Ted."'

# 4

It started to feel as though we were sisters, Norma and I, not that we were alike or aligned but that we were attached for all time. Even while I was away, she rang every Sunday. I'd always wanted a sister and particularly an older one who wouldn't fuss over me but whose version of the world would be constantly revealed, like items on a conveyor belt that I could reach for and keep or dismiss. And who would examine my preoccupations and discard them with the same few comments: 'You care too much,' she'd say, and, 'Don't worry about it.' And if I imagined a face in the bark of a tree, she'd say, 'People who see faces in everything often lack self-assurance.'

Norma was scientific in her approach to life and the world was her laboratory. She took the kettle off the boil so as not to kill the vitamin C in her Lemsip, which she drank in the afternoons because of tension headaches. She knew the body preferred acid to alkaline, but that the word 'acid' had connotations, she knew the importance of sleep for renewal and repair, especially for the eyes and smaller organs. 'Blink properly, Susan,' she'd say, 'blink so that your inner and outer lids close to keep the cornea hydrated.'

She was terribly aware of how humans are just creatures forever wrestling our instincts, like chimpanzees in bowler hats drinking from tiny china cups but all too liable to turn savage in a moment and to upend the tea table. She especially thought this of men and, with the slightest provocation, she'd try to scare me off them: 'Men are like the ocean,' she might say, 'magnificent and life-giving – but don't turn your back on them or they'll throw you about like a doll.'

'Will they throw me about like a doll because I turn my back or are they always on the brink of it?' I'd ask.

'Just stay alert,' she'd say.

I didn't want that kind of talk, not yet anyway.


Norma decided without really knowing Roy that he wasn't good enough for me. 'Surely there's a decent bloke at college?' she'd say.

'Maybe, but the ones I like would never like me.'

'What about the ones who *would* like you?' she'd say.

'I don't like them.'

Some time before Christmas she organized a double date with brothers Edmund and Joe-Tony Vangundy, whom she'd met briefly at a University of Rutland event, their father being a donor. I had misgivings. 'Wouldn't it be disloyal to Roy?' I wondered.

'No, of course not, you're not wedded to him,' said Norma. 'In any case, he's always out with other women while you're at university.'

'Is he?' I asked. 'What women?'

'Josie Jones for a start.'

'Josie Jones?' I said. 'It's not romantic with her, she's just his landlady, and they're having a pint.'

'It looks quite romantic,' said Norma.

'In what way?' I asked.

'Well, you know, sitting at one of those tables for two, gazing into each other's eyes, playing darts, and so forth.'

'No, they've been pals for years,' I said, but I can't deny it irked to hear this.

'Well, anyway, just come for a drink, as a favour to me. They're loaded, these two, real husband material.'

'Loaded with what?' I asked. I'd assumed she meant money but there'd been a lot about diminishing sperm counts on the news.

'Money – the parents own a shoe company. What else would they be loaded with?'

'Oh,' I said, 'as in the Vangundy SureFoot?'

'The what?'

'The walking boots,' I said, and I must admit, that did make them seem quite intriguing. Roy had a pair of Sure-Foots and was very pleased with them.

'You'll like Joe-Tony,' said Norma. 'He's good-looking and has such good manners. Honestly, you'll have forgotten all about Roy by Sunday.'

'Joe-Tony?' I said. 'What about Edmund?'

'Edmund is mine.'

'Why?' I said.

'He's older, he'll inherit.'

I was to meet the Vangundys at the Old Dun Cow, put them at their ease, and Norma would arrive fashionably late and dolled up. I got there a few minutes early and wouldn't have recognized them from Norma's description except one of them wore pristine walking boots with candy-striped laces. 'I'm Susan,' I said, and the one in the boots said, 'Oh, hello, Susan, I'm Joe-Tony. Can I get you a drink?' While the barman got my half-pint of bitter shandy, he introduced me to his brother. 'This is Edmund,' he said. I leaned away from the bar and smiled at Edmund behind Joe-Tony's back. He was certainly good-looking, but shy compared with his brother, and made only a cursory nod.

'I'm about to go hiking,' said Joe-Tony, tapping his heel on the floorboards.

'This evening?' I said.

'No,' he laughed, 'at the end of the month. South America.'

'So you're breaking the boots in,' I said, looking at his feet.

'No, these don't need breaking in. Good to go from the moment you put them on.' He lifted a foot and showed the boot from every angle.

I looked at them for a while. 'SureFoots?' I said.

'Yes! As a matter of fact they are.' Joe-Tony was suddenly enthusiastic. 'Do you know them?'

'Yes, of course, everyone does – "Worn by Ranulph Twisleton-Wykeham-Fiennes",' I said, quoting the adverts in the Sunday papers.

I felt fraudulent. I was coming over as the ideal girl-friend with all this boot talk. I had no intention of becoming any such thing, and that being the case made it easy to be perfect. Norma burst in looking like Sophia Loren in an ill-fitting dress, saying she was sorry to be so late and lighting a cigarette all at once, which was ridiculous because she was bang on time and then didn't inhale.

She asked for a grapefruit and soda and Joe-Tony then suggested we go on to the Amalfi Trattoria on Brankham High Street. 'I have a terrific yearning for breaded mushrooms,' he said, which was about the worst thing I'd ever heard a man say.

In the restaurant it was agreed that Joe-Tony should order for all of us, him being a regular and seeming in charge. The boys tucked in with relish and Joe-Tony regaled us between mouthfuls with tales of hiking in various hills and mountains testing new SureFoot prototypes in real terrain. 'I trod in some molten lava once,' he said, loading his fork, 'and another time, in the Andes, a blacksmith's anvil fell on my foot.' We waited then while he chewed and swallowed, before saying, 'Mmm, and I felt *absolutely nothing.*'

After the main course, he ordered two desserts and asked for four spoons, in Italian, for which he got a laugh out of the waitress. When they arrived, Edmund, who'd been entirely passive up to then, pushed one towards Norma and me, and positioned the other so it was obviously for himself and his brother. I was delighted at this arrangement, not relishing the insinuation of dipping into the same Italian trifle as Joe-Tony. Norma felt differently though, and plunged her spoon right into the middle of the boys' dish. Edmund protested. 'This is ours,' he said, moving it out of reach. 'That one's yours.' After that we ate in silence and then Joe-Tony asked for the bill, and paid it with cash. At the door, we thanked them for a lovely evening and headed off in the wrong direction.

'I *mean*,' said Norma, as we strode, 'if you're on a date with a woman and you'd rather share a tiramisu with your brother, it hardly bodes well, does it?'

'Suppose not,' I said. 'You'd probably have been better off with Joe-Tony.'

'God, no, all that talk about those damned boots,' she said.

'Well, I'm sticking with Roy.'

'For now,' she said.

Roy was at that time estate manager of Brankham Golf Club and tutor to beginners. His pupils were exclusively members' wives, girlfriends, nieces and occasionally mothers. Roy was neither a flirt nor a chauvinist and took these women seriously, treating them as though they really were at the start of a worthwhile sporting, possibly life-long, hobby. He always began each course of lessons in the clubhouse with a half-sized human skeleton and was never too self-conscious to say things like 'pelvis', 'swing' or 'muscular hammock', nor to point at its nether regions. He'd know, by the end of the first lesson (largely by assessing their attitude to the skeleton), whether they had any real intention to learn the game – few had – or were just indulging a partner, father or whomever. Being older and on what we used to call a 'career path' and having bills to pay meant that Roy unwittingly eclipsed the artsy boys at university in my mind. He meant no disrespect and neither did I. For recreation he'd go under the bonnet of his old Ford Escort, correctly believing that his companion (me) would enjoy taking the driver's seat and being told to 'press the accelerator at my command' and seeing him jump out, shocked, with a spanner in his hand after I'd sounded the horn for mischief – and this was for me ten times the joy of cleverly disrespecting Henrik Ibsen cross-legged at a party.

Back at university, the boys would be frowning into paperbacks, explaining away Blake's awful poetry (with the excuse that he saw angels in trees) writing songs and poems, campaigning against things, and marching for things, whereas there was no one like Roy. The nearest being a drunken philosophy lecturer called Don Daniels who was always rubbing his legs and described himself as a critic of the Enlightenment, which Roy actually was – not that he knew it, or said so, but simply by not knowing Nietzsche from Adam, by being far too busy to have heard of David Lynch, and by collecting Haynes car manuals for models he'd never own and reading them in bed. It occurred to me that Roy's love of golfing champ Arnold Palmer – a former paint salesman – and his understanding of what actually might happen in life, and frankly, his awareness of how to conduct himself – as a buyer, as a seller and in a pub – would surely be more pleasing to Arthur Miller than an undergraduate trotting out lines from *Death of a Salesman*.

I can't deny though that those boys in turn sometimes made Roy seem old and dull, just by using hair gel and having a high-pitched laugh. I think I knew I'd stick with Roy and his Bob Monkhouse hair, at least for a while, even though the gulf between us would widen as I made my way in the literary world (teacher, poet, journalist). I found myself looking for signs of intellectual sensitivity, like the time I'd gone to watch him run a cross-country race, through fields and woods – making up for the old days when his mother ruled him out of such activity because of a heart murmur she imagined for him.

'How did it go?' I asked afterwards as he struggled into his coat.

'It was a bit icy underfoot,' he said, 'especially where the path narrowed.'

'Oh, yes,' I said, 'on the bridge.'

'Oh, was that a bridge?'

'Funny to think you don't always know you're on one,' I said.

And he said, 'We might be on one now.'

Was he being philosophical? I hoped so, and hugged him. Or did he really think we might be on a bridge?

While my mind was always firmly in the present, Roy had a real grasp on the future. He was the first person I knew, for instance, to use the words 'logo' and 'world wide web' and 'Snickers', and has been very good in that respect, using correct and modern terminology at all times. He is one of the few people I've known to be very much a part of humanity, while also being able to comment on it, like an alien. It was as if he could step back from the world and I could only hurtle towards it. It was Roy, for example, who told me that wood-burning stoves give out minute toxic particles, which is why I've never hankered after one however gloriously soothing they seem, and that you should rinse washing-up liquid off the pots with a proper rinsing stage, and that people touch their noses when they're exaggerating.

Roy never trusted a person who didn't like their food, and I felt the same. My brother, James, had always made his Easter egg last the whole of the school holidays, nibbling it crumb by crumb, and I hated him for it, and my mother would forget to eat because of it being such a bore. Yes, the thing I remember best about Roy from our early years was his love of food. I noticed it straight away, at our first meeting and then again on subsequent dates, which were frequently breakfast because of his shifts. That was before anyone even had breakfast dates and it had been odd and exciting.

Soon after we met, he was promoted to a marketing position and moved into a flat share with a tropical aquarium, a freezer and a burglar alarm.

'How come you moved?' I asked.

'It got a bit oppressive at the old place,' he said. 'The landlady needed my room for her kid.'

If I'd asked the name of this baby he would have said Grace. If he remembered, and I'd have noticed the name, because I usually do. A side effect of the move was his cookery, his favourite, unfortunately, being duck, which he'd learned to cook from his mother who'd grown up eating only turnips and offal and now relished whole birds. Roy would buy Cherry Valley ducklings from Bejam's and sometimes a cheesecake for pudding. He'd defrost both things overnight and then roast the duckling on a high heat and, following the manufacturer's suggestion, serve it with a piquant sauce, preferably cherry because of its ability to cut through the rich gamey flavour, and if not cherry, then orange. I didn't enjoy the duck but admired the preparedness and forward planning and the lack of mystery. I'd call round and suggest a film and he'd say, 'Duckling tonight!' and rub his hands together and my heart would sink because I wanted to love Roy. By then, I really did. I wanted to marry him and have three or four children and watch him throw them up into the air, laughing, and teach them contemporary words and how a democracy works.

This might seem odd nowadays but 1990 was practically still the '80s and the 1980s is a long time ago now and many women still ate duckling they didn't want and imagined husbands being playful and good in the future. I can't pretend the Cherry Valley ducklings weren't something of an obstacle. The thought of the living, trusting, fluffy little things, almost at duckhood and then what? Shot? No, necks wrung and feathers wrenched out by a mechanical plucker, or burnt off or acid-bathed. Those roughly hewn tablets of poultry-coloured rubber were about as far from the thing they'd been in life as anything could possibly be. Why did they call them ducklings? Can ducklings be that big? I'd have felt better with the word 'duck'. All this thinking led to unfathomable sadness and yet I'd say nothing and I'd eat and smile at Roy and say, 'Delicious,' with my hand at my mouth in case he saw any morsel of duckling around my teeth, and he'd say, 'My pleasure,' dabbing at his chin with a napkin, and then, keeping his eyes on mine, take a sip of water or pale ale.

I'm vegetarian now.

# 5

At home for a reading week in early 1991 I'd signed up to work in the Pin Cushion, but on the first morning I took a pregnancy test. Only because I had one unused from a previous scare. It was highly unlikely I'd be pregnant – Roy was very good at pulling out in plenty of time. He quite liked the last part by hand. To my astonishment, it was positive. In some kind of daze I went to work my shift, with a book to read between customers, and tried not to think about it. An hour after opening I shut up the shop and spent almost five pounds on another test and did it in the shop toilet. That one was positive too. So there I was: halfway through an English degree and pregnant to a man eight years my senior whom I'd known for seven months and who, if I'm honest, suddenly seemed a bit literal and sporty to spend my whole life with. Even with two positive tests I still couldn't quite believe it, and planned to do another, a more expensive brand, before telling Norma, or my mother, or Roy. But then Norma dropped in at lunchtime to discuss the poem 'They Flee From Me' by Thomas Wyatt.

'He was rumoured to have had an affair with Anne Boleyn,' she began, 'which is intriguing, and I think that's what it's all about.'

I interrupted with the news. 'I'm pregnant. I can't believe it but I've done two tests.'

'You?' she said.

'Yes. I've done two tests. Both positive.'

She looked appalled as I spoke, and involuntarily shook her head.

'I can't believe it,' I said again.

'So careless,' she said, 'and disappointing.' I thought she might cry, and then, because I stood silent, scratching one eyebrow with my little fingernail to hide my crumpling face, she said, 'So, now what are you going to do?'

I didn't know.

'What would you do?' I asked.

'I'd never let this happen,' she said with a laugh.

'But if it did.'

'Susan, I would never be in this position.'

'But if you were?' I persisted, desperately.

'Well,' she said, 'I'd have the baby, of course!'

At the end of the day after locking up the shop I went home. Finding my mother in the kitchen, I told her too.

'I haven't decided what to do,' I said. 'I wanted your thoughts, that's all.'

She was straightforward. 'I can't advise you, but if you get rid of it, please don't tell your father,' she said, which, though worded harshly, was strangely compassionate.

I couldn't think how to tell Roy. An abortion was probably the right thing, I decided, but thought I ought to at least speak to him. I left a message at work and, when he didn't ring back, I borrowed my dad's car and parked outside the clubhouse. Roy appeared at the doors, looking serious, trotting down the steps with a folder under his arm and smoking paraphernalia in his hand. I waited for the moment he caught sight of me, the split second, I wanted to see the alteration in his expression, from neutral to what? Shock, pleasure, irritation, anxiety? He saw me and his mouth opened – he didn't even look back at the unlit cigarette that fell from his lips as they parted in surprised delight. He put the folder on the roof of the car and enveloped me and kissed me and lifted me off the ground. He was rushing though, he'd got a plan to meet friends for a meal for his birthday. 'I'd invite you along but, well, it's the boys.' I'd see him the following night anyway, on his actual birthday when I'd been invited for dinner with his family. I'd wait and tell him after that.

The meal the following evening was served in the dining room, a space only marginally bigger than the table. Once we'd all taken our places there was no moving – except for Mrs Warren who gave herself the place by the door for kitchen access. While she clanged about next door Roy introduced me to his brother, Guy, and Guy's girlfriend, Boo, short for Booboo, which was short for Bridget, and who was quite tiny and had to have two cushions. By the time we'd all said hello and how do you do? and I'd been reacquainted with Roy's father, Mrs Warren reappeared and set down a great platter with two roasted ducks and a gravy boat of orange sauce which she'd made with Quosh and a drop of brandy, and then a great metal tray of chips, but not so much as a bean or a leaf. She turned and said, to me in particular, 'I hope you like duck.'

'I love it,' I said. 'So nice for a special occasion.'

'The boys and Boo don't like veg, but I can open a tin of peas if you like,' she said.

I thanked her and said I was fine without.

It took me a while to notice the tortoise on the table. Ah, Hector the famous tortoise, I thought, and noticed Roy's father patiently feeding him salad. 'Hector's not Ted's,' I thought, remembering my last encounter with this family.

'Leave him be now, Ted, come and eat your duck,' said Roy's mother, leaning across to erect a haphazard enclosure with saucepans and ovenware. 'It's to stop him toppling off,' she said, again particularly to me. 'Tortoises don't have much road sense.'

'I love that you have a tortoise staying for dinner!' I said.

And Booboo said, 'Well, you know, it's Horace's birthday too.'

'Who's Horace?' I said.

'The tortoise!' said Booboo. 'Horace is the tortoise.' And I believe he looked up from his salad.

'*Horace?* So who is Hector then?'

And Roy said, 'I am.' And looked at me through slightly squinting eyes, watching me work out exactly what that meant.

While the Warren family discussed the time back when Roy was young, and had changed his name from Hector to Roy because he'd failed the eleven-plus and no longer felt equal to it, seeing as he'd be going to the comp and not the grammar, and the ins and outs of how they settled on Roy, because it matched his brother's name in brevity and toughness, I kept an eye on the tortoise, his jaw working methodically on the only available greenery, because it seemed suddenly very likely that he'd now tumble off the table onto the floor, and crack in half, and that someone, possibly Booboo, maybe me, would shriek, 'Hector's not Ted's!'

I must've looked stricken because Booboo said quietly, 'I get a bit claustrophobic in here, too.'

Later, driving back to Roy's new flat, I didn't speak and for a long time neither did he.

'I'm so sorry I told you that thing your mum told me,' I said eventually. 'I honestly thought she was talking about the tortoise, you know, the names both beginning with H.'

'Don't worry about it, my mum's always saying weird stuff like that. It's not true by the way, she's a fantasist,' he rambled, 'and I look just like my dad, don't I?'

I considered his silhouetted profile as we waited at the lights: the long undulating nose, the square chin and sharp cheeks, the immense geometry of it, and I remembered Ted's face, which in comparison resembled a par-boiled potato. 'Yeah,' I said, 'you're the image of him.'

We were quiet again then until he took the handbrake off and accelerated up the slight hill, and I said, 'Roy, there's something else I have to say.'

And he said, 'You're up the duff?'

And I said, 'I am actually. But how did you guess?'

'I suspected yesterday when you were waiting for me.'

'Why?'

'The moment I saw you,' he said. 'Why else would you be there, in your dad's car?'

'You seemed happy.'

'Yes,' he said.

By the end of the night we were engaged to be married. Not because he was romantic or old-fashioned or overjoyed but because the captain, Fred Fletcher, had just around then mooted the idea of the golf club becoming a wedding venue, and so ours could double as a training-day-cum-photoshoot for the brochure – we'd be doing the club a huge favour and earning Roy some Brownie points. That was our excuse, anyway, plus having heard that the Abbey National were offering low-deposit mortgages to married couples.

Roy considered Fred Fletcher an impressive fellow. His golf was pretty good and his business sense 'second to none'. Fletcher's Fine Foods supplied supermarket deli counters across the Midlands with eight different types of luncheon meat, including one with a teddy bear's face on each slice, and the mildest cheddars money can buy.

'Yeah, I'd like to help the club out,' said Roy.

'But do we want a baby?' I said.

'I don't see why not,' said Roy.

'But Norma,' I said.

'*Norma?*' said Roy. 'What's she got to do with anything?'

'She's not pleased,' I said. 'She thinks I'm an idiot.'

'Why?'

'For being pregnant.'

'You told her then?'

'I had to tell someone.'

'Well, take no notice, she won't feel like that for ever, will she?'

'I hope not.'


Norma insisted that my tutors at university would be only too happy to support me studying through the pregnancy and beyond. 'They love this kind of thing,' she said, and I hated her for it.

'No. I'm dropping out,' I said. 'I'm having a baby.'

'That's ridiculous. I mean, you're only pregnant, surely you can write a few essays and sit some exams. Because, Susan, if you don't graduate, who will you *be*?'

'Who will I *be*?' I said. 'I'll be me.'

'You won't reach your potential,' she said. 'You'll sink without a trace.'

'No, I won't.'

'I just didn't see you ending up like this.'

'Like what?' I said.

'Living with a marketing executive in Brankham.'

'Where did you see me?'

'A garden flat in the metropolis, with an electric piano, venetian blinds and the ghost of a poet. And a season ticket for the ballet.'

'Well, I might still, but in Brankham,' I said.

'Yeah,' she said, 'and within walking distance of the golf club.'

'So what?' I said. 'I think you're just jealous.'

I did drop out and went full-time at the Pin Cushion, which suited everyone. Mrs Pavlou wanted to concentrate on bespoke dressmaking in the quiet of their flat, and Mr Pavlou was keen to have her on hand for lunches and snacks now he'd got a computer and was working with stocks and shares. It benefited Norma too, if truth be told, since she was studying just up the road. I was available for in-depth book talk, which started right away with Sylvia Plath and Fiona Pitt-Kethley who were new to me and quite shocking; Sylvia so wonderfully obsessed with food and probably dead – I daren't ask, it seeming such a shallow measure of a poet, and Fiona, oh my God.

By Easter that year I'd moved into the flat with Roy and his friends, Leroy and Luke. The three of them had the television blaring in the background the whole time, which I found depressing, and not one of them wanted to do an egg hunt. Worse still, Roy liked to sit in the Brankham Arms after work for an hour or so, before going home. I'd join him, even though I was pregnant and exhausted, thinking it the done thing. 'Go home if you want, I won't be long,' he'd say, and I'd lay my head on the dark wooden table and wait. One evening I couldn't help tears slipping from my closed eyes.

'What's up, love?' said Roy.

'It's nothing,' I said.

He looked at me, alarmed. 'It must be something.'

'It's Norma,' I said. 'She's furious with me for dropping out.'

'Oh, for God's sake.'

'She says I'll never keep up intellectually. I'll be bored to death and have to rely on the radio for stimulation, like all those frustrated housewives of the 1950s.'

'Hey, doesn't she know you're marrying me?' he said, jabbing his thumbs at his chest. We laughed, but for the first time Roy realized that as far as Norma was concerned, he was the problem. 'Well,' he said indignantly, 'you can tell Bamber Gascoigne she's welcome round to ours any time for a chat and a game of Scrabble for Juniors.'

# 6

The wedding was to be catered by Fletcher's Fine Foods who were able to combine traditional and fashionable dishes in a self-service buffet to suit the golf club layout. Roy requested that we have trifle for pudding, not that he particularly liked it but because he'd heard the captain (whom by coincidence I would later know as Chair of Governors at the University of Rutland) on local radio, describing how he'd worked out how to manufacture individual layered desserts for the retail sector – the different setting times and temperatures of the component parts, jelly, custard, fruit cocktail and cream – and now saw trifles in a new light. Miraculous. A problem solved, and not to be taken for granted. Jason the barman would offer a full range of soft and alcoholic drinks served over golf-ball-shaped ice cubes, plus cocktails celebrating the sport, such as the 'Seve Ballesteros', the 'Wonky Golf Cart' and the alcohol-free 'Arnold Palmer'.

The golf theme wouldn't be limited to the drinks – there were to be tees holding the table place cards, decorative golf clubs in among the floral displays, and, as it turned out, a constant flow of gags that combined honeymoons, handicaps, the first hole, the nineteenth hole, being in the rough, and so forth. Roy was rewarded with a major promotion to *Senior* Marketing Executive a fortnight *before* the wedding day, and he and I joked that he could call it off or I could jilt him at the altar, now he'd had the raise.

When the time came to finalize the catering requirements it bothered me that Roy's guests outnumbered mine four to one, the reason being that all of his colleagues and pupils had been invited, to bulk up the photoshoot. True, I hadn't wanted to invite my friends, but now it looked like Roy was the popular one of the couple and it irritated me. I told my mother she might invite her sister and family and listed some old friends of hers from Buckinghamshire; the Steins and the Shentons, also her current neighbours, Dr and Mrs Frizzell, but she declined on all of their behalves. I told my brother he was welcome to bring his sister-in-law and family but he thought that eccentric since I'd met them only once, at his wedding, where I'd torn them off a strip for parking on a hosepipe. I hurriedly invited two old schoolfriends; one replied saying she was washing her hair that day and the other that she couldn't be relied upon to behave herself in the wedding context. I wasn't surprised – people relished declining a wedding invitation back then, especially if not themselves married. Added to which, I'd gone for laughs and let it be widely known that it was part of Roy's career plan, so it was hardly going to be a fairy-tale event.

In the end, with Norma my only non-related guest, I threw it open to her parents, her aunt and uncle, and a whole lot of cousins, who were all living close by at that time. Norma was delighted, and said we must make wedding outfits for them all in the shop, her being over-confident in that department and with all that fabric on hand.

Seeing the unknown names on the guest list, Roy asked, 'Who are Joseph, Tulpen, Denise and Ursula Pavlou?'

'Oh, they're Norma's parents and cousins,' I replied.

'Maurice and Diana Gronig?'

'Norma's uncle and aunt.'

'Are you that close?'

'They're practically family.'

I could see in the lines on his forehead that he wondered if they'd fit in with the golf club contingent. 'I hope they're going to enjoy themselves,' he said.

And I said, 'Of course they are.'

The club arranged a pub crawl for Roy's stag night and he went off a bit nervous, while I went to meet Mrs Pavlou at the shop to make the last adjustments to my wedding outfit. The dress was a copy of Catherine Deneuve's, when she'd married a British photographer, whose name escapes me, in the mid-1960s. I'd seen it in a magazine and thought to myself, if ever I get married, it will have to be in Marylebone and in a dress I could wear again and again, that doesn't just go to dust in the wardrobe. Mrs Pavlou made it, to my design, from premium silk and hand-pleated the skirt to produce a 'puffball' effect. It was adorable.

She was ready when I arrived and held out the dress for me to step into, but when she tried to zip it up, she couldn't.

'Gosh,' she said, 'you're round like a pudding. What happened?'

I didn't want to tell her I was pregnant but looking back, I expect she guessed.

'Oh, no,' I cried, 'what am I going to wear?'

Mrs Pavlou didn't panic in the slightest. She simply cut out a loose cream shift from some machine-embroidered viscose and, with pins between her lips, had it made and fitted within an hour. Just as I stepped out of the new dress, Norma and all the Pavlou women arrived, plus my cousin Timandra for my surprise hen party.

'New dress?' said Norma.

'Oh my God,' said Mrs Pavlou, 'this girl has doubled in size since I made the original.'

'Oh, that always happens to brides-to-be,' said Norma, and produced a great jug of punch with fruit and herbs.

The neighbouring shops had sent lovely things, including spring flowers with which we made corsages, a cheese board with grapes, cumquats and Carr's Table Waters, and a sign reading '*JUST MARRIED*' from the model shop, which was designed to be fixed onto the back of a car.

The bridesmaids tried on their outfits so that Mrs Pavlou could check them one last time too, and during all the on and off we saw Timandra's pubic hair hanging out of her knickers, which caused Mrs Pavlou to shriek, 'Oh my God, a lion's mane.' As if in response, Norma then stepped out of her dress, and because she never wore underwear, we could see she was as smooth and shiny as a car bonnet. Timandra stared and said, 'Good grief, do you shave?' and Norma said, 'Wax,' and we all winced.

The highlight of the night was when Mrs Pavlou presented me with a bundle of chiffon. 'What is this?' I asked.

'Your schleppe,' she said. 'It's important for the audience.'

'Schleppe?' I said. 'Audience?'

'She means a bridal train,' said Norma, 'for the congregation to admire.'

'Yes,' said Mrs Pavlou and she pinned it to her waistband and sat on the chaise.

'So, the car stops,' she said, 'someone opens the door for you, you step out – like this – and you bring out your schleppe – like this,' she carried the frothy bundle, 'and you step forward, turn around and cast it out behind you, as if throwing it away elegantly.' She demonstrated, and there it was. 'Now you try,' she said, unpinning it from herself and fixing it to me.

So I sat on the chaise, then stood, reached for the bundle, and threw it behind me. It didn't entirely unfurl. 'Ugh, I'm not sure I'll do it justice,' I said.

Norma stepped forward and shook it out. 'I'll deal with it,' she said. 'You just walk.'

The dresses and train were sorted just in time to see Roy's rowdy gang leaving the Brankham Arms. Roy was on his back in a shopping trolley, being pushed elaborately, at speed, by the club captain, until one of the castors came off, at which point they fell about laughing and eventually picked it up like a sedan chair and proceeded along to the Old Dun Cow. I didn't mind, it's just that I'd have quite liked that for myself, instead of which I ate cheese and learned off by heart a choreographed dance to 'Working My Way Back to You' by the Detroit Spinners, which wasn't nearly so much fun.

*

The reception began awkwardly. My mother had been at first surprised and then embarrassed by the golf theme and *apologized* for it to Joseph and Tulpen Pavlou.

'I believe the room came free of charge, otherwise we'd be at the Lady Jane Grey,' she said, as though she, my mother, was some kind of famous *salonnière* and the Pavlous minor royalty and expecting a more tasteful venue. The Pavlous were puzzled, not so much by the disloyalty but at the suggestion that golf might be unworthy as a theme. They'd already admired the clubhouse, respectfully scrutinized the portraits of former chairmen and VIP players that lined the walls, and read a short biography of an illustrious former captain who not only excelled at golf but was known for watercress cultivation techniques, and by the end of the evening Norma and her mother were signed up for lessons and Norma's aunt had diagnosed someone's carpal tunnel syndrome that was affecting his swing. Norma's cousin Denise is, to this day, a lady member of BRGC and herself a golf tutor and has been instrumental in Roy's summer school. Norma's uncle Brett has arranged annual golf-twinning trips with clubs in the US.

Another cousin described, to a rapt audience, the time she'd got a hole-in-one in a golf club in California: 'I hit it hard and it flew and just plopped in.'

Yet another, a cousin-in-law, mentioned that her father had caddied for the famous Brock Daniels in the 1960s when poor Brock was battling with brittle hips: 'Daddy fed calcium tablets straight into his mouth – on the green – against the rules, but the rules were an ass because without those tablets Brock would've been on wheels,' she said, and was rewarded with plaudits for her father.

Possibly resentful of the attention they were getting, my father suddenly asked in a booming voice, 'What do you people all *do*?'

'Do you mean in our work?' Norma's father asked.

'Yes,' said my father. 'What do you all do *for a living*?'

Joseph Pavlou pointed to each of his family, one by one: 'My daughter Norma makes bespoke workwear for ladies and she is doing her PhD here in this town, at the University of Rutland.'

I almost interrupted at that point, to say she was still doing her Master's, but thought better of it.

'My sister Diana is a history teacher,' he continued. 'She really knows her stuff, and brings it alive, and her husband Maurice is a civil engineer. Recently he designed and oversaw the repair of such-and-such Bridge in blah-de-blah Place. Their daughter, my niece Kimberlee, is a poultry vet, specializing in incubation techniques. She trained in Japan.'

And so it went on, with every member of the Pavlou group introduced and uniquely brilliant. He turned the question back on my father: 'And, what do *you* all do?'

And after saying my brother was currently out of work but a trained accountant, and that my mother had raised two children to the best of her ability, had been hit by a train door in 1978, but enjoyed amateur meteorology, and that he himself was retired but had been a tax accountant specializing in (what sounded like) Egyptian tax, there was a sense of anticlimax, his having failed to equal the

Pavlou accomplishments, and in some kind of bid to make up for it, my father decided to say, 'And actually, you may as well know, Susan-the-bride is expecting a baby.' And in a most uncharacteristic move, pointed to my stomach in a jabbing motion.

My mother turned to me and said quietly, 'I thought you'd got rid of it.'

And then Roy said, 'Well, thank you, Bill, we weren't going to announce it just yet, but, yes, she's got a bun in the oven.'

'Oh my God, Susan, no wonder you were too fat for the other dress,' said Mrs Pavlou, and we described the last-minute switch.

Everyone laughed and raised a glass of whatever golf-themed cocktail they were drinking and congratulated us, and Roy pulled me in for a hug and one of the Pavlous, maybe Norma, said for some reason, 'Baby Honey.' And a toast rippled round: 'Baby Honey.' 'Baby Honey,' they all said, or so I thought.

Then the Detroit Spinners came on and Norma and I and all the Pavlou women and Timandra performed the dance we'd learned the night before and, as it came to an end, DJ Leroy said, 'Let's hear it for an unorthodox first dance!'

Norma was beside herself that the Pavlou family had made such a good account of themselves, golf-wise and beyond. Best of all, though, she behaved like a true friend to me, arranging and holding my schleppe, doing the dance, and being perfectly pleasant to Roy. It was all so unlikely and a reminder to me how life can turn around.

Ah, yes, and another thing. Remember the dear little old woman, who used to come into the shop and ask us to thread a needle for her and take a Malteser? She was there too, and it turned out she was Norma's Pavlou grandmother, and when I asked Norma, 'Why didn't you say so before?' she just said, 'There was no need.'

Some months later, I was alert, awake, compos mentis, and back to my normal self within moments of the birth of our baby.

'Hey, Mr Warren,' I said to Roy, as I cradled our waxy newborn girl to my chest, 'that went well, didn't it?'

Roy did not respond, head bent, tinkering with his Canon Sure Shot.

Desperately wanting, *needing*, some acknowledgement for coming through with no complications apart from numb heels (a common side effect of a fast labour) – and *so* quickly he hadn't even had to go out for a burger – I tried again. 'Rooooyyy?' I said, and he looked up. 'That wasn't as gruesome as we'd expected, eh?' and he'd nodded his head like some kind of doped-out hippy, 'Yeah, no, good, hole-in-one.' He got the camera up to his face and before I could arrange the hospital blanket over my nipples, he'd disappeared to the worktop and was questioning midwife Carol about the placenta, winning her round with scientific talk, and then Carol was posing, holding it up, like pizza dough, for a snap, and afterwards she wrapped it and dropped it into some kind of bucket, and Roy called over, eyes wide in squeamish delight, 'Oh my God, Susan, you should've seen it,' and not knowing quite how to respond,

I shouted at the midwife, 'How dare you pose with my afterbirth without my permission?'

Roy hurried to the bedside. 'Sorry, love,' he said, and looked at the baby.

'I'm going to call her Honey,' I said.

'Who?' said Roy.

'The baby, who do you think?'

'Oh, right, yeah.'

'What's that?' said Carol.

I didn't say anything, so Roy had to.

'She's calling the baby Honey,' he said.

'That's nice,' said Carol. 'How is she spelling it?'

'The usual way,' I said. 'What other way is there?'

'Just that sometimes people go phonetic for that kind of name.'

'Well, we're spelling it the normal way.'

'Like the sticky substance found in a beehive?' Carol confirmed.

It had gone extraordinarily well, the birth, so why wouldn't Roy say so? Particularly as he'd witnessed, on the ward later, a moaning woman named Richardine, who'd had a baby they were calling Eleanor, and a dozen stitches, and couldn't stop vomiting, being presented with a garnet-encrusted eternity ring. He'd been more than happy to acknowledge that the wedding had gone off all right, and actually glossed over the awkward bits, like his mother listing all the times golf balls had injured or killed people. This continued through the early days, Roy not giving me so much as a nod. It was disheartening, and whatever the opposite of vindication is. Other than a few tiny hiccups – the pain of breastfeeding, that got worse and worse until finally Honey bit one of my nipples almost off with her gums, and I gave it up; the fact that my feet seemed to have grown half a size and my slippers were now pinching my toes; and I was suddenly afraid of mice – I was no trouble at all as a new mother, nor Honey as a baby. The worst thing, by far, was Roy's determination not to congratulate or praise me, or to appreciate that we hadn't had a three-day labour, that our baby hadn't hated us on sight and I hadn't torn to my anus. Not that I wanted praise for bouncing back with no detrimental after-effects and a completely intact vagina, but I felt it only right that he should feel lucky and blessed. In my post-partum annoyance I bombarded him with examples of the horrors he'd escaped thanks to my having done a good job.

'What about your cousin Kirsty?' I said.

'What about her?' said Roy.

'Forty-eight hours in labour and a spinal anaesthetic, then the forceps, then the ventouse suction cup, and after all that, a caesarean, and then a huge white-haired baby with a two-year headache, and a profound failure to bond,' I said. 'And to this day he won't have his hair brushed.'

Roy hated it, I could tell, but I continued. 'What about Rosemary?' I said. 'Remember, she got it into her head that Alastair was a danger to baby Duncan, and waved a hockey stick at him if he approached the bed. He had to run for his life to a neighbour,' I said, 'surely you remember your mum telling us that?'

Roy didn't remember, and just turned over the pages of a golf catalogue.

'What about the woman up the road who had to wrap her breasts in cold cabbage leaves? or the couple from the MOT centre whose baby took against them and the grandparents had to take over until it could ride a trike.'

Roy continued leafing.

'And baby Josh Williams who was allergic to Johnson's Baby Powder and they couldn't even have him smell nice,' I said. 'We've been lucky when you think about it, haven't we, Roy?'

'Very,' he said.

When my mother arrived she jigged about with the baby in her arms, the happiest I'd seen her in years.

'We're calling her Honey,' I said.

'Oh, no! Poor thing. Well, I refuse to call her that. Who do you think you are? The Geldofs?'

And with that she was gone.

Norma arrived next and gave Honey a doll-sized hand-knitted cardigan with tiny cloth-covered buttons and I really hoped that in spite of her misgivings about Honey curtailing my academic progress and necessitating a marriage, there'd be a happy transformation, that she'd hold this baby and vow to look out for her for the rest of her life, like a penitent father in a film. But that didn't happen. She didn't want to hold Honey, she only peeped at her for a moment, laughed, and said, 'Gosh, she looks just like W. H. Auden.'

And before I could say, 'Better than Winston Churchill,' which I thought showed resilience and an intact sense of humour, Norma said, 'By the way, the writer who compared women to empty museums filled with men's art was Updike, not Fowles.'

'Oh, right,' I said. 'That's good to know.'

'Anyway, how's Roy bearing up?' she asked, and I told her he was withholding praise. She drooped and shrugged elaborately. 'They go crazy after an easy birth,' she said. 'They need a drama. If all goes well, and no one almost dies, they're left with pent-up stuff.' She gave a dozen examples, including the woman from the Well-Bread Bakery, whose husband, a gentle giant, turned argumentative after she gave birth while eating a full roast. He had a tantrum in Mr Big's Menswear when they hadn't any trousers long enough in the leg. He was also suspended from work after shouting at an American client for pronouncing Leicester 'Ly-Sester', and then refused to do a structural survey on a property belonging to a pop star, and they'd had to move to a smaller house in the end. All because she'd had an easy labour.

'They shouldn't really let men into the delivery rooms,' said Norma, and I couldn't agree more.

# 7

Roy and I were able to move out of his flat share and buy our first house in Brankham when his parents gave us a cash gift. At first they tried to put the one thousand pounds into a bank account for Honey. For driving lessons, said his mother, or the trip of a lifetime when she came of age. I was overjoyed and grateful beyond belief that they felt like this about our baby and could see ahead to a lovely wholesome future in which Honey might want to drive a car or go to Australia, and need exciting things. Roy, however, savaged them over it. This is what he said to his mother down the telephone:

'What the hell are you thinking? She doesn't need money, she's an effing baby, we are living in a sh*t hole, I have to carry the pram up and down two flights of stairs every time Susan fancies an effing stroll. I'm working every hour of the bl**ding day to make ends meet, so seriously, if you want to give her something, give us the money now. Christ, Mother, we are desperate, are you insane?'

Pause, presumably while Roy's mother defended herself.

'No, Susan cannot rely on getting her job back at the sewing shop. If you really want to know, the sewing shop's about to go bust.'

I listened at the door, perplexed by every part of this drama; that there was a thousand pounds in the first place, that I'd been stupid enough to celebrate it being squirrelled away for Honey. That Roy had seen Honey's windfall from a whole other angle and had the courage to attempt to divert it away from her to us, without being devious. That the flat was a sh*t hole. That Roy was so stressed. That we were so poor. That the Pin Cushion was about to go bust – it wasn't. And why say 'two flights of stairs' when there was only one? It was a lot to take in and I found myself swaying even though I hadn't got Honey in my arms, and praying he would not let himself mention Hector not being Ted's. He didn't.

We received a cheque later that week and that resulted in us viewing properties to buy. I'd meet Roy at various small bungalows and semi-detached houses and we'd walk round opening cupboards and pretending not to like anything, and in this endeavour I found my spirit was weak. Sometimes Honey would need a bottle and I'd go and sit in the car, other times Roy would ask an awkward but very important question and the agent or vendor might say, 'I'll have to get back to you on that,' and that would put the kibosh on it. One house though, Gracedale, was perfect. It wasn't too covetable but had a nice feel about it; semi-detached, in a slightly elevated position on a small estate of newish houses, sunny kitchen-diner that went out onto a small but grassy back garden, a pretty but steep front garden that, in my opinion, cried out for an alpine-style rockery, and a third, albeit small, bedroom that would do as an office. Brankham Drive had a park one side and the vast borrowed landscape of the University of Rutland on the other. Magnolia, holly and bay formed a green arch over the campus gates, which, even though it was a most ordinary street, gave it the feel of somewhere magical and glade-like. The sharp lines of the peach-coloured houses softened by all the greenery and the puckered concrete of the road danced with leafy shadows. There was also the coincidence of the house being called Gracedale and Honey's middle name being Grace, and Grace being the name Roy would have called her if he'd cared enough to insist (it being his mother's name).

I sensed that Roy liked the house too, but I had to tread carefully. Since being a father, Roy had become a tough but nervy detective, giving nothing away and always on guard. I'd learned to say nothing even slightly positive about any house we were viewing in front of the agent or vendor, even in whispers or behind their backs as they could mind-read and lip-read.

At a previous property, at the start of our search, I'd asked the estate agent fellow, 'Is the garden south-facing?' I was imagining myself grilling vegetable kebabs on a rudimentary barbecue, Roy sipping a beer while Honey splashed about in a tiny pool – and that unspoken image had apparently been clearly evoked by my naive question and, according to Roy, put the price up by 2K.

'Why couldn't you just keep your mouth shut?' he'd asked me afterwards.

It made sense. It was the psychology of buying and selling and that, to be fair, was Roy's game.

I could tell that Roy liked Gracedale. In the garden he

looked at the sky and then vaulted up onto the fence to inspect the boundary. He called hello to the old lady next door, who we'd been told kept the hedges nice but had a cat, and then to my great surprise I saw him take a hard-boiled egg from his pocket, tap it on a fence post, peel it (careful to keep every bit of the shell), and start eating it. He held it out to me to take a bite, which of course I couldn't, it being too risky. I'd inadvertently take the whole yolk or drop a crumb on the baby's head. 'No, thanks,' I said and I smiled as he chomped, because I knew we'd live there then, I mean, who could possibly eat an egg in a garden unless they felt a sense of belonging and calm?

Two months later we moved into Gracedale and it was all going well for the three of us. For Roy, a single garage for his various pieces of motor-car equipment and golf clubs. For Honey, her own little bedroom, for which her paternal grandmother had funded top-quality bespoke curtains from Fenwick's of Leicester, depicting animals and birds, in bright though not garish colours. And for me, a new mattress, a front-venting tumble dryer, vast shallow shelving for paperbacks and nick-nacks, and as I say, the university with its trees in copper and green and lime, its turrets and clocktower on my doorstep.

The one thing I wanted to change about the house was the front door, it being like a terrible hairstyle on an otherwise reasonably handsome person. Embossed in the ugliest and most bizarre pattern as if imitating a Georgian door but made from flimsy white plastic. Roy joined in with my condemnation for the first few days and I began imagining what door I might like instead, maybe pine, I thought, with reeded glass panels and brass door furniture. I even picked up a catalogue and browsed it occasionally.

During our first week at Gracedale I donned a headscarf, knotted behind, and feeling attractive and purposeful painted over the custard-coloured woodchip in the lounge with Dulux Apple White which was white with a very, very slight green tinge. I'd chosen it partly to tone with my still life of half a cabbage but mainly to cover the yellow, which had a dreadful reputation in those days. Perfectly happy people described feeling suddenly despondent, trapped and suicidal for no reason except moving into a yellow bedroom. I should have stripped the old wallpaper off really but, well, I didn't, and as you might know, covering woodchip takes longer than painting straight plaster, on account of all the little dips and valleys that you didn't even know were there, it's a whole rugged landscape and requires a lot more paint. Also, at that time, I'd seen an advert where Ray Reardon vacuums the green baize of a snooker table with a Vax carpet shampooer and had suddenly felt squeamish about the carpets in the new house, the vendors having lived in it from newly built, and I couldn't stop thinking of all the dust and assorted dirt trodden in daily by their three children. So I hired a machine from the dry cleaner's, same model as Ray Reardon's. Honestly, hiring that machine is, to this day, one of the highlights of my life. The filth that came out of those downstairs carpets had to be seen to be believed. I made Roy take a photograph but he didn't do it justice. I had to do the whole downstairs twice – with a water change – upstairs being relatively clean due to a no-shoes policy.

The vendors were popping by to read the meters that same day, and I said to Roy, 'Don't whatever you do let them into the lounge. I don't want Mrs Thing to see the Vax.'

And he said, 'It's no business of hers if you want to go nuts cleaning.'

And I said, 'No, Roy! It would be mortifying.'

In the event, he couldn't prevent it and in she came. Norma had popped in for a coffee and luckily she flung a dust sheet over the Vax, but Mrs Thing was offended anyway, by the paint.

'We'd only just decorated this room when we put it on the market,' she said.

'Oh, I know,' I said, 'it was lovely, it's just that yellow makes my husband depressed.'

'Oh, dear,' she said, alarmed, and looked out at Roy in his blue tracksuit top.

'He's read that tragic story about the yellow wallpaper,' said Norma helpfully.

Some weeks later, I reminded Roy about us needing a new front door, but he'd changed his mind. It was, he said, 'entirely unnecessary' and after all the paint, the machine hire and new shelving for the garage, we were stony broke and couldn't even afford a few plants for the garden. I was disappointed by this U-turn, and by the sudden realization that one partner could change their mind, and curtail a plan like that, and actually, by my secret petulance over so shallow a thing. I had a feeling I'd be irritated by that door for a long, long time, and I'm ashamed to say I have been. I look at it sometimes and think, a person designed that, and another person said, 'Yes, let's make a hundred of them.' And a house builder said, 'I'll take four dozen for the new estate I'm building right by the university!' And though I like our little house, its modesty and ordinariness, I have, since the day we moved in twenty-seven years ago, disliked that door and my daily dealings with it. I've had a recurring fantasy over the years in which someone (me) slots a piece of wood through the letterbox on a chain attached to the back of a car and drives off at speed, pulling the door off its hinges and dragging it along the road like a mangled water ski. It was a scene from a film, I can't remember which, but it was very affecting.

The baby changed Roy and me, which was a shame, when you think that before Honey we'd tolerated each other's every foible. I hadn't minded Roy's rocking rhythmically in bed even though I thought it a sign of insanity, nor his need to fall asleep entwined, his philosophizing golf, his putting one foot on the crossbar of my chair, and having his shoe touch my shoe in the pub to be connected in a group, his habit of saying 'Mum this, Mum that' meaning his mother, when he should say '*my* mum' because she wasn't the only mother on the planet. I'd found these things endearing, but now I found them needy and unattractive. His holding the edge of my coat as we walked, which was – when I think back to that slight tug – terrifically irritating, but I allowed because he had his awkwardness to deal with, and gripping the coat was tantamount to holding hands without doing it. But after Honey, I had a pram to push and I'm afraid I yanked my coat free, and in so doing perhaps I cast him adrift on a stronger tide than he ever would have attempted alone. Likewise, the idiosyncrasies of mine that Roy could suddenly no longer tolerate were just as fundamental to my well-being as his to him; my need to explain myself at length, to take a long run-up to any announcement or news, however mundane, my need to talk, to ward off silence and bad feeling. Now I think about it, Roy decided to deny me *analysis* and it started immediately, while still in the maternity suite at Leicester Royal Infirmary.

My parents' unique situation hadn't prepared me at all well for marriage. My mother had been a perfect wife but after her accident she was nothing short of evil, and my father's life was made miserable afterwards until he died; I saw first-hand how grim cohabitation could be. But I knew that this was not the norm and so I think I expected more from my own marriage and not to have to work so hard at it. I'm not saying I was unhappy as Roy's wife and Honey's mother but it did start to feel as though all possibility was gone and that not having completed my degree had indeed been a huge mistake. Norma's warning, that I'd sink and dwindle intellectually, had come true – I'd stopped being curious and was entirely wrapped up in my tiny world, with fantasies about a pine door and a medley of vegetables. I didn't have to worry too much about Honey's development; she had already taken charge of her own life, and needed me for recreation and food only. I was working part-time at the Pin Cushion and was able to take Honey in with me. I had her in a papoose to start with and then, when she was heavier and more mobile, I got a second-hand playpen from a guard's wife at Gartree Prison. I could even put her for a sleep upstairs with Mrs Pavlou when need be. I was lucky in that respect, except that the convenience was a trap and I really should have moved on.

I'm not sure that living opposite the University of Rutland was a perk after all. Did it only rub it in? I'd wander about campus, sometimes with Honey in a buggy, cutting across to the high street on the other side, or just walking. There were always lovely things to see: squirrels, blackbirds, the earliest crocuses, blossoms and a rather quaint bantam house. I'd also spy occasional suited gents with books and papers under their arms whom I took to be professors, and often this same man in a fawn boiler suit, who I now know was the head of Estates – we'd greet each other and mention the weather. I joined the Sewing Circle there and over the years enrolled onto various extra-mural courses including An Introduction to the Bayeux Tapestry, which you could study without having to go and see it thanks to Stothard's facsimile. I enjoyed having a coffee in the sunshine on warm afternoons, and sometimes I'd not want to go home and I'd dawdle and smoke. Occasionally I'd attend a concert and even considered switching to UofR choir, not that it was better than the Brankham Chorus, but the setting was so glorious even when they were singing 'Yes Sir, I Can Boogie'. I think I was looking for a portal into the life I might have been living. I felt envious of Norma dashing about in a short dress with her briefcase and papers and saying things like 'discourse' and 'faculty'. She was not only teaching there – her publishing contract with the Claptrap Poetry Press made her a darling. Sadly though, the teaching and marking requirement got in the way of the poetry and stunted her creativity.

'It's all these students,' she wailed one afternoon, 'you don't understand, Susan, they're like leeches.'

I said I bloody well did understand, I had Roy and the baby, didn't I, and a plastic front door?

To which Norma said, 'Well, what did you expect?' and shot Honey a dirty look. 'I warned you.'

That was how I ended up doing some of Norma's marking for her. She'd drop essays in to me at the Pin Cushion and I'd read them and make notes lightly, in pencil. Norma behaved as though she were doing me a huge favour, which in a way she was because I enjoyed it, and I became a great expert on James Joyce, so much so that I read one of his shorter works, and answered the winning question in a literary quiz (who was baby tuckoo?) and on another course was compelled to quickly skim-read Doris Lessing's *The Golden Notebook*, which I enjoyed so much, I read it again, slowly.

'You need to keep your brain working,' Norma said, 'or you'll turn into Lydia Leopold.'

Lydia was apparently an administrative assistant at the university who could never quite keep up with her professor husband on account of having taken the vocational route in Further Education and everyone saying it was fine, but it wasn't.

'I know, what's it going to be like when I have another!'

I said, not by way of an announcement as such, but just the assumption that I ought to really get on with it. Privately, I'd only ever wanted one child, possibly a result of growing up with a brother my parents preferred, and whom I could easily have done without, for there was never any situation improved by his being in it. On the other hand, as soon as Honey existed beyond the theoretical, I hadn't liked the idea of her being outnumbered, swamped by us at Christmas, alone after an argument, or having to watch us die without a sister to make it bearable. And mostly, I realize, because it turned out that Roy and I weren't going to be entirely cheerful and loving.

'Another what?' said Norma.

'Baby.'

'*Another?*' she yelled. 'Why on earth would you do that?'

'I just think I should.'

'Why though?' said Norma. 'Do you feel any benefit from your sibling?'

'God, no.'

'Am I less of a person for being an only child?' she asked.

'I don't know,' I said.

# 8

I'd always known Honey was going to be an extraordinary person. That belief was partly to do with the Pavlous at our wedding, the way they'd joyfully accepted the invitation and dressed up in elaborate, colourful outfits and strange hats, and made the day feel like a real celebration. They'd been so pleased to meet everyone, happy to be there, and impressed with the clubhouse and all our wedding-day choices. But really the thing that stood out was the way they'd surrounded me and showered me with love on hearing the accidental announcement of my pregnancy, and how Norma, or possibly her aunt (who was younger than her and quite spirited), had shouted out, 'Baby Honey!' and there'd been a toast for the baby even though she was as yet unborn and the size of a coat toggle. It was what gave me the idea of Honey for her name and I assumed that Norma would be thrilled by this and feel an emotional connection, which I was all for, as I was going to ask her to be godmother. I was a bit late to it, and Honey already had two front teeth when Roy and I discussed it. There wasn't to be an actual christening but it seemed negligent not to tie a couple of other adults in.

Because I'd chosen Norma as god*mother*, Roy had first choice for the god*father* and asked his old friend and ex-housemate Leroy, who'd been so moved that he'd had to wipe away tears with his sleeve. He thanked us for the honour, and said he'd try to give up smoking, and within a couple of days had presented Honey with a pair of real sheepskin moccasins fit for a five-year-old, from Fenwick's of Leicester, that must have cost twenty pounds or more.

I invited Norma to tea at the Two Swans café so that we could ask her but she'd been quite hard to pin down, and put me off a couple of times. In the end I was quite forceful and said, 'I need to talk to you, Norma.'

Sensing trouble, Roy asked if he could be excused, saying, 'She might decline and it'll be awkward with all of us there.'

And I said, 'Why would she decline?'

Norma arrived late and dragged a chair noisily across the floor for her handbag and briefcase before sitting down and sighing, 'What's the big emergency?'

I began my short, formal speech. 'So, I'd, *we'd*, be delighted if you would agree to be Honey's godmother,' I said.

She appeared troubled by this, as though I'd asked to borrow money, and said she needed some time to consider it. She then tidied the tea table, stacked our plates and even wiped some butter off a knife with a paper napkin, and I didn't hear from her for, well, it must have been two weeks.

'Bloody typical,' said Roy, when I fretted about it.

'She obviously doesn't want to do it.'

'Well, tell her she's had her chance and you're going to ask someone else,' said Roy. 'You could ask Booboo.'

'Oh, God, no, I don't want Booboo,' I said. 'She likes the boxing.'

And then finally we met again, in the Two Swans. I can't remember who rang whom, but Norma was there early and hadn't ordered a beverage. I'd had a feeling it was going to be bad news so went ahead and ordered at the counter on the way in, tea for two, a slice of Swiss roll, which I knew Norma liked, it being fat-free, and a piece of award-winning fruit cake.

'I can't be Honey's godmother, Susan,' she said, within earshot of the waitress, who looked at me and grimaced.

'Oh.' Though I wasn't surprised, I needed a moment to compose myself. 'But you named her,' I said.

'What? I didn't name her,' said Norma. 'What a bizarre thing to say.'

'At the wedding, you shouted out, "Baby Honey",' I said. 'Remember?'

'No, that didn't happen.'

'Maybe your aunt shouted it?'

'No, she didn't. Roy said, "Bun in the oven," and some-one from the golf club made a joke about honeymoon sex,' she said. 'You must've misheard it.'

So it turned out that actually Honey was probably named after the tail end of a lewd joke made by Fred Fletcher of Fletcher's Fine Foods, the company who'd provided the buffet, the man who, only in his twenties, had solved the retail trifle riddle.

'Anyway, I can't be Honey's godmother, Susan,' said Norma, once we'd established that she hadn't named her. 'You and Roy are not Christian, for a start.'

'Are you?'

'Not really,' said Norma. 'That's why it's awkward. I mean, what does the job entail?'

I ended up on a monologue about not having entirely abandoned God and Jesus, just that they'd somehow slipped out of sight, like when a lorry you've been following in foggy conditions gradually pulls away from you, and soon there are only the smudgy red tail lights and then they're gone too, and it's just you, alone, going forward. I'd not taken it sitting down, this loss of faith. I'd even told my father, and he'd said, 'When God is gone, he's gone – that's my experience.' And my mother had piped up, 'For what is faith unless it is to believe in what you do not see? St Augustine.'

Norma let me ramble on for a while but finally said, 'No, Susan, I can't. It's too complicated.'

I said, 'Is it because you don't like Roy?'

And she said, 'What? No – it's because I don't want to do it, and therefore it would be wrong.'

Why had I asked her? After the W. H. Auden comment and her not even wanting to look at Honey, or pick her up, or even take a photograph. I'd asked her because I wanted to bring them together, formally, to share the burden and joy of a baby with a trusted friend, and vice versa, even though Norma had not for one moment shown the slightest interest in Honey.

'Well,' I said, 'I wish it hadn't taken you all this time to let me know. I could have asked my cousin, but now she'll know she's second choice.'

'I needed to give it proper consideration,' said Norma,

'and, if you really must know, I've had other things on my mind.'

'Oh, really, such as?'

'Such as a marriage proposal,' said Norma, 'which I've accepted.'

I cannot stress quite how absurd this sounded. Norma hadn't got a boyfriend and as far as I was aware never really had. There was a murky figure from her past, from wherever they'd lived before, who her parents had introduced her to because he was tall, and whom she referred to as Mr O'Keefe. He'd apparently showered her with attention and written sonnets about her face and ordinary poems about her mind, and she'd loved him briefly, intensely – until she'd found him one day sunning himself on a lounger and he'd asked her to urinate on him, saying he'd hose it down afterwards. But there'd been no one since. The only man she had any dealings with now being Hugo Pack-Allen, the aged, bearded investor who had initiated the partnership with Curtains For You and generally been a fly in the ointment.

'What?' I said. 'Who?'

'I am engaged to be married to Hugo Pack-Allen,' she said, as I knew she must. All the same, this news was abhorrent and horrific, and the sort of truly terrible and wrong thing that only happens in the worst, most confusing dream, and though I knew that whatever I said next would be remembered for ever, I heard myself say, 'Oh, no – are your parents forcing you?'

She looked at me for a few moments and then walked out, letting the door bang behind her. She touched neither

her Swiss roll nor her tea. She'd said neither hello nor goodbye to Honey who'd been sitting between us in a high chair, and I'd only picked at my award-winning fruit cake. I pressed my lips together and breathed through my nose to steady myself before unclipping the straps and lifting Honey up. She was practically my height standing in the high chair like that. She gave me a look of calm solidarity before saying 'Ducks' and pointing behind me to the two swans kissing.

# 9

Hugo Pack-Allen lived in an ugly house on the bypass that everyone called Frank's Place. It was said that Frank Sinatra had once spent a night in 1971 having been lured there by Mia Farrow, who had been in the area for forty-eight hours, through no fault of her own, to rehearse something with Engelbert. On taking possession of the house in 1990, Hugo Pack-Allen had converted one of the downstairs reception rooms into a pub which he called Frank's Bar. Hugo slid into my life from all directions, obviously in proposing to my best friend, but also he'd made an investment at the golf club which involved Roy, including a commitment to fund some sponsored memberships for under-privileged people who longed to play golf and get away from their families at weekends, but just couldn't manage the fees. He'd often be at the golf club on Sunday lunchtimes when Roy was teaching the recipients and I'd be there patronizing the bar in my best clothes and being a good wife and friend.

In the run-up to the Pack-Allen wedding I made efforts to get to know Hugo. I'd approach and ask how he was and strike up conversation, but however hard I tried to find evidence of brilliance, uniqueness, or in fact any redeeming quality, I could find none, other than him being slightly wealthier than other eligible men, and much older. He'd stand at the bar, hanging on one hip so awkwardly you felt for his ligaments, occasionally throwing snacks into the air and catching them in his mouth – like a dog – to punctuate his conversation, which was all very well and good except he only talked in wisecracks. I once told him that golfers had reported seeing woodpeckers on the course.

'Let me know when they see a spiny babbler, then I'll be interested!' he said, then threw some nuts, caught them, and continued, 'The only endemic bird of Nepal,' and laughed at an imagined audience.

His gaze would drift about, looking for a better companion, someone who he could talk to about business or golf. I'm afraid I decided he was shallow and pointless. You'd think Norma, now his fiancée, would be embarrassed by this, but far from it, she'd tut along happily, after her ladies' stretch class, and pickpocket his wallet for laughs, and seem wholly delighted by him, the way a well-behaved eleven-year-old might be at the antics of a disruptive classmate, doing and saying things that they would never dare. I'd seen this before – when my brother married a clinically irritating woman I very soon understood that she was by way of a weapon with which he could punish the world for not respecting him as it should. I'd watched him over the years, while she explained at dinner parties that Cliff Richard was more real to her as a child than Champion the Wonder Horse ('because Cliff is actually real and Champion isn't'), and seen the delight in his eyes as everyone squirmed.

I'd known in my heart all was not well between Norma and me after Honey was born – her never wanting to come round, go for a walk, and even declining a shopping trip to Leicester, for baby essentials and lunch, me driving – and this ridiculous engagement proved it. Knowing she'd be saddled with Hugo Pack-Allen, presumably until he died, I was almost relieved she'd spurned the offer to be Honey's godmother.

If you're wondering about Honey's eventual godmother, I asked an old aunt who at least might give us some financial help should I have to leave Roy, which looking at the stats, seemed quite probable, but she declined on the basis that she had six godchildren already and wasn't after any more. I'd only ever heard of people being disappointed *not* to be asked and took these rejections badly. In the end, in desperation, I asked my second cousin Timandra, a known lunatic, telling her it was incumbent on the chief bridesmaid to perform this duty and she said, 'But I'm an atheist!' and I assumed that meant she was declining too, so I said, 'So are we, we are total non-believers, I swear to God.'

'Oh, well, OK, if you insist,' said Timandra.

'Just be around occasionally to teach her how to keep out of the pits of despair.' I spoke like that around Timmy because that was how she spoke. 'And bung her a quid every now and then.'

'Oh, OK, yes, I will,' said Timandra. 'You can rely on me for that kind of thing.' For the next twelve years or so, until her untimely death, she remembered Honey on birthdays and Christmas and Valentine's and Easter, and would send postcards from Heraklion and Kenya and, when

Honey was old enough, would ask her, 'Honey, do I owe you any money, dear?' and make comments about global politics that weren't exactly frightening but real and arresting, and she'd say, 'I'm your spiritual guardian, what would you like to discuss?' And though they saw each other only three or four times a year, they got along very well indeed.

Norma actually marrying Hugo Pack-Allen never stopped seeming odd, as did her not telling me about any of it until it was unfolding in front of my eyes, and her still living above the shop with her parents until after they were married. Mrs Pavlou had offered to make the wedding dress but Norma said she'd rather make it herself and proceeded to do so, coming into the shop during her free hours and running up a two-piece in Dupion, black for the shift dress – with the usual unattractive sharp bust darts – and a shapeless jacket with no collar, in red. When it was completed she went behind the Lippety screen and came out, did a clumsy twirl and said, 'What do you think?'

I gave my honest opinion. 'It's not very bridal,' I said, and listed options for upscaling the outfit, such as the application of seed pearls, balloon sleeves in chiffon, or even some ostrich, just as if she had been a customer.

But Norma sniffed at these suggestions. 'Wait till you see what Hugo's wearing,' she said. 'You'll pee yourself.'

Norma didn't want bridesmaids. 'Why would anyone want a younger, prettier version of themselves, holding flowers, and looking bashful?' she said. Her flurry of cousins and aunts were either no longer nearby, or otherwise engaged, and so it fell to me and Mrs Pavlou to arrange a little hen party. Though Norma wasn't a big drinker, I arrived at the shop with a bottle of wine and somehow she and I finished it between us. We'd arranged to meet Mrs Pavlou and her friend Irina at the Brankham Arms later but first we went looking for a drug dealer Norma knew of, called Kenny Fagin, who sold marijuana cigarettes for the casual user but was also a driving instructor. We found him at the Old Dun Cow and Norma told me to walk past and give him a wide-eyed look – the sign for 'I want to buy drugs.'

When Fagin finally noticed me he said, 'Are you all right?' and I whispered, 'Can I buy a marijuana cigarette?' and he said, 'I don't know, can you?' and I said, 'I don't know, I hope so, my friend's getting married tomorrow,' and he said, 'Oh, lucky gel,' and turned away to watch the darts match.

I related this to Norma, speaking into her ear as she stared at Fagin. 'He might think you're a policeman,' she whispered back. I said, 'I don't look like a policeman, I bet he thinks *you're* a policeman,' and we laughed, and in this over-stimulated state I went back to Fagin's table and asked, 'Excuse me, who looks more like a policeman, me or her?' I pointed at Norma, and Fagin said, 'Actually, you look like a cop duo.'

'Cagney and Lacey?' I said, and he said, 'Nah, Turner and Hooch.' I thought this hilarious but when I told Norma she thought it a bit rude, Hooch being a dog or an orangutan. We left the Old Dun Cow empty-handed but as we turned the corner onto Brankham High Street someone ran up to us from behind.

'Compliments of Fagin,' he said breathlessly, handing Norma a skinny little cigarette, 'and all the best for tomorrow.' Norma put it in her mouth and the lad gave her a light. We continued to the Brankham Arms, puffing away and philosophizing about small-town life and marriage and so on when suddenly we saw, gleaming in the moonlight, as if someone had arranged for it to be there, a lone silver shopping trolley. Without any discussion Norma leaned on my shoulder and climbed in, and I pushed her along the cobbled streets and we continued our conversation. I said how sorry I was that all her lovely aunts and cousins weren't around for the hen party and she shocked me by saying, 'To be honest, Susan, I'm glad they're not here. I prefer having just you.'

And then we were outside the Brankham Arms and Norma had begun to climb out when suddenly the Pavlou cousins and aunts were all at the door. 'Surprise!' they shouted.

'Oh, no,' hissed Norma. 'Run!'

I turned the trolley and pushed it at speed along the bumpy streets. The Pavlous made chase but in their heels couldn't catch us. I dodged down a jitty they'd not know and came out onto Church Street to see them bearing down on us. Eventually, after we'd run all about the town, hiding in alleyways and shop doorways, laughing, and they'd tried to catch us, Norma's aunt Denise and cousin Kimberlee the poultry vet cut us off in a two-pronged manoeuvre and they all fell upon us and carried Norma to the pub, shrieking.

*

The Pavlou–Pack-Allen wedding was a solemn and deeply religious affair – exactly what Hugo had wanted, which was all the more infuriating when we found out later that he was a sex addict with a lifetime disqualification from driving.

I heard from Mrs Pavlou that children were not invited to the wedding service, but had pretended not to know it and on the day put Honey in her best dress and petticoat, and took seats near the back, in case she started whining, not because of any pecking order. Norma walked very slowly up the aisle beside her father and as she passed, gave me a wink and a smile, but, noticing Honey, frowned. Her suit, though ill-fitting and, as with all her clothing, short enough to show her knock-knees, was striking and somehow brilliant and when she stood beside Hugo, in some sort of faux naval uniform, I laughed. They looked just like Popeye and Olive Oyl.

It went on and on. Honey did well, bearing in mind she was still only very little. Roy, on the other hand, almost hadn't been able to hold on in church and had been about to leave in search of a toilet when it suddenly ended (the ceremony). But there was an awkward moment when the old priest asked if the congregation knew of any impediment to the marriage and the pause, which seemed to go on for ever, was long enough for Honey to notice a change in atmosphere, and looking up from her cloth book, she said, 'Yes,' and because of the delightfully echoey sound of her voice, said it again, 'Yes,' but this time in her excitement, the word came out with a slight croak, and the priest was perturbed and looked about, first at Hugo, then at

Norma, and then squinted outward to the hushed pews, casting his eyes about like a headmaster looking for trouble. No one spoke and then he continued.

Afterwards we were served meat rolls and assorted non-alcoholic drinks in St Aloysius Church rooms and Hugo's family, one brother and an aunt, shook hands with everyone at the double doors and then left in a minicab. The small grandchild of the caretaker drifted about coyly, in her own bridesmaid's dress. This annoyed Norma so much that she complained and would have had the little girl removed but for the priest mentioning compassion.

The best man, I don't remember who he was or how he fitted in with the Pack-Allens, gave a cryptic speech with a theme of opera, which not everyone enjoyed, and in a light-hearted moment mentioned Hugo training a cat to walk backwards, and I clung to that solitary charming detail whenever I felt myself disliking him, which was most of the time.

The bride and groom went to Brighton for a honeymoon weekend and stayed close to where Roy and I had had ours, which was nice because it meant I could picture it all. When I next saw Norma she couldn't stop herself telling me about the shock of it all: the shabbiness of the hotel, the faded flapping bunting that might suggest a flock of birds, or a carnival, or the start of war. The smell of the hotel soap, the clammy texture of the fabric-conditioned towels, and the dreadful feeling of being married. The dusty little jewellery shops and bad-tempered keepers, the vast pebbly beach with a road so close you heard more cars than waves. Hugo's ridiculous smile as he'd come towards her from the en-suite bathroom, his manhood swaying in front of him like a long, curved balloon, and how she imagined bursting it with a pin. They consummated the marriage repeatedly over the weekend until Hugo ran out of erection powders and poor Norma was applying Sudocrem all over her sore and rashy pudenda (her words), partly because of the frequency, and partly because her hairlessness offered no buffer. The honeymoon provided a first glimpse of the prejudice against large penises that became a recurring theme in her poetry.

Some while afterwards I bumped into Norma on campus, which as you know I treated as my own private garden, and we went to the Pineapple House for coffee.

'So, how's married life?' I asked.

And she said, 'Oh, God, don't ask!' Then, clicking a Canderel into her cup: 'Hugo's roped me into his communal recreation.'

'What does that mean?' I asked.

'Sex,' said Norma, stirring her drink, but looking at me. 'Outside, with strangers.'

'Outside? Where?' I asked.

'Car parks, lay-bys, gateways – anywhere you can park a car. Hugo mostly goes to the Holly Bush.'

It was dogging but we didn't call it that back then. I don't know what we did call it, but it was definitely a thing, especially in Leicestershire apparently, but not something I ever thought Norma would join in with. Norma who'd been shocked to hear I shared bathwater with my mother.

'Did you know about this before you married him?' I said.

'Yes,' she said.

'Oh my God.'

'Calm down, Susan,' she said, laughing, enjoying my response.

'But I can't bear it.'

'It's fine.'

'What do you mean he "roped you in"?'

'I have to drive him. Actually, that's the most annoying thing.'

'And, do you – see anything, or join in?'

'Yes, sort of, I mean, I sit in the car and that's joining in. The first time was pretty odd, like going to an auction and not wanting to accidentally bid for a Ming vase – I pretended to read while he waved his genitals at a Volkswagen Polo and then masturbated frantically with his knees slightly bent. It was all a bit – nothing.'

'Oh my God,' I said. 'I don't know whether to laugh or cry, or be furious.'

'Look, he really enjoys it,' said Norma, 'even more than golf – he looks forward to it all day on Tuesdays and Thursdays.'

'Why Tuesdays and Thursdays?'

'That's when we go, they're the good nights. Too many drunks at the weekends.'

'What's wrong with Wednesdays?' I said.

'Ah, that's when the Leopolds go.'

'The Leopolds?' I said. 'Professor Leopold?'

'Yes,' said Norma, 'and I really can't face seeing Lydia Leopold with a penis in her mouth.'

Though I wasn't well acquainted with the Leopolds at that time, I was aware of them. Norma had gossiped about Professor Leopold's conduct with the students and later, when Roy joined the university fencing club, I'd occasionally see him and Roy swashbuckling in the gym. The knowledge of his dogging or gulling, whatever it was called back then, added a strange element to the whole thing, plus, of course, the mild anxiety that one thing might lead to another and they might suddenly get their penises out.

'You seem very calm about it all, I'll say that for you,' I said to Norma.

'Well, I don't see how it's worse than what any woman has to put up with.'

'I suppose.'

'Seriously, Susan, this is what men actually want, many of them. It's just that Hugo isn't afraid to ask.'

'Oh, well, good for Hugo.'

Norma smiled.

'Do *you* enjoy it though?'

'I watch it like one might watch a wildlife documentary. They're a community just like the golf club, or the choir, or Sew & Sew, and I try to see it in those terms.'

'Oh,' I said.

'I do sometimes think the only quality Hugo was looking for in a spouse was the ability to drive confidently in the dark.'

'Why?'

'He's banned for life, remember?'

'Well, I suppose it's easier if you have your own transport.'

'As with so many things,' she said.

Norma gave me some mundane details. They'd eat their dinner half before and half after, otherwise Hugo might need a snack later and that might mean great hunks of Cracker Barrel and biscuits, which weren't good for his figure and him with a cholesterol thing. They'd jump into the car wearing certain clothing and with damp flannels in a polythene bag, Hugo raring to go and Norma wanting it over with. And suddenly it seemed like nothing.

Even the sauciest things seemed ordinary; and when she told me that one night she had herself had sex with a customer from the Pin Cushion while his wife watched through the windscreen, I only wondered, 'Which customer?'

'The one who always buys brushed denim,' said Norma, 'and metal poppers, remember?'

'Oh, her.' I remembered a woman from book club who'd not enjoyed a Beryl Bainbridge.

Some time shortly afterwards, Norma and I met again. She was equally keen to talk about this aspect of her new life. She'd reduced her involvement, she told me, to once a week and Hugo had started going alone on Thursdays (she'd drop him en route to Waitrose and pick him up on the way home, if he was done), and it seemed that this inconvenience had prompted Hugo to dream up ways of making it simpler and not requiring conveyance. He'd been exploring, for instance, the concept of 'shedding' as an alternative, popular in warmer climes, whereby participants peep through the windows of outbuildings in each other's gardens. It's important to stress that Norma spoke of this as neither right nor wrong; she wasn't disgusted or appalled by it and mostly didn't even want to giggle at it, but it was inconvenient and unexpected and, therefore, unwanted by her. Soon I merely found myself concerned that not every shed had a decent-sized window – and what about the risks posed by various garden implements in the smaller, overcrowded ones?

And taking it all in, I felt that day that a reciprocal revelation was called for and almost told Norma that Roy had started wanting to have sex on the stairs, it being easier for his knees, but not fully understanding the logistics myself, I couldn't expect her to. Instead I said, 'Roy insists on having all the lights on and one time came at me with a head torch.' It was uncomfortable talking like that, we'd not been big talkers about sex up to then, but I felt it the least I could do in the circumstances.

'Eugh!' she said. 'Why?'

'He wants to see everything.'

'Oh, Lord, no.' Norma held her hands up to her throat, and shuddered. 'I couldn't have that.'

I felt offended on Roy's behalf. Surely wanting to see everything was minor compared with requiring your wife to partake in communal lay-by sex twice a week with random rampant townsfolk, and having a pink light bulb in the shed, for God's sake? Surely wanting to see everything was a *compliment*, maybe not something a normal person – by which I mean a woman – would *enjoy*, but a compliment nonetheless.

Quite where my prudishness stems from, I don't know. I suspect I hadn't fully got over my mother's accident, seeing her knocked down like that, and never quite the same afterwards, childish and strangely sexual in her behaviour, always flashing her bust and making rude hand gestures. My father had to sleep on a put-me-up bed in the dining room then because of her insomniac demands and awful revelations that were innocent but somehow inappropriate. She would constantly mention that my father took long baths, where according to her he soaped every inch of his body twice over. I remember her letting the water cascade over her naked body, at the poolside shower, and my father rubbing his arms and legs and making a lot of soapsuds. 'You don't need to soap your arms, you know, Dad,' I'd said loudly, but only to please my mother who cackled in agreement while shampooing her undercarriage, and then the pool attendant stepping in to point at the '*No soap*' sign.

At home later, I considered telling Roy – only the bare bones (if you pardon the pun) because the subject would have intrigued him and he'd have listened avidly, which is always nice. He'd have loved hearing about the time a policeman arrived in a squad car and got out to investigate and presumably caution participants, but hadn't been able to help himself and joined in. Or the time Pete from Pete's Pets had flattened his genitals against the passenger-side window of a Vauxhall Cavalier and shouted, 'Squashed rat!' and people all around had masturbated like mad and even Norma had looked up from her embroidery and chuckled. But I told Roy nothing about it, in case he got any ideas. Overall, I was pleased Norma had confided in me, and also pleased to have been able to share the news of Michael Douglas's alleged sex addiction and Catherine Zeta-Jones's support of him, which she wouldn't have known had I not told her.

'There you go,' she'd said, clapping her hands, 'it's all the rage.'

# 10

At some point after we'd become parents Roy read something in one of his golf magazines that sparked a desire for great change. The article, by Tony Jacklin or one of the more philosophical golfers of the golden age, promulgated the idea that time intervals with more changes will be perceived to be longer than intervals with fewer changes.

'Doing new things stretches time and lengthens your life, and the ruts we get into are literally life-sapping,' Roy said, paraphrasing the article. 'Humans need the stimulus of the new.'

'What's that got to do with golf?' I asked.

And he said, 'What's true for life is true for sport.'

I felt this philosophy at odds with golf but offered some ideas that might do the trick – walk a different route to work, look for a new job, start going to bed early and reading books in translation, take up a new hobby, rise at dawn and bake – but these wouldn't do. He wanted a major life event.

'I have just given birth,' I reminded him, 'and bought a reconditioned Henry so big we have to keep him behind the settee,' but he swatted those aside. He was after something bigger. Cataclysmic.

To spice things up I invited Norma and Hugo for lunch

and served it al fresco. Norma sat awkwardly in a metal garden chair and Hugo remained standing, straining his poor ligaments. I half-expected him to suggest a mini orgy but he didn't and was actually quite nice which surprised me. He spoke intelligently about trees being anti-depressive and even described the trembling leaves of an aspen he'd planted. I could all of a sudden see that Hugo might have hitherto unknown depths.

Roy brought up the idea of great change prolonging life and Hugo was in complete agreement. We'd almost exhausted the subject when Hugo remembered an upcoming opportunity at the golf club. 'They're looking for someone to visit a canoeing facility in rural France, to look at viability in the Brankham context.'

'That would make a change!' I said.

'You could tag a few days on,' said Hugo, 'for the family.'

And so we went, and spent almost a week in the house of a friend of a friend of Hugo's who let out the top half of his house to holidaymakers. The rental part had a great terrace with views over a winding river, pine trees, a church, the whole village and distant mountains, with stone floors so cool and hard you could barely believe you weren't on solid ground, a smell of clean dust, coffee, chlorine and the faintest tang of sulphur. Elaborate metal shutters fixed over the amber-coloured windows made it very dark inside, and a recurring daydream of Honey squeezing through the balcony railings made me long to be home. I both adored it and hated it. It was called something like the House of Fury because it made the landlord furious to think of tourists living it up in the best half of his house.

Back at home, far from being satisfied by the change of scene, Roy wanted to relocate to France for ever. The French canoe centre had made noises about offering him a job, encouraged by the fact that he was not only Scottish but also almost fluent in French and good with canoes. Hey presto, this was the big thing he was looking for. He talked of nothing else for days. He wanted to live in France like I wanted a new front door. But I couldn't agree to it and knew I must not seem to agree, only to disappoint him when it came to it, and so I was unambiguous in my opposition.

'The word "relocation" sounds like something from space travel, life with no friends and no TV and everyone feeling sorry for me for being English,' I said. Then I put the blame on Honey. 'No,' I said again, 'not with her. I can't relocate with a toddler, it was bad enough having a holiday.'

He could not understand my opposition. He accused me of 'not being a Francophile' which felt really harsh. He kept up a running commentary on the joys and virtues of the country. Didn't I want to fetch bread and croissants every morning from the *boulangerie*? (Not *le depot de pain* – did I know the difference?) Didn't I want Honey to grow up French? And therefore bilingual? Didn't I want to make bread-and-butter pudding but with *brioche*? Didn't I want to get away from stuffy old England and be stylish and European?

'It's the kind of opportunity that only comes once in a lifetime,' he said. 'Surely we can't turn it down.'

'Can we *not* go to live in France but maybe get a really big parrot instead?' I said.

'A parrot?' said Roy.

And Honey, on my hip, the clever little thing, repeated the word 'parrot' like a parrot, and because she was so very young and it couldn't have been ironic, I laughed, and Roy never mentioned France again, thank God. Not in that context, anyway.

It was a relief for both of us when Roy started studying for a Master's in Business Administration through the UofR; it provided not the one new thing but two, in that he was now eligible for the UofR fencing club, which he joined immediately. It was then that the aforementioned Professor David Leopold, or as Roy called him, Dave, became a sort of friendly acquaintance. I was wary of him for multiple reasons: firstly, of course, his communal activities, and additional rumours in that department about his having sex on his desk with any student who would, but also his habit of flicking his blow-dried hair out of his eyes with a great sweeping nod of his head, like a horse bothered by flies. Actually, though, it was his insistence on being called Leo, which I heard about from Roy, that really made me dislike the man.

'Dave Leopold has asked me to call him Leo,' Roy said, one day after a friendly assault.

'What an ego,' I said.

'Oh, I don't know,' said Roy, 'he was just letting me know.'

'I hate people who force a nickname. You'd soon enough have heard others calling him Leo and switched of your own accord, but honestly, asking others to call you by your abbreviated surname at the age of forty-something seems immature,' I ranted. 'I mean, I always fancied going by the name of Sue-Faye, but no one started it.'

'He was just tipping me off,' said Roy.

Really, I was peeved that he was letting himself be out-manoeuvred by this vain, sex-obsessed peacock, and I vowed to call him David at the next possible opportunity, which, as it happened, came very soon. Norma and I were having a coffee outside the Pineapple House on campus one afternoon, her a member of staff and me a guest, when he and Roy strode past in their sword-fighting breeches. Beside Roy, Professor Leopold looked tiny and narrow.

'There's Roy,' said Norma, pushing at her hair with splayed fingers. 'Call him over.'

'What? No,' I said, 'it's that awful Professor Leopold with him.'

So Norma called out, 'Yoo-hoo! Roy Warren, are you going to ignore your wife?'

The men diverted from the main path and came to stand beside our table under the eaves. Roy seemed awkward but Professor Leopold thrust his hand out to Norma, like some kind of knight.

'I didn't know you were Roy's wife,' he said. 'I'm Professor Leopold – how nice to meet you properly.'

Norma took his hand lightly. 'I'm not Roy's wife,' she said with a suppressed laugh, and still holding his fingers with one hand, gestured with the other across the little table. 'This is Roy's wife, Susan.'

'Oh, yes,' he said, recognizing me, 'so you are, Susan, I do beg your pardon.'

'Hello, David,' I said, lunging to take the tips of his fingers from Norma.

'And this,' I said, gesturing back, 'is Dr Norma Pack-Allen from the English department.'

'Of course, of *course*, Dr Pack-Allen, do forgive me, I'm very admiring of your work,' he said. Remembering that they'd seen each other in action at the Holly Bush lay-by, I felt annoyed at the double entendre, and frustrated that I couldn't meaningfully grimace at Roy.

'Oh, how very kind,' said Norma, brightening. 'Anything in particular?'

'Your collection of exquisite love poetry, of course,' said Professor Leopold and the two locked eyes for a moment. It occurred to me how far Norma had come since our evenings spent at Genevieve's, when she'd just stare at any man who spoke or asked her to dance, as though seeing a polar bear yawning or a zebra winking.

'How cheering, I wasn't aware anyone read it,' said Norma, 'and I am an admirer of *your* work.'

Professor Leopold frowned and cocked his head to the side. 'My work?'

'Yes, I very much enjoyed your contribution to the newsletter on the subject of bicycle security.'

'How kind,' said Professor Leopold, 'I wasn't aware anyone read it.' He had comic timing, I had to admit.

'Anyway, we'd best push on,' said Roy, breaking the spell. 'We've got a bout booked.' And off they went.

Norma watched, flushed and excited, as Professor

Leopold's épée and mask bounced about at his side like the dangling genitals of a robot, and when they were out of sight, said, 'Golly, he's rather attractive.'

Unwilling to discuss the man any further, I said, 'You actually *read* the newsletter?'

# 11

One morning Roy had come in from Do It All with some bits and bobs of hardware and a packet of Cat Away which he intended to sprinkle about on the boundary with our neighbour's garden. He was annoyed and slightly obsessed by the two cats next door. Occasionally, they'd go to the toilet in our garden, but I only knew this because Roy was alert to it, and sometimes the ginger one would sunbathe stretched out on the roof of our kitchen extension. I say extension – it is only a five-foot-wide lean-to but still affording nice light. I'd put our old settee in there for reading and loafing, and loved seeing him up above me – the swirly patterns in his orange fur flattened against the dusty glass. Occasionally I'd wave at him and he'd blink in response, and watch me, and it was all very literary and reminded me of Sylvia Plath and her cat called Daddy and Charles Dickens's dear old Bob, whose paw he had stuffed and attached to a letter opener. Anyway, Roy couldn't forgive him the mess in the flowerbeds, certain that he was the culprit and up there gloating. Cats did that, according to Roy. I'm not a cat expert, so can't comment.

'It might be the other one,' I said, meaning the flower-bed messer.

'No,' said Roy, 'it's him, give him time and he'll sh*t up there, just to f*ck us up.'

Roy was checking the small print on the Cat Away packet to make sure it wouldn't poison baby Honey, who by now was scampering about, eating things – when the doorbell rang and I found Josie Jones standing there, looking furtive in a sarong, biting the inside of her cheek. She was well known to me, partly having been Roy's live-in landlady when he and I had started dating, plus she was part of the Brankham Chorus in which I was a soprano and she an alto. The altos were always aloof, and she was particularly so, and terribly over-confident, often stating, 'I could be an alto or a soprano.' She was a known over-enunciator, too. I remember her actually spoiling our rendition of 'I Saw Three Ships' by stressing the 't' in 'Christmas', which of course one is meant to, but not like that (ChrisTUMmas), practically adding a whole syllable. She frequented the Two Swans, using the kitchen, out of hours, to cook over-sized turkeys. I'd often see her heaving them out of her van and putting an 'UNLOADING' notice in her windscreen. She even once or twice popped her head into the shop to ask us to keep an eye out for wardens. It turned out to have been her who sent the cheeseboard for my hen party at the shop, left over from a catered event the previous day but still edible and very pretty nonetheless.

Josie Jones wished me a Happy New Year, and it wasn't even still January.

'Oh,' I said, 'yes, Happy New Year to you too.'

She was sorry to bother us but needed a quick word with Roy, she said.

I should have said, 'Concerning what?' But that wasn't

my style, instead I ushered her in and she stood beside the kitchen sink with her hands linked in front of her as though she were about to be filmed breaking bad news, and I, not being the sort to hang about in that situation, scooped Honey off her play-mat and left the room, lingering on the way out so that she might appreciate my daughter's loveliness.

'Say hello, Honey,' I said, and she waved a little hand.

Upstairs I felt a fluttering in my stomach, a sort of excited worry, but couldn't for the life of me work out what was going on. An affair? Surely not, she was years older than Roy – I mean, ten years or more, and so unattractive and severe. She'd once had a fight with a stall-holder on Leicester Market who'd sold her some bruised vegetables and though he was three times her size and an ex-pro wrestler, he came off worse, and rumour had it she'd once forced a boyfriend to the cinema at knifepoint to see a film he didn't fancy. That said, Norma had more than once hinted at seeing Roy and Josie behaving romantically, as you might recall. But I moved on quickly and instead recalled Josie's recent lobbying for the inclusion of Purcell's 'Bell Anthem' in the upcoming programme – in which we sopranos get only the chorus – and somehow that seemed worse.

After fifteen minutes or so I heard the front door close and, watching carefully from the window, saw her get into a horrible little car and drive off, a scrap of sarong poking out of the bottom of the door. I daren't go back downstairs straight away in case Roy was crying or stabbed to death so I read a book with Honey and pretended to fall asleep. Eventually Roy came up asking if I had any thoughts about lunch, and then, while I made cheese-and-pickle sandwiches, I asked, 'What did your landlady want?'

And Roy said, 'Tell you later.'

'Tell me now,' I said, and so he told me quite calmly that she'd come round to discuss her four-and-a-half-year-old daughter. Whom, now, all of a sudden, she claimed to be his.

'Oh, my gosh,' I said. 'And is she, do you think, I mean, *could* she be?'

'Yeah, she definitely *could* be,' said Roy, biting into a sandwich.

'Well, she probably is then.' I felt slightly wobbly for a moment.

'Yeah, she probably is,' agreed Roy.

'Wow, Roy,' I said, 'and there you were wanting a major life change!'

'Yeah. Christ.'

'Were you always sleeping with Josie when you were her lodger?' I said.

'Occasionally.'

'I can't imagine it,' I said, but actually I found I could and it was hilarious. 'She doesn't seem like your type.'

'She's not really.'

'Did you love her?' I asked.

'No!' he said. 'It wasn't like that.'

'But you liked her enough to have sex with her?'

'Yeah, she was OK.'

'Why did you stop?'

'She wanted to get serious.'

'And you didn't?'

'No.'

'So what did you say?'

'I moved out of the house,' said Roy. 'It was bloody inconvenient actually.'

'And you had no idea that the baby was yours?'

'No,' said Roy, 'not a clue.'

I looked at him. Eating crisps.

'What?' he said.

'I'm trying to work out whether you're an idiot or a shyster.'

'Idiot,' said Roy, and I believed him.

'Yeah, you must be. I mean, even though you'd been sleeping with her,' I said, 'it didn't occur to you?'

'No, it didn't,' he said, beginning to sound defensive. 'I assumed she'd say if the baby was mine.'

'So whose did you think she was?'

'I didn't think about it,' said Roy. 'I was sleeping with other people, I assumed Josie was too.'

'Hmm,' I said, 'like who?'

'Luke Walsh, Hugo.'

'Hugo?' I said. 'Hugo Pack-Allen?'

'Yes, what other Hugo is there?'

'She was sleeping with Hugo but you're confident the little girl is your child and not his?' I said, tapping the table with my index finger.

'Yes, I am. Josie checked it all out.'

'How?' I said.

'Something to do with Hugo,' said Roy. 'He can't.'

'Can't what?' I asked.

'Have a kid.'

'Oh? He can't conceive a child?'

'Apparently not.'

'Do you think it's a low sperm count?' I said.

'I don't know,' he said, now sounding annoyed.

'Well, don't you want to find out?'

'Look, in the end does it even matter that much, love?' he said, and I'd been about to say yes, it absolutely would matter to me and that it would definitely at some point matter very much to this child of his, and to Honey, but I remembered Hector not being Ted's, a subject that had been left undiscussed underneath all the tiny things we had talked about, puzzled at, unpicked and unpacked, like whether or not we could afford a new front door.

Later, when Honey was down for her after-lunch nap, I initiated sex and let Roy stare right into my vagina during the foreplay.

'But why didn't Josie tell you until now?' I said, lying in bed afterwards. 'She lives less than a mile away, you might have seen the child a hundred times and not known it.'

'It's more like two miles, actually, but yeah, I know, it's nuts.'

'But why didn't she tell you?' I asked again.

'She didn't want to burden me.'

'So why tell you now?' I said. 'What's changed?'

'We've just had Honey.'

'But we've not *just* had Honey,' I said.

'Well, I guess Josie's just found out about her, I don't know.'

'Oh,' I said. 'Might it be that Josie thought Hugo was

124

the father but then discovered he couldn't be and realized you must be?'

'I suppose that's possible.'

'What's her name?' I asked.

But Roy didn't know. He'd had enough and went off to tinker with his car. The fan belt was slipping.

Later still, I answered the phone. 'Guess where I am?' said Norma.

'I don't know,' I said. 'Work? Home?'

'Guess.'

'Home?'

'No, I'm sitting in my car on your street,' she said. 'I'm on my mobile phone.'

'What?' I looked out of the front window and there she was, waving.

'What've you got one of those for?' I said.

'I don't know, I just wanted one.'

'What for?'

'To phone people, like this, whenever I feel like it.'

'Are you coming in?' I said.

'No, I'm going into the office.'

'I need to talk to you,' I said. 'Something's happened.'

And watching Roy fiddle with his car, out of earshot, on the drive, I told Norma about the sudden discovery of this four-and-a-half-year-old he'd apparently had with Josie Jones.

Her response was almost as strange and surprising as the news itself.

'Oh, well, that's good news,' she said. 'Now you don't need to have another baby.'

'What?' I said.

'Bingo! Sibling. Job done.'

And it hadn't occurred to me, but I realized with a shock that Norma was right. I didn't need to have another. This older sister had arrived in the nick of time, whose ever she was.

During the weeks running up to our first meeting with Grace (that's what the four-and-a-half-year-old was called, which felt like proof of her being Roy's if I needed it), Roy was clearly anxious and when I pressed him he admitted to having a vague but troubling notion that this child had been born into the world with the sole purpose to kill him. By some awful stroke of luck, he had just read a long and gruesome novel with a subplot along these lines – the only way the father can survive is to exile himself in a cave and repel anyone approaching with rocks and rubble – and I was put in mind of Goya's painting *Saturn Devouring His Son* and felt sorry for poor Grace inadvertently getting mixed up with all of this when her only crime was having been begat out of wedlock to a secretive caterer. Anyway, the point is, while I was planning fairy cakes Roy was battling images of the child running at him with a kiddie fork, shouting, 'What measure ye mete it will be measured to you again.' Or trying to gouge his eye out with a doll's hand, this being the punishment the daughter in the medieval sci-fi dishes out to the father, who is then left on a coastal outcrop to bleed to death and regret his demon seed.

'Well, you will read such terrifying books, Roy, what do

you expect?' I said, my fear of horror stories vindicated at last.

'It's just such a weird coincidence,' he said. 'I can't get it out of my head.'

'Read something soothing,' I suggested, 'about a non-murderous child.'

'Like what?'

'I don't know, *Huckleberry Finn*.'

'He's a boy,' said Roy.

Eventually, I found my copy of *Anne of Green Gables* and he started reading it immediately.

We discussed back-paying child maintenance but Josie Jones's solicitor quoted her as saying she was 'sure it will all come out in the wash'. And when our solicitor mithered Roy about getting his name on Grace's birth certificate or applying for parental responsibility, Roy told him to 'chill out'. So, as you'll appreciate, it was all very relaxed, except for when Roy and Leroy brought home and assembled a huge drum-shaped trampoline with a ladder and safety netting which Roy had got from a colleague whose children had outgrown it. It took up half the garden and Norma, who happened to be there, upset him by groaning and saying, 'Have you not heard of Chekhov's gun?'

Four weeks after we'd first been told of her existence, Grace appeared in gingham dungarees with a plush dachshund, the spitting image of Roy (Grace, not the dachshund), which was reassuring. Josie gently pushed her into the lounge and then instead of leaving, as I thought we'd agreed, sat down in Roy's chair.

'What star sign are you, Susan?' she said, and when I said, 'Sagittarius,' she said, 'Oh, it could be worse, I s'pose.'

Honey sat surrounded by her toys and plastic bricks. Grace immediately squatted beside her and began building towers.

'This is Honey,' I told her, 'your sister, and I'm Susan, and this,' I said, pointing to Roy, 'is your dad, Roy.'

'Shall I call him Roy or Dad?' asked Grace, looking at her mother.

'Call him Roy,' said Josie, 'otherwise it'll get confusing.'

'Will it?' I said. 'Why?'

'She calls my fella Dad,' said Josie.

'Does she? What's your fella's name?' I asked.

'Ray!' said Josie, with a laugh. 'Seriously!'

'I think it'd be nice if Grace called Roy Dad and maybe she could call your fella Ray?'

'I'm about to kick him out anyway,' said Josie, 'so yeah, fine, call him Dad.'

'Kick who out?' asked Grace.

'Ray,' said Josie.

Grace looked up, glanced at Roy and then said to her mother, 'So you could marry Dad then.'

'Your dad is married to me,' I said, thinking I ought to make that clear.

Roy sprang up and clapped his hands. 'Cup of tea, Josie?' he said, clearly wanting an excuse to leave the room.

'Yeah, actually,' said Josie, 'Have you got chamomile?'

'No, we don't,' I said.

'All right, do me a cup of builder's.'

Roy left the room and closed the door behind him.

'Then I'll leave you to it,' said Josie.

'Yes,' I said, seizing the moment, 'it's almost lunchtime. What shall we have to eat, Grace? Soup? Or a little sandwich?'

'You're all right,' said Josie, 'I've done her a packed lunch, it's in her rucksack. All her favourites are in there.'

'You needn't have.'

'I can't leave it to chance,' said Josie, 'she's anaemic.'

Roy reappeared with the tea and Josie told us between sips about a local caterer being linked to a toxoplasmosis outbreak in the area, which she seemed quite upset by.

'Less competition for you though?' I said hopefully.

'But it reflects badly on the whole industry,' said Josie. 'I mean, imagine how Roy'd feel if another club gave everyone the squits due to poor hygiene standards?'

Roy nodded and shrugged and with that, I got up and said, 'Right, lunch.'

Josie got up too and took her mug to the sink. I followed her out to the car.

'Look, Josie,' I said, 'I know this is all a bit strange but please don't worry, we'll take very good care of Grace.'

'I know you will,' she said, with a hint of menace.

She drove away and finally Roy and I could relax. We had a picnic of flower-shaped sandwiches on the carpet and Grace opened her lunch box.

'What have you got there?' I asked.

'Pasta with pesto, erm, some spinach leaves, a little cheese, a little orange, and some raisins,' she said, rifling through. 'Shall we all share?'

'Yes, please,' I said. 'How lovely.'

The afternoon rolled along well. Grace played nicely with Honey, who was a delight. I couldn't stop looking for similarities between the girls. Grace had a strange, rather nice way of saying my name, like an elision contraction, 'Sus'n', which I thought fascinating given her mother's ChrisTUMmas elongation. I'm not saying Roy's worries fell away immediately, especially when it turned out that Grace had independent eye control, and such nimble prehensile toes that she could play the opening bars of the 'Moonlight Sonata' with them. These talents referred so poetically to his fantastical anxieties that we couldn't help but feel a bit spooked.

Josie arrived back earlier than expected and made herself at home at the kitchen table, asking nosy questions about our utility providers and grocery habits.

'Do you shop at the organic place?' she asked. 'I do, for her.'

'Some things,' I said, untruthfully.

'Like what?'

'Carrots. I've heard if you buy ordinary, you should discard the top two inches.'

'Bollocks,' she said, 'dairy is the real problem, all the antibiotics. I don't mind for me, but I don't want her ingesting a load of crap that farmers pump into their animals.'

'No.'

'Not until she's at least nine,' said Josie. 'Sainsbury's do organic milk now, and a small range of cheeses.'

'Good to know,' I said, feeling a headache coming on, and then Norma suddenly burst in through the back door with a packet of chocolate fingers and it turned into a tea party, Norma acting the host.

'Which school is Grace attending?' she asked.

'Brankham Park,' said Josie, 'lovely little school.'

'I've heard it's excellent,' said Norma.

'It is. Very high standards and a proper library.'

'Will you enrol Honey there?' Norma asked me.

Before I could answer, Josie said, 'I should think so, she'll get a priority place now, thanks to me.'

'Yes,' I said. 'I was planning to enrol her there anyway, it's our nearest primary.'

'Yeah, but now she's got a sibling there, you're in, deffo.'

'Is Grace enjoying school?' asked Norma.

'She loves it. She's top for everything, she's ahead of herself on reading and numbers and she's already started Grade One piano.'

'Have you got your own instrument?' asked Norma.

'A little electric keyboard,' said Josie. 'It does the job.'

Norma looked at me and raised her eyebrows. 'You'll need to get your piano tuned then,' she said, and turning back to Josie, 'They've got an upright.'

A few weeks later the four of us went for a walk in the countryside, Honey toddling. We were fostering a dog then, Dylan, and she must have provided a kind of buffer for Roy as he kept calling her to heel, then geeing her up and throwing things for her, and, frankly, it was awkward to watch. Eventually I said, 'Be gentle with the dog, Roy.' And moments afterwards, Grace ran ahead and picked up a small stick, and in imitation of Roy, pulled back her arm, launched it elaborately into the air, and it went off at a bit of an angle and hit Roy full in the face. He dropped to his knees, head in hands, like a professional footballer. The dog ran up to him, picked up the stick and ran proudly away, with Grace, oblivious, trotting behind.

'Christ almighty!' Roy said. 'Did you see that?'

'It was an accident,' I said.

'It didn't seem like a f*cking accident,' he said, brushing himself down.

'You started flinging sticks about – she's only copying you.'

'She's a psychopath. Just like her mother.'

'For heaven's sake,' I said, 'don't be so ridiculous.'

Grace turned and I thought for a moment she might have heard us but she smiled and waved, and I waved back.

Some weeks later, the three of us were on campus and I'd bought frothy hot chocolates from the Pineapple House and parked the buggy by a bench. Grace helped Honey with hers which I'd tipped into a sippy cup and I took photographs of them – Grace with a moustache, Honey with a beard – pleased that they'd have some early memories of each other. Strolling home I told Grace about the time, when I was little, my brother said that the guinea pig had spoken to him.

'I really believed him!' I said. 'I went out to the hutch every day, again and again, and lifted her out and spoke to her, hoping she'd say something back.'

Then suddenly Grace clapped her palms to her ears and said, 'Can you stop talking, please?'

'I'm sorry,' I said, 'it's such a silly story, I was just check-ing you understood!' We walked home in silence.

Later, thinking that Grace might have mentioned it to Roy and wanting to make light of it, I said, 'Poor old Grace had to ask me to stop talking.'

Roy stomped upstairs and dragged the poor child out of her bed so that she could apologize to me.

'I'm sorry for being rude,' she said, clutching handfuls of her nightdress.

And I said, 'No, Grace, it wasn't your fault.'

And she said, 'You were saying everything again and again.'

And I said, 'I know. I completely understand. I some-times do that. It's me who should be sorry.'

Grace went back to bed and I turned to Roy. 'That was unnecessary,' I said. 'Poor Grace.'

And I can't deny I was hurt. Not by Grace but by the fact that I'd faced a huge, life-changing event and taken it completely in my stride and was yet again receiving no acknowledgement, or praise, or thanks from any direction.

# 12

It wasn't long before Grace's presence was as normal and natural as the air, and we stopped staring at her. Honey looked forward to the sound of her bundling arrival every Friday afternoon and would race to the hall and encircle her sister with her arms, laughing. The sound of Grace's voice calling 'Sus'n' or 'Ray' or 'Honeybee', her tinkling tunes on the piano, and playing her favourite pop songs, were pure joy. The Sunday-evening departures were soon a weekly low point which felt like the sun going behind a cloud and, to some extent, we'd limp through the week until the next Friday when she'd be back. Our having her at weekends suited Josie, as she was able to grow her catering business, PardeePardee! Over the first few months we all focused on Grace – making Honey wait. Honey would toddle from person to person, with an interesting toy in her hand, try to scramble up into a chair to interrupt someone's serious talk. I taught Grace to crochet, Roy measured her for kiddie golf clubs, and Norma – who seemed often to coincide with her – answered all manner of complicated questions. Why was Sleeping Beauty asleep? And why didn't people pay their taxes? What is ink made of?

'She's so smart,' Norma used to tell me. I'd agree, she *was* very bright and self-assured. Whereas the idea of

Honey – and Honey herself, in person – slightly horrified Norma, this windfall of a child seemed to fascinate and please her. More than this even, she seemed to feel a certain responsibility for her. 'Why don't you get a telescope? As educational pastimes go, surely it's way ahead of a spaniel,' she once said, deliberately comparing Dylan, a simple dog, with a piece of intricate machinery.

Grace was such an engaging child, even my mother couldn't dislike her. She did once refer to her as 'Her Grace' but I nipped it in the bud, and turning to my father – because you can't speak directly to my mother – I said, 'If she says a *single word* like that again she will not be welcome in this house,' and my father, ashen, said, 'No, quite right.' I'd fancied a longer exchange, to be able to spin off onto other misdemeanours but my mother said, 'I was only joking.' And the next time she and my father came to tea, they brought a Vashti Bunyan CD, which Grace immediately played, and that was that.

As time went by, Grace became sisterly. If Honey whined, she'd look at her with puzzlement and ask, 'What's the matter?' as if to say, what on earth could be? And, 'Can you stop that, please?' and the whining would cease. Grace might occasionally exploit the big-sister status, in the way older siblings do – worrying and soothing her by turns – but more often she worked hard to improve her as a companion, and if I had to choose a moment to demonstrate Grace and Honey's early life together, it would be the time that Grace gave Honey, aged three or four, a French lesson, at the end of which, Honey was running around saying, 'I like bread and cheese but never give me pâté.' And, 'My name is Honey Warren and my sister's name is Grace.' In French!

When Honey started at Brankham Park primary school, Grace was still there albeit up the other end, and it made Friday pick-ups very nice, waiting with Honey at the gate, Grace rushing towards us, all arms and bags and books, and the two girls gossiping on the way home. If Grace had a lacy trim on her ankle socks, Honey would want them. If Grace had a spotty pencil case, Honey would want one, and so on. There was a slight hiccup when Honey was in Year 2, and the dividing wall in her classroom fell onto a group of pupils sitting on the floor reading, Honey among them. The children were completely unharmed but it seemed to trigger a trauma response in Honey and the day after the incident, a Friday, she'd insisted on wearing her cycle helmet, in case it happened again. Her class teacher, Mrs Kerridge, objected.

'I'm afraid Honey cannot be permitted to wear a helmet during the school day,' she said. 'If she won't take it off, she'll have to go home.'

And I said quietly, 'Are you kidding?'

'No,' said Mrs Kerridge, 'I'm not *kidding*.'

'Maybe if a wall hadn't fallen on top of her she wouldn't feel the need.'

'I wouldn't call it a wall, Mrs Warren.'

'Well, what would you call it?'

'A lightweight partition,' she said, and I laughed.

Eventually, after I said I'd go to see the headteacher, Honey was allowed in, helmet and all.

I'd had trouble with Mrs Kerridge before. One week the homework spellings had included words like 'Baboon', 'Tuesday' and 'Veritable'.

'*This week's spellings have been a bit challenging,*' I wrote in the book.

Mrs Kerridge wrote a note back saying, '*Would you like me to move Honey into the Special Needs group?*'

Later, on the afternoon of the helmet incident, Honey came out of school bareheaded, the helmet dangling off her rucksack, and we waited for Grace. When she came out, a bit late, she was silent and wouldn't look at Honey. At home it was revealed that she had been 'borrowed' from her classroom to reason with Honey about the helmet, after which it had been agreed she could wear it when sitting near the wall, and, as the day had gone on, she'd soon forgotten all about it. I was slightly peeved at this this but when Norma rang on Sunday night, she was appalled.

'How dare they interrupt Grace to do their job for them?' she said. 'That must never happen again.'

I spoke to Mrs Kerridge on the Monday. 'We'd really rather you hadn't involved Grace Jones in the helmet incident,' I said.

'Oh?' she said. 'Grace was very helpful.'

'But it wasn't her job,' I said.

'Oh, I didn't realize there were problems between the girls, you might have let us know.'

'There aren't problems.'

'Don't worry,' she said, 'I shall keep them apart from now on.'

'I haven't asked you to keep them apart,' I said.

'Well, then I'm confused,' said the teacher. 'What do you want?'

'I just think that Grace shouldn't have been involved.'

'Well, as I say, I shall make sure they have no further contact.'

And just like that Mrs Kerridge had beaten me in a game I didn't know we were playing.

I used to help out on the odd morning at school around that time and one day, clearing up in the staffroom after a tea break, saw a humorous notice pinned up on the board.

Translations for school reports:
Enthusiastic = pest
Eccentric = nuts
Unique = freak
Creative = thick
Robust = bully
Sensitive = crybaby
Thoughtful = slow, thick
Cheerful = fat
Imaginative = lying toerag
Breath of fresh air = rude
Popular = fat but generous
Ambitious = big-head
Confident = spoilt
Self-motivating = nit-ridden
Will be Prime Minister = egomaniac

I stared at it while slowly drying a dozen cups. I hung the thin tea towel to dry on a peg and then scribbled a note at the bottom of the page:

Mrs Kerridge = Robust

After that Mrs Kerridge stopped asking for my help in her classroom, and so I offered my services at the other end of the school and was soon helping in the library one morning a week with Grace's year. My duties included checking the pupils' reading diaries and that was how I came to know that Josie Jones didn't want Grace reading Jacqueline Wilson or comics.

One weekday evening I happened to drive by the Lord Lieutenant's house and saw Josie Jones's car parked outside with Grace in the passenger seat. I assumed quite rightly that Josie was delivering some catering for a party there. This must have been six-thirty in the evening and I pulled up alongside, wound my window down and waved.

'Hey, Grace!' I called. She couldn't open the window, not being on the driver's side, but she waved both hands enthusiastically. 'You OK?' I mouthed and she nodded. I drove on and did some shopping in Sainsbury's and forty minutes later, drove past again. It was getting dark by now so when I saw Josie's car still there, I pulled in behind, and went to the passenger side. Grace jumped slightly and then laughed. I opened the car door. 'Hey, you've been here a while,' I said.

'Oh, Mum's just doing the food for a moment.'

'But I saw you here an hour ago,' I said. 'How long is she going to be?'

'Not long, she's just serving the tagine.'

I went away and an hour later, couldn't help myself but drive by again and there the car still was and Grace inside, asleep. I wasn't going to march into the house and humiliate Josie in front of her customers and possibly damage her reputation but neither would I let Grace sit in the dark any longer.

Now in possession of a mobile phone of my own, I texted Josie: Hi, just found Grace in car. Going to take her back to ours. Will bring her home in morning in time for school.

Grace had taken a hot chocolate to bed when Josie rang and called me an interfering bitch and said the only reason she hadn't called the police was because of the possibility of the Lord Lieutenant being dragged into it. I said the only reason I hadn't reported her was to protect Grace, because I knew what it was like having a neglectful mother.

I texted Norma: She left Grace in the car, in the dark in the street for at least two hours. God knows how long she'd have been there if I hadn't intervened. It was pitch dark.

Norma replied: You've done the right thing. How did Josie take it?

I replied: She seems furious. I expect we'll have it out tomorrow.

Roy said he'd better drop Grace back the next morning, to avoid fisticuffs.

'Absolutely not,' I said. 'Josie and I can sort this out in a civilized way, thank you, we're not animals.'

'Well, be careful,' said Roy. 'She can be extremely volatile first thing.'

'Can she?'

'Yeah, remember when I lodged with her and had to have my breakfast in the café?'

'Oh, yes, so you did.'

When the morning came, after our porridge we set off. Grace, knowing nothing of the argument the night before, chatted away merrily. 'I hope Mum brought some leftover puddings back from the job,' she said.

Josie opened the door before I could knock, and Grace ran past her.

'She's hoping for puddings!' I said.

'Is she?' said Josie. I stood still, waiting for her to speak. When she said nothing more I asked, 'Did you bring anything nice back from last night's job?' and instantly regretted bringing it up.

'I did actually,' she said, 'profiteroles.'

'Ooh, very nice.'

'Do you want some?'

'Well, yes,' I said, 'if you've any to spare. That'd be lovely.'

'I'll bring them out to you,' she said. And though she shut the door quite abruptly, I was pleased she wanted to make amends and saw the pudding as a peace offering. I went and stood by the car on the street and gazed about. I noticed for the first time that Josie had a '*No Circulars*' notice on the door and an illustrated '*Beware of the Dog*' which implied she owned at least one large terrier, and I was pondering the implication of these signs when Josie poked her head out of an upstairs window.

'Oi, Susan!' she yelled. 'Here you go!' and threw something down, which plopped onto the car bonnet. Before

I could work out what was happening, she'd thrown another.

'What are you doing?' I shouted, staring up at her.

'You want profiteroles,' she said, 'here, have some.' She was soon bombarding me. I took cover in the car and drove away, the wipers smearing chocolate and cream across the windscreen with every swipe.

At home, Honey was sitting waiting on the doorstep, in her school uniform. Roy stood beside her, looking troubled.

'Where've you been, Mum?' said Honey, jumping up. 'I'm going to be late for school.'

'Couldn't you have taken her?' I said to Roy.

'I would have, if you'd asked,' he said. 'What took you so long?'

'I had to go through the car wash.'

# 13

I started planning a party for Roy's fortieth early in the year 2000. My idea was to have dinner at home with a few close friends and I was startled to realize that our best friends were Norma and Hugo Pack-Allen, Leroy Thomas from the golf club (Honey's godfather, and Roy's ex-housemate) and his boyfriend Dale, and Roy's brother Guy, and his fiancée Booboo. But just about the time I was deciding what we should eat and had been on the brink of approaching Josie about catering, Norma dropped the bombshell that she and Hugo wouldn't be able to make it.

'It's not really our thing, Susan,' she said.

'What isn't?' I asked.

'Being trapped in someone's kitchen-diner with a lasagne.'

'But it's Roy's fortieth.'

'I know it is, and I'm sorry to turn it down, but it's just a number after all, Susan – I wouldn't get all het up about it.'

So I switched us to a long weekend away, and chose a campsite in the New Forest that I knew from childhood and which had static caravans, free-range ponies, bike hire and direct forest access. I booked the expensive Pegasus, not only because of its integral water system, but because I thought the mythical winged horse a good omen. We drove to the village of Minstead, and took a turning near the Rufus Stone and were soon settled with the kettle on. I presented the girls each with a new soft toy for the trip: 'Ladybug' for Grace, a stylish ladybird with eyelashes, and for Honey, 'Mr Blue', a kindly hound dog with tinkling bells in his floppy ears. These two characters were arranged in the front window of Pegasus, much to the delight of our fellow campers. On the first day Grace did a watercolour of newly unfurled bracken fronds and applied blue eyeliner which gathered in uncomfortable blobs in the corners of her eyes, and somehow highlighted her periorbital veins to such an extent that it was difficult to look at her without wincing. Roy was preoccupied, planning a ladies' golf tournament, and spent much of the time shouting into his phone. I read a short historical biography of William II, aka William Rufus, who had died, aged forty, exactly nine hundred years previously, practically where the caravan stood, when an arrow deflected off an oak tree and pierced his lung. I shared the fascinating detail that the culprit, a French nobleman, had raced off to a blacksmith and asked that his horse's shoes be put on backwards so that he could not be pursued. That night, Honey wet the bed out of fear of the toilet, and I had an exciting dream about Monica Lewinsky.

On the second evening, Grace hadn't liked the look of the dinner I produced and took herself off in a huff to Tall Pines, the campsite café, with her own money. Honey gulped down a dish of spaghetti and ran out to spy on her, reporting back breathlessly that she was having cod, chips and peas (£3.95) and a complimentary tarot reading, and though my heart flipped, I admired her for it.

The next afternoon we hired bikes for a forest ride. Honey asked to stay behind and loitered inside Pegasus while the rest of us were measured at the bike shed, and emerged eventually only to be given a silly pink bicycle with a novelty bell on the handlebar. There was a resinous atmosphere on the trails and though it was springtime, it felt muggy and oppressive. We saw chestnut foals at a watering place and deer in the distance and, if I ignored Honey's too-small bike, it was pleasant enough. We saw more people than I'd expected, all of whom seemed care-free and happy. After a while, Grace turned back for the campsite, wanting to secretly put the finishing touches to a birthday cake she'd brought along for Roy, and the rest of us cycled on.

Back at camp we found Grace sitting outside the recep-tionist's office, in a foul mood. Pegasus had been broken into and vandalized, she told us, and we rushed across the site to investigate. The girls' mattresses had been slashed with a kitchen knife, and white foamy stuffing bulged from slits like cavity-wall foam. Coffee from a pot had been poured onto our bed. Ladybug and Mr Blue were trampled outside; one of Mr Blue's ears was torn and a tiny silver bell lay in the dust beside him. Bizarrely, Grace's birthday cake had been taken from the Tupperware, the candles put into holders and arranged around the edge, and tea plates laid out. It puzzled me as to why the vandal(s) would do this and not eat or spoil the cake. Hurtful words had been written on the Formica tabletop with the blue eyeliner pencil ('*No one likes you*') and some fruit including an overripe pear had been thrown about. I wiped the words away so neither Roy nor Honey would see them. Grace presumably already had.

Grace had not wanted to come in the first place and had been terribly disappointed not to be having the dinner party at home so that she and Honey could wait on table and provide some entertainment, perhaps a dance routine to one of Roy's favourite Stevie Wonder songs. She'd wanted to mimic her mother, the caterer, I realized, but too late, because when Norma declined the invitation, dinner for just us, Leroy and Dale, and Guy and Booboo, didn't seem enough of a celebration. Plus, if I'm honest, I wanted to show Norma that we didn't need her and Hugo to have a good time.

The vandalism very much upset Honey. She was confused; who had done this, and why? Roy wondered aloud if Honey had failed to lock up properly, as if this kind of violation was a perfectly acceptable outcome of that, like rain or mosquitoes coming in through a left-open window. Grace was disgusted and rang Josie from reception. I felt it was my punishment for wanting the superior accommodation, but at the same time I was slightly relieved – things like this would happen sometimes and now nothing this bad would for a while. I felt sorry for the others, though, being less philosophical than me, and I gave them a pep talk while I repaired Mr Blue's ear.

'Look, guys,' I said, 'the person who did this has nothing in their life – this is the best fun they can have.'

And Honey added, 'Imagine being that stupid.'

'And sad!' said Grace.

'And mad!' said Honey.

'And bad!' said Grace and they went on like that for some time.

The campsite staff were shocked, and kindly put us up in a giant family-sized tent which, to my surprise, was far nicer than the Pegasus, with compartments and mod cons, though cheaper because of not having a private shower. Josie Jones arrived later that evening in her swanky new van. She was angry with Roy and me; mainly because we hadn't driven home, meaning that she had therefore had to come and collect Grace, who was adamant that she didn't want to stay the last night.

'You're really staying here,' said Josie, 'after being attacked, and with the culprit still at large?'

'We've been offered dinner at Tall Pines free of charge,' said Honey, keen for Grace to stay, 'and there's a magician.'

But Grace gathered her things noisily and, without saying goodbye to Honey or happy birthday to her father, got into her mother's van, and as they roared away we heard the undercarriage scrape over the speed bumps.

Later that evening Honey asked me if I thought it might have been Grace who vandalized Pegasus.

'No,' I said, 'of course it wasn't.'

Later still, Roy, in whispers, asked if I thought it was Honey.

'Jesus Christ, Roy,' I said, 'of course it wasn't.'

'Are you sure? She was grumpy about the bike ride,' he said. 'I can just see her smashing the place up in a temper.'

I am not an angry person and can ordinarily remain

calm for the greater good. On this occasion I failed. I clapped my hand hard over Roy's mouth and told him to 'bloody well shut up'.

It's ridiculous but I have thought about the vandalization of Pegasus, specifically Roy's suspicion falling on Honey, a lot over the years – probably too much – because I knew she'd never do such a thing and his not knowing that troubled me. I didn't think about it much in the days immediately afterwards because when we got home, Josie Jones had let herself in to our house, and was waiting for us, and for something to do had tidied our cutlery drawer.

Seeing her there, hands linked loosely in front of her, looking absolutely distraught, I thought she might be about to launch a verbal assault along the lines of 'How dare you drag my daughter on such a lamentable holiday, when she didn't want to go in the first place?' Or was she about to say that Grace had confessed to the vandalism? Or that she had seen Honey do it? Or that she'd found out about Jacqueline Wilson, or, God forbid, Jilly Cooper?

'Josie!' I said. 'What's wrong?' I braced myself.

'It's Hugo Pack-Allen,' she said. 'He's dead.'

# PART TWO
# Work
## 2000—2019

# 14

It hadn't been one of Norma's nights for driving so Hugo had taken public transport to the Holly Bush roundabout to get to the lay-by and then left on foot, walking beside the A46 to reach the bus stop; and hearing the bus approach, he had started to run, and as it neared him, he'd apparently had a wardrobe malfunction, and after some staggering, had toppled into its path and been killed instantaneously. Josie was the type to go into the finer detail, and I could picture it clearly. I recalled my mother's transport-themed emergency – passengers agog at the windows, commuters stepping over and around her prone body – and I felt sorry for Hugo and for all concerned. Now he was dead I could see him as a human being. Someone with hopes and dreams, not just someone who'd forced us to stock the Ronco Buttoneer; had us sell yarn by the *hank*, not the ball or skein, because it saved money; who coaxed Norma into a threadbare marriage; and who was so desperate for group sex that he'd declined the invitation to Roy's fortieth. I pitied him and my hard feelings were now directed towards Norma; if she'd had one shred of loyalty to me, she'd have willingly helped me celebrate Roy's birthday, and we wouldn't have had to go to the New Forest. Hugo wouldn't have been running for a bus with his belt undone, he'd have been eating lasagne in our kitchen-diner, and even if Pegasus had been vandalized by a random stranger, our family wouldn't have been the victims of it. I didn't actually blame Norma, I simply hoped that all this occurred to her.

Anyway, this was the news as we returned, and Josie seemed terribly distressed by it, which surprised me, her being the sort to accept that there was always some kind of juggernaut on your heels and it was up to you not to fall under it.

'If only he'd done his belt up properly,' she said. 'It just goes to show.'

I felt I had to invite her to stay a while and gave her a cup of tea with non-organic milk. Then it came out that Hugo had invested in her catering company, PardeePardee! and that's how she'd got the van and had its sign written and illustrated with anthropomorphized capsicums, ditto the paella pans and the crêpe stove. She was worried she'd have to pay it back, all at once, especially now she'd got Grace starting at Brankham Girls'. It would ruin her. Roy said he doubted that very much and suggested she carry on as normal, he'd be surprised if anything changed. I was shocked, firstly by Josie's detailed knowledge of the tragedy and her entanglement with Hugo, but secondly by Roy's confidence on the subject, and the revelation that Josie planned to send Grace to the posh secondary school.

I drove to Norma's house and knocked at the door. She was upset of course but surprised me by saying she hadn't ever imagined they'd grow old together, and seemed mostly troubled by it being such an odd and unnecessary accident, and for it to happen beside a notorious lay-by and for so many to have witnessed it. I stayed the night in the spare room and thought I heard Norma on the phone in her bedroom. The next morning I asked who she'd been speaking to.

'Myself,' she said.

We met a couple of days later in the Two Swans and at one point she told me in a croaky whisper, 'I can't bear that people are laughing at him.'

'No, Norma,' I said. 'For goodness' sake, give people some credit – a man died, people don't find accidents like that funny.' I was lying. Of course people were laughing; even Roy's mother had put her hand to her mouth and said, 'Oh my God, I'd never live it down if my husband got run over by a bus.' My mother-in-law, a benchmark of propriety.

I was curious about Josie's connection with Hugo and probed rather rudely. 'How did Hugo know Josie?' I asked.

'He knew everyone in town.'

'But he seems to have been bankrolling her business?' I said. 'And she's very upset about everything.'

Norma shrugged.

'I think Roy and I have a right to know,' I said.

'There's nothing much to know. We invested in Josie's business at the start when the bank wouldn't help, that's all, like Hugo did with the Pin Cushion.'

'We?' I said. 'You said "we".'

'Well, yes, what was Hugo's was mine.'

Over the next weeks Norma discovered the extent of Hugo's investments; how many fingers he had in how many pies, and it cost her hours and days of admin, and nights of worry, to get it straight. Some of the deals weren't entirely official and Norma's solicitor had to undertake a certain amount of clever jiggery-pokery to untangle the murkier ones. However, Norma had inherited the house, Frank's Place, which was all paid up, over one hundred thousand pounds in money and some shares in a shoe factory. It might not sound much now, but back then it was a lot more, and taking into account how modest we all were, it was life-changing.

Roy was both right and wrong about things carrying on as usual. Right, in that nothing changed for Josie except that she put money aside, just in case. Wrong, in that things changed for Norma and for me.

'What animal do you see him as?' Norma asked us at dinner one night. She was writing a eulogy for Hugo.

'Hyenas were his favourite,' I said, and realizing that wasn't a pleasant image, added, 'but I see him more as a St Bernard.'

And then Roy said, 'Isn't that only because he looked like Bernie from Mike and Bernie Winters?'

And I said, 'No,' and gave Roy a frown.

Then he said 'Bull?' which seemed insensitive, and made worse when he switched to buffalo.

Honey said she saw him as a caveman in a suit, but Norma ignored that and settled for a St Bernard.

Norma asked for our first impressions, hoping for something amusing, but this was difficult because I'd disliked him from the off, and actually so had she. Roy told an anecdote about the time his remote-control golf caddy had gone berserk in the car park and ended up on its side in the flowerbed. This didn't seem funny so I interjected saying I'd been impressed by his imitation of a crying baby, not that it was enjoyable but because it was authentic and haunting and somehow tragic. I had always wondered how he knew he could do it. Had he just never stopped crying as a baby or had he suddenly been gripped by the ambition?

The funeral at St Aloysius was a sombre affair. Norma read one of her own poems, 'See Below' (that was the title), which seemed to be comparing Hugo to Robin Hood crossed with the Good Samaritan and a St Bernard. Her eulogy, which described him as 'eager to belong and to help people', continued the theme. 'He preferred to say he was banned from driving for life than to tell people he didn't want to drive,' she said, as if that was anything to be proud of. As soon as probate regulations allowed, I helped Norma clear Frank's Place so she could put it on the market decluttered. It was the best house in town, albeit slightly on the outskirts. Big, solid, and with many good features, it should have been nicer than it actually was. In fact, it felt cold and bleak and only the constant rumble of lorries on the bypass that necessitated triple-glazing offered any kind of comfort. It struck me that Hugo had surprisingly few belongings for such a wealthy fellow, and I noticed he and Norma slept in separate rooms; his bed made up with black sheets, and his bedside book, the memoirs of an American who'd gone through life never saying the word 'no' and eating only corn pone and grits. Norma's room was brighter, with Sylvia Plath, Matthew

Arnold and a notebook of her own scribbles on the night stand.

'You've been happy here, though?' I said. We were having a cup of coffee in the kitchen, black, as there was no milk.

'No. Not really.'

'Oh, but it's a lovely house.'

'Would you want to live here?' she asked.

I thought for a moment she was about to give it to me and I panicked. 'God, no,' I said, 'I could never live in the best house in town.'

'Wow!' said Norma. 'The best house in town would always be my first choice.'

'I couldn't handle it,' I said.

'Why?'

'I wouldn't want an orchard if the neighbours only had bins and a rabbit grave.'

'This sounds like a lifelong obstacle to your acquiring anything,' said Norma, and I had to agree.

'What is it you fear?'

'Other people's resentment manifesting as an arson attack or a brick through the window.' I told her about my mother at the bring'n'buy. How she erected her trestle table outside the village hall, laid a cloth over it and made a display of all our games, books and nicest trinkets: a model hermit crab, an antique popcorn tin my father had brought home from New York, my doll called Lorraine whose hair grew at the push of a button, her own doll from the 1950s called Wetsy Betsy who urinated, a drawing of a cat that I'd done and won a prize for, three bottles in different-coloured glass, a condiment set in pale blue from Copenhagen, a china figurine of Hunca Munca and her cradle full of baby mice, teacups, and just about every nice thing we owned. A woman called Cynthia marched up to my mother and told her she had no right to set up outside by the doorway and that she must pack everything away and take her table inside, with all the others, otherwise she'd be at an unfair advantage.

My mother refused. 'What advantage?' she asked. 'Proceeds all go to the medical missions, don't they?'

But Cynthia knew full well, as did my mother, that there were rewards to be had in clearing one's table, and some indignity in being left with unsold jumble and having to see it all again, at home. After some altercation, Cynthia took hold of two corners of the tablecloth and pulled it off. I remember comprehending her intention a split second before she did it and rushing forward to intercept the china ornaments, but managed to save only a plant pot in the shape of a sombrero. I scooped everything up into the tablecloth, flung it over my shoulder like a swag bag, and walked home, leaving my mother and the woman shouting at each other, and went back later to find them watching the piano-smashing contest, a fete staple back then and more depressing even than the earlier fight.

Norma listened and, for once, looked at me with something other than complete bafflement. 'Aren't we all so silly!' she said, and went on to tell me of her own irrational fear of 'finger strike' – a thing where a person thrusts their fingers into another person's throat and blocks their windpipe – or being struck in the throat with a kung-fu kick or a swift punch. 'I feel the need to cover my suprasternal notch at all times,' she said.

I said I'd noticed this over the years, but thought she'd grown out of it.

'It's back,' she said.

'That's not surprising,' I said.

'Oh, no, it's not Hugo, it's because I saw it enacted in *The Matrix*.'

We laughed and couldn't decide whose phobia was the most bizarre. The spell was broken when Josie Jones pulled up on the drive beside Frank's Place and loaded her van with everything that wasn't plumbed in.

# 15

Norma went to live above the shop, which was quite distracting for me working below as she'd suddenly appear in the middle of my assembling sewing kits, or stocktaking the threads, fastenings and quick-unpicks on the spinner which required the dead quiet of an empty shop, and I'd have to stop and make her a mug of black coffee, which she'd hold in both hands while she talked about her plans.

The shop lease was up for renewal not three months after Hugo's death, Norma told me, and the family had decided to sell the business. There was some brief talk of my buying it as a going concern but Roy and I would never have been able to raise the cash and it came to nothing. If I stayed on I'd be at the mercy of the new owner, if they even wanted me, and so I had no choice really but to say goodbye to the florals and ginghams in five different colours, and the candy-striped seersucker, the balls of wool, the talk of summer dresses and christening gowns and babies' cardigans and culottes, the bias binding, the curtain rings, the multi-drawer counter cabinet in smooth oak from Dutton & Walton of Manchester with its brass inlaid measuring tape sixty inches long, the spools of lace, the smell of indigo and the gentle hum of the radio, and to look for a job in the real world.

In the end there was no buyer and the shop closed

down without so much as an '*Everything Must Go*' sale. I took two bolts of my favourite chenille for future cushions and replenished my sewing box. Norma gave the sewing patterns to Oxfam and the hardware store took everything else in return for tidying up. Norma's parents, who were suddenly shockingly old, had already moved to Godfarthing, a supported village with all mod cons and a medically trained resident warden, which Roy called 'God's waiting room'. I drove over there with Norma to take them the giant wooden bobbin and they'd been thrilled.

It was more difficult than I'd expected to find a job. I went for various shop and factory positions but having one child seemed to put them off me, as if I might at any minute go on leave to have another. One day, while I was having a cup of tea with Norma on campus and she was leafing through the interdepartmental newsletter as we chatted, I saw the word 'Opportunities' and it occurred to me just how terrific it would be to work there, at the university – not just terrific, but *obvious* – and I interrupted our conversation to ask if there was anything going to suit me.

'What do you mean, "going"?'

'Jobs,' I said.

'Oh, nothing appropriate.'

'*Nothing?*' I said. 'Are you sure?'

'Yes,' she said. 'There's a librarian position that requires education to degree level, and a cleaning job, that's all.'

'Oh. How many hours is the cleaning?'

'Sixteen, but you can't apply for that, Susan.'

'Why not?'

'It's for cleaners, people who do that kind of work.'

'Yes, me,' I said.

'Can't you see how awkward that would be?' she said.

'No.'

'Look, Susan, if you'd finished your degree, you could've applied for the library job, but you can't just take other people's work. Can't you see how arrogant that would be?'

'But I *didn't* finish my degree, I was pregnant, and now sixteen hours' cleaning would suit me down to the ground.'

'I can't forbid it, obviously, but I'd rather you didn't.'

'Well, could you put a word in for me at the library, then,' I asked, 'explaining that I'm a keen bibliophile but didn't graduate for personal reasons?'

'That would be inappropriate,' said Norma, 'as well as unprofessional.'

I didn't apply for either in the end because a position came up at a local supermarket, managing refrigerated desserts, and although it entailed a drive to work, it was a surprisingly responsible role, with better pay than the university was offering.

Then, only days after I started my new job, Norma announced that she was leaving to take a sabbatical in Copenhagen and would not therefore be at the University of Rutland for at least a year, probably more. I was devastated at the thought of her absence and cried in front of Roy.

'It's the idea of it,' he said. 'Norma's just an illusion.'

I had never known him so perceptive and haven't since.

*

Life was to change for Grace, too. In the autumn of that year she started at Brankham House School for Girls. This had been mentioned in the spring when Hugo had died and Josie was so anxious about money, so I was surprised to come home a few days before the start of the new school year to find Grace twirling in an ugly tartan kilt and green blazer in our sitting room and Roy saying, 'Very smart.' I was appalled. It wasn't just the impact this might have on Honey later, though I did worry about that, it was more that I felt I should at least have been consulted. There was the money side too – everyone knows it's not just the fees when it comes to private schools, it's all the equipment they need: lacrosse sticks, broomsticks, funny clothing, money for horse-riding lessons which the less posh girls particularly need, to make up for being ordinary. Did Josie and Roy think Grace would have an easy time of it? Her mother running a catering business, her father a golf instructor and me, a part-time supermarket worker? And the fact that, if all went well, Grace would have to at least start believing herself to be superior to us, and then what? Would Honey have to go to Brankham Girls' too?

I said all of this to Roy.

He shrugged and said it was Josie's decision.

'But will we be paying?' I asked.

'No,' said Roy.

'Good,' I said, 'because we can't afford it.'

'I just told you, we won't be paying.'

'Well, who will then? Because Josie hasn't got that kind of money or they wouldn't have plastic grass in the yard.'

'She's got some kind of patron who helps with that kind of thing,' he said.

'Who has?'

'Josie has.'

And if Hugo Pack-Allen hadn't died that year, I'd have put two and two together. As it was, I just hoped to God none of Grace's classmates would recognize me in the dairy aisle.

# 16

Shortly before Norma left for Copenhagen we had tea together at the Two Swans and I took the girls along. It was during Grace's short angry phase and she barely spoke. Honey asked for a second slice of cake and stupidly, I refused, and so she went into a huff too. To show her displeasure at this, Norma sat in sarcastic silence and so, since no one else had anything to say, I told of my own adventures in Denmark. My father had taken us there for occasional holidays in the 1970s and '80s, it being a good place to go if you feared flying, or worried that one of your party might have a mental breakdown. It was there, in a modest hotel run by two brothers, that I first ate marmalade.

'They'd run out of jam, you see, and this was a blow because in Denmark the jam was so pungently fruity, with great big chunks of fruit, and addictive – that, and the butter being so much nicer than at home, you could almost taste both things before you got the bread to your lips. My mother – Granny,' I said, 'ate the jam in such quantities that I remember praying the hotel brothers wouldn't notice and start to hate us.' I laughed and continued, 'Anyway, one morning they'd run out of strawberry and with no other jam available my mother sprinkled her bread and butter with sugar but I tried the marmalade and though I didn't particularly like it, the sweet bitterness was interesting.'

I paused at that point in case anyone else wanted to speak, but no one did. 'The next day the strawberry jam was back but, just as I'd been about to take a spoonful, I knew I wanted marmalade again. It was a real coming of age,' I said, 'and I often think that had the strawberry been constantly available I might never have tried the marmalade, and now, oh, my goodness, marmalade is honestly one of the best things in my life.'

For some reason, I'd become slightly emotional and the others were looking anxious, so I laughed. I didn't mention the little mermaid, which I'd actually had in mind to discuss, but had been waylaid by that jam shortage. Hey ho. We left the café then and I sent the girls ahead, to walk home across the university campus, and dawdled with Norma who was going to call in to her office for a final time.

'Can I help with anything?' I asked.

'Nope,' said Norma, 'not now you've opened my eyes to the delights of Danish marmalade.'

I looked at her, and felt tears prickling. 'I'm really going to miss you,' I said.

'I'm not dying, Susan,' she said. 'I'm going away for a while, that's all, and I'll be back in no time.'

I found I couldn't contain my emotions; my mouth trembled and I had to dab my eyes.

'Come over and stay as soon as I'm settled,' she said and patted me on the shoulder.

Then Norma was gone and so were the Sunday-night phone calls. To begin with we emailed at the weekend instead. Me wanting her opinion (should we go private for

Roy's hernia operation?) and sharing news (replacement hoover won't pick up rice) and she'd reply with local news (Danish film has won a prize) and personal updates (been fined for jaywalking, which isn't prostitution, just crossing the road on a red man).

I'd write very formally and at length about books: Am loving Ishiguro's When We Were Orphans, I remember telling her. Don't let the reviews put you off, especially the one that admonishes him for not using phrasal verbs.

Norma kept to more domestic themes and told me quite early on that she'd had some kind of intrauterine device fitted and then I replied that a colleague at the supermarket had done likewise and had gone off red peppers and sex overnight, and was as hairy as a monkey within a month. Norma ignored this.

How's it going with the coil? I'd written.

It is wonderful! she'd replied. No periods, no babies.

Mentally, emotionally, and in the head though?

Happy in the knowledge I'll never use another tampon.

Do you still love red peppers though?

No further details.

After she'd been away almost a year, I went to stay in Copenhagen and found her living with a man called Ole Bobby Olsen many years her senior who had a small braid in his beard and swore a lot but in a non-aggressive way. There was much birthday paraphernalia around the apartment and Norma explained that Ole had just celebrated his birthday, and he was sixty, which though very old for Norma was young for Denmark. Ole was a literary professor who took additional work translating plays from

English into Danish. His translations were known for having more hinted darkness and lust than the originals, and fewer jokes, which 'spoil the drama', he said. 'We don't need laughs here.' He sat in the kitchen overlooking a cobbled square, eating slices of salami out of a paper bag, which he offered around every now and again like a packet of crisps, and Norma would go behind him in his chair and press her hands down on his shoulders in a quite sexual way.

At breakfast on my first morning Norma, who was in her dressing gown brewing coffee and putting a jar of flowers on the table and assorted pretty crockery, said, 'Tell Ole your Danish marmalade story, Susan.'

'Oh, no,' I said, 'it was nothing really.'

But Ole protested. 'No, I'd like to hear it,' he said.

So I told him about the jam and marmalade at the hotel in 1980 and he asked, 'Do you remember which brand?' I didn't, except that the logo was in capitals and included the fruit in question, which Ole seemed to recognize, and said, 'Yah, very good jams.' And then Norma presented a tray of hot baguettes and two opened jars of jam, one strawberry and one orange marmalade, and to everyone's delight, they were the exact same jams as in my story, which was if I remember correctly, DANISH SELEC-TION, and I shrieked and we all dug in. I felt flattered by the attention, and glad for her, because surely only the happiest couples go to such concerted efforts to tease a guest.

They had an apartment with floor-to-ceiling windows and huge, heavy, lined curtains, matching hammocks strung up in a V-shape in the tiny garden, and though Norma didn't seem like her old self, she was light-hearted. The visit flew by. We cycled to the university and met some of Norma's colleagues who were sitting in the sunshine on a bench sharing a cigar and reading poetry. We went to the butcher's to get assorted cooked meats for Ole, who was working on a Michael Frayn translation. Ole offered to take us to the newly opened Øresund Bridge and I jumped at it, really for something to tell Roy and so as not to meet any more colleagues, but Norma didn't fancy it – 'It's just a bridge,' she said – and I remembered there were bridge builders in the Pavlou family, and it wasn't all that much of a treat, so we cycled about town. I bought Norma a copy of *Amsterdam* by Ian McEwan, which she read immediately and loved. She bought me a bleak Danish novel about an experimental school, which I didn't enjoy at all.

On my last evening Norma told me she might never return to the University of Rutland, and though it was sad to contemplate, it was also liberating. I'd have her friendship still, but in Denmark, where it worked better and where Norma felt free to joke and smoke cigars, and when Ole said goodbye to me, he said, 'Come back in December, and see the play in Danish.'

And Norma said, 'Come for Christmas, bring Roy, Grace and . . .'

'And Honey?' I said.

'Oh, yes, Honey. Sorry, yes.'

## 17

Working with refrigerated desserts was like working in the Arctic: my nose was red for almost the whole of 2002, my rhinitis often flared, and my gloves always smelled cheesy. I didn't dislike the job overall but did come to resent individual dairy pots and anyone who bought them, especially if they bought four. I had studied 'buying behaviour' as part of my induction training – which explained that customers might require the small pots for 'portion control' or packed lunches, or out of concerns about freshness. This only made me wonder why customers couldn't spoon out the right amount into a dish, or lidded Tupperware, and then I wouldn't have to be forever rebuilding towers in the chiller, and removing the ones with compromised foil. My video training programme focused particularly on dairy storage with some nutrition analysis. Yoghurt, I was told by a white-coated presenter, had suffered an association with the cranky health food movement of the 1970s but now, thanks mainly to innovative German manufacturers, it was beginning to advance into the luxury sector and comfortably straddled the two, and therefore part of my job was to be poised to help customers on this seesaw.

Müller's Fruit Corner, for instance, being lower in calories than a banana, but not to be confused with a low-cal yoghurt choice such as a fat-free or probiotic option. Müller *rice*, different again, and not strictly speaking even a yoghurt but displayed nearby in order to establish it as an everyday, convenience dessert. Rice was starting to be favoured by athletes over energy drinks, this of course being of great interest to Roy, but stocking refrigerated produce alongside canned and bottled drinks being impossible, as cans and bottles were not permitted on the cold shelves, we weren't able to exploit this in-store. No one was allowed to say 'Greek' but only 'Greek-style' and we weren't allowed to say 'live' without quote-mark gesturing. Medical enquiries were supposed to be met with the reply, 'I'm sorry, I'm not medically trained. Please try the pharmacy across the road.' It was generally believed that refrigerated desserts had more customer–staff interaction than any other section, bar alcohol.

One day, towards the end of my shift, a customer approached for advice. I assumed by her manner it would be about vaginal thrush, but actually, it was that her husband had been prescribed an antibiotic. Was it true, she wanted to know, that a live yoghurt taken in tandem (her words) could help prevent unpleasant side effects? I made my unqualified disclaimer before saying I'd heard this was the case, and that, in fact, my own husband had had the same situation some months previously and not only had the yoghurt seemed to help but that we'd both felt the benefit so profoundly, we'd eaten it daily ever since.

'I can hand on heart say it has literally changed our lives,' I told her.

'In what way?' she wanted to know.

And I said, 'Digestively.'

She got my meaning and took two large pots.

Then, some weeks later, Roy and I had had to attend a harp recital at Brankham Girls', Grace's school, and during the interval I saw that same woman. I knew her but couldn't place her and she the same: we smiled and frowned quizzically at each other.

'Who is that woman?' I asked Grace.

'That's Mrs Koto, she teaches me Latin and Japanese.'

I turned to Mrs Koto and said, 'Oh, nice to meet you, I'm Grace's stepmother.'

And then she said, 'Oh, my goodness, I remember you now, you're the yoghurt lady.' She grasped my forearm. 'We have it every morning, religiously, and, just as you said, it's changed our lives.'

'A lot of people find this,' I said with pride.

As much as I enjoyed my time on refrigerated desserts, moments of professional validation and recognition, like that described above, were few and far between, the money didn't quite compensate for the hard work, constant acrid smell, and the short but grim commute out to the superstore, with nowhere nice to go for breaks, and after a year and a bit I noticed a vacancy for a job in Estates at the University of Rutland. It wasn't a long contract but a Grade 6 appointment so it paid well and would mean only a few minutes' stroll to work each day. Apart from the money, and the much-needed change, there'd also be the added bonus that I wouldn't be on my own all day, stacking tiny pots, checking sell-by dates, or, as previously, unfurling bolts of calico, selling ribbon by the metre, and sometimes only seeing two customers all day, one to buy a zip, the other to ask about denim shrinkage. I'd now have colleagues and maybe make a friend or two.

I mentioned the position to Norma in an email and she wasn't enthusiastic.

She seemed to believe I'd chosen the job over our friendship. Won't it be awkward when I return? she said. I promise you academics and professional services do not mingle.

You're not here though, I replied.

I could come back at any time.

This seemed unreasonable – she'd been gone so long her replacement was on a permanent contract, and hers was the longest sabbatical in university history. Plus, hadn't she told me she might never return? I reminded Norma (and myself) that she didn't own the place; if anything, I had prior claim, living practically on campus and knowing the grounds like my own garden. So, with some misgivings, I applied.

At the interview Michael Pascoe, head of Estates, proved my point when he said he saw me so often he assumed I was *already* a member of staff. 'I guessed you were a lecturer in Health and Social Welfare,' he said, which I took as a compliment. After two interviews, I got the job.

Having accepted the position of Estates assistant over the telephone I had to present myself to Joyce Ho, head of Human Resources, to fill in forms, show my ID and that kind of thing. While I waited, I gazed at a large wall-mounted aerial photograph of the campus and noticed that viewed from above, the university grounds formed the shape of a bottle-nosed dolphin. Its beak (correct terminology) pointing towards my little house, which as you know is on a small 1960s-built estate flanking the campus. Brankham House sits where the flipper joins the body, and the original garden (now mostly a car park) is the flipper itself. The newer teaching blocks form a gentle arc below the dorsal fin. Finally, nestled in the cleft of the tail sits the Gate House, residence of the Vice Chancellor. I estimated that I'd walk the path across the dolphin's back from my front door to the Estates office in eight minutes, ambling, not rushing. I expected that at a jog I'd do it in three. By car it's a lot further away, door to door being in total 1.6 of a mile due to the one-way system plus a busy chicane by the park gates.

I remember tracing the periphery railings with my finger, trying to locate my house, and suddenly finding it, camouflaged by tree canopies, just as Joyce Ho called me through to her office.

'If you'd like to come in, Mrs Warren,' she said.

In my excitement I'd said, 'You can see my house on this photograph,' and I pointed.

But her face remained stern and she only widened her eyes momentarily in mock surprise and said, 'How convenient.'

Joyce took a polaroid for my staff lanyard and, glancing at it, said I had a look of Martha Gellhorn, and I'd agreed, not 100 per cent sure who she was. Later, after typing her name into the internet, I saw that she was a famous war correspondent and that because of the way I'd done my hair that day – with curling tongs – I did indeed look just like her. Afterwards Joyce Ho asked me to wait again in the reception for the VC to welcome me, in person, to the institution. I went back to studying the aerial photograph, and, following a bend in my road, thought to myself how odd that it seemed a very definite curve in the picture and yet was almost a straight line in actual life, and how it is often the case that although it feels as if you're travelling in a straight line, on and on, from a different perspective you've veered way, way to the left, or don't know any more.

Leafing through the prospectus with my ankles crossed, I read about the university motto, *One Day I Shall Astonish the World*, and its history, which felt wonderfully inspiring. I sensed my old self awakened, the me who'd imagined I might run for my country (400 metres or hurdles), or write a play or a novel or even a TV theme tune, or produce a tapestry so compelling or socially disruptive that the British Museum would insist on displaying it in the entrance hall so that even the people going only to the gift shop might see it.

As I was thinking all this, a shaft of sun pierced the fanlight above the door, the stained glass making the light extra yellow and illuminating thousands of tiny floating particles, which in the moment seemed like glitter but must have been dust. There was a slight kerfuffle to my right and the VC was approaching majestically, with an arm outstretched (one arm, not two), and though I'd seen him numerous times previously, getting into a car, or weeding his gravel, or shopping for drinking yoghurt, it was as though I'd been allowed into heaven and he, a high-ranking angel, or even God, was accepting me, even though I no longer believed in him. I appreciated at the same time that he was contractually obliged to appear from doorways, to glide and sparkle on behalf of the university, and that was fine too. I didn't need to feel special – *he* was special and that was enough.

'Mizz Warren?' he said.

I took his hand and said, for some silly reason, 'Professor Willoughby, I presume!' and saw his genial smile grow into an almost grin. He had something of Gabriel Oak about him, from Hardy's *Far from the Madding Crowd*. The corners of his mouth spread slowly towards his ears, and his eyes twinkled like tiny black gems while the wrinkles deepened around them, 'extending upon his countenance like the rays in a rudimentary sketch of the rising sun'. In other words, I liked him straight away and have ever since. He is good; the type of man one saw in the movies growing up, and expected to see a lot of and hoped and wished for, but hardly ever did when it came down to it. Confident, kind, not particularly clever, but enthusiastic and warm and personable, engaging, trustworthy. Not health-conscious; possibly partaking of an oil capsule for joint health, a twice-weekly swim, healthy breakfast aims but in truth probably toast with a lot of butter and jam.

I can't pretend that, over the years, the VC hasn't put Roy in the shade because he has. It's no one's fault. Not Roy's, not the VC's and not mine, because believe me, I am fully aware of how easy it is for the VC to be wholly good. What's the saying about it being easy to be magnanimous if you're privileged? Well, that was applicable here.

# 18

The campus is set back from the main street and fronted handsomely by wrought-iron railings – made to the same design as those surrounding St Paul's Cathedral in London and with matching lamp posts and high arched gates, and bearing the coat of arms of the Brankham family, which consists of a funny-looking pine cone and a crow of some sort. The circular drive, previously a deep swathe of warm beige gravel that crunched pleasingly under the tyres of the VC's car, was tarmacked over recently to prevent students throwing handfuls of it at the official car during the row over the VC's salary, though some say it was to protect the heels on Joyce Ho's shoes. Whatever the truth, the tarmac is an ugly solution to a temporary problem, like so many things in this world, and if I'd been in post longer I should have opposed it. The driveway – with its sloped terrain and free-ranging pedestrians – is a challenging negotiation for any driver, always necessitating first gear and frantic looking about in all directions and mirrors, and a reminder of the need to maintain neck and shoulder suppleness as well as lumbar and lower-back strength. Running over a student is sadly not unheard of. (Note: the Grantham Institute driver who knocked one down while retuning the radio.) Some years into my career at the university, having been given some driving assignments, I, myself, once stalled the engine of the official car with a visiting dignitary on board and though I can't, for legal reasons, say who, suffice to say it was a VIP on a par with Archbishop Desmond Tutu or Nigella Lawson, and in my keenness not to roll back, I had to rev the engine rather aggressively.

Brankham House, the main building and heart of the university, is built from Bath stone, and its tall bays and architraves make such an imposing first impression that prospective students used to decide, on the driveway, to apply for a place, imagining themselves drifting about in its shadow, rushing to a lecture with books under their arms. Like choosing a spouse on account of his dimples or eyes or beard – yet to learn what lies behind. Through the central hallway you come to an attractive glass-and-steel conservatory dating to 19-something, between the wars. The main building was previously home to the Brankham family who were entirely unimpressive and presumably quite mean, since there are no reports of any-thing philanthropic, and they don't seem to have donated so much as a bench to the town. In the late 1800s the house was acquired by the Church of England and run as a school for boys who wanted to go into the clergy. Later, it became a hostel for Belgian soldiers, and then it was sold back to a distant member of the Brankham family who, having no living relatives, bequeathed it to the University of Somewhere or Other, possibly Nottingham, or Derby, who set it up as an outpost for academically minded locals who didn't want to leave home. No one from beyond Rutland, Leicestershire or Northants ever seemed to be admitted, possibly because no living accommodation was provided – the town didn't want any of that. Since the sudden growth of the institution in the early 1990s Brankham House now accommodates only the library, the offices of the VC and the Dean, and the head of IT and her department who need the wide doorways for wheelchair access.

The Mitfords used to stay here in the 1930s and '40s, the nice ones, apparently, not the Nazis, enjoying the famous pork pies and cheeses which are plentiful in the county, and the better-than-average plumbing that the Brankhams had installed. Recently someone from UofR 'reached out' to the Mitford estate hoping for permission to call a building the 'Mitford Something'. A reply came, denying knowledge of any such friendship.

Behind Brankham House is an assortment of less attractive, more modern blocks, used for teaching. These, now listed, feature high ceilings, gloss-painted interior brickwork and exposed pipework, flat Crittall windows, narrow echoing stairwells, linoleum flooring and those municipal cork boards with perished edges and craters made from clustered pinholes, displaying ancient information, locked behind the glass with now long-dead extension numbers and obsolete words (disco, beer, book sale). These buildings have no pleasant outlook at all.

The grounds are impressive by any standards (open to the public during daylight hours), the Brankhams having been great arborists and shrub collectors and friends of Brown, Jekyll and Virginia Woolf's friend whose name escapes me at the moment. Recent visits from Beth Chatto disciples have climate-proofed our bedding and I'm happy to say we have not used a watering can or hosepipe since 2017, barring the window boxes at the front – unlike our neighbours at the golf club, who have sprinklers going even through hosepipe bans. As for the Elliott Huts situated in the now slabbed-over paddock; yes, they're something of an eyesore but they demonstrate the expansion and success entirely down to Professor Willoughby.

Some notable pieces of art grace the walls at the institution. The most significant being an architectural drawing with a railway theme by George Stephenson which is so faded, and the paper so yellowed, you can barely make it out, priceless but gifted by the Stephenson family for some obscure reason and from where the motto originates. The second is a tiny still life in oils of a local cheese and a knife painted by an artist known for bigger scenes but gifted to us on account of the dairy connection. The third – a huge Twombly-esque painting – was acquired by Vice Chancellor Willoughby in his first heady year and mounted in the reception hall. Titled *The Busy Mind*, it is a huge rectangle of jarring purple, black and red scribbles like a child's drawing of its mother's hair; or someone went crazy holding three felt tips at once.

# 19

My role as Estates assistant entailed regular light cleaning, some operational management and generally being poised to respond, as and when, to the everyday crises that inevitably crop up in an establishment of that type. Say one of the cast-iron windows jammed; it was my job to look into and establish our obligations vis-à-vis repair within the strictures of the building's listed status. My manager, Michael Pascoe, head of Estates, was also driver to the VC and often out and about, thus giving me managerial experience.

A minor but perpetual concern was the control of graffiti. The university's progressive attitude tolerated imaginative offerings, in the name of art and free speech, but allowed the speedy removal of anything unattractive, straightforwardly offensive or extremist. And it was my job to recognize which was which and above all be on the alert for cryptic assaults on members of staff.

For instance, '*Daddy Warbucks*' and '*Overweight, overpaid comb-over*' in white bubble writing outlined in red, which appeared on a side wall, seemed quite jolly to some but not to my trained eye, particularly appearing so soon after the VC's salary increase was leaked to the press.

Another confusing example was '*WHY DO YOU*

*LIKE HOUSE MUSIC?*' in large wobbly letters, with the reply, '*WHY NOT?*' which had, I thought, an obscure, possibly drug-related insinuation, and I'd been about to scrub it off with soda crystals but it turned out to be an art student's project entitled 'Why Do You Like House?'

I had an ongoing battle with taggers called Meringue and Betty. I very much took against Betty, for a lack of talent and wit, whereas Meringue was amusing, and had written ahead of a visit from our local MP Edward Garnier, '*You're Not Worth It*', which made me think he or she was probably a business student and I rewarded them by leaving it be.

After I had been a few weeks in post, my boss, Michael Pascoe, was cautioned for driving over a colleague's foot for a wager; this was uncharacteristic to say the least, but resulted in my doing much of the official driving, not just for our university but on occasions loaned to the University of Leicester. I was soon chauffeuring female VIPs who visited the half-dozen or so Higher Education institutions in the area. I was a popular choice after an incident in which a celebrity chef became alarmed when her male driver stopped for no reason beside a river.

With passengers on board, especially VIPs, the thing is to say very little and let them start the conversation (or not). I like it when intriguing things come up naturally like they did when I was driving Canadian poet, novelist and literary critic Margaret A. to her London hotel after an event. I wouldn't as a rule reveal a guest's identity but on this occasion I know she wouldn't mind.

I said to Margaret, 'What actually is a bilberry?'

And that led to a most interesting conversation about gooseberries and other pudding fruits. She spoke at length about the rhubarb triangle and homicide rates therein.

I had to say to her at one point, 'Margaret, I'm really sorry but your voice is sending me to sleep.' Which, as soon as the words were out of my mouth, sounded terribly rude. But she is robust, and didn't take offence. We spoke once more during the journey, most intelligently, about *Anne of Green Gables* and other important Canadian literature.

I thought I'd misfired with VIP Sandi T. It is my habit to have things up my sleeve, ready to trot out, if necessary. Sandi seemed to want to chat and if a VIP wants to chat then chat you must. She'd asked me a couple of polite questions about driving; I seem to remember she said something about jackknifing and I had to explain that that could only happen when one vehicle was towing a trailer of some sort on a close coupling. I took this to mean she didn't drive, and if I hadn't researched her the evening before I'd have been stumped for anything more to say. In the event I was able to bring up the fact that I have been a regular visitor to Denmark over the years and am therefore familiar with the various sweet jams and marmalades, as previously mentioned, and a certain nursery rhyme, '*Klappe, Klappe, Kage*', which was sung to me by a dear old family friend. Sandi knew all about the marmalade but couldn't remember the nursery rhyme, she said, or perhaps she didn't recognize my pronunciation. So I sang it:

*Klappe, klappe, kage*
*I morgen skal vi bage*
*Én til mor, én til far,*
*Og én til lille Sandi!*

I sang it, glancing into the rear-view mirror occasionally as I did, and saw Sandi's frowning face. She still didn't remember it.

'It's similar in theme to the English pat-a-cake song,' I told her.

'Oh, so I hear,' she said, 'but I don't recall it.'

I thought she might be disgruntled and slightly regretted it until she suddenly said, 'Sing it again, will you, it's rather soothing.' So I did and Sandi was impressed and smiling, and with her head nodding, went back to her knitting.

A driver should by all means make light conversation but never raise topics or mention things that might jar, or cause anxiety or offence. I remember the driver from a neighbouring university telling me that during his waiting times he'd got to know all the footpaths and bridleways for a twenty-mile radius of his institution, and kept a small machete in the boot for reclaiming neglected paths, and that it was his dearest wish to find a portable chainsaw small enough to carry in a rucksack for such work. He's no longer a university driver after a hoo-hah about the machete which he stupidly mentioned to an East Anglian sculptor and she reported him. Although I didn't for one minute suspect him of anything, I do often recall the incident, just to remind myself to watch what I'm saying and to never talk about, say, J. G. Ballard or Stephen King.

Most of my time behind the wheel, though, I was taking the Vice Chancellor to meetings outside the institution, and these were the nicest trips. He had an aura of well-mannered importance, smelled of cedarwood, and always chatted so nicely.

'I'm a great friend of Norma Pack-Allen,' I told him on one of our first official trips together. He only vaguely remembered her, that's how junior she was and how long she'd been away. 'She's on sabbatical at the University of Copenhagen.'

'Ah, yes,' he recalled. 'I do hope she's getting on well.'

'She's teaching the Romantic poets to highly motivated Scandinavians,' I said, 'goes everywhere by bicycle and has a secure place to lock it outside her apartment. And they have such nice jam over there.'

And the VC said, 'Ah, that might explain her reluctance to come back.'

I spoke at length about Norma, not because she was particularly interesting but by way of flagging my intellect. 'It was me,' I told him, 'who encouraged her to read John Donne in the first place, and now look at her!'

Likewise, I wrote to Norma on the subject of her estranged colleagues.

Telling her, for instance, that Joyce Ho had not only worn a jumpsuit to an official event but had been heard saying that the institution was 'spiritually adrift'.

Norma replied that she could never wear a jumpsuit due to being long in the body, which rang true when I pictured her in my mind, and was why she always stuck to dresses and skirts. I replied, reminding her that *short* torso length ran in my family. My mother having such a low-sitting ribcage that she hadn't been able to drive more than a couple of miles, couldn't comfortably wear trousers, and had to switch from piano to violin as a child.

People with regular body length don't know how lucky they are, I wrote.

I particularly enjoyed telling her all about the Vice Chancellor.

Drove the VC to UCAS yesterday. Discussed the bovine contribution to climate change. Arrived early so played chess.

The subtext being: the Big Cheese and I manage to get along reasonably well in spite of my lowly status.

Be careful, Susan, it sounds like you might be falling in love with him! Norma emailed back.

No, of course not. (Well, a bit, I'm only human!) I wrote back.

What about poor old Roy? she replied.

No threat to Roy. The VC is a charming companion whom I admire and am paid to look after occasionally, that's all.

So you're not about to jump into bed with him?

No, I wrote. Definitely not!

Norma barely remembered him. What's he like? she asked. How old? How tall? What star sign? Politics?

Born 1958, handsome, widower, Sagittarius, Conservative but nice, interests include agriculture, I wrote.

Ooh, widower? wrote Norma.

We talk about you a lot, and Copenhagen. He's fascinated. Doesn't remember you very well but does remember Hugo.

Her response to this was brusque. I'd rather you didn't discuss me with the Vice Chancellor. Please stop.

\*

I missed Norma tremendously but looking back, I see how Grace, by then a young adult with a wise head and sense of fun, began to fill the gap. An example of this being the time Roy had got Saturday matinee tickets for an ethical circus which was supposed to be the most exciting show outside London. When the day came, Honey was unwell and had a temperature. Roy said he'd stay at home and that Grace and I should go, just the two of us. On the way to the venue, it occurred to me that it would make Grace very happy if we invited her mother to join us, as much as I disliked Josie. Grace was overjoyed and used my phone to call her. We swung by to pick her up, and I felt virtuous. The circus was indeed spectacular, with tightrope walkers, human cannonballs, acrobats, escapologists, contortionists and clowns and we left in very high spirits. On the way out, at Josie's suggestion, we had a burger and then a go on the dodgems. At first Josie let me take the wheel and, thinking the aim of the game was to dodge the other cars, I steered us around the edge. Suddenly, the ride operator who was standing on the body of his car, and steering with his foot, deliberately bumped us quite forcefully, and we ended up in a heap. His spiteful laughter rang out in time with the rock'n'roll and Josie seized the wheel. 'Right, you lousy little bastard,' she said, and went after him, hitting his dodgem hard from behind. Because he was standing, he almost fell, and spat his cigarette out. He then came after us again, at speed, knocked us into the skirting and disappeared. Josie spun us around, hunted him down and jammed him between two cars, before coming back round for a second smash. This went on for some time before the power stopped abruptly and the session ended. We were almost sick with laughing as Grace and I stood on our wobbly legs and began to clamber out.

'Wait,' said Josie. 'Let's ride again.'

'We can't,' said Grace. 'We need to get back to Honey.'

'OK, see ya,' said Josie, staying put.

'Sorry about Mum,' said Grace on the way home.

'Are you kidding?' I said. 'She's fabulous.' I didn't mean it. I actually thought her a menace.

'Oh, she is,' laughed Grace, 'but God, it's been nice having you as well.'


Some months later there was a visitor to the golf club from its twin course in the USA. He'd been supposed to stay at the Brankham Arms but something went wrong with the booking and because there was a blue cheese convention in town, he ended up lodging two nights with us. I remember it being something like an Alan Ayckbourn play. First, I'd been mortified because Roy's friend Leroy had been at the digging stage of constructing a rockery in our front garden, and there were piles of earth and stones all about, and however carefully Leroy worked, small clods of gingery clay were trodden into the paths for yards around.

This golfing visitor went by the name of John John-Jessop with two Johns. I imagined his first name was double John but it wasn't. He'd been christened Wesley

John John-Jessop but switched to his middle name, he said, 'for obvious reasons'. Anyway, apart from golf, the thing that most preoccupied John John-Jessop was his desire to live to a ripe old age and not die needlessly, and he liked to quote the stats. 'In eighty per cent of men who pass away under the age of sixty, it's a plain case of too much sugar, too much alcohol, too much tobacco – so cut it out.'

On meeting Honey, 'How old is she? Ten, eleven? Yah, out of danger, most kids that die, die before two.' It occurred to me that this might be quite triggering for Roy vis-à-vis his catastrophizing mother and I did my best to make light of the subject. On the second morning at breakfast Triple J said, between mouthfuls of muesli, 'Yah, what you *really* don't want, is a mutant influenza, like that from, say, bird to human, or turtle to human, that can wipe out whole communities.' And the very next day, John John-Jessop still with us, news of bird flu broke.

'If I were you guys, seriously, I'd get to the mall and stock up on canned fish and comestibles before the panic hits,' he said. 'Don't mess about.'

'Really? You think there'll be food shortages?' I said. Roy looked stricken.

'I couldn't say, ma'am,' said Triple J, 'but on an island that relies on imports, I wouldn't take the risk. And another thing – buy it, hide it, bury it, whatever, but don't draw attention to it, you don't want to be looted.'

I thought him a crank but bought an extra can of tuna and a bag of brown rice we didn't need, and after he'd left for the airport I admitted it to Roy. He beckoned me through to the garage and lifted a piece of tarpaulin to reveal a whole wall of cans.

'Oh, my goodness,' I said, 'where did all that come from?'

'I bought it this morning,' he said. 'I'm going to hide it.'

# 20

Honey didn't put up a fight for Brankham Girls' and for that I was grateful. The fees were exorbitant and she hadn't a cat in hell's chance of getting a scholarship. For her first year at Rossington Comprehensive, Grace was up the hill at Brankham Girls' and they'd occasionally meet at the ice-cream van in the high street and walk home through the campus grounds; Grace in the Brankham tartan and tam-o'-shanter, Honey in navy blue and an anorak. Of course people commented. 'I see Grace is up at Brankham Girls',' they'd say, meaning: and poor Honey's not.

When, aged eleven, Honey had had to plan and write a term-long assignment entitled 'The Person I Most Admire', she chose her godmother Timandra Cohen – and had compelling reasons. 'Timandra is adventurous and brave. She is alone. She will not be told what to do by anyone,' was how she explained her subject in the one-to-one planning session with her English teacher, during which she was encouraged to switch to Florence Nightingale. Honey declined the advice and took the case to her personal tutor who felt she had to agree with the head of English: Florence Nightingale was a better bet, the problem being the dearth of research opportunities and archived sources on Timandra who was, it was fair to say, just an eccentric family member who liked travelling. Her suggestion that Honey go with the person she second-most admired resulted in a very impressive project on Barbara Hepworth which focused as much on her cigarette-smoking and having triplets as her sculpting.

Then, soon after Honey's twelfth birthday, and only months after the project was completed, Timandra was found dead in a hotel bedroom a few miles from our house. My mother's reflection that it was 'always on the cards' made me want to scream. There was a suicide note written for Honey which I didn't want her to see until she was older, it being lovely but I thought a bit upsetting, and so I filed it away with other family correspondence. On hearing of the death Honey said, 'If only I'd been allowed to have her as "The Person I Most Admire".' I can't deny I'd thought the same thing. I mean, imagine being admired by a wonderful child and knowing that maps and stories of your travels were displayed on the walls of the class for all to see. Surely that would have helped. I don't know. But Honey spoke to her English teacher about it and we had a letter home.

Afterwards I worried about what might become of Honey if Roy and I died, not because I thought it likely but if it did happen then Honey would have to go to live with James and his wife by default, him being my brother and them having a three-bedroomed house with welling-ton boots in the porch and a good standard of living. Frankly, I wouldn't wish that on anyone; my brother is and was a cold-hearted man who revels in the awfulness of his unintelligent wife, with no children to share the load.

Also, it hadn't been long since James had made a Nelly the Elephant joke about Honey, which Roy didn't hear, and which I ignored until the next day when, unable to get it out of my head (such a catchy tune), I drove to his house and on the doorstep said, 'I've come to tell you never to disrespect my daughter again.'

He acted the innocent until I reminded him. 'I didn't mean anything by it, for God's sake,' he said. 'It was just a joke.'

And I actually felt sorry for him; usually so serious and reserved, to have his rare attempt at humour end like this was unfortunate. Nevertheless, I continued, 'No wonder Jennifer doesn't want children with you.'

'What?' he said.

'There's something wrong with you, James.' I said.

He looked at me in disbelief, turned to look up and down the road, then put his hands on his hips and looked at the floor, shaking his head, and made a false little laugh, which I took to mean he was hurt and surprised at my saying such a spiteful thing. I was of course sorry and regretful but didn't say so. I hurried back to the car and drove home.

That afternoon I spoke to my solicitor, instructing her that should Roy and I die before Honey got to eighteen, my brother was not to have her. 'I'd rather she took her chances in an orphanage,' I said.

She suggested I seek an alternative adult to be Honey's official 'in loco parentis' because, in all honesty, it seemed a bit odd to request that she be made a ward of court, and so there I was, back in my best man/godmother situation all over again, and with no better option, I approached Josie Jones.

'Josie,' I said, 'would you take Honey if Roy and I went under a bus?' I regretted putting it like that, obviously, but once Josie had recovered from the wording, she said, 'I don't see why not – if you sort me out financially.'

Norma had always said she was going to kill herself before she turned forty and I believed she actually would, not that I thought about it often, but it was just there in my head. So when she announced she was leaving Denmark and meeting with Joyce Ho to discuss resuming her position at UofR only months before her birthday my main thought was, is it worth it? You'll be dead before Christmas, but I didn't say anything, of course. I told her she was welcome to stay with us while she house-hunted as long as she didn't mind that Honey was now beyond the age of giving up her room and that she'd have to squash herself into Grace's little room which doubled as Roy's study.

Norma arrived from Copenhagen with a folding bicycle and really it wasn't much fun having her as a guest, her taking such an interest in Grace, even though it was Honey who'd recently made the transition to big school and who'd had all her hair cut off by mistake.

'I hope they're putting Grace in for the Oxbridge exams,' Norma said one day.

It irritated me so much I said, 'Hold your horses, Norma, she's only just chosen her A Levels.'

'She needs to be well prepared.'

'She doesn't want to go to bloody Oxford or Cambridge,' I said. 'Back off.'

Of course, when the time came, Grace attended an open day at Wadham College and then applied to read law at Brasenose.

After staying with us the best part of a month, Norma finally found a nice apartment backing onto the canal with an old grain chute fashioned into a pretty balcony and views of waterfowl and the odd barge. She'd been snapped up by the UofR and reappointed on a 0.6 teaching contract, in other words, three days a week. The new position allowed her to come and go as she pleased, honoured her publishing commitments, and took into account her allergy to small groups of young women.

When it came to it, far from killing herself Norma threw a party, catered by Josie Jones, and invited colleagues, family and Roy and me, with the proviso that we didn't have to attend if we didn't want to.

'Of course we want to,' I said, 'as long as you're not planning to throw yourself off the balcony into the canal.'

Norma ignored that.

On the night, I put on my party clothes and got there early to help. 'Oh, thank God,' said Norma at the door. She was in her loveliest dress, green with tiny white spots and an asymmetric hem with flamenco frill. She ushered me in and popped an apron on me and worked me like an ox. By the time I'd finished moving furniture and wiping glasses I was exhausted, quite red in the face, and my lace sleeves had gone baggy through being pushed up above my elbows. 'What now?' I said, hoping Norma would say, relax with a drink.

But instead she said, 'Get the canapés off those platters and onto my nice plates, but warm them first, and scatter halved tomatoes in among them.'

'Didn't Josie do all that for you?' I asked.

'No, God, no, I didn't want her hanging about,' said Norma. 'You don't mind helping a bit, do you?'

When the guests started arriving it was me who took their coats and laid them on Norma's bed and then me who offered them a drink. It got quite busy and at one point a visiting lecturer said to a colleague, 'Do you know if there are any soft drinks?'

And the colleague said, 'I'll ask the waitress,' then turned to me and said, 'Do you know if there are any soft drinks?'

I said, 'I'm not the waitress, but I'll ask the host.'

'Oh, I'm sorry, it's just –' he gestured – 'the apron.'

I called out to Norma, 'Are there any soft drinks?'

Norma said, 'Oh, yes, in the fridge, just arrange an assortment over there, please, Susan, thank you.' And she continued explaining her fondness for *The Count of Monte Cristo* to a little group from the English department. 'Revenge is so very human!'

Later, herself circulating with canapés and seeing me chatting to the VC, she handed me a plate and said, 'Come on, Susan, people need food.'

After what seemed like hours of going around with mini fishcakes and potato wedges I stopped for a drink and found myself chatting to the VC again.

'Such a fascinating old building,' he said.

'Isn't it!' I said. 'Sacks of grain would've been loaded from where we're standing onto narrowboats and then taken away to who knows where to be milled.'

And he said, 'Gosh, yes, how cheering, and then on again to be baked into loaves of lovely bread.'

'I'm in heaven here,' said Norma, butting in with a plate of mackerel-and-gherkin bites. 'You see, I just love living alone.'

'Oh, do you?' said the VC, frowning.

'Yes!' said Norma emphatically. 'How people cohabit, I really do not know.'

'It's sometimes a matter of economics,' I said.

'But you've never lived alone, have you?' said Norma.

'Not as such,' I said, and was about to compare Norma to Diogenes in his little terracotta dwelling when she handed me the plate.

'I need a break, Susan, do you mind?'

And what could I say?

Professor Leopold had been recruited too but it was different for him. He didn't mind being interrupted by Norma and enjoined to work, or even told off – he was quite happy pirouetting about and saying, 'Can I tempt you to a nibble?' He came across as less like waiting staff and more like the host's secret lover, which he was.

Honey had always seemed like a natural linguist and would often as a child make up her own special languages. Not silly ones, like 'argy-bargy', but beautiful, intuitive systems, whereby yellow or silver things were called 'bright-ings' (one word) and big things were 'gee-ant'. It was like a prettier version of Esperanto devised by a creative six-year-old – I always supposed this to be a lovely long-term effect of Grace's early language lessons.

When French and German classes started in earnest at secondary school she had a good attitude and plenty of confidence, and when the school announced a French trip for the following year, we let Roy's mother contribute and economized ourselves, so that when the time came she'd been looking forward to it for almost a year. I was surprised and sad when, on the second day of the trip, we received a long-distance call from the head of Languages. All wasn't well, and the upshot was that Roy had to drive over to France, to the town, I forget its name, twinned with Market Harborough, to bring Honey home early.

I'd never heard of such a thing happening. It had horrible echoes of Grace's early departure from our New Forest trip. When they got back, Honey was subdued and odd. I was angry at her classmates, assuming they'd been mean to her, and knowing that a common secondary-school solution to bullying is to remove the victim. But Miss Bryant, head of year, told a different story when we met with her the following week. Honey had been disruptive from the off; liberated from her shyness in the French language, she'd mocked the riders on the Tour de France and called them 'dopers' and declared everything '*merde*', and, worst of all, she'd done some kind of 'lesbian dance' in the dorm.

'Lesbian dance?' said Roy.

'With another pupil?' I asked, hoping.

'No,' said Miss Bryant, 'on her own, while the other girls were trying to get to sleep.'

Roy took against Miss Bryant. 'What in God's name is a "lesbian dance"?' he demanded.

'Leave it, Roy,' I said, thinking it inappropriate to expect any further description.

But Roy wouldn't let it drop. 'Well, hang on, she says Honey's done a lesbian dance, so how is it a lesbian dance, if she's done it on her own?'

'Roy!' I said. 'Leave it.'

I wondered if it might be a delayed reaction to the death of her godmother, my cousin Timandra, and raised this with Miss Bryant. To my annoyance, Roy tutted.

Anyway, Honey was different after the French trip. She started whistling elaborate old tunes, like a man, the whole time, and it seemed like a non-verbal message that things had changed. She also started playing the more perplexing Beatles songs, and laughing for no reason. I'd imagined her watching romcoms, microwaving popcorn, and drawing dolphins and girls with big eyes until the age of eighteen, and then taking ecstasy at Reading Festival, and developing bulimia, getting a boyfriend who wasn't very bright, and painting her bedroom either a very dark colour or white; and that would be her passage into adulthood. But because of that stupid French trip she was branded eccentric, and by gosh, lived up to the label.

I told Norma about the lesbian dance as we sat on her leafy balcony watching amusingly named narrowboats chug past, one called *Chillax* and another called *Not to Worry* and one with a whole herb garden on the roof.

'Roy says her reputation will be in tatters,' I said, 'and that every single pupil will know all the gory details. He called her an official pervert.'

'Poor Roy,' said Norma. 'This is precisely why I never wanted children – you just don't know how they're going to turn out.'

I thought this a bit rich coming from her and got up awkwardly from my deckchair.

'Honey has turned out great, thank you very much, Norma,' I said, and she raised one eyebrow.

I picked up my things to leave and Norma said, 'Don't be so defensive.'

And I replied, 'Well, maybe show some compassion?' I cantered down the stone stairway and slammed the door.

Grace had just arrived when I got home and though I hadn't intended to I raised the lesbian dance. 'I feel that I should mention it,' I said, 'in case it reaches you on the grapevine.'

It had reached her already and she was very mature about it.

'Honey sometimes acts strange when she's anxious,' she said.

'Will she be ostracized, do you think?' I asked. Grace didn't quite know the meaning of the word and though I felt this was a sign that she was too young for me to be burdening her I continued anyway. 'Will the other pupils exclude her because of it?'

'No more than they already do.'

I must have looked distraught because Grace squeezed my arm.

'Don't worry,' she said, 'I'd rather she wasn't such a weirdo, but I'll always love her.'

What seemed like a troublesome spell for Honey at Rossington Comprehensive lasted from Year 8 to the end of Year 10, when, to our amazement, she was appointed Head Girl for Year 11. It seemed – I don't know – *wrong*, even to us. Honey had survived the previous three years in blinkers, neither befriending anyone who didn't temporarily need a friend, nor expressing herself, nor joining any clubs, nor being a part of the establishment in any way other than attending and hating it. We, as a family, were too ordinary, neither posh enough nor sufficiently underprivileged, to warrant the odd choice. Honey, wilfully unsporty, lacked confidence, was neither geeky nor popular. Her only memorable achievement having been the infamous solo dance which had so scandalized the girls' dorm on the French trip at the start of Year 8. Nor was she one of those invisible hard workers – upon whom teachers rely – who need no attention or encouragement and who hate school but stoically get on with it. Honey was outspoken enough to set others off, she was lazy, and she never wore regulation shoes.

Neither Roy nor I knew quite what to say.

'Have you? Gosh!' I said eventually, after slightly too long.

'You sure you got that right?' said Roy, his face dubious but hopeful. He was thinking about the lesbian dance, that it must now be water under the bridge. I immediately thought of the two poor girls who seemed much more obvious for the role: Lorelei Palmer-Smith, whose father Seb was at that time our solicitor and lived in a house with five-hundred-year-old beams that meant Honey could never go there, being squeamish of ancient things, and to whom Roy had just that week complained regarding the deeds to our house; and Heather Something, who worked hard and did voluntary work with stray dogs.

'Of course I'm sure,' said Honey.

'I bet Lorelei Palmer-Smith's parents will be disappointed,' I said.

'They've lodged a complaint with the Deputy Head,' said Honey.

'Why not the Head?' asked Roy. While he and Honey discussed the situation I wondered what it was that made Roy ask such bizarre, beside-the-point questions. Presumably the same thing that caused him to photograph the placenta when only five feet away was his newborn daughter.

'The Deputy Head is in charge of prefect stuff,' said Honey.

'How did you get the position?' I asked. 'I mean, what did you have to do?'

'I had to apply in writing.'

'You applied *in writing*?' said Roy, now looking shocked.

'Yes, Dad, I applied in writing. I can write, you know.' And with that Honey left the room.

I wished we could start the whole subject again, but we couldn't, obviously. Instead I made dinner a little early and produced an orange and ginger ale punch with sprigs of mint. I proposed a toast, 'To Honey, who beat stiff opposition to be awarded the coveted position of Head Girl at Rossington Comp,' and Roy joined in, 'Yeah, Hun, very well done!'

'Thanks, cheers!' said Honey, slurping her drink. 'I had to submit a piece of written work, a personal statement, and a reference from a job.'

'What job?' said Roy.

'Well, because I got sacked from the petrol station, remember, I couldn't ask them but Grace wrote a reference about my role as her sister instead.'

'Oh, Hun,' I said, quite stunned by this, 'I'd love to see that some time.'

I watched her help herself to a second glass of punch, and saw her in a whole new light. I saw the school in a whole new light, too. Instead of the brutalizing sausage machine, they seemed suddenly human, compassionate, nurturing. They'd picked Honey. Difficult, angry, killjoy Honey, and now here we were, raising a toast to her success. Honey got up, left the room and stomped upstairs, and reappeared a moment later with a piece of paper, which she propped up on the pepper grinder.

*Honey Warren is my half-sister. I first met her when I was nearly five and she was one. I disliked her. I never intended to like her but she liked me. I'd turn up at my father's house and she'd run towards me with open arms and I would delight in turning away. This went on and on until one day, years later, when she was nine or ten and she'd got hold of her emotions and would only smile instead of running to me. I told her then that the only reason she'd been born was to provide donor organs should I need them medically. She listened intently and said, 'Oh, no, Grace, are you ill?' And I replied, 'Not yet.'*

*Going to visit my father, stepmother and Honey every other weekend was sometimes pleasant, but going home again was always difficult. Honey has been the constant in my life, the cleverest, kindest person I've ever known. I have been the thorn in her side, but she hasn't had to forgive me because she never saw me like that and though we are chalk and cheese, I wholeheartedly recommend her for the position of Head Girl at Rossington Comprehensive.*

Roy read it and laughed. 'Nice one, Gracie!'

I left the room as soon as I could, to have a little weep and text the good news to Norma.

Honey has been appointed Head Girl at Rossington! I wrote.

Norma replied, Quite right too! which I thought an odd response, but kind.

I replied with other news: Did you see in the papers that Ian McEwan has admitted to stealing pebbles off Chesil Beach?

Norma replied: So what?

I thought you'd be interested. You told me about this problem, years ago.

Don't remember, but loved the book.

What book?

His new one. On Chesil Beach.

Oh, yes, silly me!

The Brankham Chorus started a new term and knowing I'd see Josie, I decided I'd tell her about Grace's good deed. Before we got going on the rehearsal of Karl Jenkins's *The Armed Man,* I went towards her, smiling. This was such an unusual occurrence that she looked behind her to see who I might be approaching. I began by commenting on how splendidly Grace was doing at university and then said, 'Also, I wanted you to know that Grace was very supportive of Honey recently, when she was going for Head Girl at school.'

When Josie looked blank, I continued, 'Grace wrote her a glowing reference.'

'Oh, did she? That's nice,' she said, tipping the dregs of tea from her thermos into the cup.

'It really was,' I burbled. 'I mean, Honey's not exactly Head Girl material, but, yeah, she got it!' I beamed and shrugged at the same time.

'Wonders will never cease,' said Josie.

I took from my pocket the post-it note on which I'd scribbled down a couple of lines from Grace's reference, assuming she'd be happy to think the sisters had a relationship that might last a lifetime.

'*I told her then that the only reason she'd been born was to provide donor organs should I need them, medically,*' I read.

Josie guffawed. 'Yeah, I told Grace that!'

'What do you mean?'

'I told Grace that,' she said.

'Told Grace what?'

'What you just read, about donor organs.'

I'd been going to walk away, but instead I questioned her about something I'd always wanted to know but had never before quite had the nerve to ask.

'Why didn't you tell Roy about Grace from the start?'

She looked baffled.

'I mean, why did you wait nearly five years?'

'He wasn't mentally up to it.'

'Who wasn't?'

'Roy wasn't,' she said, 'and I didn't want him involved.'

'So what changed your mind?'

'Your friend from the shop came over to the Two Swans and had a word.'

'What friend?'

'Norma from the sewing shop. She came across, and said you'd had a baby, blah, blah, and that I should let Roy know.'

'Norma?'

'Yeah, Norma.'

'Norma,' I said, again. 'What did she say *exactly*?'

'I dunno. "Now might be the time to let Roy know about the kid" – something like that.'

'But how did Norma know?'

Josie shrugged. 'No idea.'

'And that's why you came and told Roy?'

'Yeah, I got the feeling that I if didn't, she would.'

'Come to think of it, how did you even know Norma back then?' I said.

'She'd started going out with Hugo and came to see me to check everything was in order, you know.'

'Like what?'

'Like had I finished with him.'

'And had you?' I asked.

'Yeah.'

There was some noise as choir members moved about. Josie scrumpled her KitKat wrapper in one hand and dropped it into the empty flask.

'Good evening, everybody,' the conductor called out, tapping his baton on the stand. We took our places for the warm-ups.

When Norma phoned on Sunday I asked her straight out why she hadn't told me about Grace when she first knew.

'Josie says it was you who made her tell Roy about Grace,' I said.

Norma sighed and I could imagine her hand going to her throat.

'Well, is it true?'

'The minute I found out I told Josie to tell Roy immediately,' she said, 'and she did, literally, the next day.'

'Why didn't you tell me?'

'I knew Roy would.'

'No,' I said. 'No, no, no. You should have told me the moment you found out!'

'You're wrong,' said Norma. 'It was better coming from Josie.'

'You really let me down.'

'No, Susan, you're wrong.'

'So why do I feel tricked?'

'I honestly don't know,' said Norma, 'but you really need to let it go.'

I put the phone down.

## 21

Roy's routine hernia surgery at St Lucy's day-case unit in 2012 had gone perfectly well, only the surgeon, just prior to Roy's discharge, made a silly joke and it fitted exactly into a tiny space in his mind and then the wind must've changed direction because it got stuck, and sparked in Roy a quest for longevity that took him over almost completely.

It went like this. I'd arrived early to collect Roy and seeing me floating about in the corridor, the ward sister had ushered me in. So I'd been there when Roy came round, blinking his hazel eyes, muddled and childlike, as his limp, hot hand reached out to find mine and to be held. Happy, relieved, and pleased to see me, still in his surgical gown and stockings, chalky dribble on his chin and his hair tousled. Then struggling to sit up a bit, Roy spotted the surgeon beginning his post-op rounds, and exultant that all had gone well he called out, 'Hey, doc, how did it go?' pointing to his slightly exposed, shaven tummy.

I saw the irritation flash across the little man's face, his twitch of annoyance, like a stab of neuralgia or a hurtful nickname. I saw that Roy had, in not being more reverential, inadvertently dented this man's esteem.

He won't have known that to me – and the nine or ten men whose hernias and gall bladders and anal polyps he'd removed, corrected, cauterized and stitched up again that day, and who he had brought out mended to St Christopher Ward to wake up and slip into their new cotton dressing gowns – he was the hero, and to call out to him like that was a salute. We didn't mind that he'd not been doing open heart surgery or separating conjoined twins or operating on the hippocampus; God, we were glad of it. But he'd been cross at Roy's manner, his lack of post-anaesthetic modesty, and in front of the nurses, a young, pretty one and the sister. And he'd not been best pleased at Roy calling him 'doc', like something out of *M\*A\*S\*H*. So he knocked him down a peg.

'Well, buddy, I thought we'd lost you for a moment back there but you're a fighter!' he said, with great seriousness, before moving on to the next bed, beside which a middle-aged man who'd had a hernia repair was already sitting in a chair in his dressing gown.

Hearing this, Roy was stricken, and the surgeon smirked.

'Jesus, Susan, did you hear that?' he said.

And I said, 'Oh, he was only joking.'

'Joking? He's a surgeon, he's just cut me open. Surgeons don't joke about life and death like that.'

'Surgeons constantly make jokes like that. They pull organs out and pretend they're speaking like Homer Simpson, to make the nurses laugh – they swear and all sorts.'

'Where the hell did you hear that?'

'I don't know, novels I suppose?'

'Novels? Jesus, Susan, I died in there, I died and came to back to life.'

Later, ringing my mother at my brother's house, I got my sister-in-law, a medical person, and she asked how Roy's surgery had gone.

'Fine,' I told her, 'but the surgeon implied that he died and came back to life, so he's a bit overwhelmed.'

'They're always saying things like that,' she said. 'Gallows humour.'

'I wish he hadn't.'

'Minor procedures on old people, though,' she said. 'It's like a pilot having to drive a bus.'

The following day, still obsessing, Roy phoned St Christopher Ward for an explanation and when the feedback didn't mention this alleged emergency he emailed the clinical manager at St Lucy's asking for clarification.

Mr Roger Barrington-Easterfield spoke to me on his ward round and implied that something had gone wrong during my hernia repair surgery. I'd like to know what exactly happened and why, wrote Roy.

A letter arrived a week or so later: *Nothing out of the ordinary was noted by the surgeon regarding your hernia repair procedure. It's possible you misinterpreted comments from Mr Barrington-Easterfield, which can happen after a general anaesthetic.*

Roy read it out to me. 'But you heard him, didn't you, Susan? I was pronounced dead.'

'No, I didn't hear him say that. I heard him make a stupid joke.'

'No, Susan, you heard.'

'No, I heard you say, "Hey, doc, how did it go?" and I could see it had irritated him so I turned away and I only heard him make a spoof reply.'

'Spoof?' said Roy. 'What does that mean?'

'A leg-pull, satire, I don't know.'

The result of all this was that by August of 2012, Roy was possessed of a fervent ambition to live to a hundred, and went part-time at work in order to concentrate on veteran sports and optimum health and, as if that weren't bad enough, took up the trombone. He was fifty-two years old. Before you think me callous, I did my best with his resurrection anxieties. I could see how believing you'd been brought back from the dead might make you re-evaluate things and, seeing him gearing up for big changes, I rather hoped he'd regret being such a joyless father and would write letters to that effect to Honey apologizing for his dismissive attitude vis-à-vis her impending jewellery degree, tattoos, speaking voice, literary and dietary choices (eating croissants with a knife and fork) and her dislike of team sports, and for basically treating her like a dysfunctional golf partner, but he didn't. Instead of getting therapy or turning over a new leaf he read a book called *99 Ways to Reach 100: Step-by-step advice for a long, healthy, happy life* and started to reuse teabags.

I wasn't concerned about Roy's state of mind as much as our joint income, so was interested to see the notice for the position of PA-cum-driver to the Vice Chancellor and, noting the salary, applied immediately via the intranet, slightly over-egging my love of motor driving. I didn't think about Norma and her complicated ideas about status and friendship in the workplace – frankly, I had more pressing concerns. She had by that time been promoted to senior lecturer, and had a second publishing contract with the Bloomsbury Press; she was doing well, and in any case, I wasn't over the revelation that she'd known about Grace and hadn't told me. And even when she called the following Sunday I didn't tell her, but asked her to meet me for coffee on campus the next day. I was going to put the blame on Roy and didn't want him to overhear.

'Roy's gone doolally,' I told her, 'and so I've applied for a promotion. We need the money.'

'Oh, what's the position?' she asked, no concern for Roy.

'PA to the VC.' I grimaced while I waited for her to respond.

'A big leap,' she said. 'Don't you need a degree for that?'

'Apparently not, and now that Roy's gone part-time and Honey'll be gone, I just feel the time's right.' I was defensive, over-explaining.

'Sounds like you've got it all worked out.'

'I probably won't even get the job,' I said, 'but if I do, I think it'll be fine. There's no actual law against being inter-departmental friends, is there?'

'Well, good luck,' she said. 'I know you're obsessed with the place and with me – I just hope it's worth it.'

'What? God, Norma, I know you think you're the centre of everything, but on this occasion you're not. I need this job because Roy wasn't sufficiently deferential to an angry little surgeon, and now we can barely afford to pay our bills.'

Neither of us spoke after that. She finished her drink, said, 'Bye then,' and left.

We'd get over this disagreement, I thought, and though she wouldn't want to flaunt our friendship, we'd meet up, say, once a fortnight for soup and salad. In the event, my move to the Vice Chancellor's Office, which was announced in a staff newsletter email, was barely noticed by anyone, and Norma – one of the few to read it – wrote saying only, 'Congratulations on your appointment!'

One night, some weeks after I'd started in my new job, someone stole the barley-sugar edging surrounding our front garden and in so doing compromised the rockery we'd put in some years previously. The perpetrator was presumably a gardening type, aware of the rarity and value of antique terracotta, and though the garden now lacked its pleasing border, I thought little of it other than the ordinary annoyance one feels at a violation of this kind. I still wasn't really speaking to Norma, otherwise I'd have told her and maybe we'd have gone to Barnes's Scrap and Antiques Yard to find something to replace it with. Knowing my luck, I'd buy back the very bricks that had been taken.

Some weeks later, after a night of torrential rain, I woke to Norma ringing to tell me the road was blocked. Our whole front garden had been washed away in a landslip. I ran to the bedroom window, and there it was: a heap of soil and great jagged alpine boulders, all strewn across the street. I stared in disbelief. It reminded me of the time when we'd first moved in and our dustbin had gone over in a storm; a week's worth of our rubbish had blown about and caught, like trout escaping a fish farm, in the railings and shrubs on the campus boundary. I'd gone out in the gale-force winds to pick up the items we'd thrown away: panty-liners, mouldy bread slices and a whole 70p iceberg lettuce, gone black in its plastic covering. That publicly wasted lettuce haunted me for months, years.

I got dressed quickly, put on my anorak and went out. Norma was already at work, soaking wet and ankle deep in mud.

'Have you got another shovel?' she called.

'Oh, Lord,' I said, and rushed to the garage.

When I got back to the scene Norma was digging about in a pile of what looked like muddy cans.

'What's all this?' she shouted.

I leaned closer to look: tuna, sardines, stewed steak in gravy, beans with pork sausages. I gasped and covered my mouth. It was Roy's bird flu stockpile. I began throwing them into the barrow.

'What are they?' shouted Norma, and then, seeing my face, began loading more quickly. 'I'll pile everything inside the campus gates,' she said, 'behind the rhododendron, for now. OK?'

'OK,' I said. I wiped my eyes, and could feel the mud smearing my face. 'Thank you.'

It took almost an hour to properly clear the road of all the soil, shrubs and tins. We'd had to carry some boulders between the two of us and walk them through the gates. Afterwards, Norma swept the road and with the rain lashing down it was soon quite clear and the patch of raw earth in front of our house was the only sign that anything had happened. Norma and I stood staring at each other, muddy and drenched.

'So what's the story?' asked Norma, just as Roy appeared at the front door, dressed for work.

'I can't talk about it now,' I said urgently. 'Please don't say anything.'

'What's going on?' called Roy.

'Mini landslide,' I said, 'but all sorted and stable again.'

He came out and began poking at the soil with a bamboo pole and, satisfied that nothing was amiss, and presumably that his stash was well underground, went back inside.

'So who buried the tins?' she asked.

'Roy,' I said, my voice wobbly.

She looked at me some more. 'Roy?'

'Yes.'

'Why?'

'He got it into his head—' I began, but paused to collect myself, and just said, 'Avian flu.'

'*Roy* had avian flu?' said Norma, aghast.

'*No!*' I said, and we began to laugh and laugh at the misunderstanding, and, imagining it would be disguised by all the rain and mud and hilarity, I let myself cry as well and then I couldn't stop.

Norma hugged me hard. 'Go and have a shower. I'll get that stuff moved.'

I trudged up the steps and looked back at her. 'It's going to be fine,' she said.

# 22

Finally, in September 2012, Honey was off down south to study jewellery design. She was twenty years old though she seemed younger. She'd got her place and arranged her accommodation and her loan, but even so, I couldn't believe she was actually going. I'd thought she'd never leave, like Doris Lessing's son, Peter, who lived with her his whole life and was with her when she heard she'd won the Nobel Prize for Literature. The image of him alighting from a taxi holding an artichoke and a string of onions had haunted me. It was so odd and unabashed, so Honey.

'Jewellery design! For the love of Mike!' Roy had said, in my hearing, on the phone to Grace.

And Grace had replied, also in my hearing, 'But that's a lovely thing to be studying – she'll be happy and that's what matters.' Roy's attitude made me very sad, but that might have been my general state of mind. I mean, my father had recently died, Roy was optimizing his physical health to the detriment of everything else in his life, I'd suffered a fungal toenail infection which upset my equilibrium, started a demanding new job, and apart from dramatic interludes, my best friend was cold-shouldering me.

I would've offered to let Honey drive some of the way for practice but she'd given up official tuition when her driving instructor said to her, 'Don't look so worried, I'm not going to molest you.' At which she'd made an emergency stop so sudden and so hard he almost went through the windscreen, and damaged his spectacles, and that was that, and apart from the time she stole Roy's car to get a pizza, she remains a non-driver to this day.

I'd wanted Roy to come too, partly to shore up their relationship, partly to share the driving, and if I'm honest, partly because I worried Honey wouldn't let me leave without her if I was on my own. But Roy was training for a triathlon, the silver lining being all that extra space in the car for baking equipment and a beanbag. We were in the car and ready to go as dawn broke and it was all feeling positive and happy. Roy came to the window. 'Heinz ratatouille with grated cheese. A good cheap square meal,' he said, then patted the side of the car and jogged off for his morning run.

Before Honey and I left the driveway we sat for a few moments, admiring the beautiful markings and quivering antennae of a huge moth that lay flattened against the windscreen – it might have been a tawny moth – and then, thinking it would flutter away if we moved off, I started the ignition and to my horror the wipers came on instantaneously and smeared the poor thing across the glass. Honey and I both screamed and threw up our hands.

'Oh my God, Susan! Why did you do that?' said Honey. She called me Susan at times of high stress. 'I'm traumatized!'

'NO! I didn't mean the wipers to come on,' I said. 'I'm so sorry, it's this fucking car.'

I drove away, feeling wretched that our bright start had

been destroyed. I changed the subject but Honey observed that it was a sign of our privilege that we might never see anything worse than that. 'I mean, like, how many human beings in the world can say that's the worst thing they'll see until their parents die?'

I had to agree.

As we sailed along empty roads, Honey nodded off, and I stashed away subject matter for my next journey with the VC: the clearness of the roads (a topic in itself), a misused apostrophe on a lorry that should have known better, a fleet of handsome Eddie Stobart trucks, bumping into Dr Chandra from the department of Materials Science and Engineering at the petrol station. I wouldn't mention Honey sleeping for the first hour or so, white-painted lashes on her olive cheek, Mr Blue in the crook of her neck. I wouldn't dwell on the parent/child side of things, the VC not having children, which might be a sadness for all I knew. An hour into the journey Honey woke when a slight hissing noise began and the car filled with a smell of sweet peaches body spray.

There! I thought. That'll go down a storm with Professor Willoughby. It's the kind of thing people like the VC really enjoy; something modern and tasteless coming a cropper.

We arrived at our destination surprisingly quickly considering I stuck rigidly to the speed limit and we'd had a longer-than-planned stop at the services – and were soon marvelling at the loveliness of the sea air, the boho atmosphere, the endless junk shops and quaint little places, all of which would suit Honey down to the ground. I realized I'd dreamt the night before of being here and buying some potions and oils and so I did and the dream came true.

After a walk and some lunch we began to unpack Honey's things in the little flatlet at the halls of residence. We were the first, and it all felt rather nice. Her room had a desk across the wall with a view of a steeply descending terrace of houses and a feel of being very much in the thick of it.

'I'll get going when your flatmates start to arrive,' I said, 'and let you get on.'

At which point a perfect, confident girl appeared: 'Hi, there, I'm Alice and this is my mom, Anoushka,' she said.

The mother was self-deprecating: 'I'm hopeless at all this, Alice has nothing of any use, I'm such a ditz,' she kept saying, when she saw e.g. Honey's IKEA slimline laundry rack, or non-stick frying pan/wok hybrid, and hob tool set. I didn't care that she was probably speaking in code, meaning, 'Aren't they common!' I just wanted it all to be lovely, so spoke in my poshest voice and made mint tea without even asking if they wanted it. Honey retreated to her bedroom and I followed.

'Right, I'll get going,' I said, and after a long, long hug, I went to leave the room. But she clung to me.

'I can't find Mr Blue,' she said. After a thorough search we decided he might have fallen out of the car at the services.

'I don't want to stay here, Susan,' she said.

'You'll be fine.'

'No, no, I'm not ready. I want to come home with

you – just for a couple of days,' she said. 'I'll try again next week. I'll come by train, you needn't even come with me.'

I was reminded of the time I'd nursed a fledgling thrush to health and walked out to the middle of a field to release it, whispering into my cupped hands, 'Time to fly, have a wonderful life,' and lifted my open hands to the skies. 'Fly, baby bird!' I'd said out loud, and off it had gone, up into the blue, quite high, and fluttered about in mid-air; and to my squinted eyes it seemed to be gone but then it came back on the breeze and sat on my shoulder, all dusty, ungainly feathers. It took two more attempts, and I remember thinking I should have thrown higher and harder the first time.

'But next week will be too late, Hun, everyone will be settled into their cliques.' I shouldn't have said 'cliques' because she flinched. 'We can't come all the way here and then go all the way back,' I said. 'It just doesn't make sense.' And it was true. I couldn't. I simply could not walk back into the house and have her still with me, like Peter Lessing. I want to claim that Roy would have been disappointed, that he'd been looking forward to her leaving since the day she was born, that he'd be bound to say something fatal – but it was as much me who wanted a new, dependant-free chapter, organizing the VC and helping the smooth running of the university.

But neither could I leave her there, alone, trembling and tearful, calling me Susan, and tapping her upper and lower incisors together, like my father used to do when concentrating. I booked us into a Travelodge nearby and we drove back to Pease Pottage services where we found Mr Blue.

He'd been run over but was in one piece. Back at the hotel we bathed him, and went out to walk by the sea, and actually it was a good thing. Honey got her bearings, playing the slot machines in the arcade while I sat on a bench nearby. She won a plush duckling which she put in her hoodie pocket like a baby kangaroo, and I went into the Old Rock Shop and bought Roy a stick of rock with 'Roy' written all through it, and because they didn't have a 'Honey' I ordered one to be made especially and mailed to her new address within a week. Thinking that a good omen.

The next morning we returned to Honey's accommodation and finished her unpacking. I pulled clean, dry Mr Blue from my bag but Honey said to take him home – she had the duckling now and two soft toys would look sad. The girl Alice said nothing about Honey's disappearance the day before, only offered her a Ribena and introduced us to Ursula and Bethany, and while Honey wasn't looking I walked quickly out of the flat and away along the street, almost without breathing.

In the car I took my phone from my bag and texted: Hun, I'm off. Are you OK?

And she replied: where r u

And I replied: In car.

And she replied: k bye ty

Whatever that was supposed to mean.

I drove in the drizzle, looking for an '*All Other Traffic*' sign. The wipers came on intermittently, smearing the windscreen with the first drag and then clearing with the next, and I thought of the moth. To cry on top of all this would have been untenable visibility-wise so I pulled into a spot against a stone wall beside a sports field until a lot of young men in football kit started to drift by. I dried my eyes and texted Roy:

Honey settled. Am now leaving.

Alone?

Yes.

Good work.

I was suddenly desperate to speak to Norma. The landslide emergency had felt like a reconciliation of sorts, but it occurred to me that we hadn't really spoken since then. I think I'd felt a bit raw and exposed afterwards. I called her from the car, expecting to leave a voicemail, but she answered.

'Oh, hello,' she said, 'what's up?'

'Nothing, I've just left Honey at her university halls.'

'How is she?'

'A bit wobbly.'

'But OK?'

'Yes,' I said, 'the halls are right next door to your and Hugo's honeymoon hotel.'

'Oh my God,' she said. 'Did you get a photograph?'

'Yes.'

'Ha!' said Norma. 'And how are you feeling?'

'A bit sad and weird, you know.' Trying to keep my voice level. 'But I'll be back by six. I'd love to meet up for a drink.'

'Oh, I can't tonight, sorry, I daren't leave the flat. I'm up to my ears in admin for the new term. Let's have a coffee tomorrow.'

\*

The weather brightened on the journey northwards, which was helpful, and by the time I was home the sun was shining. I was glad to be back without Honey but then, smelling her vape and a specific shoe smell, went to her room. A shrine to the puerile: the picture rail featuring a line-up of novelty cigarette lighters, and a whole collage of photographs of herself in silly poses, one in a pram, one being piggy-backed by a smaller girl and another of her, nude with smiley stickers covering her nipples. I held an abandoned sweater to my face and breathed in. It smelled like Ritz crackers.

Downstairs I could hear Roy playing ping-pong against himself in the garage and so I slipped out to walk on campus alone with my thoughts. The grounds were at their most beautiful: the beech leaves glinted like treasure, and painterly shadows made the sandstone building more magnificent than it already was, while the wisteria swayed pleasingly like pretty curtains in the breeze. Clusters of montbretia, late sedum and nerines dotted the scenes with colour and all in all it was a joy to behold. To cheer myself further I strolled over to the east side, really just to necessitate a walk past the VC's cottage, in which I felt he appeared like a tableau vivant. Inside, there was always the smell of hickory smoke, beeswax and ripe apples, and outside, the tangy aroma of azalea, thyme and rain-wetted shingle. Its frontage resembled a kindly face – the thick stone lintels were its eyelids and the deep-set dark windows its smiling eyes; the overhanging slate roof was a friendly mop of grey-black hair and most glorious of all was the red gloss door, its mouth open in greeting: 'How lovely to see you.'

The whole thing was conducive to learned thoughts and poetry. Maybe I'd see him in the front garden, raking the gravel or reading the *Sunday Times* or the *Dairy Farmer* on the curved metal bench; if so I might tell him about the aerosol setting itself off on the drive to Brighton, the mislaying of Mr Blue, and Honey's success on the slot machines. Drawing closer, I saw the flash of mustard that was his sun hat and from his movements I guessed he was pottering with a hoe or secateurs. I'd rather have been meeting Norma but the VC was a very good next best. When I reached the picket fence, I could see he was dead-heading a late rose.

'Hello,' I said. 'Lovely climber, a late bloomer?'

Hello, Susan. Yes, it's Snow Goose, I think it's a wayside rose,' he said, snipping a spray and handing it to me. I breathed in the light musky fragrance and felt a wave of happiness.

'Yes, I've just driven up from the coast where it was *pouring*,' I said.

'Ah, yes, you dropped your daughter at university.'

I felt flattered that he'd remembered.

'Yes, a tough day.' I made a weary gesture. He glanced back at the house, which I thought might mean he was about to insist on making me a restorative cup of tea.

'Good, good,' he said. 'Well, I'd better let you get on.' And on he went with his cautious pruning.

'Yes,' I said, 'have a nice evening.'

I walked on and just as I passed the front gate something caught my eye. I went closer and moved the bough of another late-blooming rose, and there beside the wall, laid out on the garden bench, bare-legged, one arm flung out with a glass of something, was Norma Pack-Allen, in the green spotty dress I knew so well, floppy hat over her face. I rushed on before being seen. And of all the awful things to have happened that year, I'm ashamed to say this was the most painful.

I met Norma the following day for coffee as planned, but got myself an orange juice just to unnerve her.

'So what's new?' I asked.

'Nothing, just lots of rather boring prep. Tell me about Honey.'

'She didn't want me to leave her in the halls so we had a night in a hotel.'

'Oh, so it all went well, then,' she said. 'Great, good for her.'

'No. It didn't go well. It was horrendous. Honey was fucking traumatized.' I was almost in tears.

'Oh, no, I'm sorry.' She went to take my hand but I moved it out of reach. This version of us – her, wise and mindful; me, fragile and pouring my heart out – was suddenly disagreeable.

'Have you heard from her today?' said Norma.

'No, I haven't,' I said, 'but I'm sure she's fine.'

'Well, send her my love.'

'Actually, I'm going to go and ring her now.' I got up abruptly.

'OK. Bye then.'

If Norma wasn't going to tell me that she'd started some kind of affair with the VC she was no longer a friend. I ignored her call the following Sunday and the next. I was angry with myself too, for not foreseeing it. Hadn't I had a fleeting thought after she'd asked me not to discuss her with him? I counted myself lucky to have discovered it, though – if I hadn't, I'd have been wrong-footed when some weeks later I arrived at the Gate House to take the VC to an extremely smart dinner hosted by our Professor-Doctor Supal-Singh, when Norma appeared in a spectacular evening gown and got into the back seat of the car, the VC's companion for the evening. She'd been about to say, 'Evening, Susan,' and to enjoy my surprise, but I beat her to it and said, 'Oh, sorry, Norma, would you mind sitting on the right-hand side?'

'Does it matter which side I sit?' she'd asked.

'Yes, if you wouldn't mind.'

And instead of getting out and walking round the car she shuffled over, like a child.

I could feel her watching for my reaction to her presence and my being entirely unfazed, chatting about the evening traffic and the difference in symbolic significance between an acorn and a fir cone. 'Poor old fir cone!' I'd said, laughing.

We'd been warned in advance that celebrities such as David Attenborough, Sting, Joanna Lumley and other A-listers would be in attendance, and lots of press, and during the afternoon the VC had twice referred to 'String' and so on the journey I was able to make a joke that went straight over Norma's head. Before arriving at the venue I gave my passengers instructions on their entrance. 'Norma, if you could please remain in the vehicle until the VC has alighted for the press photographer, and when you do alight, Norma, please step away from the vehicle quickly so as not to spoil the shot.' I gave her a big smile. 'OK?'

The shortlist for the Preece Poetry Award 2014 comprised:

*The Flying Horse*, Norma Pack-Allen (Bloomsbury)
*Curly Locks*, Della Wong (Bloodaxe)
*OK, Forest, OK!* J. G. Woodfine (Claptrap Press)

> *Who rides Pegasus, Medusa's foal*
> *made from droplets of blood*
> *Epsilon Pegasi also known as Enif.*
> *Younger brother Equuleus*
> *tail like a fountain, wings like ears*
> *Gallops to heaven swifter, stranger, brighter than sungold*
> *Ridden by the poet with smoke in his hair*
> *Nostril flaring, daring, bearing.*
> *Look, O Pegasus, no one likes you.*

Norma and I were barely on speaking terms but I
impressed myself by feeling pleased for her (being the
eventual winner), and considered hers the only work of
real beauty and truth. I was certain the title poem 'Pegasus'
referred to the mini-break Roy and I had in the caravan. It
pleased me that Norma made such good use of the memory even though she hadn't been there, and she might
have asked. Other poems in the collection seemed to refer

to the death of her late husband, Hugo, which, as you might recall, happened while we were away on that trip. One titled 'Under the Bus' particularly, which the judges praised for its blend of comedy and tragedy.

Also, as if winning a prestigious poetry award wasn't enough, by the January of the following year Norma and Vice Chancellor Willoughby were engaged to be married. It was proof of how bad things had got between us that she and I still hadn't discussed her relationship with the VC. How it had started, how it was going, what my role should be, any of it.

'I thought you'd like to know,' she said, 'we're getting hitched in the spring.'

'Why?' I asked, hiding my distress.

'Well, it'll be announced in *The Times* and the *Mercury*.'

'No,' I said, 'I mean, why are you getting married?'

'Because he likes being married. And not, by the way, because I'm after the cottage. I hate it.'

'What about your affair with Professor Leopold?' I asked.

She pretended not to hear, but I detected a slight shake of her head.


A week or so before the event, Norma called me during work hours. I thought she might be about to ask my advice on some aspect of the VC's life, or to check his preferred buffet foods, or to say she'd got cold feet, but it was in fact to give me a 'to do' list. I wasn't sure whether this was in my capacity as PA to her fiancé or as her friend, but she seemed quite blasé about it. One small but time-consuming job was to collect the wedding dress from the bridal shop in Leicester, in university hours, and drop it at the Gate House in time for her mother to fit the lace bolero and possibly make a schleppe. Tailored by the Gris Frères, to a design by Norma herself. The assistant at Happy Ever After fetched it from the back and held it up reverentially, declaring it the prettiest she'd ever handled and, imagining me to be the bride, said how lucky I was. I didn't disabuse her.

'Would you like to try it on one last time?' she said, holding aside the brocade curtain of the changing room.

'Maybe I should,' I said, and stepped inside.

The assistant followed and laid the dress on the chaise longue, before stepping out again and arranging the curtain into neat, even folds.

I held it up against myself and stared in disbelief. It was a faithful copy of the Catherine Deneuve dress that Mrs Pavlou and I had designed all those years ago, for my own wedding. The dress I couldn't squeeze into and had to forgo. I mean, it was *exactly* the same: tight bodice, cap sleeves, hand-pleated to produce a 'puffball' effect in the skirt, except made from the most luxurious ivory silk taffeta and antique lace, and unique in colour ('Mistletoe Berry', I later discovered), and with extra tiny flourishes that I hadn't imagined, and perfect minuscule buttons instead of a zip. I slipped into it, the assistant returned briefly to help fasten it at the back, and I looked at myself on tiptoe in the huge gilt-framed mirror. I tousled my hair, and angled my head about. The dress suited me very well – in fact, it fitted perfectly. I took some photographs on my phone.

'How does it seem?' called the assistant.

'Yes, fine, thanks,' I answered.

'Can I bring you some shoes?'

But I was already out of the dress and keen to be on my way. She reminded me under no circumstances to hang or fold it, but to place it flat, so as not to compromise the skirt. I carried it through town over my arm and then, in the car, laid it out across the back seat where it looked like an overdressed child counting to one hundred for hide-and-seek, and all the way home I expected it to shout, 'Coming, ready or not,' spring up, and stab me in the neck.

The actual wedding was a private affair, just the two of them with two witnesses apparently dragged in off the street. The party was held at the Gate House and spilled into the garden on account of unseasonably warm weather. Norma's parents were there, and Joyce Ho, whose husband told a terrible story about his teenage son from a previous relationship peeing from the balcony in church as he and Joyce made their vows below. Joyce changed the subject quickly to their dog, which she referred to not by its name but as 'our rescue Golden'. Norma's editor, Simone St John from the Bloomsbury Press, was there, with her wife, celebrated novelist Diggory O'Farrell – who'd been in the news for arson but had presumably got away with it – and her daughter who kept talking about the joy of flea markets, which I found awkward, not knowing what a flea market was. Most surprisingly, the Leopolds were there, him dressed up like a tiny Johnny Hallyday. Apparently the VC had invited them, whether in a spirit of generosity or conquest, I'm not sure.

The VC's wedding present to Norma was permission to create her own lily pond in which she wouldn't be permitted to keep fish, due to the likelihood of students entering the garden to steal them, but he had budgeted for waterlilies and bullrushes and a faux bridge – in other words it was to be an improved copy of the existing pond in the back garden. Norma's gift to him was a bottle of vintage Château Margaux dating to the year of her birth that he'd always had his eye on and now displayed in an alcove at the cottage that was the exact size and place to exhibit such a thing and get a bit cobwebby and look the part. On the first day of every month he'd turn it on its side for the count of twenty, to keep the cork damp.

The VC and I rarely mentioned Norma and I was determined not to let the fact of their marriage spoil my enjoyment of the job. Norma asserted herself from time to time, though, which was frustrating but I suppose quite validating. Take, for instance, the occasion I'd arranged for us to attend the Cheltenham Literature Festival, which coincided perfectly with a meeting at the University and College Admissions Services (UCAS) which is based on the outskirts of the town. I'd got tickets to see one of his favourite authors.

The subject came up in conversation one day while I was driving the two of them to an evening event.

'Oh, which writer are you going to see?' demanded Norma, as I knew she would.

'I don't recall,' said the VC. I stayed quiet and changed gear to seem preoccupied.

'Susan?' said Norma.

'Andy McNab,' I mumbled. But we were approaching a hump-backed bridge and I'd sounded the horn almost as I spoke so Norma didn't catch the name.

'Did you say McEwan?'

'That's right.'

'Oh,' she said.

I expected the VC to pipe up and put us straight, but he was in a world of his own.

Shortly before the day of the literary festival Norma texted to say that if I didn't mind she'd like to drive her husband to UCAS and then attend the festival, unless I was desperate to go, in which case we might go together and the VC would be content to wait in the bar.

'Be my guest,' I replied. 'I have plenty of admin to get on with.'

And off they went. I gather the VC very much enjoyed the event. I never heard whether or not Norma did.


Barely a year after the wedding Norma walked out on the VC (with suitcases, in daylight hours) and went to live in a borrowed apartment in a swanky block with balconies overlooking the River Soar, an integral gym and an Italian-style coffee bar. Professor Leopold was back in the picture (was he ever out of it?) and they'd been seen in a West End theatre, watching an Ibsen play, laughing and sharing a box of chocolates. Who laughs at Ibsen? Lovers, that's who.

I called Norma. 'I'm only ringing because I thought you ought to know the rumours that are going around,' I said.

'Thank you, Susan, do tell.'

'You've left Professor Willoughby for Professor Leopold and you're living in an apartment with a river view and a gym.'

'Wrong,' said Norma. 'I've left him, that much is true, but not for anyone else, and there's no gym.'

'So you have left him then?'

'Yes.'

'I can't believe it. You've hardly given him a chance.'

'Ugh,' she said. 'I really have. I'm sorry you're so disappointed, Susan, but honestly, marriage doesn't have to be for ever, even for you.'

'What do mean by that?'

'I mean, if you think he's such a great prospect, you try him out. I'm sure Roy will manage without you.'

'My marriage is fine, thank you.'

'Thanks to you having put up with iceberg lettuce all these years,' she laughed.

'How do you know about that?' I said, dismayed.

'You never stop complaining about it. And, by the way, top tip – Crispin loves spinach and garlic makes him frisky.'

I winced at the VC's first name being used, and the unwanted detail. Neither of us spoke for a moment.

'I never thought you were much of a wife to him,' I said.

'You don't know what you're talking about.'

'I mean, like never sending sandwiches or phoning to see how he is after a big event, or putting a cushion in the car for his sciatica, and the way you've scruffed up the garden with that pond.'

Norma made a noise somewhere between a tut and a laugh.

'Honestly,' I said, 'I used to not know whether to congratulate myself or congratulate you, you did so little.'

'What year are we in?' said Norma.

'Yes, I buy iceberg lettuce, but I'd never tell Roy I put his preferences before my own. He has no idea that I crave other salad leaves.'

'Do you know just how crazy that sounds? And for such a paragon, isn't it odd that your husband was so traumatized that he buried tins of food in the garden, like Samuel fucking Pepys?'

I hung up.

In the days following the phone call, I let myself imagine I was the VC's life partner (or wife); not that I was in love with him, I was simply trying it out for size for a few days and it struck me that his character flaws were the kind you could happily ignore and his errors, if not bearable, were easily remediable. In a closer relationship I might encourage him, for instance, to shampoo more frequently and maybe switch to a more modern hair preparation, or change from his David Niven style to a shorter, more manageable crew cut. I might steer him away from entering the National Punning Championships, not to denigrate the skill, but to claw back the month lost in preparation every year, and the misery of it.

At the end of the week, for our Friday meeting in his home, I stepped up the garden path in a yellow tea dress. I never used the lion-head door knocker, it being so harsh and loud and not the kind of announcement I'd ever want for myself. Instead, I rapped a friendly four-beat tune with a single knuckle (rat-a-tat-tat), and I shan't give you the whole soup-to-nuts, but briefly, the VC greeted me at the door with great excitement and ushered me through to the sitting room. He'd known for some time but was now at liberty to share the news that he was to be awarded an OBE, apparently in recognition of services to education, but I suspect it was more to do with research he'd done on behalf of DEFRA concerning bovine health and mega-dairies, and frankly, it was the least they could do after the brickbats it earned him from local vegans – three verbal assaults, a death threat and some very robust graffiti – and I wasn't the least bit surprised having liaised closely with DEFRA regarding the nomination.

I listened to his trilling commentary on who he thought might have put him up for it, and how terribly proud his parents would have been had they not been dead, and what it might mean to the institution as a whole. I gazed around and noticed, with great relief, how tidy the place was, presumably since Norma's departure. No tea towels draped over chairs, no old coffee cups, no dusty chunks of volcanic rock collected in the Canaries, no scarves or hats strewn about, and best of all, no downtrodden Taz of Tasmania bedroom slippers. The curtains were fully open and the light poured in. The VC himself looked alert and reasonably clean too, if you ignored the collar curls and gardeny fingernails.

'Please email an announcement to VAG in the first instance,' he said, with a hard G, referring to the Vice

Chancellor's Advisory Group, and then, almost as an afterthought, asked if I'd consent to be his guest at the Palace. I was so shocked I leapt at it in rather an undignified way.

I should have said, 'But what about your wife?' which would have been professional, but to be fair I did then add, 'Are you sure you shouldn't keep it open?'

And he said, 'No, Susan, I'd like you to be there.'

# 24

I knew not to say anything publicly – partly because of implications about the state of his marriage but mainly because I doubted I would get to go to the Palace. I ran up a simple but stylish shift dress and matching shrug in shot silk, midnight blue, knowing it would tone with any one of his suits, but I didn't go as far as a handbag or new shoes. Two weeks before the event, I headed over to the VC's cottage for our Friday diary meeting, and as I walked up the path there was Norma squatting beside the pond, in cargo pants, chopsticks in her hair, planting irises and swearing.

'Hello, Susan,' she called.

'Oh,' I said, 'you're back.'

'Yes, I am, back and raring to go!'

I knocked at the door and the VC answered it; he seemed awkward, and couldn't help himself but glance out to Norma, who now stood full height, hands on her hips.

In the study, before I'd even poured the tea, I said, 'I see Norma's back.'

'Yes,' said the VC, 'and straight to pond maintenance!'

'But, back though?'

And he said, 'Yes, apparently.'

'Will you want me to put her name on the Buckingham Palace guest list? Instead of mine?'

'Yes, I think that would be – yes, thank you very much, Susan.'

And, because I couldn't bear the disappointment, I excused myself from the meeting and got up to leave, adding, 'I think I'd better get straight onto the Palace administrators this afternoon.'

And he said, 'Of course,' and bowed slightly.

As I say, I wasn't in love with the VC or anything, but I can't deny a certain disappointment. For a few days afterwards I found myself troubled by sad but unrelated memories. For instance, the baby squirrel that had bothered my parents just weeks before my father's death back in 2012, and for some reason I brought it up on the telephone with my mother. 'What was that thing with the baby squirrel?' I asked her. 'Around the time Dad died.'

'It crawled up my trousers at the bus stop.' My mother was almost hysterical in the recalling of it. 'I shouted at Daddy, "Get it away from me, Bill!" but he wasn't firm with it because he wasn't well enough and it came back and back until finally the bus came and we jumped aboard and the doors closed just in time and we got away and watched the thing running after the bus in the middle of the road.'

Imagining my parents staring out of the back window of the bus, like Dustin Hoffman and Katharine Ross, as they escape the misguided affection of a tiny lost creature, almost made me cry, but a snort of laughter came instead.

'I'm glad you find it amusing, Susan,' said my mother. 'That was the last time your father left the house alive.' And that made me laugh properly, not because it was funny but because it just kept getting sadder and sadder and that seemed to be the way of things. Why had a little lost baby squirrel chosen my mother? Why had she been wearing trousers? Why had that incident made my father give up on life? Why do we choose the wrong people? And what is it with Norma Pack-Allen and that bloody pond?

I was still required to drive the VC and Norma to London and back. The VC protested – they'd easily manage to get themselves there by train and taxi if necessary, he said – but for some reason I had insisted. I looked carefully at the directions on how to approach the Palace – which gate to drive through, where to drop recipients and guests, where to park, where to wait, and so forth. I rather wished I'd agreed to let them go by train and taxi, and mentioned this to Roy.

'What you so worried about?' he asked.

'All those roundabouts and one-way streets,' I said, 'and getting to the right gate.'

'But Norma will be with him. You'll be fine.'

'No, Roy, Norma being there *is* the problem. God, how do you not know that?'

'Oh, yes, I always forget – you two fell out.'

On the day I had no need to consult a map or have the TomTom going. I picked them up and felt immediately resentful of Norma for getting to meet the Queen, and to have this memory for the rest of her life. For being allowed back into the VC's life after humiliating him, and for saying she couldn't have the heater on or she'd get carsick. She'd brought with her an enormous scarf of rich orange and apricot colours, and I watched in the rear-view as she arranged it across herself, and sat back, cosy, with her eyes closed, practising the therapeutic breathing that I thought Roy had probably taught her. Professor Willoughby, beside her, sat uncovered in a light wool suit, and likely a bit chilly. I glanced back again, really to take another look at the scarf, and she was staring right at me. We locked eyes like cowboys in a saloon.

I pointed out landmarks along the way. 'Lord's Cricket Ground,' I called, 'Speakers' Corner.' The Dorchester. Canada Gate. Look, Professor, the same designer as our own gates.' Norma resolutely kept her eyes closed and her hands in her lap, but the VC turned and twisted to see everything. We arrived in very good time of course and when they alighted to make their entrance, Norma folded the lovely scarf in a certain way without even looking, a sort of half-fold here and doubling-up there and calmly arranged it about her neck; the result was like something out of an expensive catalogue and presumably why other idiots go around with great rugs around their necks, hoping to look like that.

I leapt out after them and took a photograph with the Palace in the background. Such an unprepossessing building , but never mind. They smiled and laughed and looked surprised, it being against the rules really. I heard other drivers that day saying to their passengers, 'Wish Her Maj a happy birthday from me,' and so forth, but things like that never sound as funny or original as you imagine, and can seem disrespectful.

So I steered clear and just said, 'Have a good time,' looking first at Norma, and then at the VC.

He nodded.

'And send me a text message when you come out.'

Back in the car, I watched as they were ushered quickly along by a suited old man weighed down with multiple tabards and a medal, Norma in her loose silk navy-blue dress (good for curtsying, I suppose), the orange-and-apricot scarf, heels and a low bun, the VC in a good, plain suit and a tie with tiny ginger corgis on it (a gift from Human Resources). They made a handsome couple, I couldn't deny it, and Norma seemed quite excited which was a relief because on the journey I'd detected a satirical attitude, something you'd expect of a celebrated and slightly radical poet from humble beginnings, but not from a friend or wife. Anyway, in they went, arm in arm.

I found the correct parking place, ate my scone and had a few sips of tea. Then, after clearing it with Palace security, I walked quickly to Hertford Street to see if I could get the photograph printed and framed immediately at Snappy Snaps. I could, and in a spirit of mischief I ordered a set of six coasters as well. I wasn't sure Norma would know these were meant ironically but I didn't care, and then I wondered if she'd think the framed photograph ironic. I certainly didn't mean it to be. It's tricky these days, I thought, knowing when to make a gesture and when to make a joke, when to quietly acknowledge the significance of a thing and when to poke fun. But I was over-thinking it and getting resentful, so I pulled myself together because this was the VC's day, and to some extent mine. I chose a dark blue frame for the photograph to tone with Norma's dress and had the coasters mailed to my home so I could think it through some more.

Back at the Palace gates, out of breath, I showed my ID and couldn't resist telling the security man what I'd been up to.

'I've run all the way to Snappy Snaps on Hertford Street to have a photograph developed,' I said.

He tutted. 'There's a branch just round the corner in Victoria Street,' he said, and waved me in, shaking his head pitifully.

Driving home I heard that HM the Queen had looked the VC straight in the eye, which he thought impressive. She'd said, 'I'm a huge lover of cows.'

Norma guffawed on hearing this and without opening her eyes said, 'Oh my God!'

Norma had made a beeline for a pop star who was getting a gong and him told him she'd had a poster of him in a glittery top hat on her bedroom wall when she was a teenager, and the pop star had been very gracious and said she didn't look old enough and they'd joked about hair dye.

'I referenced Peter Pan,' said Norma, 'and he referenced Dorian Gray and I said, "You obviously haven't read the book," and he owned up and I admitted to hating Peter Pan and he said, "Don't be mean about Cliff Richard," which was hilarious.'

The VC laughed but I didn't – it just wasn't funny.

'Norma can charm the birds off the trees,' he said.

Norma caught my eye again in the rear-view mirror, and then, thank God, slept for the rest of the journey, so the VC could give me some more details. They'd had teatime foods, he told me – lots of rather small strawberries with the leaves still on and quite a bit of parsley, a slimy mousse cake and buttered scones – and there was talk among the honorands about previous recipients, Sue Barker and Chris Froome, who were said to be the Queen's favourites. Sensing him running out of steam, I put on a Schubert CD and not long after it finished we pulled up outside the Gate House.

Before Norma woke, I handed the framed photograph to the VC, glancing at it before handing it over. It really was a lovely shot, both of them looking surprised and happy and Norma leaning slightly in to him. The VC took it from me and looked at it for what seemed like a whole minute – he was speechless.

To fill the silent moments I told him about my jog to Snappy Snaps in Hertford Street, and he was moved, almost to tears, and had to shuffle about in his seat to get his handkerchief from his pocket to blow his nose.

'I hope you like it,' I said.

And then Norma woke and mumbled, 'Why are we just sitting here?'

'Look, Norma,' said the VC, handing her the frame, 'look at this.'

'What?' she said, yawning. 'Good God, where the hell did this come from?'

'Susan ran all the way to Snappy Snaps in Hertford Street,' said the VC, with a note of caution in his voice.

'Isn't there one nearer?' she said.

The coasters arrived a week or so later. I've still got them.

# PART THREE

# Marriage

## 2019–2020

## 25

I'm with Dr Z. Tang again. I had the blood test after all, and it confirms that I am indeed menopausal, or perimeno-pausal. Dr Tang raises HRT as something to consider. I tell her I'll probably tough it out: the cracked hands, the night-time fearfulness, mood swings, etc.

'I don't get on very well with medicaments,' I say.

She cocks her head, obviously not remembering the time I'd had to interrupt a course of antibiotics after a sudden-onset persecution complex. How could she not? (I'd packed a bag for prison.) I remind her and then, to lighten the mood, recall the time my anti-fungal prescription made me laugh hysterically at men's faces for two weeks until I switched to a topical solution. She turns to her screen and scrolls for mention of this in my notes.

'Ha! Yes! Here we are,' she says, delighted. ' "Fluconazole, hysterical laughter." 2012.'

'That's right, in 2012,' I say. 'I ruined the London Olympics.'

I gather my things and stand to go. Dr Tang says, 'Just a thought – could your feelings be a reaction to the situation with the Vice Chancellor?'

'What situation?' I ask, suddenly alarmed.

'Well, his leaving the university,' she says, flaring her nostrils.

'*Leaving?*' I say. 'Who is leaving?'

'The Vice Chancellor. I believe it's a year at Westminster – I assumed you'd know.' Her hands on her knees rise up onto fingertips, like two cats stretching.

The thing about Dr Tang is that she doesn't seem like a gossip, but she is. Doctors aren't supposed to be, but she's clinical, dropping out the occasional tip of an occasional iceberg. Since I've been taking the minutes for the governing body I've seen her in action: the puzzled expression as though she's not in control of the secret that unfurls from her lips. It's like a hiccup. Take last month's quarterly meeting; as she and I watched the Chair of Governors get into his *new* Jaguar, she voiced a tiny thought which expanded like modern polyfilla and when examined in detail shifted Fred Fletcher from recent widower to question-mark sex pest.

'Good to see Fred's moved on,' she'd said. 'Maybe he wants to start a family.'

'No, I didn't know,' I say now, meaning the VC leaving. 'I had absolutely no idea.' Is she allowed to tell me this? Maybe it's OK because we're coming to the end of my consultation and we're laughing about my fungal medication, like friends? The two of us lock eyes for a moment, and press our mouths into lines, hers in sadness for me and mine in disappointment at her.

'I think it's still confidential,' she says and she puts her finger to her lips.

I thank her and leave via the pharmacy where I buy another tube of hand cream. I sit and think about this bombshell. Is it decided? Who knows? 'It's still confidential,' means I am probably the first to know, well, the third, no, fourth to know. Actually, I'm probably the sixth, counting the Chair of Governors and the boss of wherever he is going, Dr Tang, Professor Willoughby himself and Norma. But then Professor Leopold must surely know, and possibly Lydia Leopold. So I'm eighth. That's fine.

I drive away from Dr Tang with troubled thoughts. Why hasn't the VC told me his news? Who will take his place? Will I still be needed for driving and admin? What about Norma? Is it really a year with the government, or a recurrence of the breakdown when he kept smelling smoke?

When I get back from the doctor's, in turmoil over this VC leaving news, Roy comments, out of the blue, on how healthy he's feeling, how well he's been sleeping, how clear his head, and so on, and gives all the credit to lifestyle guru Wim Hof.

I can't help myself but say, 'It's not Wim bloody Hof, Roy, it's your vegan decaf diet.'

And Roy says, 'What? I'm not vegan decaf.'

And I say, 'Actually, you are, practically.'

'What are you talking about?'

So I explain. It just seemed ridiculous to keep buying such a wide range of foods when Honey is vegan (except for tuna because she can't give up Costa Tuna Melts), so I switched us all to Linda McCartney sausages and these pies that seem like meat but are actually a type of fast-growing eco-mushroom, and soon we were all practically vegan, apart from cow's milk for Roy's Nutty Grainz and my custard, and since Honey's counsellor, Meeghan, advised her to avoid caffeine I'm no longer buying three different types of teabags, and I've just switched to Clipper organic decaf, tea and coffee.

'I didn't mention it to you because, well, I wanted to ease you into it, and then when you didn't notice I just thought I'd let sleeping dogs lie,' I tell him.

He just stares at me, open-mouthed, for a while. Then he calls me a poisoner and threatens to call the solicitor, but rings Grace instead.

I go and make some tea. 'I can't believe you rang Grace to grumble about me?' I say when the call's over.

'I wanted to know where I stood legally,' he says, 'and you're lucky I can't be arsed to sue.'

I'm reminded of a neighbour who took an action against his wife for not fixing their decking steps properly and causing him to twist an ankle; he was awarded an undisclosed amount from their home insurance. The pair had a holiday on the proceeds and spent most of the week in a hot tub. I stand my ground.

'For God's sake, Roy, I haven't fed you anything you don't ethically believe in,' I say.

But as always, it's my not being contrite that infuriates him and he strays from the specific 'You're a poisoner' to the more general 'You're a nut job' and then lands on other assorted crimes, culminating in the observation that I am the reason that Grace never comes to stay with us. 'She can't stand your yacking.'

'Not true,' I say. 'Grace doesn't come because she's busy and if it's anything else, it's that she can't stand your boorish behaviour.'

He shakes his head pitifully and laughs. 'Ring her up,' he says. 'Ask her.' And the way he says it sounds as though he's breaking a confidence. 'Remember the first time you met her?' he says. 'She begged you to put a sock in it – she was only four years old?'

'She was nearly five.'

'Four, five, whatever, a little kid having to block her ears,' says Roy, shocked at himself for being so rotten, but enjoying it. I don't retaliate. I lean on my knuckles and hope he'll leave the room which he does but continues on the way out, 'You drive people nuts – you never stop – yack, yack, yack.' He makes a quacking duck beak with his hand.

It's Honey having come back to live at home that has caused discord between Roy and me, just as it had when she was born. She and her friend Darnley, a research student at UofR, seem always to be here, lounging about, laughing and causing mild chaos. One minute baking, decorating and filming delightful-looking cakes. The next, making the most extraordinary and often disturbing art. Having her home, after years of calm and quiet, is an upheaval. I try to focus on the positives: she's in full-time employment, managing the Pineapple House café at the university (a job I fixed up for her), and though Roy calls it 'sh*tting on my own doorstep', the fact is she fits in really well; she looks like a student for a start, with holey tights, ironic patches ('*Fries before guys*') on her jacket, a grill on her teeth and so on, but being that bit older makes her something of a bellwether. It's Honey who has got the students all bringing in scraps for the hens and joining in with the caring wall, and switching to Oatly. She's blossoming under the UofR development scheme, attending marketing lectures and study modules.

Even with this godawful row going on between Roy and me, she's at the dining table compiling SWOT analyses of high-street retailers. 'Which would you invest in, Mum?' she asks, 'Googly-Eyes or Th\*\*\*ton's?'

'Well, Th\*\*\*ton's is a well-established chocolatier and Googly-Eyes is just two grubby women in a booth by the Corn Exchange!'

'No, Googly-Eyes are a lean and nimble outfit compared to Th\*\*\*ton's who are far too reliant on a handful of supermarket clients and therefore super-vulnerable and could go bust any minute,' she says.

I prefer Th\*\*\*ton's, vulnerable or not, because of the name Googly-Eyes, but I don't say so. Instead I say, 'You're a chip off the old block, Hun.' Hoping to engage Roy.

I pick up the phone and redial the last number. Grace answers. 'Hello, Grace, it's Susan,' I say. We chit-chat for a moment, she laughs about the vegan diet and then I say, 'I meant to grab the phone from Roy. I just wanted to ask whether you think your mum might like to give us a quote for a gala dinner at the uni next year.'

I don't actually need a quote from PardeePardee! as we'll almost definitely use Fletcher's. I've asked because I want to make Grace happy, and to irritate Roy.

'Oh, my gosh, yes, that would be amazing,' says Grace.

'It's not until March, and it'll be in a marquee,' I say, 'and we'll get a few quotes, so no guarantees.'

'Oh, Susan, that really would be great. Shall I get her to ring you?'

'Yes,' I say, 'get her to do that.'

We chat a bit more and I send love to her partner, Marcus.

'Thank you, Susan,' she says. 'Thank you *so* much for thinking of Mum.' There's real warmth in her voice.

I long to phone Norma and tell her this whole vegan saga. How she'd laugh. But I realize I haven't spoken to her properly since, oh my God, when? Buckingham Palace. And then I remember that the VC is leaving, and suddenly Roy suing me for turning him into a vegan seems like small potatoes.

## 26

'Ah, you've just missed Norma,' says the VC, which he does every Friday afternoon, as she studiously avoids the time of our weekly meeting. We always have tea and cake or easy peelers while we liaise diaries for the following week, and on sunny days we might sit in the garden – an oasis of loveliness, secretly tended by the head of Estates but credited to Norma. On this day however, the day after my visit to Dr Tang, in which she recommended hand cream and blurted out that the VC was leaving, we sit by the old log burner in his study and for something to say, as we cool our lapsang with gentle puffs before sipping, I update him on our Deputy VC's freak accident, which in retrospect seems like a colossal mistake – my mentioning it as well as his doing it.

'You remember Dr Junction did a roly-poly down a hill at a stately home?' I say. 'Well, it turns out he's split his liver in half.'

'Liver in half, good grief!' the VC cries, more horrified than I'd imagined – I'd had a day or two to get used to it. I reassure him that Dr Junction is doing as well as can be expected and that colleagues have clubbed together and sent him a book on fermentation techniques in food preservation (vis-à-vis his pickling hobby) but that he'll most likely be off work until Easter.

'We'd better send him a card. Can you, Susan, please?' he says.

'Already done. And an email to his partner.'

We sit in silence for a moment after that, the VC in a sort of daze. I gaze out of the window and make diverting observations, how funny it is, for instance, the way a single blade-shaped leaf might tremble or even thrash about unilaterally when others in the clump remain quite still, as if a naughty elf were out there making mischief. Getting no reply, I turn to see him staring at his phone calendar (how these men stare at their phones), scrolling forward, year by year, on and on, to the next and the next and the next. His index finger striking the screen with the insistent rhythm of a jazz percussionist.

'Professor?' I say quietly, and he comes to his senses and lets the phone clonk onto the desk and, finally, begins the run-up to the news that I already know but need to hear from him. It's worse than I'm expecting.

'Eddie Stobart's are on the brink of collapse,' he says.

'Roy thinks someone will step in.'

'Do you think so?'

'Yes, they'll be back in profit this time next year,' I say. 'It's just a cash-flow thing.'

Pause.

'Professor, are you going to tell me about your secondment?' I say.

He's surprised. 'Yes, but how do you know?'

'I just do.'

'Yes, well, I shall be taking a year out.' He tilts his chin up.

'What year?'

'Next year,' he says.

'Academic year 20/21,' I say.

'No, the calendar year from January.'

I sit up shocked. '2020?'

'Yes, 2020,' he says firmly. 'I wanted to tell you before it's official.'

'Who knows?' I ask.

'Only Norma and the Chair of Govs, so far.'

And the doctor, I think, but don't say.

He is to be seconded to DEFRA for post-Brexit planning, which is not to be sniffed at. No, I have to admit, this is a once-in-a-lifetime opportunity and it's only right that he should rise to the challenge and do his bit, especially in view of his recognition in recent honours.

Being among the first to know is always good for self-esteem. It means I'll be able to surprise selected colleagues with the news, and feign indifference or pride, depending on how the story unfolds. It being 'only a year' is small consolation though, knowing that a year can so easily stretch into two or three or four – like the time we fostered that cat for a biologist who went to Calgary, and the time Honey came home for a week at Christmas. Both are still with us. I have to face it, the VC might never come back, except as a distinguished guest or a portrait in oils. I say nothing, fearing I might let myself down and the VC makes one of his high-pitched, fake coughs and gently bridges his fingertips, imploring me to say something, and so, as always, I oblige.

'Well, crumbs, congrats, how exciting,' I say, and then we sit in silence drinking our tea.

I always imagined I'd start to like lapsang at some point, like one does with olives and stilton and at a push, fresh figs, but sadly I never have and probably shan't now the VC is going. What are the chances the next one will serve it? I wonder. Can you still get PG One Cup? Such a clever invention, ordinary teabags being too strong for a single mug but awkward to use for two because the first cup gets the strength, colour and caffeine while the second only gets the flavour, and all the dripping as you hook it out of the first cup and swing it into the next. I know because Roy used to do this and when I objected, started saving once-used bags for reuse. And I said to him, 'For God's sake, Roy, tea is all I have.' I think he took it on board.

The fire crackles in the grate, and the slight nasal whistle of the VC's irregular out-breaths interferes with the rhythm of the mantel clock, and then I can't help myself but say, '2020, of all years.' He puffs out his cheeks and nods slowly and I think he's going to cry.

The year 2020 is to be a gala one for the university, and for the town of Brankham itself; it's also significant personally for the VC and Norma, it being their fifth wedding anniversary in the March, and for me too as June will mark my eighteen years at the institution. Since I've done much of the planning and organizing of the gala already and always with Professor Willoughby in mind as host, I can't quite come to terms with the idea of anyone else, none of the Pro-VCs possessing the blend of charisma, modesty and grace required.

'I've managed to book the superior jazz band,' I say, 'but I suppose it's none of your concern now.'

I must sound forlorn for he goes upbeat: 'The gala will be a triumph, Susan, you'll see to it, and Dr Junction will be splendid in my place.'

'But Dr Junction won't be here,' I remind him. 'He split his liver in half, remember, he'll be off for months—'

'Indeed,' the VC interrupts, not wanting the details again. 'Yes, poor chap – well, whomever the governors recruit.'

'Dr Chandra, perhaps?' I say.

The VC pauses. 'Possibly,' he says.

'But if not Dr Chandra, then who?'

'Well, we may have a more qualified man – or woman – right under our noses,' he says.

As I leave through the back garden, I hear the VC whistling 'Happy Days Are Here Again!' which would have been upsetting except I know how relieved he will be, to have broken the news and that I've taken it on the chin, pretty much. Seeing a small mound of gravel beside the pond, I kick it sideways with enough force that much of it sploshes into the water, an act that could have seemed accidental should anyone be watching.

The VC's pond – the original one, that has been there since ponds were first fashionable – is a perfect and constant joy in my life: tadpoles in spring, pond skaters and dragonflies in summer, irises in the autumn, and now the crisp reflection of bare winter trees. The very existence of it always surprises me because one of the things I first noticed when I joined the university was the intellectual dismissal of animals and nature – that scholars acknowledge them only in ancient myth, or carved into frescoes, or in laboratories, or poems, or interspecies relationships, or languishing in mega-dairies. They ponder on why birds sing? what makes ants collaborate? how do salmons navigate? and what's going on with the elephant graveyards? But if you, yourself, admit to owning a living breathing pet, or mention a beloved dog from childhood, you're nothing more than a deluded fool. Especially the self-consciously arty ones, like Norma, who has only ever had an outdoor guard dog and can only countenance tadpoles and invertebrates, and even then only as a metaphor for change and because of an early fascination with and repugnance for frogspawn. Her own copycat front garden pond is a haven for frogs.

Maybe liking animals seems spoilt and entitled. After all, every Queen of England since Elizabeth I has loved and obsessed over animals. Horses, pigeons, birds of prey, corgis and the Loch Ness monster. But be fair, queens can trust animals; even the cleverest corgi in the world couldn't understand the sequential hierarchy of the Royal Family and so if a dog likes you best, it's pure, true love, not guile. I am the same (as those queens) in my fascination and wonder. Magic for me is seeing a deer in the wild or a snake zigzagging up a drystone wall, or a tiny wedge-shaped wren sideways on the trellis, just knowing there's a nest in a certain tree, and even a ladybird that could be mistaken for a lacquered cufflink – though one of these once temporarily paralysed a friend of Roy's when he allowed it to crawl across the back of his hand, to admire its iconic good looks, and it bit him.

Intellectuals will try to pull the rug out: for instance, they'll claim that your dog only likes you because you feed it. That it'd run off at the drop of a hat if someone better came along – say, a pack of dogs with plenty of obvious resources – and that guinea pigs don't give a damn about anything except staying alive.

And that *you* only like *them* because of Bambi's long eyelashes and that spaghetti scene in *Lady and the Tramp*, and because Disney's Robin Hood the fox was really good-looking.

I walk home, and the wind comes in great rolling clods as though bowled straight at me by a giant. I imagine hoardings coming loose and flying about, and some unfortunate person's life being ruined in a ridiculous accident, flattened by the Fletcher's Fine Foods billboard (which actually happened one time in chaotic weather), or knocked unconscious by a train door, or tumbling comically to your death under a bus, trousers round your ankles and your Y-fronts showing, poor Hugo. All in all, things aren't going well. I list my woes and realize the worst thing by far is not the VC leaving, nor poor old Dr Junction, nor the compromised centenary gala that I'm now going to have to plan without the VC at the helm, nor the marriage that neither Roy or I seem to care about one jot, nor my daughter's counsellor digging about in my psyche. It is that I kicked that gravel into the VC's pond. I am turning into a monster.

At home Roy is in the kitchen. 'Good day?' he asks, without looking up from his device, and I begin telling him; not about the VC's secondment, which I can't be bothered to hear myself explain, but about Dr Junction's roly-poly liver.

'Poor devil,' Roy says, wincing. It's the third time I've heard him called a poor devil in the space of an hour.

I arrange my tender stem broccoli and pak choi in a Waterford crystal vase, a wedding present from the Pavlous, and get the wok smoking.

## 27

The next morning I wake early to the familiar sensations of Roy's morning routine and I am cast immediately into a pit of despair – an overreaction, I admit, but I can't be blamed for what comes to me before consciousness. He takes long, deep in-breaths, the type that, if he were a woman, might indicate that something serious was about to be said, something funny and scandalous, that they've lost something you lent them. Soon, I know from the way the tension in the mattress shifts, he's holding the out-breath (two full minutes). It's not like holding an in-breath, it's harder and more panicky for the brain. We're accustomed to holding the in-breath; we've done it all our lives; timed it and swum like mad and broken the surface to exhale, but this is not allowing a breath in and you're holding empty lungs.

He'll time it on his device but I like to see if I can accurately count it. Towards the 100-seconds mark, he fights his urge to breathe, like someone trying not to cough at the theatre, or drown in an Italian lake in full view of party-goers on the shore, which actually happens, until it ends and he takes a great breath in (through the mouth) and goes limp, followed by a period of otherwise organized breathing – in through the nose and out through the mouth – and then some rhythmical leg and hip flexing that actually pre-dates Wim. And soon his feet are sliding up and down on the cotton sheet, up and down, up and down, with the timbral quality of a kazoo which sounds like laughter, but is also slightly worrying.

How would Dr Tang like this? I think, and I remember that she is enrolled onto our new part-time Life Writing course. It occurs to me that should she ever publish her memoir Roy and I might well find ourselves there, albeit unnamed, but with my quips and adverse drug reactions, and Roy's quest for longevity and tragus-pressing and hatred of veg, and it makes me wonder if Dr Z. Tang might be the nearest thing I have to a friend these days. What a thought! I see her six times a year at most – twice in her GP capacity and then in the quarterly governor meetings – and don't even know her first name, except that beginning with Z it's probably Zoe or Zara.

Waiting for Roy to finish his hip-swivels so I can tell him about the VC's secondment, I wonder if maybe I should go back to discuss the HRT further, and while I'm there, suggest coffee? But no. Dr Z. Tang wouldn't make a good friend. Her gossiping would be off-putting and her niceness unbearable, and you'd never know what she was really thinking which is what I dislike about nice people: having to wonder if they secretly despise you or feel bitterly jealous, or just think you common but want someone to go to the cinema with, or need help with their computer or for you to befriend their child. Is Roy the nearest thing I have to a friend? He's funny, or used to be, knows roughly what's going on in the world, and is so good with computers. Why am I wasting him?

Maybe a functioning professional relationship will always put a marriage in the shade? I mean, neither the VC nor I would dream of sticking our fingers in our ears, nor expect a mannered conversation in which you are supposed to wait for the other person to pause before speaking, interruption being a true sign of engagement. If he and I do a crossword together, we don't wait for the other to answer; if we know, we know, and we shout the answer.

Yes, the chatter can be pointless.

I might say, 'Monday morning again, Professor!'

And he might say, 'Ah, washing day!'

And I might recall my granny's old twin tub and he might say, 'Oh, golly, my grandmother had a mangle.'

I'd say, 'Argh! Terrifying things,' and we might marvel at the memory of the soapsuds, bubbles, soap flakes and scrubbing brushes of days gone by and their place in the comedy canon, and we'd just chirrup on: Daz, Fairy Snow, Omo. The VC's pride in Norma buying only the amphibian-friendly detergents might come out.

Then I might say, 'Quite right, good for her, she's always liked frogs.'

And he might add, 'She's very caring.'

And I might think, yes, about frogs.

The above meditation, however long it has been, say fifteen minutes, is the time it takes Roy to stretch and relax every muscle in his body and bring his frontal cortex to peak awareness and his brain to life. Now he's up out of bed and running on the spot. Then shrieking from the cold shower and at last downstairs, dressed in breathable utility clothing, with his vitamin D oral spray and a mix of cereals with additives and low-fat live yoghurt. It occurs to me this morning that if he's going to live to a hundred, he'll have forty more years of this and, as things stand, I'll have it the rest of my life. I join him downstairs; he's made me a cup of tea, as always, and I'm about to speak but recognizing the threat, Roy frowns so hard his eyebrows tremble. I cannot inflict a conversation on him now, I realize; he's just done his Wim Hof, I'd be ruining the vibe. I point to a squirrel on the bird nuts instead.

'Look,' I say.

I've taken the first steps to improving the marriage, by not speaking. I feel quite satisfied and proud, and think, gosh, how easy, and just wish there was someone I could tell.

# 28

I have booked tickets for *The Favourite* which is showing at Tuesday film club and have a feeling that things are on the right track. But then, on the Monday morning, Michael from Estates emails asking me to meet him in his office, and everything isn't OK.

Security cameras have picked up footage of Honey on campus.

'Obviously, I shouldn't really be showing you this,' says Michael as he clicks, drags and enlarges a section of the screen. 'But that's your girl, isn't it, the one with the blue hair in the golf-club hoodie?'

I laugh. 'She wears it ironically,' I say. There is Honey with a group of students, smiling and huddled together under the eaves at the side of the café. 'Yes, that's Honey,' I agree, rather pleased that Michael has recognized her, and even more pleased that she seems to have some friends, smiling and huddled.

It has been easy to underestimate her recently; her self-consciousness and wilful incoherence making her seem less intelligent than she is, and her world view, which can seem naive, being so clear-sighted and often absolutely right in the long run. Where I see a painting of a pretty girl in a toga trailing her foot in the water, Honey sees a prisoner with no escape: 'Look, there's no way out, just a wall.' Where I see a landscape with a man and wife and their dog, Honey sees the patriarchy, discrepancy and sadness with a hint of hunting. She can no longer love the books that gave her so much joy in childhood because the living author is on the wrong side of history. On the other hand, she rails against the oddest things and, I'm afraid, sometimes makes a fool of herself. She once called a radio phone-in and after convincing the researcher she had a bona-fide question about pruning fruit trees, told a panel of celebrity horticulturalists, on air, that bonsai was cruel to plants, and burst into tears.

'I've really agonized over it, Sue,' says Michael, 'but in the end, I had to say something, you being on the safeguarding committee and everything.'

'What do you mean?' I ask.

'She's selling drugs, Sue. Her dealer name is "Miss Honeypenny" and I've been tracking her. I'm sorry, as I say, really agonized.'

'No, of course, yes, absolutely,' I say. 'I'll speak to her and put a stop to it straight away – I mean, not that I was aware of it, obviously.'

Michael is very kind indeed. 'I've really agonized over it,' he says for the third and final time, and that's a huge part of the episode – Michael's sensitivity, his caring about me, albeit calling me Sue, which, as you know, is not my preferred name. I'm like Susan Sontag in that respect.

'No, of course, of course,' I say again. 'Does anyone else know?'

'No,' says Michael. 'And I'll delete this footage, but you've got to swear you'll never say anything, Sue, and you'll speak to her, and – you know what I mean – tell her she can't be doing that, not on campus. I mean, I can only turn a blind eye once, and only because she's your kid, Sue.'

'Yes, of course, I will, and thank you, Michael, thank you so much, I'm so grateful for your kindness.'

Honey is not the druggy type, let me make that clear. She enjoys her food, for goodness' sake, she goes to bed early, she has no friends apart from Darnley, and they bake cakes and watch cartoons, and I'm certain she doesn't take drugs. I'd know, wouldn't I? Walking home after work, I decide I'll take the softly-softly approach, bide my time and be pragmatic. I will not raise it straight away, I'll wait until we're out together, when she's more likely to want to discuss it. Certainly not before Cheltenham with the VC and our trip to Gustav Holst's house. I'll snoop and look for signs, and then tell Honey the game is up and she'll be relieved and glad to stop, it all having been a silly mistake, and she'll see the error of her ways. I'll make absolutely sure she knows how much I love her and how brilliant she is at marketing, because she is. I definitely won't tell Roy.

The moment I step through the door, though, and take in my home's particular aroma – dog, cherry vape, coconut hair products, coffee, Honey's trainers – I need it off my chest, and go straight upstairs, in my shoes, scrabble my fingertips on Honey's door and go in without waiting.

'Hi, hi, how are you?' I ask.

'Fine, wow, what's the matter?' she says. She's lying

diagonally across her bed, straddling her comfort maggot and watching an American sitcom from the 1990s that I literally can't bear, and tapping on her phone.

'Look, I know it's probably just a silly mistake, Hun, but . . . the security people, well, Michael Pascoe from Estates has got some webcam footage that looks a bit funny.'

'Funny?'

'Suspicious,' I say.

'In what way?' Honey continues tapping the screen of her phone with two thumbs.

'They think it looks a bit like you're dealing drugs.' I droop. 'Ugh, I know it's ridiculous.'

'Oh my God, is this for real?' says a voice, but not Honey's.

'Wait, hang on, Darn, I'll call you back,' says Honey, and I realize they're FaceTiming or whatever. 'Breathe, motherfucker!' she says, which is their way of saying goodbye, and comes from the Wim Hof Method. I don't like her mocking her father like this, except privately to me, and I frown hard.

'Yeah, harsh. OK.' I peer at the iPhone and see Darnley gurning.

'Hi, there' I say, and Darnley starts to say, 'Breathe, motherfuck—' but freezes, eyes half-closed as if ecstatic, and is gone.

'So what was that guy saying?' says Honey.

'Well, that guy, you mean Michael – your boss, Michael Pascoe from Estates – has asked me to ask you to stop dealing drugs on campus.' I say it slowly and calmly.

Honey tuts. 'Yeah, Michael, but what does he say?'

'He's not going to say anything for now, but only if you stop, otherwise we might be raided.'

Honey laughs. 'What?'

'The university might be raided.'

'What, for swapping meds with some third years, seriously?'

'And actually, I want to know what's going on. I mean, is it a mistake, or what?'

She makes a little shrug, burps politely with her hand to her mouth, nails so long, polish so chipped, cuticles so bitten and sore, and silver rings buried in her chubby little fingers so horribly oxidized.

'You're not a drug dealer are you, Hun?' I ask. 'Please tell me you're not.'

'I am a bit though, not gonna lie,' she says. 'Everyone is.'

'Well, can you stop doing it in our workplace, please.'

'Yeah, no, OK, fair enough.' Honey taps her screen.

The next day I drive the VC to Cheltenham and home again. I'm preoccupied with the question of where I might have gone wrong as a parent, and my mind lands on a memory from a couple of years previously when Grace (qualified in law now and living with kind-hearted Marcus) said they were planning to call their firstborn child Barney.

Hearing this, Honey sniffed and said, 'I'm calling mine Kult.'

And my response, 'But what if it's a boy?' had Honey rolling about under her weighted blanket, laughing at me, and at Grace, future Barney and the whole world, it seemed.

I do my best to think of something interesting to say to the VC and dredge up from the far recesses of my memory that he is preparing a presentation on 'The Global Transportation of Meat' or some such grim thing, and though I have no interest in the subject, mention an article on container ships I've seen recently in Roy's *Economist*, describing particularly the diagrams and photographs that illustrate the size of these things.

'I mean, a thousand times the size of a double-decker bus, bigger than a whole village, literally huge,' I say. 'Talk about unattractive and un-shiplike and monstrous – great big rectangles of *stuff*.' I pause then, to let him contribute, and glancing in the rear-view see he's fast asleep.

# 29

The VC's secondment has been announced officially this morning. I've already told Joyce Ho myself, which felt like a bit of a coup to be honest, her being the head of Human Resources and us always slightly vying.

'Do we know who'll step up to acting VC?' I asked her, disingenuous.

'What are you talking about, when?' she'd said.

'Oh, sorry, don't you know?' I said. 'Professor Willoughby is having a year at DEFRA for post-Brexit planning.'

'Oh, Christ, no, really, what year?' She was pink in the face.

'Calendar year 2020,' I said breezily, as if I didn't have any feelings about the news either way. She rushed off, baggy court shoes dripping off her heels.

'Well, we may have a more qualified man – or woman – right under our noses.'

It's been over a week since the official announcement and now that everyone knows the VC is going a gloomy atmosphere prevails, not helped by the news of Dr Junction, because of course it should be him stepping up, and he'd have been a jolly good acting Vice Chancellor, but it's not to be; he's on an Ensure diet and unable to move very far from his recliner. I've been having catastrophic dreams in which I interrupt Roy's breathing exercises, pull the plug on his apnoea machine, and come face to face with Dolly Parton without a wig. While awake, I've not been able to stop wondering: if not Dr Chandra, then who? The other obvious candidates are Professor Jennings (science and scientific perceptions). It can't be her though as she's about to go on maternity leave and the twins aren't even due until February, so no chance of her returning to host a gala event in March however much she might love to. And Professor Leopold (sociology) whom I dislike for a number of reasons as I'm sure you'll recall. It wouldn't be him surely, how could it be? I mean, how ghastly if, when invited to take a companion to an event or dinner, he took the current VC's *actual* wife – how awkward and embarrassing, we'd be a laughing stock with Leicester, Nottingham and De Montfort.

So I'm assuming it'll be Chandra. He held a senior management post at De Montfort prior to moving to us and has published an impressive number of peer-reviewed articles. One publication that we hold in multiples in the library is an edited collection about vehicular visibility, entitled *Windows on the Move: From airline to spacecraft*, in which his own chapter concerns aeroplane construction (atmospheric pressure change, perimeter seal, desiccants). I read this through quickly and found his style a bit long-winded but was able to appreciate the main point: windows on aeroplanes must be firmly in place and double-glazed and must not fog up because this could compromise safety and passenger experience. I drifted a bit on some passages and ended up recalling a time I'd spent an entire flight to Spain watching beads of condensation trapped between the double-glazed cabin window dance about, join and separate, run terrified to the bottom corner and then shimmy upwards in a line and so forth, and how mesmerizing it was and how mood-altering. It was a bad start to a holiday.

But then I run into him and see the fear in his eyes and remember just how lacking in charisma he is (the VC himself has hinted as much). That said, I've read enough on vehicular windows to enable me to chat intelligently, should the need arise.

But what did the VC mean, 'more qualified man – or woman'?

Ruling out Leopold and Jennings, could the 'more qualified man – or woman – right under our noses' comment have been a tactic to stop people scrambling for Dr Chandra's affections? Because if not Chandra, it left only a ragtag bunch of lecturers who wouldn't have a clue how to take the helm. You see, this has been going round and round in my head.

And there's also the question of what Norma intends to do while her husband lives in London Monday to Friday (aiming to come home most weekends). Michael Pascoe has been asked to look after the cottage garden and keep an eye on the place if necessary, but no one knows her plans. My guess: she'll be like Melania Trump and just stay put, and we'll be seeing a lot of Professor Leopold dashing up the garden path with carrier bags full of alcohol and sex toys. I sincerely hope this turns out not to be the case.

During the lunch break before the next VC's Friday planning meeting I sit in the car, it being a private space where I can have my salad and few sips of custard in peace and not have anyone bothering me for an update on the VC situation. I ring for an appointment with Dr Tang, to discuss HRT. While on hold, it strikes me to wonder: am I the more qualified man – or woman – right under our noses? Could I step up to acting VC? In practical terms there is no doubt I could do the job blindfolded – the VC will know that – but ceremonially, I have no letters to my name other than certificates from the Institute of Advanced Motorists and St John's Ambulance; although my recent reading of *Coming Up Trumps*, the memoir of Baroness Trumpington who literally went from heating up fish fingers to flicking the Vs at the House of Lords just by having guts and a deep voice, has given me ideas. I should at least offer to job-share with Dr Chandra? Or maybe suggest that the VC continue nominally in the role with me his right-hand woman, on the ground.

I cut Vivaldi off before speaking to anyone at the surgery, stride to the Gate House, and in a change to usual procedure, knock with the knocker. I'm early but, as always, the VC has prepared a tray of tea, and I let him burble awkwardly on the subject of Westminster's relationship with the dairy farmer, and the supermarket stranglehold, while I pour two cups and wait for his whole attention before bringing up my thoughts on his successor; but when the time comes I find I can only talk about practicalities for the week ahead and, to finish, bring him up to speed on Dr Junction's liver. I am about to put on my coat when he clears his throat and raises the subject himself.

'We've a significant downturn in student applications and the dropout numbers are very concerning,' he says, 'and so this means that whoever steps up will have to attend to the problem as a matter of urgency ... and unfortunately Dr Chandra has ruled himself out, because of publishing commitments. The governors are very concerned and in fact, last night, they called a special meeting and the upshot is they have appointed an acting VC to get cracking straight away.'

'Appointed someone?' I say. 'Who?'

'They have appointed Norma.'

'*Norma?*'

'Norma Pack-Allen,' he says, in case I might think he means Norma Nagel from accounts.

'Norma,' I say again.

'Yes, she has agreed to take it on.'

Before I know it, the meeting's over. I'm leaving the Gate House, and without even glancing at the pond, I walk home across the campus. Roy is in the lounge, practising putting.

'All right?' he says, without looking up. A golf ball rolls slowly into a paper cup and he punches the air.

'No,' I say. 'Norma has got the VC job.'

'Oh, heavy shit,' he says and stands upright. 'Are you going to have to drive her about and clean her specs for her?'

I shrug, and not wanting further discussion, go upstairs and shower. Afterwards, I Google 'Norma Pack-Allen/ images' and there she is, very lightly airbrushed, resting her chin on her knuckles, with a more formal shot of her in spectacles in an article about cuts to arts funding and another about culture and the mental-health time bomb. There she is on her wedding day (to Professor Willoughby) in the Catherine Deneuve dress and it looks baggy. I search my phone for the photograph of me in that same dress and I look better in it. It fits me. It's actually the nicest I've ever looked.

I go back to Google and read a short biography detailing her rise through the ranks of the arts sector, with commendations for her work abroad (especially that of inspiring word art in the inner cities). I discover nothing new except that her interests apparently include aquaponics and scuba diving. I watch a YouTube video showing her in a wetsuit and breathing apparatus, with others, all surrounding a giant tuna fish and giving each other the thumbs-up. I remember our trips to the pool for fitness swims, and that she never once put her head under. I wonder if I've ever really known her.

Roy calls me down. We've started watching films together every Friday night, taking turns to choose. The previous week, I chose *The Phantom Thread* which I'd been longing to see for all the haute couture, tiny waists and invisible stitches, but frankly there wasn't enough of that and Roy said it was mostly a show reel for Daniel Day-Lewis's hair. Tonight it's Roy's pick and I must admit I quite enjoy the opening scenes of *Lawrence of Arabia* which he considers a masterpiece, but soon I can't bear the augmented blueness of Peter O'Toole's eyes and the constant assault on the camels. I mean, Lawrence never stops whacking his and shouting, 'Hut! hut! hut!' Roy agrees, it is a bit much, and tells me that during the charge on Aqaba in real life, Lawrence had become so frenzied he accidentally shot his camel in the head. We pause the film and have tea.

Roy pulls me in close and I say, 'Yes, I will have to drive Norma about.'

'You'll get used to it, love, but, yeah, it's a rum do.'


First thing Monday morning, I spy Joyce Ho through the window of the Pineapple House, so I nip in and get myself a peppermint tea, and on the way out, go over to her table. She brings up the subject in hushed tones.

'I suppose you've heard?' she says, with raised eyebrows.

'Yes,' I say, looking about.

'Odd choice, don't you think?' says Joyce.

'Well, she's had no experience at that level representing the institution, but I suppose she'll pick it up as she goes along.' I'm shrugging so hard my shoulders ache.

'Beggars can't be choosers, apparently . . .' Joyce opens her eyes very wide and I can see much mascara clumping and swollen lids. 'Chandra dropped out, bloody wimp, Jennings is out with twins, Junction is on long-term sick leave, heart attack, and that leaves only Leopold or Triggs and they're both –' she pauses, picking up her tea, and says out of the side of her mouth – 'friendly with the VC's wife.' She takes a long sip and sighs.

'It's actually his liver,' I say. 'Dr Junction, he's off with his liver.'

## 30

Darnley arrives to stay for the weekend but doesn't want to eat with us even though I've done tuna pasta bake especially. After Roy has spooned himself a large helping, Honey takes the rest up to the bedroom. 'Darnley's been struggling with an eating-type thing,' she whispers on the way upstairs, with pasta, two forks and a bottle of Diet Coke, using the waistband of her sweater as an oven glove.

Darnley is still with us a few days later and starts joining us for meals, which feels rather nice, though Honey announces that Darnley would rather we didn't have tuna again – it makes their teeth squeak – and then reminds us that Darnley's pronouns are 'they/them'. I expect Roy to find this difficult but he is surprisingly relaxed, only staring at Darnley in a bewildered way for a few moments before saying to Honey, 'I thought you were vegan?'

'I am except for tuna,' she replies.

Over dinner one evening Honey and Darnley discuss a proposed a life swap (part of Darnley's thesis) which will entail filming themselves living in each other's parental home for a week, alone. I'm keen to know which way round seems the most absurd.

'Will your parents get along with Honey OK?' I ask.

Darnley and Honey roar at the idea of this and talk

excitedly – about why it would be hilarious – with their mouths full.

'Oh my God, though, the thought of my dad with Honey.' Darnley's eyes open wide and Honey fans herself and feigns choking.

After pudding, Darnley shows us, all three of us, their most recent art project: an eight-minute film montage of people struggling in sinking sand, plus a clip at the end which features a close-up of their parents' faces as Darnley tells them some important personal news (we do not discover what exactly the news is).

The mother's head and torso fill the screen, she nods gently for some time, and then says, 'You what, love?' and you can see where her spectacles have dented the bridge of her nose.

And then the father leans in and says, 'Have you fallen behind with your rent, Heather?'

This seems hysterical to Darnley and Honey but I'm not sure what's going on, and I daren't laugh in case anyone involved is about to cry, and in the end my own eyes well up.

Darnley looks at me and says, 'I know, right?'

'Darnley got an A plus for that,' says Honey with pride.

'I'm not surprised,' I say, dabbing under my specs, 'it's very poignant.'

'Remember when we were video-calling and your mum came at you like, "Stop dealing at uni",' Darnley laughs.

'Stop WHAT?' says Roy.

'Don't worry,' says Honey, 'it was only mushrooms.' And she changes the subject. 'By the way, Dad, what was your old name, before you switched to Roy? Wasn't it something like Heather?'

'No, it was Hector.' Roy is self-conscious but smiling.

Honey nods slowly. 'Oh, yeah, *Hector*.' She and Darnley exchange a look.

'What's so funny?' I ask, unhappy at them laughing at Roy's discarded name.

'We're not laughing, Mum.'

'It's just that mine was *Heather*,' says Darnley quietly. 'You know, and it's quite similar – Hect-or, Heth-er.'

'Darnley was Heather at Rossington Comp,' says Honey.

'Oh, I see – and did you know each other back then?' I ask.

'Mum, Darnley was up against me for Head Girl,' says Honey, with much drama.

'Yes,' says Darnley. 'Oh my God, remember?'

'Were you friends?' I ask.

'NO!' says Darnley. 'Honey was a little freak, she should never have got Head Girl.'

'Ugh,' says Honey, 'you were so stuck up.'

'You borrowed my Tupperware cake transporter and never gave it back,' says Darnley.

Honey laughs hard.

'Oh, is that yours? I didn't realize,' I say. 'We've still got it.'

'It's fine, no worries.'

'You can have it back.'

'No, really,' says Darnley, hands in the air, laughing.

'Where did the name Darnley come from?' I ask. 'It's very . . . catchy.'

'He was a husband of Mary Queen of Scots,' says Honey.

'Oh, yes, the Duke of Albany – didn't he push Lord Bothwell down the stairs?' I ask.

'No, Darnley was pushed,' says Darnley. 'Bothwell did the pushing.'

'Bad luck,' says Roy.

'Doesn't the name Roy mean King?' says Darnley.

'Yes,' says Roy quietly.

'You remember serving Mum in the Apple shop,' says Honey, 'don't you, Darn?'

'Oh, golly,' I say, 'I hope I didn't show myself up.'

'No, not at all,' says Darnley, 'not really.'

Honey defends me. 'Mum's always nice. She wants everyone to like her, it's her thing.'

Roy nods. 'True.'

Darnley nods too. 'Yeah, I liked her.'

I feel unaccountably happy and hope Meeghan the counsellor has heard this analysis.

I try to place Darnley in the secondary-school years and picture them, back then. 'Is it your mother who had a corgi, Darnley?'

'No. She doesn't drive.'

'She means a dog, Darn,' says Honey.

We all laugh except Roy who hasn't quite followed, and it goes along like that. Me laughing at Roy with the two young ones, and then laughing at the two young ones with Roy. But kindly, and it's much like being a referee in a friendly game, amusing but exhausting, and the young ones, who are actually both twenty-eight, seeming like eighteen. Darnley leaves the room to have a private call with their parents and Honey smiles at Roy and gives me a kiss on the cheek.

It looks like Darnley will be staying a while, which suits me, them being a true scholar and yet so modern in their ways; able to talk about William Blake having pretended to be a chimney sweep, or Kate Winslet's refusal to read a single Iris Murdoch novel before depicting her in the biopic *Iris*. Apropos of nothing, they might suddenly say, 'Poor Keats, died at twenty-five after bad reviews, and that bully Byron was behind it, you know?' As if it has all been in the news that week, and then make us all feel better with the revelation that Keats was contacted in a seance at Oxford, where someone present was able to tell him, 'Nobody reads Byron nowadays, he only has a few cheap streets named after him. It's you, John Keats, whom we turn to for truth and beauty and all we need to know on earth.'

It turns out, to my slight annoyance, that Darnley is a huge fan of Norma, or 'NPA' as the students call her.

'She's a legend,' says Darnley.

'Oh,' I say, 'is she your personal tutor?'

'Nah, but we're really tight, she gets me, you know?'

'Mum and Norma are best buds,' says Honey.

'OMG, seriously?' says Darnley.

'Yes, we go back years,' I say.

'Cool,' says Darnley, 'she's amazing.'

'You ought to tell her about the Keats seance,' I say. 'She'd be intrigued, I'm sure.'

'It was her who told me!' Darnley laughs.

Later, I text Norma to say we have Darnley staying. I do this partly to make real the claims of our friendship, partly to pass on the compliments, but mostly to boost Honey in Norma's estimation. Norma replies, saying Darnley is 'a total marvel'.

I agree and quote Darnley's observation that we must all love each other or die.

Norma doesn't reply.

# 31

I'm to say a few words at the VC's farewell drinks and realize with something of a shock that it'll be my first speech. I didn't even speak at my own wedding even though I was a feminist. I'd had a few sentences ready (memorized) but the master of ceremonies, Roy's brother Guy, had gone from applauding the best man, Roy's colleague Leroy, to introducing the father of the bride. He spoke at length about cricket and said what a fine pair of batsmen Roy and I were, and that he'd always hoped I'd find a partner who'd stretch me but not run me out, etc. and then said, 'Actually, I'll stop using this metaphor because as far as I know, Susan has never lifted a cricket bat.' And then he proposed a toast and, before I could get to my feet, the cake appeared, and we were to cut it quickly before the photographer left the venue for another job at the town hall photographing a balloon-modelling festival. So the bridesmaids, my cousin Timandra and Norma Pavlou (as was), were not officially thanked and I had to give them the specially chosen swan brooches, that I would have referenced in my speech, privately in the toilets afterwards, and though Timandra hadn't minded at all, Norma had seemed downcast at not being publicly acknowledged.

'They missed you out,' she said bitterly, and I thought it a bad omen, but shrugged it off.

Now I experiment with different styles, but my speech will keep sounding as though I am the VC's manager, or that it will be *me* taking over from him, which of course makes complete sense but can never be. While making notes, I recall and dwell on an excruciating moment from a few days previously. We'd arrived for a carol service at the cathedral, not quite early enough for a game of chess and, for something to occupy his mind, the VC picked up the novel I had stowed in the glove compartment. Usually I'd be delighted by this, keen for a book discussion, but not on this occasion. Not that the book is junk, far from it (it won the Guardian First Novel Award, that accolade being the thing that had initially drawn me to it), and I was very much enjoying it and, as they say, 'couldn't put it down'. Anyway, I watched the VC read the cover blurb, and then open it at the places I'd dog-eared, and saw him involuntarily flinch, and a look of mild terror in his expression. I have to assume he was reading, 'I want to fuck you till your ears drop off.' There are other words on the page but that sentence, I happen to know, is on a right-hand page, surrounded by white space, and positioned exactly where a reader's eye first lands in search of meaning. I wonder now whether this is accidental or intended for moments just like this one.

'It's a Lucy Ellmann,' I said, taking it gently from his hands.

Since then, I've begun to see his departure as a kind of release. Freedom from the obligation to collude with his niceness and his rose-tinted view, from worrying about his teeth, bowel and lumbar region, his awful written grammar and his missing the point in almost every speech we attend, along with his frustrating obliviousness to the brutal spikes in his wife's poetry. It was similar in the days leading up to Honey's departure for university, when I'd suddenly taken hold of myself and said, 'Enough of weeping and tears – you will no longer have to see cake at the breakfast table, and biscuits for lunch, and Pringles after dinner, and if she insists on swaddling herself in fleece and hunching in front of a screen every single evening, it'll be out of your sight.' In other words, my brain had managed to see a silver lining around that most gloomy of clouds.

I strike through my notes so far and begin again.

Later, I read it to Honey. 'OMG, Mum, you two sound so cute together.'

'Yes,' I say, 'we were.'

I email the speech to Joyce Ho – everything has to be run past her in case of impropriety, like the time Professor Leopold announced Norma Pack-Allen's shortlisting for the 2017 Kono Poetry Prize that hadn't been officially announced, and the only way he could possibly have known being via Norma herself. Joyce replies immediately, checking that the VC will be OK with the line, 'Don't come back until you've sorted out Brexit.' I assure her he'll love it.

The next day, I arrive at the Pineapple House twenty minutes early, and while loitering by the bookshelves have a chance to leaf through recent staff publications including another of Dr Chandra's, this time on the subject of plexiglas and volatility. I don't look at the notes for my speech as I have it memorized to the extent that I can say it straight off, as if it were all just coming to me as I stood there. Colleagues begin to amble in, take a glass of something and stand around talking; mainly academic staff and a few PhD students whom Professor Willoughby has up to now supervised, along with reporters from the *Leicester Mercury* and *Harborough Bugle*. That damned Pete Dwight is here too, the journalist from the *FT* who gave the VC a bad review. I'm just wondering what the heck he's doing here when he ambles up and introduces himself.

'Do you live locally?' I ask.

And he answers, 'Yes.'

Honey is here, wearing a crisp white blouse, in quite a senior role, making sure the students from Hospitality & Catering are circulating with trays of food and drink. 'Miss Honeypenny' is gone for ever – she's given Michael her word, and he's given her extra responsibility to show his faith in her.

Joyce appears in the distance, tall on account of her heels, and spotting me, throws her hands in the air and staggers in my direction.

'Oh, good, Susan,' she says, 'I need a word.'

And then, lowering her voice, she tells me that, regarding the speech, actually, Dr Pack-Allen is going to say a few words about the VC, 'To wish him well and so on.'

'OK,' I say, 'mine's only about two minutes, if I talk quickly.'

'No, Susan, no, Dr Pack-Allen is going to speak *instead* of you,' says Joyce, 'not as well as.'

'Oh.'

'I know it'll be a relief, and thanks so much for sending yours over last night, it was a jolly good read.'

'Wait,' I say, 'it wasn't inappropriate, was it?'

'Gosh, no, it's not that, it was great, I forwarded it to Dr Pack-Allen for ideas,' she says. 'But you know how the academics get twitchy if they're not up front, doing the blather.'

Just then Fred Fletcher, Chair of Governors, taps his wine glass with a biro. You might recall that Fred is the former captain, chairman and mainstay of the golf club – where Roy has worked all of his adult life – and proprietor of Fletcher's Fine Foods. 'Hello,' says Fred, 'if I can just get everyone's attention,' and the conversation fades. 'Good evening, and thank you, thank you all for coming. Now, I think Susan Faye Warren would like to say a few words about the Vice Chancellor.'

But Joyce Ho rushes forward: 'Sorry, sorry, change of plan, Fred, actually Norma Pack-Allen is going to say the words.'

And so Norma steps up and faces the room, clutching a sheet of paper and wearing an ill-fitting Evangeline dress in jade with a lace collar – I know the pattern well. She's cut it for a 14, which is at least one size too big. The adage about dressing well pops into my head, and I think it through a few times until I have it right. 'Dress shabbily and they will remember the dress, dress impeccably and they will remember the woman.' And I probably wouldn't have remembered her speech at all except it is my speech, the one I'd learned by heart, and she has it practically verbatim, and it's the oddest thing, because only someone who'd travelled the highways and byways of the English Midlands with the Vice Chancellor, stopped for refreshments, played chess to calm his nerves and switched him to sugar-free Smints to safeguard his bridgework, could have written that speech, and even though she's his wife, she can't claim that. I gaze about at the smiling, half-listening audience. I look at the VC, who is staring at the backs of his hands, probably running his own few words over in his mind. 'So, bon voyage and good luck, Professor Willoughby,' says Norma. 'Don't come back until you've sorted out Brexit.' Here she blows a kiss his way and does a kind of curtsy.

'Bon voyage!' she calls out again and swoops her empty tumbler into the air. The audience clap, laugh, raise their glasses and repeat, 'Bon voyage!'

There's a lull and a pause before the VC steps up, and during that time, I text Roy: Joyce asked Norma to speak instead of me (sad face).

Roy replies with a single, pluralized, word that I shan't repeat.

Now Professor Willoughby is centre stage, smiling modestly. He thanks the Board of Governors and his wife for encouraging him to take up the opportunity to work with government, and then thanks a few individuals, including Joyce and me, and finally says, 'Most of all, I'd like to thank Norma for agreeing to step up and hold the fort, and for her supportive words just now.'

'Written by Susan Faye Warren though,' says Honey, audibly, without missing a beat. Everyone turns to look at Honey and then I feel their eyes on me.

## 32

Norma has requested a meeting in the Two Swans café. I'm surprised at first and then curious. Maybe this bad news is actually good news in disguise. I get there early. The Two Swans has in fact been a Caffè Nero for at least five years now, but old-timers still call it by its original name. They've replaced the romantic swan mural with a blurry photograph of stereotypical elderly Italian men with no teeth, laughing over their coffee and backgammon, and, on the back wall, where there was previously a map of the Grand Union Canal, there's a giant Magic Eye poster, which to me looks like a lot of tiny rust-coloured dots. No one, and I mean, *no one*, can see the hidden image, except for Honey who has described it to me in great detail. I think about this as I wait for Norma, about Honey's perception, the way she sees things that can at first seem worrying, or neurotic, but almost always prove truer vision – and then I remember her glasses.

I knew Honey squinted a bit and even pulled her eyelids to narrow the aperture when looking at the television, but she was young and neither Roy nor I wore glasses, so I ignored it. Eventually, because Norma mentioned it, I took her to Specsavers and hey presto, she was terribly short-sighted.

'Do I need glasses?' she asked after the examination.

'No, I shouldn't think so,' I said.

And the optician said, 'Er, yes, actually.'

And I said, 'Really?'

And she said, 'Very much so.'

And Honey said, 'I told you, Mum.'

But then, downstairs in the spectacle showroom where they had a section for young customers, she was quite anxious. While she tried various frames I entertained her with the tale of my Aunt Bernardine who had put her own spectacles on her dog (Jojo) to take a funny polaroid to send my second cousin who although quite posh was in jail for fraud. She could tell in that instant that Jojo could suddenly SEE because he looked about the place, surprised by his surroundings, and even barked at the furniture. She let him wear her spare pair as often as possible after that. And far from worrying about the names she might be called at school for wearing glasses, Honey wondered with me what it must be like for a beagle to suddenly see a nest of mahogany tables and van Gogh's *Sunflowers*. Because it might be rather like that for her. That was how I put it anyway.

Soon afterwards we collected Honey's tiny purple-rimmed specs, and she was thrilled to see the giant ice-cream cone outside the Two Swans.

'I always thought that was a litter bin,' she said.

At home, though, seeing Honey in the glasses, Roy began to cry.

'She's not dying,' I hissed at him later, 'she's short-sighted, that's all.'

He then accused me of having Munchausen's syndrome

by proxy. Or maybe not by proxy. Whatever way, the point is, it was easier for him to imagine I had Munchausen's than that his daughter had less than 20/20 vision. I was surprised and disheartened by his response and called him whatever we said for 'ableist' back then. Honey liked her specs and looked after them incredibly carefully for a seven-year-old, always putting them into the little case at bedtime in a most grown-up manner. I used to look at her in those days, her great mounds of hair, the smooth skin, thick black lashes and over-sized tear ducts. Why were her tear ducts so big, so open? How could she not become an MP or surgeon or writer in those tiny spectacles, wiping them with the glass cloth, her little sleeves rolled up for business, swallowing her saliva before speaking? She was a serious contender for life.

Roy made her take them off for photographs, and then, in Year 10, he took her to Granby & Wise to choose a nicer pair, and soon she had frameless, with non-reflective coating, barely there, that made her look like a Swedish football manager. She was immediately appointed Head Girl for Year 11.

I snap out of this reverie when Norma bustles in. She's wearing ill-fitting culottes that she's made herself, a size too big in over-pressed linen.

'Congratulations on the appointment,' I say as she drags a chair out and plonks herself down.

'You've already congratulated me, but thank you,' she laughs. 'Mind you, I don't suppose anyone else wanted it once we'd had the application and dropout stats.'

'No,' I say, meaning, of course other people wanted it.

'So, Susan,' she says, 'we find ourselves thrown together again.'

'Yes,' I laugh. She's taken on a new, formal way of talking and this unnerves me slightly.

I consider telling her about 'I want to fuck you till your ears drop off' but decide she's probably not in the mood.

'The thing is, I was reading recently about the advent of the motor car,' she says. 'You know, a hundred years or so ago, the effect on the working man's psyche, the difficulty they had making the transition from an actual living breathing horse to a metal machine.'

'Yes, I can imagine.'

'In particular, the grooms and stable boys,' she goes on, frowning, concerned, 'found it almost impossible to change their habits, with the new technology.'

'Oh, right?' I say, nodding in agreement.

'The master would arrive home in the motor car and leave it at the front to be dealt with – put away in the garage, wiped over, whatever – and the poor grooms would feel compelled to rub it down with hay and throw a blanket over it, ha, as if it were a weary animal.'

'Oh, how poignant.'

'Yes, charming,' she says. 'I'm mentioning it because it occurred to me that it might be a bit like this for you when Crispin – Professor Willoughby – goes and I step up into his place.'

I tilt my head.

'I mean,' she says, 'because I won't be like him, and I hope that won't be too much of an upheaval or disappointment to you.'

'You won't need hay and a blanket?'

'Precisely,' she says, picking up her coffee cup. 'I won't need hay or blankets, or any fuss.'

We sip our coffee and she squints past me at the Magic Eye behind. Her lips and eyelids move very slightly while she tries to find the image.

'When you say "blanket" what exactly do you mean?' I know what she's saying but I want her to elaborate.

'I mean, simply, I shan't want much looking after,' she says, 'unlike my husband.'

'In what way?'

'I'll be more independent.'

'So I'll just drive.'

'I mean, really, I won't need you to check my teeth for sesame seeds,' she continues, 'or to offer me a piece of thread from your blouse to floss in the cloakroom. I shan't want to play chess, and, because I intend to work during car journeys, I shall probably not want to chat, and I shall never need your thoughts on, for instance, container ships.'

She's saying this quite casually and peering behind me at the Magic Eye, apparently still unable to see it. The container-ship comment lands hard and I almost flinch.

But instead I say, 'It's a long-haired woman riding a Eurasian dragon.'

'Can you see it?' she asks.

'Yes,' I say, 'the sky's on fire.'

# 33

Our centenary year, 2020, begins oddly. I do not quite know what is expected of me, except that I'm not to make a fuss. Norma's attitude before we broke up for Christmas made it clear I am to be lumped in with everyone else and there is to be no special relationship; this feels like a relegation, and though I've had practically the whole of December to get used to it, the sight of her swivelling and moving about the office in the VC's leather chair is disconcerting. I've mentioned the chair activity to Michael.

'You might have to get us some carpet protection mats,' I say.

'Uh-oh, who's motoring?' he asks.

'Norma Pack-Allen. She's like Harvey Smith.'

Michael goes into the office to monitor the situation at some point, and when we meet again he agrees with me on the protection front; the sisal is already churning badly under and around her desk.

'If we let her carry on like this she'll be down to bare boards,' he says, quite rightly.

I think I'm allowing this to get to me. It's reminding me of the time I walked with my mother past our old house in High Wycombe and she couldn't reconcile herself to the fact that while it *was* our old house she wasn't able to go in and remove the floor-length nets the new people had put up at the porch windows. It was as though she'd lost her mind, which I suppose she had. Frankly, I'm counting the hours until Professor Willoughby returns and Norma goes back to the academic offices on the ground floor, where the chairs aren't on wheels, and the surfaces don't require coasters.

For all that though, I have to admit Norma's first inter-departmental meeting goes well. She won't be making 'any sweeping changes' she tells us, which is wise because no temporary leader ever says on Day One they're going to make changes without it provoking a mutiny. Her priority, unsurprisingly, is student applications, and she schedules a special meeting for the following week at which she'll require contributions from all departments on the subject of how to maximize the effect of the open days.

Afterwards I meet her in the kitchen and refer to our time at the Pin Cushion when she was reluctant to stock the Ronco Buttoneer and refused to make house calls to measure for curtains.

She's puzzled. 'I don't remember that,' she says.

'But how could you forget the Ronco Buttoneer?' I laugh, and she shrugs.

When Roy asks me later how I am getting along with 'the new broom', I don't say that the main difference between her and the old VC is that it always seemed as though he couldn't face the world without me, and she seems to wish I didn't exist.

'Yeah, fine,' I say.

'See!' he says. 'I knew you'd settle in.'

*

Our first outing together is a trip over to UCAS in Cheltenham. Our email exchange on the subject the day before began with Norma requesting a nine o'clock departure, which I countered with a suggestion of eight-thirty at the latest, and she came back with, I suppose you know best. Arriving at the car park early I'm dismayed to see Norma already in the back, laptop open and AirPods in her ears. Professor Willoughby was never early, nor did he wear headphones of any kind. She's declaring something – it's not to be a skirmish, but a long, cold war. I get into the driver's seat and twist round to face her.

'MORNING!' I call.

'Yes,' she says, touching her earpiece, 'I can hear you.' She's not as glam as usual but has gone more formal in an overly stiff, tight trouser suit in a royal blue and honest to God she could be a KwikFit Fitter.

'This is your eight-thirty ride to Cheltenham,' I say, as I reverse out of our spot, and add, 'I always confirm the destination before departure.'

'Very wise,' she says, and looks down.

I've to turn a broken friendship into a tenable professional relationship, and have given myself a pep talk on this subject. I know to chat strategically, to say only interesting or useful things, tailored to the moment. In my mind I have reduced her, as far as possible, to the velvet-phobic snob who lacked the confidence to cut fabric, and had a frogspawn obsession, not out of disrespect but so that it shouldn't feel awkward. I have some pertinent topics of conversation planned, some mild advice about making journeys bearable in her new role, and have primed myself to not mention Professor Willoughby unless an opportunity arises in which we might mock him in a gently conspiratorial – and therefore bonding – way. Still, it seems absurd to be driving Norma in the official Audi and I can't help feeling self-conscious, as though I am wearing my mother's high-heeled mules to school, or having a telephone conversation that might be recorded for training purposes, or when, during sex, Roy suddenly looks like the Archbishop of Canterbury.

Seconds before we exit the gates, Norma decides she wants to put a bag in the boot. I pull over and pop the lid, and she gets out and fiddles about for a few moments before banging it down so hard, manually, that the whole car jolts, and I have no choice but to ask her not to slam it like that again, it being automatic, and though German-made, the mechanism quite delicate.

She resettles without acknowledging her mistake or my request, but only says, 'We'd better get going, I don't want to be late.' As if I was the one rearranging luggage at the last minute.

I see Honey vaping under the eaves with Michael Pascoe; she's about to open the café and there's a group of students waiting to go inside. She waves, I wave back, and seeing her broad, calm smile I feel better.

'There's Honey,' I tell Norma, and she touches an AirPod. 'What's that?' she says, but I swing out onto the Brankham road and we're away out of town.

At some point that day I notice in Norma's tote bag a book by Rachel Cusk, the Canadian-born novelist whom

I've never really fancied, but, in pursuit of good relations, and something to talk about, I think I'll give her a try. I say nothing. I just drive and enjoy the sounds of the road. The car tyres on a new surface make the sound of something being very slowly torn apart, like pulling a great, long, and in this case, never-ending, strip of masking tape off the edge of a carpet after painting a skirting board. It's a thing I've always enjoyed, the clean edge, the paint-spattered smooth side of the tape and the adhesive side covered in spaniel hairs and dust. I will be more selective, I think, more relevant and concise.

'Are you enjoying the Rachel Cusk?' I ask, a day or two later, as we cruise the A6 on our way to the Confucius Institute.

I spent almost ten pounds on the tiny paperback and since Norma is close to the end, I've galloped through it so as to be ready to bring it up today. Yikes, what a book! Still, I've spent the money and put in the hours, I'm damned well going to mention it.

'Yes!' she says. 'I've just about finished it, have you read it?' She seems surprised, forgetting it was me who got her onto Iris Murdoch all those years ago, and Toni Morrison and Jayne Anne Phillips, when she was still only plodding through abridged Dickenses.

'Oh, yes,' I say.

Thankfully she doesn't ask if *I'm* enjoying it because I am not. In fact, I feel personally attacked by author Rachel Cusk and quite honestly it's as if she's joined a queue to judge me harshly for just being me. Thinking this, it dawns on me that Norma might easily have set me up to buy and read the Cusk, like the sort of ex-friend you might encounter in one of her novels.

'Isn't it fabulous?' says Norma. 'So cleansing.'

'Yes, so cleansing,' I repeat.

I'm taking the minutes at the special open-day meeting. It's a whole-morning affair and includes a coffee break with biscuits. Norma starts by outlining the problem and talking us through a selection of graphs on the giant whiteboard.

To put it simply, our open days are not stimulating the expected spike in applications and we're here to discuss why we're failing and how to fix it.

The president of the Students' Union goes first. 'Students want a university with a conscience. One which is prepared to disinvest from fossil fuels, which addresses its legacy of slavery and confronts institutional racism head on, delivers a student experience free from harassment and sexual violence, takes the future of the planet seriously, and commits to sustainability as a guiding principle in all its activities. They want to be sure we will put equality first, whether by ensuring a level playing field for students with additional needs, or by taking gender equality seriously whether someone identifies as male, female or gender non-binary. In short, students want to know this university cares, and that it lives up to its values.'

Norma nods vigorously. 'Thank you,' she says, 'but other than our statement in the prospectus, how can we flag those aims at an open day?'

One of the governors says she's a mother of three, and wonders if students might have more personal concerns at open-day stage. 'I mean, of course they want integrity but before a nice café? I don't think so.'

The head of Catering goes next and apologizes for the café being closed during the last two open-day events; this time they'll take on extra staff and offer free pastries with every beverage.

Norma can hardly contain herself. 'So you're telling me that the café wasn't open during the last open days?'

'Yes,' says the head of Catering, 'it was unavoidable, we had staff shortages.'

Norma moves on and asks about maximizing the university's USPs: the building, the grounds, the history, the town, well-known academics or alumni, etc.

'I didn't know we had any famous academics?' says Fred Fletcher, Chair of Govs, and Norma clears her throat. 'Oh, yes, beg your pardon,' he says.

There's a lot of talk about inviting an ice-cream van into the car park, or even letting the farmers' market spill into the grounds, as well as about the most effective and impressive approach to the main building: can the guides please not use the back entrance. Finally I mention the university motto, *One Day I Shall Astonish the World*, the story behind it, and my feelings upon first reading it all those years ago. I speak briefly and concisely, and make no mention of sunbeams. Norma seizes on it, and tells of her own experience, that day in 1990 when I'd minded the shop single-handed while she was interviewed for the MA; she doesn't mention any of that, of course, but I know it. Joyce Ho then pipes up. She remembers first reading it in the Latin, *Me quondam mirabitur orbis*, as *she* waited to be interviewed by the Deputy VC, and looking up had seen a ray of light, which, as you can imagine, makes me wish I'd mentioned my sunbeam first. Michael from Estates lowers his khaki work shirt to reveal that he has the original version tattooed on a shoulder blade. Almost everyone present feels the motto speaks personally to them, which, though good in the circumstances, is rather dispiriting on a personal level.

Michael says, 'What about social media?' and everyone groans.

'What?' he says.

'We have a slight problem with the Marketing team,' answers Norma.

'Do we?' he asks. 'What problem?'

'They've all resigned in protest at a certain colleague being promoted to head of Marketing in spite of the complaints,' says Joyce.

'What complaints?'

'Not for public disclosure.'

'I can put Honey Warren onto it, if you like,' says Michael. 'She's an expert.'

'Oh, yes, brilliant,' says Norma, 'I'll contact her.'

Norma closes the meeting and asks us to reconvene on Tuesday. Afterwards, I'm putting the cling film over the remaining biscuits, Norma is writing her notes, and I briefly mention the scroll Honey painted some years ago on a huge piece of plywood that Roy is now using as a rudimentary ping-pong table.

'Scroll?' she says.

'Yes, with the motto painted on it.'

This is of great interest. 'I'd love to see that,' she says.

'Well, it's upside down in our garage at the moment,' I say, 'but I'll get Honey to dig it out.'

I am thrilled by this turn of events and at home later, I want to run in to Honey and blurt it out. But I don't. After dinner, I go and look in the garage. It's exactly as I remember, upside down, balancing on two trestles. I decide to say nothing until Norma asks about it again. While I'm there, though, I find an old flower press. I bring it back inside and call Honey to come down and open it with me. In truth, I'm not terribly keen on dried flowers as a rule but these are personal relics and so I'll love them however dusty and grim. I call again: 'Come down, Hun, I've found something interesting.'

She appears in dark eye make-up. 'Oh, cool – wait, what, is this mine from when I was a kid?' she says, unscrewing the wing nuts on each corner.

She's being a bit heavy-handed and not quite keeping it on the level, so I say, 'Yes, it is, but be careful, darling, the flowers inside are twenty years old.'

And she says, 'I *know*!'

'Hey?' says Darnley, who has appeared out of nowhere wearing a short kilt and the same panda eyes as Honey. 'What deviousness abounds?'

'Mum's found this creepy-ass old thing with dead flowers in it, from my childhood,' says Honey, her way of not seeming too enthusiastic in case it's a flop.

'It's Honey's flower press,' I say. 'An historical artefact that might remind Honey of her wholesome childhood.'

'Oh, wow-ee,' says Darnley.

The wing nuts are all undone and Honey lifts off the top. The first layer reveals seven or eight flattened celandines, still just about yellow in colour, some perfectly flower-shaped, others with petals folded over, and some grasses, very delicate and pretty. I could cry. Honey gently lifts a blade of grass.

'Oh my God, look, Darn, I pressed grass.' She is genuinely delighted at the simplicity of this and so am I.

We look at each other and smile and Darnley wonders out loud, 'Hey, though, what if grass didn't exist, would the whole earth be all brown tundra.'

And Honey replies, 'Probably, except for deserts,' and then, 'Tundra can be grassy, but usually treeless.'

Darnley looks through a magnifying glass at a wafer-thin buttercup and comments that cellulose is the most abundant biopolymer on Earth. Honey agrees, and they continue like this, throwing out words like 'extracellular', 'biological', 'ecotone', 'reed-beds' and 'terrain', as we carefully uncover the dried flora of our past, layer by layer. I think, take that, Meeghan the counsellor. At the very bottom there are a few mischievous-looking violets and a contoured feather from a blue jay and I'm reminded of the time Honey ran a hundred yards, barefoot on hard sand, to the wrong woman on the beach, thinking it was me, to give her a feather she'd found. This was the very one.

I'd been slightly, privately offended at the time, not

because the woman was so much prettier than me but because Honey had realized, at the last moment, it wasn't me but had gone along with it, because why spoil it after that long run? And when I appeared on the scene, and the matter was cleared up, the woman handed the feather to me. I realized I didn't like feathers, I mean, yes, feathers on birds, but not fallen ones, and Honey pointed out a tiny dot of blood on the tip of the quill and said, 'Look, Mummy, the feather died.'

Anyway, I don't know whether or not Honey remembers the detail of the incident, but I've got it covered. Darnley gently lifts a pressed four-leafed clover, which I remember was actually a common-or-garden three-leafed clover but I'd added the fourth leaf before pressing. Now Darnley prises it off the parched paper and it remains intact; the extra leaf having fused itself over the years.

'Hey,' says Honey, 'this is why I've been so lucky!'

Literally at this moment, an email pops up on her phone, from Michael inviting her to do some social media research for the Vice Chancellor's Advisory Group (VAG). She's to meet him and Norma first thing, and she's over the moon.

# 34

I'm at the open-day meeting part two, feeling nervous because Honey is in attendance after doing some preliminary research.

She seems confident though and said to me on the walk in, 'Don't worry, Susan, I've taken a couple of Darnley's beta blockers.'

Norma begins the meeting by announcing that she is looking into commissioning a chandelier for the main hall. She'd like teardrops, not sharp-edged shards, and unlike the one at the railway station where there are wires everywhere, detracting from its beauty, she wants a seemingly wireless model. This is for next year, she says, but she wants it minuted and to discuss it with the Arts department and head of Alumni. Fred Fletcher looks dubious and gazes about, before eventually speaking.

'Hang on, we have a problem with student applications and you think a chandelier might help?' he says. 'It doesn't make sense.'

Fred's a restless man, with a square jaw, dark hair and a strong Derbyshire accent, and since his wife died he has lost weight and started to resemble Harold Pinter. He has a habit of tapping his pen and rustling his papers when other people speak. He is, I think, like men used to be. He is, I realize, what Roy might have become, left to his own devices.

'The chandelier is for the future but I bring it up now for a reason, Fred. A chandelier is one of a handful of things proven to affect post-open day applications,' she says.

'Where's the evidence for this?' asks Dr Tang. I glance at her and she does a tiny extra frown, just for me. It's the first time I've heard her speak out in a meeting and I notice her collar has flipped up as though she's angry.

Norma Pack-Allen slaps down a copy of Honey's notes. 'Honey Warren has analysed the social media posts of prospective students attending open-day events here and at twenty of our nearest rival institutions over the last twelve months. So, let's have a look at the things deemed worthy of posting.' And there is Honey's work, up on the whiteboard.

**4,123 images posted over 42 open days with institutional hashtags and location tags:**

20% Chandelier or elaborate lighting, on campus

12% University buildings, especially with large windows

12% Lake or large pond with wildlife, on campus

10% Café or bar on campus

10% Sports facilities on campus

10% Significant work of art (with political/cultural theme)

5% Stairwells and signage on campus

5% Science labs in action

5% Local graffiti

**Instagram posts of students visiting the University of Rutland:**

25% The Corn Exchange in town, including buskers (not on campus)

22% Chandelier at railway station (not on campus)

20% Front of Brankham House

18% Graffiti on the railway bridge WELCOME TO HELL (not on campus)

5% Campus hen house

'The worrying thing here,' says Honey, 'is that prospective students visiting UofR open days are posting images but many not of the campus, and of the on-campus images they do post, five per cent are the hen house, which suggests that students are desperate for interesting images, but can't find any. The campus is boring.'

There are murmurs at this.

'Also, it's noticeable that the UofR prospective students posted less than prospective students at other institutions, probably because the café wasn't even open and that's when they might have sat and played with their phones and posted stuff.'

Dr Tang raises a hand. 'Is this really relevant?'

Honey smiles politely. 'Look, we're concerned about applications, Zeinab, [Zeinab!] and I think we might be out of touch with what students are actually looking for at this stage. They're young, remember, and the open day is where you imagine yourself in a new life, and that means you notice tangible things, like, you know, coffee bars, and the idea that you might have fun, life will be good, there are quirky backdrops, and nice places to hang out with alpha people.'

Fred Fletcher looks baffled and raises a hand. 'Isn't it all about the league tables and reputation?'

'No,' says Honey, 'they've already decided on that stuff, that's why they're visiting. This is about day-to-day life.'

'So,' says Norma, 'we need to make it an interesting and enjoyable day out?'

'Yes,' says Honey, 'I think so.'

And so we go through department by department.

The head of Student Services is upbeat and describes having a fleet of smartly dressed helpers to meet and greet at the station, and guide parties up the hill and in through the main entrance to get the best view of the house. The head of Sciences will conduct some friendly risk-assessed laboratory entertainment. The head of Art will recruit students to encourage visitors to use pavement chalks and easels outside the café, and as an afterthought, will remove the portraits of a dead dove currently hanging on the wall outside the studios, and so on.

'And I think we need to ask staff to stop wearing gilets on open days,' says Honey, 'and reward visitors who come by train, with a free Frappuccino or something, and offer a menu that's not just rank meat pie and chips.' Fred Fletcher bristles at this and looks hard at me.

The meeting ends with Norma announcing that the ceremonial hanging of the university motto, painted by Honey Warren, will take place in the main hall the following day at eleven o'clock and will be in place for the open days over the weekend of 29th February and 1st March.

*

Another meeting. On the agenda this time, the centenary gala.

'Susan Warren is going to bring us up to speed on the centenary gala,' Norma says, gesturing to me: 'Susan.'

I quickly run through the guest list, catering, entertainment, speeches and car parking. After we've thrashed everything out Fred Fletcher wants to focus on the caterer, which is the last thing I want.

'PardeePardee!?' he says, frowning. 'Isn't that Josie Jones's outfit?'

'Yes,' I say.

He taps his pen loudly.

'Have we used them before?' Norma asks.

'No,' I say, 'but we decided to try someone new.'

'Who decided?' she says.

'The Vice Chancellor and I did.'

'Right. OK. What's on the menu?' she says, looking at her phone and presumably Googling PardeePardee!

'I was wondering that too,' says Fred Fletcher. 'What are they going to serve?'

Ignoring him, I remind Norma that the catering has been planned and approved for months.

'But what will we be eating?' she persists.

'Multi-course small plates of warm, mainly vegetarian dishes,' I say.

'So, tapas?' says Norma, frowning harder.

'Tapas, but high-end.' I am feeling under attack. 'The style is undeniably Mediterranean, but with less sausage and more vegetables, and the little plates come out piping hot. It's easy to self-serve and build up an assortment of highly flavoured foods, and easy to eat – no cutting required that the side of a fork can't handle. It's all very modern and on trend.'

'It's a gala event, Susan, we can't have a bunch of kids serving up patatas bravas. The guests will be expecting a lamb shank and pavlova.'

'PardeePardee! is ideal, being modern and easy to serve,' I say resolutely, and I think that's an end to it.

After the meeting Fred and Norma stay behind, and a governor called Barb Flynn who's driving Fred home afterwards. Fred strongly recommends I cut my losses with Josie, by which he means cancel her and forfeit the deposit. I'm not to worry about the late notice, he says, his company will cater – same fee, minus the deposit.

I object. I'm satisfied with PardeePardee! 'They're a good local firm,' I say, 'and to switch now to Fletcher's might smack of something.'

'Smack of what?' asks Fred.

'Cronyism. You being the Chair of Governors and your business getting all the catering contracts.'

Irritated by my non-compliance, Fred clamps his jaw and scratches the back of his head. 'Look,' he says, 'I've heard something on the QT – this firm isn't up to the job.'

'What d'you mean?' I ask.

'A guest found a drowned mouse in a crème brûlée at a PardeePardee! wedding a couple of weeks ago,' he says, in tragic tones. 'They plonked it down in front of her with the tail hanging over the side of the ramekin.'

'The side of the what?' says Norma.

'Ramekin,' I say, and turn again to Fred. 'I don't believe it. I mean, apart from anything else, is a ramekin even deep enough for a mouse to drown in?'

'Er, yes, a human can drown in a saucer of water,' says Fred.

I'm annoyed now. 'No, they can't,' I say, 'unless they've already had a stroke, and frankly if this dead-mouse rumour is true, which I doubt very much, so what? A recent PR disaster like that makes PardeePardee! exactly the company to use. They'll be hyper-vigilant.'

Fred Fletcher doesn't agree with my thinking. 'No, this outfit cuts corners. The owner's a known reprobate,' he says, and gazes about for corroboration until Barb Flynn pipes up that she knows someone who saw the dead mouse.

'It was very upsetting,' she says. 'The guest put her dessert spoon in and — well, it was awful and some people who'd already eaten theirs were sick.'

'To be honest,' I say, 'crème brûlée isn't that difficult to sick up.'

'Ew!' says Barb Flynn.

I continue with an anecdote about an acquaintance who moved her life savings into that bank that had to be saved from collapse in 2008, on the basis that it was now the safest one in England.

Fred Fletcher kisses his index knuckle and says, 'So, are you going to get in touch with PardeePardee! or am I?'

I say I will, though I'm bloody annoyed. I honestly

think it's Honey's 'rank meat pie' comment from the previous meeting that has riled him.

The next morning is chaotic. Roy rather resents the makeshift ping-pong tabletop being removed and wants to know when he'll get it back. He stops protesting when Michael from Estates arrives (to help, he says, but it's probably to check it's a viable project) and soon Roy's as excited as the rest of us because it really is a lovely thing. Michael, Darnley and Honey carry it from our garage over to the workshop on campus where Darnley touches it up with red, gold and black enamel paint, Honey adds shadows for impact, and Michael cuts it to shape with a jigsaw, sands the edges, reinforces it and attaches six picture-hanging brackets. And then, as announced, it is mounted in the entrance hall opposite the main doors, in the place of the Twombly. The Twombly will go up somewhere more fitting but for the time being it leans against the wall beside my desk. Everyone's acting as though it is an actual Twombly.

Though everyone's busy at eleven and there are lectures about to start, a crowd gathers and frankly it feels momentous. Norma has been on a call with Fred Fletcher and I text her saying, It's up, and after a moment she appears at the open double doors and walks towards it, sun behind her, heels clip-clopping and mouth in open admiration.

She looks at Michael and he gestures to Honey, both hands as if presenting her, and Norma says, 'Oh, Honey, this is marvellous.'

Joyce Ho says, 'We should've had an official unveiling and got the *Mercury* in.'

And Honey says, 'That's not the point, Joyce, this isn't for the mainstream media, it's a surprise for the open days.'

Grasping that Honey is in the know when it comes to all this, Joyce does not demur.

# 35

I'm at my meeting with Meeghan the counsellor in a wooden cabin at the bottom of the long, slim garden behind her house. Yes. I agreed to come.

I can see her small children with someone, presumably their grandmother, going about their business inside the house. They're drawing pictures on the window glass so fledgling birds won't fly into it. It's all rather nice. I'm here, I realize, because I miss Norma.

'What a lovely set-up,' I say.

Meeghan looks quizzical and I wish I hadn't said 'set-up'. 'The garden and the cabin,' I say, 'and the children inside.'

'Oh, yes, it is. I'm lucky. But I gather you've got a pretty good set-up too?'

'Well, I can walk to work.'

'Good. Anyway, Honey wanted us to meet,' she says.

'Right.'

'She was keen that I speak to you.'

'Yes,' I say, 'I've been a bit worried, to be honest. I prevented her seeing a suicide note her godmother left for her, but she was only just twelve.'

'She's aware of the note,' says Meeghan, 'and I think understands why you kept it from her.'

'In retrospect, I suppose it might have helped. I think I

probably envisaged the wrong future for her, I mean, she has rejected the life I imagined for her – the little house, seedlings, two kids [heck, I'm describing Meeghan's set-up]. Not that there's anything wrong with that life but just that, well, she doesn't imagine hers like that.'

'No, she doesn't.'

'I've been guiding her to a future I thought was good and right and she's rather proved it all to be somewhat illusory.'

'Illusory?'

'Well, not necessarily worth striving for, exclusively.' I'm sounding anxious and confused.

But Meeghan says, 'Well put.'

I tell her about us doing a quiz to see which member of the Royal Family we're most like, Honey coming out as Charles, and me the Queen, whom I'd been trying for. We chatted some more until I told her about the bedroom makeover when we'd put a plain burgundy roller blind at Honey's window and I'd offered the old curtains to a neighbour a few doors up whose young son slept in the equivalent bedroom to Honey. So I knew the curtains would fit exactly. I had reason to believe that those curtains were the single most expensive thing we bought when we moved in, or ever. I could have run them up myself for a fraction of the cost, especially as I worked at the Pin Cushion and had a discount on fabrics, but Roy's mother, on the lookout for ways to compensate for not having put any money away for the baby, insisted on buying curtains for her room. If Roy had known the cost, he'd have blown a gasket.

Anyway, when they came down I did think, golly,

someone must want these – adorable animal print, subtle but charming colours, blackout lining, beautifully made – and mentioned them to this neighbour and she bit my hand off. A day or two after she'd put them up, she and the child appeared at the door with some cookies and I had no option but to invite them in for a cup of tea, and I called Honey down to join us.

'We wanted to say thank you for the lovely curtains, didn't we, Matthew?' said the neighbour to Honey.

'No problem,' said Honey.

The child listed every animal depicted.

'Rhino,' said the little kid (not even three years old).

'Endangered,' replied Honey.

The little kid continued – panda, tiger, turtle, leopard, gorilla, polar bear, red squirrel, African elephant, a certain kind of penguin, a certain kind of moose, whale, wolf – and Honey responded to each – endangered, clinically extinct, improving, soon to be endangered, safe (which only applied to the penguin). She didn't speak rudely, or aggressively, or with spite or malice, or under her breath, just matter-of-factly, between bites of cookie.

After the neighbour and her son had gone, I said, 'Gosh, I hope he still likes the curtains.'

And Honey said, 'He should bloody well cherish them.'

Relating this episode to Meeghan, I don't tell her I'd hoped this interest in conservation and zoology might develop into an academic pursuit, so that her knowledge about extraordinary things didn't merely drag her into sadness, but that's, I'm afraid, where her curious intelligence got her every time.

'Honey is a very clever young woman,' says Meeghan, and we continue, heaping praise on her for approx. twenty minutes until we're both saying the same thing, which is that Honey is simply one of the best and wisest humans ever born and everyone else is less so.

I tell her how relieved I am that she hasn't blamed me for the difficult aspects of Honey's life and she says she'd be happy to have a longer chat some time if I'd like, and I say I'll think about it. But secretly I don't really think counselling is for me. I've seen what it can do: previously bearable people marching assertively up to dear old friends saying, 'You owe me 27p,' and that kind of thing. I think I'll tough it out. We say goodbye and smile at each other warmly for so long that we laugh and Meeghan holds my upper arms for a moment and blinks. It's been nice.

At home I run upstairs in my shoes and coat and fling myself onto Honey's bed. She's watching *Kimmy Schmidt* and eating Walker's Sweet Chilli Sensations. She bangs the space bar as I land beside her and Kimmy freezes mid-smile.

'Oh, Mum, fuck's sake,' she grumbles, 'what you doing?'

I drum my feet and laugh. It doesn't seem so long ago that every bedtime we'd lie side by side in this bed and Honey would read her book to me, and it would have the effect of a tranquillizer drug, and often Roy would have to come and wake me up, either to watch a thing on TV that I'd agreed to, or to go to my own bed, and each time I'd just want to stay where I was, next to Honey.

'Oh my God, I forgot. How'd it go with Meeghan the Stallion?' she asks.

'Really well, I think.' I help myself to a Sweet Chilli Sensation. 'I was worried.'

'Were you?' frowns Honey. 'Why?'

'I thought she might tell me off about the oinking pig fridge magnet and the portion plates.'

Honey laughs and says, 'Lol, no, she wouldn't, she loves you.'

'Well, she thinks you're marvellous,' I say, 'and you are.' I take another Sensation.

'Did you tell her about my involvement with the open days?'

'No, I thought you'd like to.'

'Ah, yeah.'

'I wish Meeghan could see us now,' I say.

'She can!' says Honey, taking a photograph, and there we are, Honey, me and Kimmy Schmidt, blurry but clearly ourselves, and then Meeghan has apparently seen us and replied with heart eyes, and I wonder if that's ethical.

Honey looks closely and says, 'Meeghan says if it's OK can you give her a five-star review.'

I don't think I've felt happier in my life.

# 36

## *Tuesday 3rd March*

I'm outside the VC's cottage, waiting to drive Norma to Birmingham NEC for an education management conference and, as it turns out, to drop Professor Leopold at the airport next door to catch a plane to Italy to give a couple of lectures. Norma doesn't come out in spite of my text messages, and I'm forced to go up the path and knock at the door, which I do, loudly, with the knocker. The garden is untidy, the gravel not combed, and a faded Bag for Life containing old trainers hangs on a hook that used to have an evergreen foliage basket. Norma has asked Michael to concentrate on the campus grounds in the run-up to the open days, and not to worry about the cottage. This might seem magnanimous but it's really so he doesn't notice Professor Leopold's almost constant presence.

Eventually she comes to the door, opens it and retreats back inside. 'Come in,' she says, 'we won't be a minute.'

The hall console is piled with books, periodicals and mail. In the study, Professor Leopold is sprawled over a leather sofa moaning softly to Fleetwood Mac, there's a two-bar electric fire going, and in the semi-darkness I can make out cups and plates and bottles and candle stubs on the low coffee table, while through the gap between the half-closed curtains, there's a discarded dish of some kind of curried peas on the windowsill.

The Professor sees me and says, 'Hi there, let me get you a cup of tea.'

I don't know why this particularly irritates, but it does. *He*'s offering to make *me* a cup of tea, as if he belongs and I'm a visitor.

'What happened to the bird?' I ask, pointing to the unprotected stuffed woodcock that had previously been covered by an antique glass dome.

'It died,' he says, and laughs at his joke.

The debris by the fireplace suggests they've tried and failed to light a fire, and I realize they must have stopped the cleaner too. There's no need for me to be here so I say I'll see them at the car. On the way out I notice that the little alcove, where the Château Margaux usually stands, has a cup in it. I look back at the coffee table, and there's the bottle, uncorked, empty.

En route to the NEC, Norma is irritable and they bicker.

'I'll come straight to the cottage from the airport,' announces Professor Leopold.

'No,' she says, 'it's not that simple. Just wait to hear from me – I'll let you know. Do not just turn up, Leo, OK?'

'Well, don't leave it to the last minute, I don't want to be hanging about.'

'I don't think you should even be going, actually,' she says.

'What? You want me to let them down?' he says.

I can't be bothered to follow the conversation any further – to be honest it's making me sleepy. I accelerate, and venture out into the middle lane. I want them gone. I drop them both in the same spot outside the Novotel. Norma asks me to wait a few moments, they walk away and then she's back saying she doesn't think she'll attend the conference after all, she'll email to let people know.

'Do you want to email before we set off?' I ask.

'Yes,' she says, 'otherwise –' She mimes carsickness, and it's testimony to the frailty of our friendship that the gesture seems warm and kind.

'Indeed,' I say and wait while she taps away.

At home, later that day, Honey reads from her phone: 'It could be as severe and prolonged as the 1918 influenza pandemic,' she says, 'when between twenty-five and fifty million people died.'

'It won't be that bad,' I say. 'We're in modern times.'

'Yeah, but one guy's got it who hasn't even left the house or seen anyone.'

## Wednesday 4th March

I rarely take single days off. I prefer my leave in two big chunks, same as Professor Willoughby. But I have booked this quiet Wednesday for a change, to spend some time with Grace and go to the Picasso exhibition. We're meeting early, and if it turns out that I have time to pop over to Westminster for a coffee with the VC, then so be it.

'Should you even be going to London at the moment?' asks Honey on the day.

I think for a moment. I've made the plan now, I'd feel

silly cancelling. I send Grace a message anyway, blaming Honey, in case she's unsure: Your sister is wondering if we shouldn't be staying at home . . . re this Coronavirus. What do you think?

Grace responds: Still up for meeting if you are, but let's not shake hands!! x

'Grace isn't worried,' I say.

Honey twists her hair. 'I am,' she says.

And she is. I know for a fact. Her old drug-dealer pseudonym 'Miss Honeypenny' has reappeared as the narrator of her blog, or vlog, on current affairs, specifically public health. I've seen one post, on the Coronavirus, in which she spelled 'dinosaurs' wrong and I hadn't the heart to read on.

In London, I'm very early so browse the National Portrait Gallery first, looking particularly at Thomas Paine sitting for his portrait as if everything is fine and then a tour guide comes along and speaks of exile, betrayal and jeopardy. What a lovely job, I think, all those rapt tourists taking in every word. I was expecting Grace to have Marcus with her, as a buffer, but when I meet her she is alone which I take as a compliment. I am like Lesley Manville in a certain role, I can't recall which, and I speak very little, only questions concerning her job, Marcus's job, their skiing holiday in Italy. She spies my copy of *Bleak House* and I enjoy her thoughts on Charles Dickens having a good grasp of the law as it pertained to the masses.

'"The one great principle of the English law is, to make business for itself",' she quotes and I heartily agree. '"There is no other principle distinctly, certainly, and consistently maintained through all its narrow turnings",' she continues.

'Good old Dickens,' I say, but stop there. I say nothing

whatsoever about myself though, for at least the first thirty minutes, and only go slightly off-plan because Grace is so nice, and I tell her about Norma Pack-Allen stepping up as VC.

'Oh, good for her!' she says.

And my shrug surprises her. 'Oh, is it awkward?'

'Yes, it is a bit.'

'But you two are such friends, aren't you?'

'Not really, we haven't been for a while now.'

Grace is shocked. She lists a dozen times Norma has been kind and supportive over the years, to her and to Honey, and I'm momentarily humbled. 'She was so helpful when I wrote the letter to Rossington Comp when Honey was up for Head Girl.'

'Was she?' I say, incredulous.

'Yes, it was Norma who encouraged Honey to go for it,' says Grace. 'Didn't you know that?'

'No,' I say, 'she's always a bit cloak and dagger.'

Grace changes the subject. 'Mum's so excited about catering for the gala, thanks so much for fixing that.'

'Absolutely no problem,' I reply, which is ironic, but what else can I say?

When we finish our cake and tea Grace says, 'Thanks for coming, Susan, it's been lovely.'

'Oh, yes, it has,' I say, and we hug goodbye.

As I walk away I think about cancelling PardeePardee! But what will my excuse be? I'll tell Josie the truth, that Fred Fletcher has hygiene concerns, and maybe she'll go round to his house and bombard him with crème brûlée. Pleased at this thought I head over to Smith Square. After a while, I stop at a bench, look at my phone to check the exact location of the VC's new office, and seeing it's a short walk I text: In your neighbourhood, visiting St John's. Have spare 15 mins. Fancy a coffee?

I can't imagine him here, it's all too frenetic and slightly risky. Outside, I stop and check my phone. Nothing. I text: Hello? and again, nothing. I browse the trinkets on a tourist stall and buy a tiny ashtray for Honey and look at alphabet keyrings. They're very attractive, in a glossy fairground font, heavy and double-sided and yet only two pounds each.

The stallholder nods. 'They're good quality, they are, two pound each or five for a tenner.'

I select R, H, G, D and S.

I give the VC ten minutes more, but still, nothing. He must be in a meeting.

At St Pancras, with time to kill before my saver ticket is valid, I go to the British Library and look at stamps. The VC never does reply.

At home Honey is excited. She's emailed VAG with open-day stats, and though it's too early to tell, it seems that engagement is sky high. Instagram shows a huge interest in Norma's lily pond (now fully visible without the picket fence), the café, and the science lab demos, but by far the most images, including selfies, feature the motto scroll. The hashtag #OneDayIShallAstonishTheWorld which Honey worried would be too long has been abbreviated to #AstonishTheWorld and has been used over two hundred times. Even Grace has seen it and she's barely on social media. This will take her mind off the Coronavirus, I think.

# 37

## *Thursday 5th March*

Norma has called me eleven times, no exaggeration. I've failed to notice because for sanity-saving reasons I'm not looking at my phone as much. Anyway, I finally ring back and she wonders if I might be available for a driving job late this afternoon, now-ish, and can I meet her straight away at the Two Swans? I go there immediately and there she is.

'I need a huge favour,' she says, her voice close to panic. She needs someone to collect Professor Leopold from the airport.

'Could Michael go?' I ask.

'I can't ask Michael,' says Norma, 'I'm asking you.'

'Why can you ask me but not him?'

'OK, fair enough,' she says, getting up and walking away quickly. I do the Wim Hof breathing because I really want to remain calm and in control, but I run out after her, catch up and we have a whole conversation, walking quickly along, with a prong of her umbrella tapping me lightly on the head every other step.

'The problem is that Crispin has announced he's coming home for the weekend and I wasn't expecting him,' she says. 'And I've just spoken to Leo at the airport and he's – well, he's drunk.' There's a pause while I frown, look at the ground, and think it through.

'I'll do it,' I say, 'but for Professor Willoughby's sake, not yours.'

When I get to the airport I park and wait. I'm early, but not that early. And I'm not going into the terminal – he can come out.

I open an email from PardeePardee! wanting to confirm the gala starters menu, and when I see the word 'burrata' I close it again quickly. I really will have to cancel tomorrow.

Then I open an email from Joyce, with an attachment concerning the recent open days which I can't open, but her summary is heartening: The trend is undeniable, she writes. The spruce-up has been hugely successful, over 40% of Instagram, Facebook and Twitter posts feature Honey Warren's UofR motto artwork.

Professor Leopold texts to say he's landed. I text back telling him to head towards the Novotel opposite arrivals, which is where I dropped him on Tuesday, and I watch the doors. Eventually there he is – I recognize the camel coat. I stand beside the car and wave with both hands. He doesn't notice and walks falteringly in slightly the wrong direction, then stops, looks all around himself, causing a bit of a bottleneck, then sees the Novotel, and then me, raises one arm to wave back and sinks onto a metal bench by the bus stops. I go to help him.

His bag of goodies, which contains wine, vacuum-packed cured pork and golden-wrapped sweeties, tips over and spills out across the pavement.

Someone says, 'Oh, no, mate?' and another stoops to help pick it all up.

He apologizes and wipes his face with his hand, takes the bag, then doesn't know what to do with it. I think of his manifestation in Norma's erotic verse: the strength, the muscular, horselike lips, the small but satisfying penis, etc. but all I can see now is a film of perspiration across his waxy cheeks and the redness of his neck under the woollen collar of his greatcoat.

'Sit tight,' I say, 'I'll bring the car round.' It's all of fifty metres, but takes some time.

Once in the car, he sits in the back and I ask if he's OK for me to drive.

Yes, he says, he's fine.

'How was Italy?' I ask.

'Super,' he replies, and then says he's not feeling well.

'We'll soon be home.' I ask for his address and he seems unsure. We leave the NEC area and soon we're travelling northbound on the M42.

'Erm, could you drop me at the VC's cottage, please.'

'No,' I say, 'I can't take you there. You'll have to go home.' I explain that Professor Willoughby is back unexpectedly. We say no more about it for a while.

'The thing is,' he says then, 'Lydia's thrown me out. I can't go home, I need to go to the Gate House.'

'No, you can't go there, I told you – Professor Willoughby is home.'

'Oh, Christ.'

'So where shall I take you?'

He slumps back and pinches the top of his nose and

says nothing. I pull over onto the hard shoulder, get out of the car, and ring Norma.

'He's unwell,' I tell her, 'and Lydia's thrown him out.'

'OK,' she says quietly.

'So where am I taking him?'

'Susan, I don't suppose you'd put him up for the night, would you?' she says in a low voice. 'I'd be very grateful.'

Flecks of oily drizzle swirl about, the wet road amplifies the evening traffic, and my throat tightens. I don't want Professor Leopold in my house, it will be humiliating. There's my mother's sideboard that doesn't fit in the lounge but which for some stupid reason I haven't disposed of and it makes us seem so lowbrow. Roy will say 'yourself' instead of 'you' and talk about cars, but I'll be the real culprit, unable to bear the sense of worthlessness elicited by not having huge fluffy white towels, as if what's the point of me if I don't make life bearable and beautiful for people? An Eddie Stobart flashes its headlights to guide an overtaking Downton truck into the lane in front of it, the Downton thanks it with a honk. And I realize I'm going to say no.

'No,' I say.

'What do you mean?' says Norma.

'No, I can't put him up for the night.'

'Why?'

'Why should I?'

'Because of our friendship.'

I make a sound – a half-gasp, half-laugh that comes out as a cry. It's the sound of someone hearing something that is both terrible and true. I switch my phone to the other ear and push my wet hair away from my face.

'But you haven't been a good friend to me,' I say, 'and – you should have agreed to be Honey's godmother.'

Norma says nothing and I change the phone back to my other ear.

'Why didn't you tell me about Grace when you first knew about her?' I ask.

Norma doesn't answer.

'Are you still there?'

'Yes, I'm here,' she says. 'I did.'

'Tell me the truth,' I say. 'Did you think Grace might be Hugo's?'

'Yes, very briefly.'

'And you were disappointed when you realized she wasn't?'

'Yes.'

There's a moment of silence.

'OK,' I say, 'I will put Leopold up for one night. If – and only if – PardeePardee! can be reinstated.'

'If what?'

'If PardeePardee! get to do the catering for the gala dinner.'

Norma sighs and mutters. She's irritated and there's a long pause while she mulls it over. 'No, no, I can't agree to that, Fletcher's are doing it now.'

'Fair enough,' I say. 'In that case I shall drop Professor Leopold at the university. Hopefully Michael from Estates can do something, maybe you could ring ahead and warn him – but look, Norma, I've got to go now, I'm on the hard shoulder.'

'All right, *all right*,' she says, 'you can have your caterer, for God's sake.'

'Can you email confirmation, please?'

'Sure.'

'Now,' I say.

'What? Now?' she says.

'Yes, now, I'm not driving him to my house until I've had an email confirming that PardeePardee! are doing the gala catering – and copy Fred Fletcher in.'

While I wait for the email, I ring Roy to explain and as we're speaking, I tap on the rear passenger window and hold up my index finger to Professor Leopold inside the car, meaning, one minute.

'It's an emergency,' I tell Roy. 'It's Professor Leopold – Leo – I've got him in the car and he's unwell, and needs a place to sleep.'

'What?' says Roy.

'He's ill, or drunk, or both, and Lydia has thrown him out.'

'You sound stressed, Susan, are you all right?'

'I'm fine.'

'Do you want to wait there and I'll come over and drive behind you?' he asks and his kindness slightly chokes me. He's done this for me before, when I've had to pick up the VC from an evening event in the dark, and driven over to guide me home – not because I'm a woman, but because it helps.

'I'll be OK, it's all well-lit roads. I'll be back in less than an hour,' I tell him. 'And Roy, put an extra pillowcase on, he might have this virus and I don't want it seeping through in his saliva.'

Back in the car, I tell Professor Leopold, 'I think it's best if Roy and I put you up for the night.'

'Oh, that is sweet of you and good old Rob,' he says. 'I'm much obliged.'

'*Roy*. He's getting his office ready for you, you can just flop when we get back.'

'Yes, yes, of course, Roy. Roy the boy,' says Professor Leopold, with his eyes closed. 'OK, home, James, and don't spare the horses.'

A little further along he speaks again. 'Can you talk to me, Susan?'

'Talk to you?' I say, eyeing him in the rear-view. 'About what?'

'Anything. Please, I'm not feeling so good and it's soothing.'

'OK. Are you aware that Norma and I used to be good friends? Do you remember that the first time you met her she was with me?'

'I'd knew you worked together as kids,' he says.

I laugh. 'We were *best* friends, went to each other's *weddings*.' Then after a pause, 'I went to her *first* wedding.'

'She was married before?'

'Yes,' I say, 'to Hugo Pack-Allen.'

'Oh, yes, so she was,' he slurs. 'So what happened?

'She just went off me.'

'No, no, I mean to the husband?'

'He died in 2000,' I say. 'How do you not remember? He fell under a bus near the Holly Bush lay-by.'

'Good God,' he says, 'of course, that was him. Jesus Christ, poor chap.'

'Yes, that was Norma's first husband, died after dogging,' I say, and pause to let it sink in.

'And now Copenhagen?' he says.

'Copenhagen? What about it?'

'She's saying she wants to bugger off back to Copenhagen, but, shhh!' He puts his finger to his lips. 'It's a secret.'

'When?' I ask.

But he's asleep, head lolling.

'What about Copenhagen?' I say again, more loudly, looking at him in the rear-view mirror. 'Professor Leopold, Leo?'

When I look back at the road, I'm a bit close to the car in front.

I finally get home. Norma is there, outside. Professor Leopold is asleep in the back seat. She leans in and shakes him: 'Leo, *Leo*, wake up.' Finally she drags him to the edge of the seat, lifts him like a sleeping toddler, and carries him up the path.

Roy is at the front door. 'Put him in my office,' he tells her, and she goes in sideways to protect his head.

Norma comes downstairs again afterwards. 'I can't thank you enough,' she says, breathless, looking at me and then at Roy.

'No, not at all.' Roy picks up his cup of coffee, and reveals the coaster underneath. Bless him, he doesn't even take a sip before putting it down again. Too late, though.

'Oh my God,' says Norma, 'what was that?' Roy lifts his cup again for her to look at the picture of herself and the VC outside Buckingham Palace.

'How bizarre!' says Norma.

'Well,' I say, 'let's hope it's not the Coronavirus and we don't all die.'

And she says, 'I really don't think it is, he's just drunk, he was drinking in Bologna.'

## Friday 6th March

Professor Leopold is in bed in Roy's little office. He's been asleep for approx. ten hours. I'm thinking I'll wake him with some clanging about. It's on my mind that he might have preferred a firmer pillow. How he came to be here is proof of my devotion to the institution and Roy is pretty miffed on my behalf, which feels quite vindicating.

Roy peeps in to see if he'd like a cup of tea and comes away grimacing. 'He looks pretty rough, Susan.' Over breakfast he is curious about Norma and Professor Leopold's affair. Since when? And how come I haven't told him before now?

'It's common knowledge,' I say. 'I *have* told you, Roy, it's just that you don't always hear everything.'

Is the Professor hungover or is he poorly? we wonder. Should we call the doctor? Just as I've decided to call Dr Tang, Norma phones for an update and tells me under no circumstances to do so.

'Think about it, Susan, she's on the Board of Governors.'

She suggests Roy goes in and wakes him properly with paracetamol and a glass of water. A few minutes later she arrives to have a look for herself and after banging around a bit, tells him quite loudly to get up and dressed.

'Might he have the Coronavirus? It's just that Honey was saying that Italy has high infection rates,' I say. I want Norma to feel uncomfortable. 'They've gone from the containment phase to the delay phase, apparently.'

'Look, it's possible, I suppose,' she says, 'but he hasn't got a cough or a sore throat, so I doubt it.'

'It does seem more like a hangover than a virus,' Roy agrees, but we exchange a look and I know he's thinking about John John-Jessop and the bird flu.

## Saturday 7th March

'The *Guardian* says the number of confirmed cases of the Coronavirus has jumped to two hundred and six,' I tell Honey, thinking it doesn't sound too bad.

'Yes,' she says.

'Not too worrying,' I say.

'It's a twenty-five per cent increase on yesterday,' she says.

## Sunday 8th March

Honey greets us at dinner, saying, 'There are seventy more cases and three deaths.' This news starts Roy coughing.

# 38

## Monday 9th March

Roy definitely has a dry cough. I've told him to drink more fluids and I get him some barley sugars with the shopping. He wants to be well enough to go to his dad's eighty-fifth birthday tea.

## Tuesday 10th March

Roy is poorly today. He wonders if it's wise that Fred Fletcher and some of the golf club have gone to Cheltenham for the races. I agree, but am secretly relieved; now, if we all go down with the Coronavirus, it won't be my fault for going to see Grace last week, or bringing Professor Leopold home for the night – who, by the way, is back at work and looking quite grey in the face.

## Wednesday 11th March

Roy is still poorly today. I ring Dr Tang to see if we can get a test for the Coronavirus, which we're now calling COVID-19, but there are none available. She says paracetamol is better than ibuprofen, and makes the comment, 'I thought Roy was so fit and healthy.'

'Well, he is, but he's got this cough,' I say. 'Should we isolate?'

'Wash your hands frequently, and don't shake hands with anyone,' she says.

Confused, I hang up.

I ring Joyce Ho. 'What do you think?' I ask.

'Your decision, Susan,' she says. 'If it were up to me, I'd say come in. I mean, it's not as though we can all just stay at home.'

I go in but tell Joyce from a distance that I can't share an office with anyone. I lock the office door and wear Roy's woodwork mask for the toilet.


## Thursday 12th March a.m.

Norma is working from home with a bad back, probably caused by heaving Professor Leopold up the stairs. I'm talking across the corridor with Joyce Ho. Michael from Estates is hanging the Twombly in a place where it can be seen from reception. Maybe it is a Twombly. I'm saying to Joyce that we should start thinking about a scenario in which we send the staff and students home. Joyce, irritated by my hysteria (her word), parrots the Chair of Governors: 'the show must go on until the government advises to the contrary.'

'I mean, seriously, Susan, they're not going shut the universities down,' Joyce reasons, 'or they'd have to shut the whole country down and they're not going to do that.'

'They might have to,' says Michael from Estates.

Later, Joyce sends round the latest guidance by email which advises us all to continue as normal but wash our hands, singing happy birthday, and use gloves for certain jobs. The Chair of Governors replies, saying he's going to Liverpool that afternoon to see a football match and that all's well. I pop my masked head round Joyce's door to ask about the gala dinner and notice she's suddenly childish, making loud pronouncements, whizzing about on her chair from her desk to her assistant's, flapping papers about, as if it's a modern ballet. Whizzing about in chairs is all the rage now that everyone's seen Norma doing it. God help the carpets.

'We really should discuss the gala dinner,' I say.

And she says, 'Yes, yes, yes! The gala's going to be great, don't worry. As soon as Norma's back, we'll discuss it.'

'I think we have to face it, Joyce – we're going to have to cancel, aren't we? It's hardly a necessary gathering.'

She spins around in her chair, agog. 'What? No way!' she says, walking her chair across the room towards me. 'They didn't cancel Cheltenham, we're not cancelling the gala dinner.'

I back away and she follows.

'I mean, after all the work you've done?' she says.

I grab the headrest of Joyce's chair and inadvertently some of her hair, and push her away.

'What the hell are you doing?' she says.

'Joyce, we have to cancel. Or we're putting people at risk of serious illness.'

'You're being obsessive.'

'The 1920s jazz band has cancelled.'

'We'll get the students to play.'

'You told me at my interview, all those years ago, that the health and well-being of students and staff was paramount and that was why the governing body were planning to rip out the green island even though it had a protected tree on it.'

'You're being ridiculous,' says Joyce, waving me away, pretending to read a document.

'Now we're all at risk from this virus and you don't seem to care. Just as long as you can entertain the Chair of Governor's customers.'

'It's completely different,' she says. 'We have no reason to cancel. The government guidance is to continue as normal, as per my email.'

'Joyce, I've been to London. I met Grace, she's just back from Italy. The whole family has had a high temperature. Professor Leopold's been in Italy, half the governors at Cheltenham bloody races.'

Joyce swivels. 'You've been to London?'

'Yes.'

'Well, for God's sake, don't tell anyone, Susan.'

'But Joyce, this is why we must cancel.'

'We can't. Fred's adamant. By all means you stay away,' she says. 'But as far as I'm concerned the gala is on.'

I pick up a telephone receiver and glancing at a list on the wall dial the secretary for the Chair of Govs. 'Hello, Veena, it's Susan here, from UofR. I need to speak to Fred, please.'

Fred's not available.

'Tell him it's concerning the gala night here. I honestly think we have to cancel – it's highly likely people on campus have been exposed to this virus, tell him.'

She says she'll get him to ring me back. He never does call.

# 39

## *Friday 13th March*

Roy still has a sore throat. He says he feels quite normal and isn't feverish, just slightly short of breath. Should I go to work? I wonder. Before I've finished thinking it through properly I find myself in the Brankham House library looking for a book for Darnley. I see Professor Leopold, who seems perfectly well. I catch him up.

'How are you now?' I ask.

'Oh, fine, thanks, and thanks so much for putting me up. I must bring you a bottle of something.'

'Do you think you might have had the Coronavirus?'

'It's possible,' he says, 'but not likely, I don't think.'

'But Italy?'

'I haven't been in Italy,' he says. 'Where did you get that idea from?'

'Oh, I don't know,' I say. I walk away, puzzled. He *was* in Italy, I know he was, but his denial is reassuring.

Instead of cancelling the student statistics meeting, Michael provides us with masks and hand sanitizing wipes and we're sitting as far apart as possible. We're in Meeting Room G listening to Norma's upbeat presentation when someone appears at the door, face wrapped in a huge scarf.

'Sorry, 'she says, 'is Susan here?' and I realize it's Honey.

I get up, mumble apologies, and leave the room. We stand outside in the cold sunshine. She's been ringing me repeatedly but my phone has been off because of the meeting. Roy has worsened rapidly – she actually says 'worsened rapidly' because she's been on so many phone calls with people trained to ask medical questions, one of which is, 'Has he worsened rapidly?'

'He was struggling to breathe, Susan.' She tells me this tearfully, and that an ambulance arrived at 14:05 and took him. They wouldn't allow her to go with him, and they couldn't tell her anything, not even where they were taking him.

'So where is he?' I ask.

'What d'you mean?'

'Where did they take him?'

'I told you, Susan, they wouldn't tell me.'

'Oh my God.'

'They've got his details, they wrote it all down, and his phone is in his dressing-gown pocket in a plastic bag. I got him ready before they arrived.'

I make her tell me everything again, slowly, step by step. She says the paramedics weren't jolly or kind, but serious, like robots, and they kept telling her to stand back. Keep back. Stand back.

'It was dystopian, Mum,' she says.

She tells me that June from next door approached to ask if Roy was OK and then, realizing it wasn't a heart attack or a broken neck, staggered away, terrified. A detail that stands out is that Roy seemed delirious, breathlessly

343

talking about murder hornets and then quiet, except for terrible breathing, and as they waited for the ambulance he'd said, 'I knew Grace would be the death of me.'

We walk home amid plumes of Honey's cherry-flavoured vape, and I ring Leicester Royal Infirmary on the way. The receptionist at the Royal can't locate Roy on their system but explains that that doesn't necessarily mean he's not there. They also say that it's possible they've been diverted to Kettering, and that we'll hear in due course.

I think that's the moment when, hearing they might have diverted to Kettering, I know this thing, this whole thing, is serious. It's not a feeling I recognize, not knowing who to believe, not knowing who to trust. I realize with a thud in my heart that Honey is, and always has been, right. People are going to die. Maybe Roy is and maybe I am. Honey makes me some tea with oat milk.

The phone rings. It's Roy's mother wondering if they should cancel Grandpa Ted's eighty-fifth.

'With this virus going around,' she says.

'I think that would be wise.'

'Yes,' she chuckles. 'We can postpone to the end of the month and you know what that is, don't you?'

'Roy's sixtieth?'

'And Horace's one hundredth!' she says triumphantly, meaning the tortoise.

'Oh, is he really a hundred?'

'Yes, I'm hoping to get him in the paper.'

'Go for it,' I say.

'Are you all right, love?' she asks.

'Yes, I'm just a bit up to my neck, you know.'

'Oh, aye, I'll let you get on then,' she says. 'Love to all.'

'Love back.'

Honey looks stern.

'I couldn't tell her,' I say. 'Not yet.'

I ring the GP practice but Dr Tang isn't available. I tell the receptionist it's 'extremely urgent' and she says she'll get her to call me as soon as possible. When Dr Tang returns my call, half an hour later, I explain the situation: we don't know where Roy is. Can she help track him down? She says I'm not to worry – he'll be at either Leicester Royal Infirmary or Kettering. Someone will be in touch. She gives me Roy's NHS number to write down and says that Honey and I should self-isolate from now, if we have symptoms, and not leave the house or go to work or have anyone in.

I know this, but for some reason, in spite of everything I believe, I hear myself say, 'But the gala dinner!' and feel immediately ashamed for mentioning it at a time like this.

But Dr Tang is thinking the same thing and says, 'I know, such rotten timing.'

I ring Joyce and explain. 'Roy's been rushed into hospital,' I say.

'Rushed?' says Joyce.

'Yes. Rushed.'

'Do you think it's Coronavirus?'

'Well, yes.'

'Is it confirmed?'

'No, but we have to assume that it is,' I say, 'so I'll not be in for a while.'

We discuss briefly my working from home and Joyce returns to the subject of Roy.

'How do you think he came into contact with it?'

'I went to London,' I say, 'Fred went to Cheltenham, and Mrs Miggins went to effing market.'

My phone goes again. It's not the ringtone for Roy or Honey or the VC but the default ring that I never usually hear and my gosh, it's the ghostly chiming from a fever dream – how appropriate, I think. It's the Royal. Thank God.

Ward Sister Bettina George says, 'Hello, Susan Warren? I'm calling from Cinnamon Ward at Leicester Royal Infirmary. It's about your husband, Hector Warren.'

'Is he there?' I ask.

'Yes,' she says, 'he's here, Mrs Warren.'

'HONEY!' I shout.

I can't help but cry because in the back of my mind the robot ambulance men have dumped his body in a pit with other sick people, and left him to die, and he's going to be outlived by his tortoise. I haven't spoken any of this out loud, of course. Honey comes thundering downstairs, dragging her blanket behind her.

I put Bettina on loudspeaker and tell her, 'My daughter is listening as well.'

'How old is your daughter?'

'Late twenties.'

Ward Sister Bettina confirms that Roy has suspected COVID-19 and is quite ill, but stable.

'How is his breathing?' I ask.

'He's breathing with some help,' she says.

'Is he on a life-support machine?'

'Erm, no, he's just getting some oxygen and intraven-ous medication.'

'Is he conscious?'

'He's sleeping most of the time.'

At the end of the call she says we must not come to the hospital, gives me two numbers I can call for updates, and says, 'Ring any time after two, but remember we're very busy, and we will keep in touch with you.'

'Is he going to be OK, Bettina?' I ask.

'I think so. He seems strong, Mrs Warren. Amazing, actually.'

And her saying he seems strong makes my eyes fill with tears again. He seems strong. He'd be so pleased with that observation.

'Oh, he is strong,' I say, 'very.'

'We'll keep you informed,' she says. 'He has the same name as my father.'

'How funny!' I say. 'Though actually he goes by the name Roy mostly. Can you call him Roy?'

'Oh, heavens,' says Bettina, 'my father also goes by Roy.'

I'm flabbergasted and almost make a joke but don't.

'I'll look after him, Mrs, Warren, I promise he's in the best place.'

I thank her and say goodbye.

Darnley has appeared and thinks I should have told Bettina that Roy is hoping to live to a hundred. We debate this at length. I mean, doesn't it sound a bit greedy, to say to a ward nurse that you're hoping for another forty years?

Honey thinks Darnley is right: 'Anything that gets the nurses rooting for you.'

Honey has lost her sense of taste and smell, which she puts down to eating pine nuts, and is having feverish spells. We can't have a test. There are no tests, apparently.

She and I speak to Grace on the phone. She is ill too, but not very; both she and Marcus have sore throats and headaches, they're self-isolating and taking lots of vitamin C.

'Oh my God, Susan,' she says, 'do you think I gave it to him?'

'No,' I say, 'he could've got it from anywhere. People at the golf course were at Cheltenham races, and a member of staff has been it Italy. We just don't know.'

'What about the gala dinner, is that going to go ahead?' she says. And then, 'I don't want Mum doing the catering, it's just not safe.'

I tell her I'm hoping they'll cancel it. 'Surely they must,' she says.

I send an email to Norma, Joyce, and Michael from Estates, to update them on Roy. Norma sends a message by return, which makes me almost cry:

Hold tight, Roy is strong. Nx

Later, I don't really want to go to bed but Honey and Darnley have insisted on staying up as long as I do. I know they'd rather take mug cakes upstairs and watch TV in bed but they feel they should keep me company. Darnley talks about the plague in literature, and Shakespeare's Sonnet 65, which they know by heart, and claims its themes are decay and the inexorable march of time. Personally, I've always believed it to laud the enduring nature of the written word, but I haven't the energy to discuss it. Finally, we play Bot or Not and can't tell the difference between Emily Dickinson and a computer.

'I'm going up,' I say. 'Night, night, you two.'

'Night, night,' says Honey. 'Better news tomorrow.'

I spend what seems like hours writing to Roy. I've been sending short supportive texts all afternoon, with no response, and imagine his phone to be in his dressing-gown pocket in a drawer. But now, knowing he'll never see it, I write him a love poem.

I tidy our bedroom and start making a pile of items to take to the charity shop. Clothing mostly and some unopened pairs of opaque tights in bright colours that I've never quite risen to. I take down a textile wall hanging we got in the Ardèche, featuring roe deer, and see for the first time that the decorative border is a ghastly tangle of fir boughs, skulls and *rifles*. I add it to the heap. I don't feel it an omen until I tidy Roy's chest of drawers, and opening his top drawer to drop some elastic bands in, I'm startled to see a silver gun. I turn it over in my hands wanting to enjoy the weight of it but it's no heavier than a spoon. It's just his starting pistol. Even so, two weapons in two minutes seems portentous. I snoop further and detect three books buried beneath the various oddments. An Edgar Allan Poe, a James Herbert, and Hilary Mantel's *Beyond Black*. Roy has hidden them from me so that I won't scare myself by reading them, so I'll not even *see* them and therefore I shan't have even a moment's unease.

I text him about this: I found your horror stash and am crying with joy that I'm married to a man like you.

Soon it's one o'clock in the morning. How lovely it would be right now, I think, to wander about downstairs and perch on a wooden chair in my nightie until I'm thoroughly cold right through and then come back to bed, with Roy, warm, in a deep sleep, on his back, arms out like an arrowhead, the reassuring hum of his apnoea mask. He'll be fine though, I trust him – all this health nonsense will pay off. Roy is Strong. Roy is Strong. I go to bed and fall asleep thinking about the time Honey and I took the same train as the art historian Sir Roy Strong, from Paddington down to Devon. We'd sat opposite him, a table in between us. Honey, a teenager then, took out her travel watercolours and the detergent ball she used for water, and began painting. I willed Sir Roy to look over and encourage the young artist at work, but he wasn't interested, being preoccupied with his ticket, the timings, his poorly ankle, and whether a man called Justin was going to be there to meet him at Newton Abbot.

# 40

## *Saturday 14th March*

I wake early and Roy Strong pops into my mind again, and I realize it wasn't him on that train, it was Brian Sewell, and somehow it makes more sense, and then, as I'm remembering it all again with the correct person/face/aura, there's a knock at the front door. None of us answers it but we watch from upstairs windows. It's Norma. I open my window and she waves. She's left a box of groceries on the step: 'Just some bread and cheese,' she says.

There's a lot of talk about leaving it there for three hours, or wiping it down with alcohol, but in the end we all want toast, so Honey brings it in. It does contain bread and cheese, and oat milk and cow's milk and daffodils, tiny tomatoes and a whole lot of salad leaves and red pepper, spring onions, marinated tofu, a bunch of coriander, and a box of Maltesers.

Norma doesn't know I went to London, she doesn't know Grace was in Italy. She thinks this is her fault. The day goes by. I ring the infirmary. They do not return my call. Honey reads the news. Darnley bakes.

## Sunday 15th March

I wake and notice that Roy's not here; I don't feel the mattress tensing as he holds his out-breath, I don't have to creep away or remain still for his meditation. I don't have to see his striding about with a coffee-coloured towel around his waist. On the other hand, I have dreamt about him speaking from his hospital bed.

'Finally you've talked someone to death, Sue,' he says in the dream, with a painful, hoarse laugh that turns into coughing.

I ring the infirmary and get through to a very nice ward manager called Cheryl Lam. She says there's nothing to report except that Roy 'has moments of lucidity' and is not in distress, and I think for a moment I might joke, 'Lucky him!' or 'Tell me about it!' but this is a new world in which one doesn't make quips about one's husband. Cheryl Lam can't tell me any more because he isn't officially 'on her case load' and she can't speak for long anyway, because they're so busy. 'He's doing great, Mrs Warren,' she says, 'he really is.'

Later, Honey, Darnley and I FaceTime with Grace.

'How's Dad?' she asks.

'Stable but critical,' I say.

'*Critical?*' she says. 'Oh my God, might he die, Sue?'

'No, he won't die,' I say, choked.

Honey butts in. 'Yes, he might. He's critical. Of course he might die – that's what critical means.'

'He won't die, he's strong,' I say, and we all agree.

And then suddenly, with no warning and apropos of nothing, Grace says, 'It was me who messed up that caravan that time.' She covers her face with her hands.

'You vandalized Pegasus in the New Forest?' I am really just translating it into my own language. It's strange, because in one way I've been waiting twenty years to hear this and in another, I think it immaterial.

'I don't know why I did it,' she says slowly, crying, 'and I've never done anything like it again. I mean, I've not even, oh, I don't know.'

'Grace, you were a kid, it was a tricky time.'

'But I can't bear that I did it.'

Honey seems entirely unfazed by the revelation but Grace is making quite a bit of noise and blowing her nose. We soothe her and say, repeatedly, it doesn't matter one bit, it was a long time ago, these things happen in families, on holiday, and so on, and when the call ends Honey scratches the side of her head and Darnley says, 'What was all that about?'

I make some mint tea and we explain Pegasus.

'She really ripped it up,' says Honey, 'and wrote this fucked-up message in eyeliner.'

'Well, yes, she did,' I say, 'but finally we know the truth, which is good.'

'There is no truth, only perception,' says Darnley.

'I knew it was Grace, though,' says Honey.

'How did you know?' I ask.

'I saw her inside, writing the message, "No one likes you".'

'"No one likes you"?' repeats Darnley. 'Harsh.'

Honey explains that, having found herself back at the campsite and knowing the passcode for the key box, she had gone in for a wee and left it unlocked, then waited on the steps of the clubhouse and seen Grace appear, try the door and go inside. 'It only took her a couple of minutes to do all that damage,' she says, impressed.

I'm flabbergasted, not that Grace did it, but that Honey has known all this time.

'Why didn't you say anything, to me, or to Dad?'

'I couldn't've snitched on her, she's my sister.'

'But – Honey – you were never in the clear yourself,' I say. 'You remained a suspect.'

'Hang on, you mean, you thought I did it?'

'No, no, no,' I say, 'definitely not. I always suspected Grace.'

'So Dad thought it was me?'

'Well, he thought it was most likely one of you girls.'

'Oh my God, all these years Dad thought I did it, hasn't he?'

'I don't know. Possibly.'

'Oh my fucking God,' she says.


## Monday 16th March

Telling people about Roy's situation is horrible but they need to be told. It's not just that someone they know or love is dangerously ill, it's part of a bigger, more frightening thing. My brother rings before I get to him. He's already heard from someone at the golf club.

'I heard Roy was rushed to hospital with Coronavirus?'
He says it in a worried, slightly accusatory way.

'Yes,' I say, 'it's true.'

'But I thought he was supposed to be so fit and healthy,'
says my brother.

I don't know what to say to this, so I say nothing and
remember that he never thought much of Roy.

'Hello? Susan?'

'Hello,' I say.

'Is Roy going to be OK? I mean, how badly . . . ?'

'He's in ICU, so pretty bad.'

'Where did he pick it up?' he asks.

'I don't know,' I say, 'I'll ask him when he gets home.'

I email Joyce Ho with details of my self-isolation.
We've spoken about it on the phone but I think I'd like to
have everything in writing. She responds, asking if there's
anything she can do and whether Roy's made a will, and I
want to reply, 'Why would he? He's got another forty-plus
years.'

Honey emails Mike from Estates. He replies asking if
there's anything she needs.

Norma Pack-Allen leaves another food box on the
doorstep.


## Tuesday 17th March


Leicester Royal Infirmary phone every day at least once,
which is incredibly good of them. Honey, like me, is certain Roy will pull through, even though the people ringing

with updates always sound as though he won't, however much they stress he's doing great.

'He's doing well at the moment,' they say, 'but you must prepare yourselves for things to deteriorate.'

Honey asks today, 'Is he speaking?'

And the person on the phone says, 'He occasionally speaks, yes.'

This shocks us.

'What is he saying?' asks Honey.

'I'm afraid I don't know that.'

For a while now, since before Roy's illness, Honey has had an interest in the last words spoken by dead cultural figures; there's a Wikipedia page on the topic. She knows that Truman Capote said, 'Mama, mama, mama.' Allen Ginsberg said, 'Toodle-oo.' And Nabokov said, 'A certain butterfly is already on the wing.' But this hasn't inspired poetry or an interest in palliative care, only a morbid fear of being mis-recorded on one's deathbed. Now, she's wanting to keep tabs on Roy, in case he utters anything of interest, or admits to more children, having a favourite, or being gay. I just hope he's asking for me.

### Wednesday 18th March

The infirmary ring. It's Ward Sister Bettina George. She's sounding quite chirpy. 'Great news,' she says, and my heart skips a beat. 'Roy is no worse.'

'That's good,' I say. And I tell her that I've heard on the news that Princess Beatrice has cancelled her planned wedding reception in Buckingham Palace Gardens because of the Coronavirus.

'That's a shame,' says Bettina George.

## *Thursday 19th March*

I phone Joyce Ho to ask if the gala dinner is still going ahead. Yes, she tells me, it most certainly is, the marquee is up, the faux palms have arrived and the concert stage is being erected as we speak. I mention Princess Beatrice cancelling. Joyce ignores me and says she has a call coming in on another line.

I phone PardeePardee! and Josie tells me the university have sent someone to collect ingredients for the gala food this morning after she told them she wouldn't be able to attend in person, or supply waiting staff, because of the risk to health. They asked for a retrospective discount but Josie only laughed.

I track down the replacement jazz band, a bunch of students who go by the name 'Nice'. They are going to play, all bar the vocalist who has underlying health conditions and doesn't want to take the risk.

Honey copies me into an email to Michael from Estates saying she needs to slightly renovate the motto scroll before the gala, but since she's self-isolating, would he mind taking it down and leaving it in the porch at the café for her to collect. Michael is happy to do this. She and Darnley go to collect it and walk it through the grounds in the dark.

I send an email to everyone in my work mailbox:

## Important re. University of Rutland Gala Night Dinner

Despite there being innumerable SUSPECTED CASES OF CORONAVIRUS the Board of Governors are determined to go ahead with the gala night celebrations TOMORROW. Since I organized the event and it is my name on the invitations, I want it known that I shall not be there in person because my husband has contracted the virus and was admitted to Leicester Royal Infirmary on the 13th of March. He remains there in intensive care and I am self-isolating with my family at home in accordance with medical guidelines.

It is my opinion that the event should be postponed until gatherings of this kind are again safe and I urge you all to stay at home.

Yours,
Susan Faye Warren
Vice Chancellor's Office

# 41

*Friday 20th March 6 p.m.*

Honey has chained the gates at the back entrance with a combination padlock (1234). The three of us go by car to the front gates where we park right up against the entrance. Honey and Darn (we're calling them Darn now) have fixed the motto scroll on the car roof with a balancing leg so that it sits up there without toppling over, like a Domino's Pizza sign. It's back to front, though, and now reads, '*COVID-19 infection here*'. There are red crosses on the car windows.

Guests start arriving and we urge them to turn back. We can't get out of the car but we toot the horn and call from the open windows, 'Please don't go into the gala dinner, there's a risk of infection.'

Some ignore us, others stop and ask for details, and Honey tells them, 'We are part of the university. Two of us work here, the other's a student, we care about this place, my mum has been planning centenary events for a year now, but my dad is in hospital. Please don't take the risk.'

Some thank us, reverse out of the drive at speed, and leave. Others thank us but continue, while many take photographs.

In a lull between arrivals, I see Joyce staggering towards us in a 1920s-style silk dress.

'What the hell's going on, Susan?' she shouts. 'Have you lost your mind?'

Darnley yells back, 'No, she's lost her husband.'

And so Joyce assumes Roy has died, and claps her hand to her mouth. I have to say, 'He's not dead yet.' And Joyce takes her shoes off and sits on a bench with her head in her hands.

Another car pulls in and the nearside window opens. The passenger is Norma Pack-Allen, and the driver is Professor Willoughby.

'What's going on?' Norma is looking at Joyce, but then sees me. 'Susan?'

'It's not too late to cancel,' I say. 'Just leave your car there and we'll turn people back.'

'Just cancel!' Honey calls. 'It really is insane that you're going ahead.'

'Please move your car,' says Norma.

'We're not on university grounds,' says Darnley. 'We have every right to be here.'

'But you're obstructing the gateway,' she says, 'and on double yellow lines. We can have you removed.'

The VC, who's been quiet up to now, leans forward to catch my eye. 'Susan, this is absolutely preposterous. I demand that you stop this nonsense and go home.'

Norma turns to him. 'For God's sake, Crispin, shut up! She has every right to protest.'

I can't think of anything to say, so I gaze at him benignly, and soon I'm worrying that if he's not careful he'll let the car roll backwards – it's a tricky slope, as previously mentioned – and then Norma speaks again, to Joyce.

'Go inside and call the police to get them moved, meanwhile ask Michael to come out and dismantle that thing.' She points to our COVID-19 board.

There are two or three cars behind the VC's now, and so I hold my hand on the horn and in the din and the dusk, while Joyce puts her shoes back on, I lock eyes with Norma as their car glides in through the archway.

The next to turn in is Pete Dwight in a jeep. He peers at me: 'Hey, what's going on?'

'Have you heard about this Coronavirus?' I ask.

I'm being sarcastic but he just says, 'Yes, so what's happening?'

'Staff, including me, have been in contact with this virus,' I say. 'My husband is—' I can't finish.

Honey continues for me: 'Yeah, well, my dad's ill with it, he's in hospital. So we want to warn people.'

Pete Dwight holds up his arm. 'Good on you, can I take a picture for the papers?'

'Yes, definitely!' Darnley calls back, and they pose, Darnley on the bonnet, Honey on the roof pointing to the sign. I'm in the driver's seat, chin on knuckles, frowning.

'Thank you, guys,' says Dwight, and he reverses out of the gateway and drives away tooting his horn.

The police arrive. There are two of them; they're perfectly nice and reasonable, both males. Darnley tells them why we're here. They're sorry to hear about Roy, nevertheless they ask us gently to take the sign down and to go home. We say we shan't stay long, as most of the guests will be inside by now, and we don't want to make trouble for the sake of it. They believe us, ask us to move back by a few inches, and leave.

Michael from Estates appears. 'They've sent me out to dismantle the sign,' he says.

'Oh, Michael,' I say, 'I'm so sorry.'

'Don't come near us, Michael,' says Honey.

'Don't worry, we're about to go,' I say.

'Stay as long as you like,' he says, and pats the car bonnet. 'You're doing the right thing, Sue.'

Cars drive slowly past to gawp at us and toot. 'Oh, we missed a trick,' says Honey. 'We should have a "toot if you don't want to catch the Coronavirus".' One driver slows right down, it's Dr Z. Tang. She waves and gives us the thumbs-up and drives on. Then Josie pulls up in the gateway in her PardeePardee! van with its dancing peppers. She's playing *Don Giovanni* through her speakers and she turns it up loud.

# 42

*Pegasus*

*Saturday 21st March*

Honey and Darnley are on a high after the protest. We've got pizza and we're chatting about Roy. 'I cannot wait to tell him,' says Honey. I recall her jeering at Roy once, from a friend's car, like one of Bertie Wooster's friends, and snatching the golf cap from his head as they sped by. Honey reminds me of the time I got up at 3 a.m. for cornflakes and Roy thought I was a burglar and came down with a baseball bat, saying, 'I've called the police,' and now every time Honey sees me eating cornflakes she says, 'I've called the police.' And then we feel sad and say how hard it must be being a man of his type and mistaking wives for burglars, because if it had been a burglar, the burglar would have scarpered and it would've been a heroic act instead of a laughing matter. Of course, if I'd said, 'I've called the police,' to Roy by accident I'd laugh at myself and enjoy the attention – but then I can laugh at myself because I'm female and we've less to lose.

Honey mentions Roy being so cross about everyone having those puffy down jackets. 'They're ubiquitous!' he says, peeved because he had his before anyone else.

'People used to admire it,' says Honey, sad on her father's behalf. I remember him seeing them on sale for £29.99 with genuine down and saying it wasn't right, and that in the old days duck and goose down were a by-product, whereas nowadays the carcasses are the by-product. This is one of the few areas of agreement.

'You're talking about feathers, right?' says Darnley.

'Yeah, it just gets to him, the whole puffy-jackets thing,' says Honey.

My mother is the same about Venice, I tell them. It used to be wonderful in the old days when only a few went. You could wander around and look at the art and be the envy of all when you came back with photographs. Nowadays it's all queues for gondolas and being a gondolier is no longer a revered occupation – they're just wide boys, she says, and they never sing any more, because of the Cornetto advert, and it's a forty-five-minute wait for spaghetti vongole and then it's out of a bottle. It's nothing but a theme park, like St Ives, or Lindos on the island of Rhodes.

'It's not the same at all, Mum,' says Honey.

Honey chunters on about funny, charming things Roy has done, like the time he sided with her about parsley the herb being overrated – and then someone puts the *Mercury* through the letterbox.

## WIFE AND KIDS OF SICK MAN WARN PARTY REVELLERS OF VIRUS RISK

While Susan Warren's husband of almost 29 years clings to life in Leicester Royal Infirmary, she and her daughters take to the streets to warn partygoers of the risks of COVID-19. Many of the 200 ticket-holders ignored the trio but others, grateful for the tip-off, will be hoping to get their money back. "We spent £200 on tickets for the gala dinner," said Lucy Greenwood from Market Harborough, "but we didn't want to risk it. We'll be asking the University for a full refund."

"The Board of Governors have behaved irresponsibly, when they know staff have been exposed. It's disgusting," said would-be partygoer Mrs G. Gwilliam of Fleckney.

Josie Jones, proprietor of PardeePardee! was due to cater and waitress this event. "I provided the food but not the staff," said Josie. "I'm not mingling in a tent with people who have been exposed to a deadly virus. I think they got some students to do it."

A gentleman who didn't want to be named said he'd take his chances. "Otherwise, where does it end?" he said.

## Sunday 22nd March

Ward Sister Bettina George phones. Roy is better today, so much so that she'd like to schedule a FaceTime call. She tells us to be prepared for him to seem weak and very poorly. When the call comes, he does indeed seem weak and poorly, and the nurse is not Bettina George, and it's hard to stay cheerful.

After a while Honey says, 'Dad, I want you to know it *wasn't* me who vandalized the caravan, campervan, whatever, Pegasus.'

Roy waves it away and coughs.

Honey continues, 'And I've just realized you guys might've thought it was me, and so I want it out there that it really wasn't, OK?'

'I know it wasn't you, love,' says Roy, sounding exhausted. We all lean in to the screen. 'It was Grace.'

'What?' I say loudly and put my hand to my mouth.

'You knew it was Grace,' says Roy.

'I suspected but, hang on, Roy,' I say, 'you never said *you* knew it was Grace.'

He'd known all along, and there he is now: hospital-gowned, with pillow-flattened hair and drugged-out eyes. It's time to let go of this obsession. But I can't.

'Anyway, how are you feeling?' I say, but I'm struggling and signal with my elbow for Honey to take over.

'How are you feeling, Dad?' she asks.

'I'm, I'm, mmm, tired,' he says. 'It's very warm.' He pulls weakly at his gown.

Honey asks some questions about the medical machinery. Roy lifts his arm in response to show much bruising and a cannula, and seems to say he might be allowed home next week, but the nurse looks surprised. He freezes briefly there and I wipe my eye with my sleeve.

Honey holds up Mr Blue, and Roy's back, straining to see, but he's had enough and a nurse leans in.

'Dad!' says Honey urgently. 'Breathe, motherfucker!'

Roy smiles. The screen freezes on the nurse's horrified face.

'Only in the agony of parting do we look into the depth of love,' says Darnley.

# 43

## Monday 23rd March

'Hello, hello,' says Norma, on a crackly line, 'I'm in Denmark.'

'*Denmark?*' I say.

'I've come to Copenhagen to be with Ole.'

'Ole?' I say. 'I thought he'd died.'

'*What*' says Norma.

'Nothing, sorry. How long are you going to be away?'

'For the time being,' she says. 'How's Roy?'

'He's breathing on his own so they might let him come home next week. It's going to be a long old haul. He's like a skeleton,' I say, 'but he's over the worst, and he's alive.' I'm almost tearful but pull myself together.

'That's such good news, Susan, I'm so pleased,' she says. 'So, so pleased.'

'Are you planning on staying in Denmark for good?'

'No – I don't know. The borders are closed, it was hard getting in,' she says, 'but the point is, Susan, I spoke to Fred and Joyce last night to let them know that I'm asking you to act on my behalf.'

'What do you mean?'

'You're going to have to close us down.'

'What do you mean?' I ask.

'I mean, you were right,' she says. 'Liaise with Fred and

Joyce,' she says, 'but handle everything yourself. I mean, write a formal newsletter, explaining how the university is going to proceed.'

'OK.'

'You can do that, can't you?'

'Of course,' I say, 'but why can't you?'

'I just can't, but you can.'

'Can Professor Willoughby not step back up?' I ask.

'No, he definitely can't, no.'

'Why? What's wrong with him?'

'Nothing, but anyway I don't want to ask him to step up,' she says. 'I'm asking you.'

'Are you all right?'

'Yes, I am. Are you?' she says.

'Just about.'

'I have regrets, Susan,' she says.

'I have regrets too.'

'When this is over will you come and visit and have the nice jams?'

'Yes, definitely,' I say, 'but Honey says it'll be a year or more.'

'I think she's right,' says Norma. 'She's a very credible young woman.'

'She is.'

We pause there for a moment.

'Let's speak on Sunday evenings,' she says.

'Yes. You ring me.'

'OK.'

'I'll get this newsletter written straight away and let you see it before I send it out this afternoon. OK?'

'All right,' she says. 'Bye then.'

# 44

## The Vice Chancellor's Office

### *Tuesday 24th March 2020*

Dear All,

We find ourselves in an unprecedented situation and I appreciate how worrying and unsettling things are. Many of us have had to quickly adapt what we do, and I have been impressed by the flexibility, hard work and dedication of staff across all areas of the University over these last few days.

The health and well-being of staff, students and our wider community will always be our number one priority. We are working closely with the public health authorities and would urge everyone to heed the advice that has been given and which can be accessed on our Coronavirus web pages: *www.rutland.ac.uk/coronavirus.*

As confirmed in my earlier communication, the University has now implemented online teaching, and exams scheduled for April and May will be conducted remotely. I recognize that there is so much that needs to be done to prepare for these; however, I am confident that thanks to the creativity and resourcefulness of colleagues we will be able to achieve what we are aspiring to, in what is the most challenging set of circumstances the University has ever faced.

The coming period will be extremely difficult for all of us, but we will get through it by working together and supporting each other. Please do contact me if you have any concerns.

On a more personal note, I'd like to thank everyone for their concern about my husband Roy Warren, who, after two weeks in intensive care at Leicester Royal Infirmary, was moved last night, on his sixtieth birthday, to a regular ward. I attach a short film of him *here*.

With my very best wishes to you all and your loved ones,
Susan Faye Warren
Acting VC

I send the above email to Norma for approval.
She replies immediately:

Hi, Susan. This is fine but I suggest you cut the bit about Roy and the video before you send.

God, he looks terrible.

Shall I phone on Sunday?

I reply:

Disagree re. cutting Roy. Have left him in and sent to All Heads of Department, President of Student Union, and Governors. It should be in your inbox now.

Yes. Do ring!

# Acknowledgements

Thanks go to:

At Jo Unwin Literary Agency: my brilliantly supportive, wise and wonderful minder, Jo Unwin, and the team, especially Nisha Bailey and Donna Greaves.

At Penguin Books: my editor, Mary Mount, for excellent editorial guidance, for being a complete delight to work with, and for proving, yet again, to be the greatest living human.

I'd like to thank the whole team at Penguin behind this book. Especially **Early readers:** Isabel Wall, Karishma Jobanputra. **Managing editorial:** Natalie Wall. **Copy-editing:** Mary Chamberlain. **Proofreading:** Sarah Barlow and Kit Shepherd. **Contracts:** Sofia Karjoy-Wennerström. **Design:** Julia Connolly. **Illustration:** Sarah Madden. **UK Sales:** Samantha Fanaken, Rachel Myers, Kyla Dean, Eleanor Rhodes Davies, Tineke Mollemans, Andy Taylor, Alun Owen. **International sales:** Linda Viberg, Guy Lloyd. **Production:** Charlotte Faber, Jane Delaney, Anya Wallace-Cook. **Publicity/Marketing:** Olivia Mead, Poppy North, Anna Ridley. **Rights:** Amelia Evans. **Audio:** Meredith Benson.

Family and friends, especially: AJ Allison, Elspeth Allison, John Allison, Paul Beaumont, Ollie Day, Sam Frears, Adriaan Goldberg, Margrit Goldberg, Victoria Goldberg, Fiona Holman, Stuart Lord, Countess Kristina Lutkevitch,

Keith McGarry, Wendy Nicolson, Alfred Nunney, Anya Ostwald-Harper, Jon Reed, Jeremy Stibbe, Tom Stibbe, Eva Stibbe Nunney, @CostumedVole, Mary-Kay Wilmers.

Special advisors: Emma Beddington (tortoise behaviour), Malcolm Cowan (university driving), Stella Heath (university life), Cathy Rentzenbrink (miscellaneous).

Finally, to my husband, Mark Nunney, for wisdom, loveliness and general brilliance, and for saying yes to another dog.